Futuristic

Love in another time, another place.

ALL'S FAIR

"What will you do if my father refuses to give you the equests?" Tia asked.

"I pray he won't." Dare turned his face away, not wanting her to read the truth in his eyes. He'd already sent a message to the Grand Elder that, if any of his men were harmed, Tia's life was forfeit.

"That's no answer. What threat did you use to force payment of the equests?"

"I don't make threats, as a rule," Dare said ominously.

"You haven't answered my question," she whispered hoarsely.

"If your father refuses to send the equests, my dealings with him are at an end."

"But what about me?"

"What about you, Tia? If I send you back without compensation from the Grand Elder, my people will lose faith in my leadership. Does your happiness depend on scurrying home to papa?"

"You are cruel!"

"Life is cruel, Tia. I can't make it easier for you, but I don't take pleasure in your pain."

Other *Love Spell* Books by Pam Rock:
MOON OF DESIRE

Love's Changing Moon

Pam Rock

LOVE SPELL NEW YORK CITY

To Warren

LOVE SPELL®

July 1994

Published by

Dorchester Publishing Co., Inc.
276 Fifth Avenue
New York, NY 10001

Printed in the United States of America.

Love's Changing Moon

Chapter One

Tia's tears froze before they could trickle down her cheeks. The frigid air burned the exposed skin around her eyes, but she hardly noticed the stinging pain.

For all of her twenty full-cycles, Doman had been her shadow-keeper, her guardian, and now she was the cause of his death.

She knew crying was as futile as her long pursuit of the killer beast, a vicious bernit, had been, but still the bitter flood of tears continued, blurring her vision like a sheet of ice obscuring the water on a pond.

She'd been backtracking for hours, trying to find the trail where the giant white-furred bernit had slaughtered her mount with a single slash of its razor-sharp claws. She'd been moments from death herself when Doman courageously jumped from his fleeing equest and attacked the beast with a cudgel, the only weapon defectives were allowed to carry on the planet of Thurlow. The contest ended with one deadly swipe of the beast's front paw. Then, to her horror, the bernit had clamped its huge jaws around Doman's struggling form and lumbered away on all fours.

She'd followed on her footsleds until her calves cramped with excruciating pain, but the wind wiped out the beast's tracks before she could catch up. Now a dark blue mist closed in around her, making it seem impossible to find her way back.

She'd failed Doman, but she couldn't fail in her urgent mission. Somehow she had to find a way to cross the Frozen Desert without her shadow-keeper, but she'd never before been alone in a strange place.

Icy pellets of frozen moisture added weight to the lepine-skin greatcoat that swathed her from the top of her head to the thick oiled boots on her feet. Nothing looked familiar in the furiously blowing storm. She closed her eyes tight to stop her tears and tried to wipe away the frozen rivulets on her face, wincing when they broke away, taking skin with them.

The bernit had attacked within sight of Ringfort, the remote outpost she'd hoped to reach before dusk gave way to the eerie blackness of a polar night.

"Help me!" she cried out, hardly able to hear her own voice over the shriek of the wind. "Help me! Help me!"

Screaming made her throat feel raw, but she continued calling out, stopping only to catch her breath. She had little hope of her cries being heard in the desolate place, but desperation made her keep trying.

Never before had she so fervently regretted not being able to call upon her father's strength and wisdom. Logan, Grand Elder of the Zealotes, would never be so rash and foolish as to be lost so close to an inhabited place.

She concentrated with all her remaining strength, hoping that some latent spark of her father's great courage would give her guidance. Icy pellets were bombarding her, robbing her of all sense of direction, and she was afraid each step she took might take her farther from Ringfort.

A faint, distant sound reached her over the noise of the storm, but she was afraid her imagination was playing tricks because she was so desperate for help.

"'Allo!"

Was she receiving spiritual comfort in her dying moments? The darkness closing in around her confused her senses.

"Help me!" she cried again, but in her confusion she was calling out to her father, yearning for his forgiveness if she died in this horrible place. Had he known about it, he would never have permitted her to undertake this reckless quest, not even to save his life.

"Keep calling so I can find you," a stronger voice commanded.

"I'm here! I'm here!" The distinct words made her realize how urgently she wanted to live. Her life was only beginning, and she was horrified by the thought of her mother, Calla, mourning the death of her only child.

"I'm here!" she cried again.

"Have you taken leave of your senses, wandering off on a night like this?" a man's gruff voice demanded from behind her. She was caught in an iron grip, powerful hands holding her arms against her sides.

"I had to. . . ."

"No explanations now. If the storm worsens, not even I can find the way back to Ringfort," he said, coming around to face her.

At least she knew he came from the frontier post. She started to thank him, but her rescuer suddenly became her captor, coiling a rope around her body and binding her arms to her sides.

"No, don't!"

"No time for foolish struggling. Follow me."

He was wearing short wooden footsleds like her own, but he glided over the icy ground with ease, forcing her to struggle to keep up. Twice she stumbled, and twice he jerked her upright by pulling on the rope, saving her from falling at great cost to her dignity.

Her breath stabbed her lungs, and she almost preferred abandonment to this headlong dash through a curtain of searing ice pellets.

"Please go slower," she cried, then hated herself for showing weakness to the beastly man who was dragging her forward without regard for her waning strength.

Blinded by the storm, she didn't see the dim blue lights until she nearly collided with a rough-hewn plank surface.

Indifferent to her weary shuffle, he followed a wall broken only by a few narrow slits showing pale rectangles of eerie light.

Ready to drop from exhaustion, she was barely conscious when he lifted a heavy wooden bar and opened a door in the wall.

Inside the crude fortress the wind howled around shadowy buildings with narrow slitlike windows showing the same bluish light.

Leading her to a low structure nestled against the wall, he opened a door and shoved her into a dimly lit room.

The puzzling blue light came from a wax stick burning inside a transparent blue globe. The ghostly light illuminated a rude sleeping chamber with three narrow cots covered by thick, shaggy white skins. Shuddering in distaste, she recognized them as bernit furs.

"Untie me," she demanded, trying to disguise her fear with anger.

"I expected gratitude, not commands," he said, throwing back his fur hood.

His sarcasm stung, and she watched in sullen silence while he threw off a robe of tawny fur and hung it on a thick peg near the fireplace. With slow, deliberate movements, he kicked off his varnished footsleds and stomped his boots to shake loose the icy residue. Freed of his cumbersome garb, he bent beside the hearth of a jagged rock fireplace and added small sticks to the glowing embers to produce a blazing fire. Then he slowly added large chunks of dark, slower-burning fuel of a type Tia didn't recognize.

As the fire flared, she saw her rescuer clearly for the first time. He was younger than his gruffness had led her to expect, certainly less than thirty full-cycles. His hair was tawny, lighter than the robe he'd discarded, and hung down his back in an unruly tangle, golden in the fiery glow. His features were comely but spoiled by the angry set of his full lips and the scowl etched on his high forehead. Back in the Citadral where her father ruled

11

as Grand Elder, she would have had the luxury of secretly admiring his powerful shoulders, bare under a loose-fitting vest of dark brown leather. But now she only saw an unexpected enemy.

"Will you please untie me now?" she requested with poorly concealed disdain. "Surely you're not afraid I'll overpower you?"

"Can you see my fingers?" he asked, holding his hand close to her face.

"Of course I can," she said, although, in truth, his image seemed to shimmer in front of her aching eyes.

"I thought you were suffering from polar blindness. If you knew you were straying from the trail, then I've risked my life to save a fool." He loosened her bindings, letting the coil of rope fall in a circle around her feet.

He bent to retrieve his rope, and she tried to back away, tangling her unwieldy footsleds in the coil and falling backward, destroying her last shred of dignity when she landed with a thump on her backside.

She wanted to cry and be comforted; she wasn't ready for a harsh life of adventure! A telltale sheen of tears further clouded her vision, but she heard his laughter crackling louder than the roaring fire.

"You can't abuse me like this!" She tried to pull off her footsleds, but her gloved fingers were so stiff she couldn't manipulate them.

"That's where you're wrong," he said with grating cheerfulness. "I found you in the wilderness. You belong to me now."

"You don't know who I am!" she cried out, panicked into an arrogance her parents would have severely rebuked.

12

"I don't," he agreed, stooping to remove her footsleds. "Nor do I know how you came to be wandering in this ungodly place during the season of endless nights. I was returning to Ringfort when I saw a slaughtered equest. Against my better judgment, I followed your trail until the wind wiped it out." He tossed aside the footgear and pushed her hood back from her face.

Standing, he gently lifted her to her feet.

"Suppose you enlighten me," he said, deftly unfastening the catches on her black lepine greatcoat. "I'd like to know your name if I'm to be your master."

"My father is my only master!" She backed away, but there was no escape. His tall, muscular body was firmly planted between her and the door. Even if she could find a refuge elsewhere in the fortress, she couldn't be sure of a safe welcome.

"What kind of father lets his daughter come alone to a place like this?" he scoffed.

"I wasn't alone! My shadow-keeper was carried away by the beast that killed my equest." She slumped down on the closest cot, her spirit ravaged by an overwhelming sense of loss.

"And you tried to follow alone without a weapon? Were you going to charm a bernit into releasing your shadow-keeper?"

He was ridiculing her, and no one ever showed disrespect to the daughter of the Grand Elder. She wasn't as defenseless as he thought. Her eyes strayed to her right boot.

Before she could react, he pushed her back on the furry blanket and yanked at her left boot, pulling it away from her numb toes in a single tug. Quickly searching the interior, he tossed it

13

aside, pinning her legs down with one arm and removing her other boot.

"Is this what you expected to use on the bernit?" he asked, holding up the thin-bladed dirk she'd bought from a merchant, breaking her father's stern rule about steel weapons.

"Give me that!" She tried to sit up, but he held her down with unruffled ease.

"I think not." He slipped it into the top of his own wet boot. "Now tell me who you are and why you're here before my patience is completely exhausted!"

"It doesn't matter who I am." Her heart was pounding, whether from fear or anger she wasn't sure. "I must find a man called Dare Lore."

"For what purpose?"

"That's for his ears only."

She trembled, not from cold alone but because she lived in fear for her father's safety. Even now, as he was trying to negotiate with Thurlow's corrupt government, an assassin might be stalking him. She had to find the only man who could help him.

Dare shrugged, determined to conceal his curiosity about the dainty little creature he'd saved from certain death. Stripped of her costly, sleek greatcoat, she was only a girl, albeit a shapely and provocative one. Flattened as it was by her hood, her hair still curled around her face in a heavy mane of sable with red highlights. Her face was a perfect oval, beautiful in any man's eyes, but dark violet eyes were her most arresting feature. Set off by shapely brows and improbably long lashes, they sparkled with anger now, suggesting a passionate nature that could only mean trouble for a man like him.

"Then your secret is likely to die with you. You'll never find him."

"My shadow-keeper was sure he could find him. Defectives have an instinct for locating people."

"You were traveling with a defective?" He couldn't imagine this exquisite creature with such an inadequate guardian.

"Defectives have hearts and souls like any other person on Thurlow!"

"They also have misshapen heads, tiny, pointy teeth, and no more intelligence than the animal that once wore that skin," he said, pointing at her coat.

"You're wrong! Doman once saved my father and mother from dire danger. He could reason and speak, and he watched over me from the moment of my birth."

"A defective with intelligence? Next you'll tell me your equest could talk!"

"You're cruel to mock the creatures I love! Do you know how it feels to lose those who are close to you?"

"No, I don't," he said bitterly, furious because she'd touched a raw nerve. Snatched from his parents at birth by the ruthless Zealote Warmond, Dare had never known what it meant to belong to a family, to know his rightful name or enjoy the pride of kinship.

"This is my room," he said harshly. "You will stay here until the darkness lifts enough to send you back where you belong. Under no circumstances are you to venture out alone. I don't intend to rescue you twice."

"I'm not going back. I have to reach Norvik."

"You won't be welcome at that northernmost settlement, and you can't cross the Frozen Desert alone. Believe me, no one here will take you there."

"You can't be sure of that. I can pay well." She stood and faced him.

"I am sure," he said gruffly, still smarting because she'd accused him of being cruel. "Lie down. Rest. I'll bring you some hot food and a soothing unguent for your face."

He took a heavy woolen jacket from a wall peg and pulled it on, lacing it up the front over his broad, naked chest.

Teeth chattering, shivering convulsively, she didn't know how he could expose his flesh to the chill air in the barren room. Not even the steady warmth of the fire could stop her chills.

Feigning compliance, she slid under the fur robe on the nearest cot, wishing she could sleep for a hundred hours. She closed her eyes, pretending to doze but struggling to resist it.

"I won't be long," he warned, his voice soft because he thought she was close to losing consciousness.

She moaned sleepily, hoping he would be deceived as he closed the door behind him.

Tia longed to stay where she was, snug and cozy under a furry covering that no longer seemed repulsive. Instead she wearily rose to her feet, unsteady from shock and fatigue. She had to hire a guide while her captor thought she was too weak to venture out. She couldn't trust him not to keep her prisoner if he knew her intent.

Her greatcoat was heavy with moisture and her boots stiff with melting ice, but she pulled them on, afraid to step outside wearing only her violet leather tunic and body-hugging black leggings.

She might not be able to return to this warm haven, so she put her footsleds in the deep pockets of her coat, regretting that all her other supplies were with her poor slain equest.

Stepping outside took all her courage. She knew frontier fortresses were hiding places for the most despicable criminals. In case of trouble, her only chance for help was to search out a member of her father's sacred cult, the Zealotes, many of whom had scattered to the far reaches of the planet when her father's new rule began. Even if these black-clad, hooded refugees opposed her father's liberal, noncelibate policies, they would respect his office. She could trust them.

She'd stopped in many remote outposts on her long journey, and without exception each had a place where men gathered for companionship and strong drink, an alehouse. Although it was as black as the bowels of the planet beyond the little oasis of light, it was still midday, a time for wakefulness and work for those who had duties. She'd learned, too, that idleness was the curse of these frontier posts; this gave her hope that a competent guide would gladly accept her generous payment.

Finding the gathering place would not be easy. The narrow wall slits were high above her head, and no building was graced by a sign. She knocked on several rough plank doors, but no one answered, not even when blue lights clearly showed through the openings. Either the wind had muffled her raps or the inhabitants were too hostile to open their doors to unexpected visitors.

Stiff with cold and near the point of panicking, she at last saw a dim shape entering a long

17

shedlike structure built against the wall as many of the buildings were, perhaps to save precious wood by utilizing the fortification on one side. She followed this person's example and pushed open the door without knocking.

Her eyes clouded over in the densely packed room. As she'd suspected, many inhabitants were gathered in this low-ceilinged room, some puffing on small gray pipes that caused a smoky fog to hover over the small, scarred wooden tables. She searched for a familiar black robe, trying to ignore the curious stares that followed her progress through the room. A motley assortment of rough men put down their drinking mugs or stopped their gaming as they watched her move through the long room.

She spotted a black-robed figure leaning against the back wall, holding himself aloof from the others. He frightened her more than any man in the place, perhaps because he seemed to look through her, surprisingly indifferent to her approach.

"Pretty one, let me buy you a mug," an oafish man with a great red beard called out to her.

She shook her head and approached the black-robed one.

"Are you a Zealote?" she respectfully asked.

"I am." He still looked beyond her, and she suddenly realized the man was sightless, his blind eyes fixed upon some scene only he could see.

"I'm Tia, daughter of Logan," she said. "For my father's sake, I beg a word with you."

"Beg all you like," he said indifferently.

"I need a guide to take me across the Frozen Desert."

"And I need one to take me to the privy," he said bitterly. "Why bother me?"

18

"All I'm asking is the name of a trustworthy man."

His laugh was chilling, and she felt demeaned by it.

"You've lost your sense, girl," a grizzled old man called out to her. "No one's going to cross that frozen hell, not even for the use of your sassy ass."

"I have enough to pay a dozen men to act as guides," she said, her face hot with resentment.

"A dozen, you say," the red-bearded oaf taunted. "You won't want a dozen once you've been ridden by the likes of me!"

She'd suffered her share of vulgar suggestions in the course of her journey, but never without Doman at her back, his cudgel warning off the more offensive tormentors.

Her eyes ached, and seeing through the noxious haze was difficult. She'd never felt so helpless, but her mission was too vital to give up. If the Zealote wouldn't help, she'd have to ask every man in turn until someone agreed to guide her to Dare Lore's remote polar outpost.

"I can pay well," she said, approaching a table with two men wearing the dark green uniforms of the government patrol police.

"Can you now?" asked one of the policemen, a swarthy giant whose open tunic was straining at the seams.

"Name your price," she said, mentally tallying the funds secreted away in the money belt around her waist.

"Just name your price," his companion mocked, "then tell us how a dead man can spend it."

"I see you're cowards," she said, hoping to shame them into entering her employ.

19

Before she could back away, the large man flicked his wrist faster than her eye could follow, and a rawhide whip snapped around her body, capturing her as effectively as her rescuer's rope had. Only her thick coat saved her from searing welts across her back and arms.

"If you were a man, I'd have you by the throat," the first man warned.

"Let her go, Guston."

Tia knew without looking behind her that she'd been rescued a second time by the tawny-haired man.

The policeman released her without comment, shrugging and refilling his foul-smelling pipe.

"So you're willing to make a man rich if he'll take you to Norvik," the tawny one said. His eyes were icy blue, more threatening than the swarthy man's whip.

"Yes." She met his hostile gaze, sensing he was testing her in some way.

"I'll be your guide, daughter of Logan, for a price I set."

"You heard me talking to the Zealote."

"Yes, I know who you are now. You left my quarters against my orders. Didn't you know I'd find you in this confined place?"

She didn't respond to his question and instead said, "If you've changed your mind about guiding me, I'll pay handsomely for your services."

"My price is twelve equests from the Zealote stables, the best of the breed, all broken to the saddle. Two stallions and ten mares."

Every man in the room stopped speaking.

"You're asking the impossible," she gasped, knowing that a single equest trained by the

20

Zealotes was beyond the means of all but the richest citizens. Who was this man, that he'd even think of asking for such steep payment?

"Maybe the Grand Elder isn't your father?"

"I spoke the truth; he is. But Zealote equests are rarely sold outside the Order."

"I said nothing about buying them."

"No, but—"

"But you want a man to risk his life for mere money. I wonder how highly your father values your 'mission.' "

"He doesn't know about it," she let slip, hating the way this man made her heart beat faster and her throat constrict.

He stared for a long moment as though he could peel back her fair skin and read the secrets stored in her skull.

"Let me ask you this. What would the esteemed Grand Elder pay to have his daughter restored to him?"

"You can't let him take me hostage," she cried out, appealing to the crowd around them.

As though animated by an invisible puppet master, every man looked away and feigned great interest in drink, dice, or pipe.

"I warned you not to leave my quarters," he whispered angrily, grasping her arm and propelling her toward the exit.

She dug her heels into the hard-packed dirt floor, but he forced her forward as though she were a rag doll.

"It seems," he loudly pronounced, "that I've struck a very advantageous deal with the lady." Under his breath he added, "Let them hear you call me master."

"No . . ."

21

He yanked her into his arms, crushing her mouth against his.

"Say it!" he hissed.

Through her thick coat she could feel the pressure of his fingers on her arm.

"Master," she said, saying the word but giving it a meaning of her own.

He threw open the door and flung her through it with such force she fell forward onto the ground.

"You have no right . . ." she cried out, blinded more by anger than the swirling frozen droplets.

One moment she was shrouded by darkness and the next illuminated by bluish light. Her captor had slammed the door shut, but some curious spectator had opened it. The tawny one reached down and picked her up, slinging her over his shoulder like a sack of fodder.

She heard laughter and obscene jests, then dizziness drained away the last of her resistance as he carried her head-down across the compound.

"If you're the issue of a Zealote," he said, dumping her on the cot where he'd left her, "then it was an evil day when the Order stopped imposing celibacy on its members."

"You have no right to interfere with my mission!" she cried out, so angry she thought her heart would burst.

"You have no mission! Don't you see you're asking the impossible? A man can freeze to death in midstride trying to cross the Frozen Desert on foot. Those ruffians were only toying with you. Not one of them would risk being swallowed up by a swirling snow mirage or falling into a bottomless ice crevasse. Nor would they work for a handful of currency."

"If Dare Lore and his men are hiding at Norvik, there must be a way to get there."

"What do you know about Dare Lore?"

"I know he's the leader of many young men. As children they were destined to be Zealotes, but they were stolen by Warmond when he was the Zealotes' Master of Apprentices."

"If this Dare Lore does lead an army of rootless men, what is it to you?"

"I can only speak to him."

"So you say." He cupped his bristly chin, letting his long locks fall forward in a wild cascade. "Are you really Logan's daughter? Or did you make that claim to further your own ends?"

"I spoke the truth, although I can see there's no advantage in your knowledge of it."

"Then you have access to the riches of the Order."

"I only have my own savings from gifts my parents gave me over the years. I have enough to make a man wealthy."

"I don't want money. I want something money can't buy: your promise I'll receive a dozen equests."

"I don't have the authority to make that promise."

"How much does your father value your life?"

She was afraid to answer, even though she knew her father loved her beyond measure. She was the only child of his loins, although he had adopted her cousin, Fane, when he was only nine years old after his parents had perished in a fire. Fane was her mother's nephew, and her parents had met when the Zealotes sent Logan to investigate the Master of Apprentices, Warmond, on one of his "summoning" journeys to find newborn males to be raised by the celibate Order. In some villages it had been considered a great honor to place a child with the Order, and families willingly surrendered their newborn sons because, as Zealotes, they would be exempt from government-mandated service in the hyronium mines.

Unfortunately Warmond had turned to kidnapping when healthy offspring became few and far between on Thurlow. Once a man began his servitude in the mines, his exposure to the poisonous gases destroyed his ability to father any children but defectives. With her sister's mate away serving his time at the mines, Tia's mother had pursued Warmond and her sister's abducted child across the planet, rescuing the babe Fane and returning him to his parents. She had also won the heart of Logan, who aided her and later became the Grand Elder of the Zealotes. Although Logan had won the acceptance of the Zealotes for his reforms, especially an end to celibacy, he himself had only one offspring, Tia. Her father lived in hope that she would someday give him a grandson.

"Answer me," Tia's captor ordered, glaring at her with narrowed eyes.

"He loves me well enough." His eyes had inky depths that compelled her to speak the truth.

"You have three choices. Set out alone on foot, and you'll freeze to death. Stay here, and you'll be at the mercy of the patrons of the establishment you just visited. Some of them haven't seen a female in many moon-cycles." He rubbed one finger tenderly along her jawline, flicking a strand of hair from her cheek. "If you're as innocent as you seem, I think you'll find a fast death in

Love's Changing Moon

the storm more merciful than what they'll do to you."

"What is my third choice?" The warmth of the room was making her feel light-headed.

"Agree to my price."

She weighed the urgency of her quest against her reluctance to lie. There was no way she could guarantee a payment of twelve equests, but her father did dote on her. When she'd gotten into mischief as a child, he'd rarely showed the stern side of his nature. He was reshaping the future of the Zealotes—and the whole planet—but with his wife and daughter he was tenderhearted and indulgent.

"I don't know. . . ." she said, stalling for time to make a decision.

She was acting without her father's knowledge, but the need for Dare Lore's help had assumed new urgency when she learned of the threats against her father's life. Logan had been planning to contact the leader of the Wanderers himself, but now there was no time to wait until his negotiations were terminated. An Earth colony, Thurlow's only worth was its hyronium, which was transported by Earth spaceships and converted to energy on the home planet. Thurlow's hyronium was discovered more than a thousand years ago by a survey probe searching for new power sources for the dying Earth, whose oil and uranium resources had been exhausted. The hyronium miners were now revolting, chafing at the enforced terms of servitude. Her father's spies within the Senate had warned that Earth was bringing weapons to help prop up the shaky Thurlowian government, on the

25

condition that the rebellion was quelled and the hyronium was available when their space-ship arrived.

For centuries Earth had denied Thurlow access to its technology, preferring to keep the planet primitive and easier to control. Only one man had enough weapons and an army to challenge the corrupt government on Thurlow: Dare Lore. Tia thought it was well worth risking her life to enlist him on her father's side in opposing the government's stranglehold on the planet. But would her father forgive her for acting without his permission or knowledge? Would he honor a debt she contracted?

She was challenging her father in the worst possible way: thwarting his plans for her and putting her own life in jeopardy. Could she count on his forgiveness?

Maybe she was foolish! If she died, her mother would carry an unbearable burden of guilt for not watching her more closely and restraining her freedom to come and go as she wished. Calla would never have allowed her to undertake such a journey. No matter how much he loved her, her father would never forgive her for throwing away her life instead of carrying on his bloodline as he so desperately wished.

Compared to the horrible possibility of ruining her parents' lives, a broken promise to this over-bearing outcast seemed of little consequence.

His eyes never left her face, and for a frighten-ing moment she wondered if he were an empath like her father. If he sensed her deceit about the equests, her quest was hopeless.

"My name is Tia. What is yours?" she asked, still hesitant about agreeing to his outrageous price because a deliberate lie was so foreign to her nature.

"You don't need to know it."

Only a man with a criminal past would be so secretive about his identity. The other men had seemed wary of opposing him, and she didn't dare imagine what horrendous deeds had brought him to Ringfort in the dark season.

"I'll call you Yellow Hair," she said, expecting him to object and tell her his given name.

He nodded. "Do you agree to my terms?"

"Twelve equests." She took a deep breath, trying not to imagine the consequences of giving him a false pledge. "I agree."

"You may still perish," he said, "but you won't die alone. We'll leave when you've regained your strength."

"Leave me now. I'll be ready to depart in a few hours."

He regarded her with his icy gaze. "You've struck a bargain for passage over the Frozen Desert. You still belong to me—and I don't take orders from my captive."

"Our agreement—"

"I will take you to Norvik. First eat and drink." He gestured at the broth and flat bread he'd set out on a small table by the fire before he went to find her. "Then sleep."

"I'll rest," she said, too exhausted to refuse, "but only when you've left my quarters."

"Your quarters! Your existence depends on my goodwill. I'm not going to bunk with a dozen filthy renegades so you can sleep in solitude."

"I can't stay in this room with you!"

"Be assured, Mistress Tia, you're as safe with me as you can be in this outpost. My only interest

27

is in your father's equests."

He took her arm, firmly but not roughly, and led her to the stool where he'd provided the best meal available.

Watching as she drank a few swallows of the meaty broth, Dare wondered how long he could pretend indifference to her charms. Her skin was soft and dewy, except for the raw patches around her eyes where the wind had seared it. A woman's skin aged quickly in the dry, frigid air of the far north, and her hair became brittle and lifeless. He knew of only one female as beautiful as his captive, and her spirit was as twisted as her evil father Warmond's.

It soon became clear that Tia lacked the strength to eat, and he led her to a cot, pulling off her boots for the second time. He rubbed her feet over her weak protest, then applied a film of soothing ointment to her face. She was asleep before he finished his ministrations.

Far into the night, Dare lay sleepless on the cot beside hers, hearing her soft cries and imagining the fearful dreams that disturbed her slumber. He'd made a rash promise—to take her to Norvik. He couldn't foresee the consequences, but he feared more was at stake than the dozen equests he planned to demand as ransom for his hostage.

Chapter Two

Dare tossed restlessly, knowing the men from the alehouse would soon challenge him for possession of the woman. The longer he delayed leaving Ringfort, the more liquid courage the ruffians in this frozen hell would consume. Eventually some would decide Tia was worth a confrontation with Dare Lore, the leader of the Wanderers: Lore's Lost Ones, some called them.

Journeying alone was always risky, but the few close companions who knew about his second encampment had been needed to keep peace at Norvik. Several malcontents were spreading dissension, complaining that Dare didn't have the courage to seize a homeland from the Zealotes.

He sympathized with their impatience. Many had been refugees as long as they could remember. What they didn't understand was that the Wanderers had to be strong enough to win before making demands of a Grand Elder as powerful as Logan.

Crawling out of the nest of furs, Dare rose to his feet and shivered as the frigid air assaulted his naked body. The hard-packed dirt floor felt like ice under his soles, but he didn't reach for his boots or clothing. Instead he went to the large glazed clay bowl he'd left near the fireplace before going to bed. The fire had burned down to glowing embers, and he had to rap sharply to break the film of ice on his bathwater.

Dare cupped his hands and splashed icy water on his face, gritting his teeth to keep them from chattering. He bathed his arms and torso, scrubbing hard to encourage a powerful blood flow in his veins. It was misery to splash water under his arms and between his legs, but he did it stoically, then rubbed hard with a rough scrap of toweling.

When he was dressed, his skin still tingling under his travel-worn breeches and vest, he stood over his captive. She had burrowed under the bedrobes, and all he could see was dark hair spilling over the edge of the fur.

"Tia." Her name sounded stiff and foreign on his tongue. "Tia, wake up."

He wasn't surprised by her deep sleep. The extreme cold affected people differently, but almost no one could be exposed to it without ill effects. Some slept like the dead; others shivered convulsively for hours on end. The most serious effect was polar blindness, a loss of sight that could be temporary or permanent. Unlike blurred vision caused by looking at the sun, polar blindness shut down the optical system after exposure to swirling ice pellets and unbearable temperatures. Dare feared it more than any other danger on the Frozen Desert.

"Tia," he said more emphatically, reaching down to touch her shoulder.

She stirred but didn't awaken. Folding down the fur to see her face, Dare found it hard to believe that the daughter of Logan was his hostage. Was he gullible to believe what she told him? Why was the pampered daughter of the Zealote's Grand Elder in this remote outpost?

The female could be deceiving him, pretending to be Logan's daughter to further some end of her own. He moved the shaggy white skins away from her shoulder and wished he could read her thoughts.

"Tia, it's time to wake up."

She murmured but was still lost in sleep.

Her hands were tucked under her chin, and her body was curled into a ball under the fur, the sleeping position of an innocent child. He watched for a moment, wishing he could let her sleep off the polar fatigue, but delay was too risky. He wanted to be long gone before the bullyboys of Ringfort rolled out of their sleeping sacks to face another dark, purposeless day. Without a true dawn to lift their spirits, most of them would be in ugly moods.

"Crazy girl," he muttered aloud. "Coming alone to a place like this."

An army of defectives wouldn't intimidate the fugitives and outlaws who took shelter in Ringfort, yet she'd come with only one as a shadow-keeper. The few patrol police charged with keeping order at the outpost were little more than time-servers, doing duty on the frozen frontier to earn double pay with very little labor. Only a fool—or a naive innocent—would expect any protection from them.

"Tia!" he said more sharply. "Wake up!"

She stirred, and her long dark lashes fluttered, but her eyes didn't open.

"Wench, we have to leave," he said, not sure how to rouse this reluctant female.

His words didn't seem to penetrate her dreams. Impatient to be gone, Dare yanked off the heavy skins, hoping the cold air would shock her into wakefulness.

She only curled into a tighter ball, mumbling incoherently.

He knew well enough how to rouse a lazy bedlover, but he couldn't bring himself to smack her pertly rounded bottom. She was smaller, more delicate, than he remembered, but the shapely curve of her hip and the swell of her backside were seductively feminine.

His chest ached staring down at her, and he didn't like the way her beauty confused his senses. There were women at Norvik, most the offspring of fugitive Zealotes and slave women, but Dare usually thought of them as sisters-in-peril, fellow sufferers. He had never shared his bed with a woman like this.

Maybe she really was the daughter of Logan. If so, she was a prize beyond price, possibly the key to his plan to secure land for his Lost Ones.

Did any of the drunken rotters she'd approached in the alehouse believe her story? If only one man awoke with a clear head, he might decide to make a fortune for himself by holding her for ransom.

"Get up!" he said urgently, rolling her onto her back.

"Oh!"

She looked startled and defensive, but he didn't have time for gentle coaxing.

"Unless we leave within the hour, you may spend the rest of eternity on your back. There are more than fifty men here, and not one woman. Even I can't guarantee your safety with those odds."

He looked away, but not before he took in the perfection of her calves in the black leggings and the way her breasts swelled under a thin white top.

She sat up, shaking her head as though confused about where she was, then rose unsteadily to stand beside the narrow cot.

Dare donned his leather jacket and fur greatcoat, but he looked at her one more time to be sure she was fully alert. Her hair was in wild disarray, a rich brown halo around the heart-shaped face of an angel, but he shook his head impatiently, trying to push aside the vision of her nipples hardened by the cold under her silky garment.

"Yellow Hair," she said, sounding more coherent. "How long have I slept? I wanted to leave right away."

"It's still the time for sleeping," he said.

It would easier to hear her reason now for wanting to talk to him, rather than play out the charade that he was only a guide taking her to Dare Lore. But then she would not have to go to Norvik if she knew his identity and could speak her piece right here. Revealing his identity now wouldn't be wise, as his plan's success might depend on her being held at his polar stronghold.

He had to let her think he was only a paid guide, even if it meant deferring to her arrogant Zealote ways.

"I'll bring my team and swoosha. Listen for my signal: two knocks, a pause, then one more. Don't open the door until you hear it. Be ready to leave the instant I get back."

"I have to collect my gear."

"You'll have to make do without it. I want to be well on our way before anyone wakes up."

"It won't take long. My saddlebags are with—"

"No," he said impatiently, beginning to realize how hard it would be pretending to defer to her wishes. "Your equest could be totally buried by now or dragged away by the bernit. We can't take time to search for the remains."

"If we'd left last night when I wanted to—"

"We would have had a horde of angry men on our tail. I command enough respect to be allowed the first night with you, but no one here would grant me exclusive rights."

"You agreed to a deal! Twelve equests . . ."

"Men say things to a woman when they want a willing playmate."

"Is that all your word meant?"

"No," he said, angry because he had to waste time explaining. "But when I carried you off, the others took it as a great joke at your expense. No one believed I'd actually guide you to Norvik. They entertained themselves by imagining how I'd use you—and anticipating their own turns."

She felt woozy, wanting to disbelieve him but too alarmed to challenge his assessment of the situation.

"I'll dress quickly," she said, hating the fear that made her sound meek and compliant.

34

"There's bread left. Eat your fill. It will take me a while to harness my beasts and lead them here. Just be ready when I knock."

He was scaring her, and she was glad to see him leave. But as soon as he was gone, she felt abandoned and vulnerable, missing Doman so much she couldn't hold back tears that smarted on the raw skin under her eyes.

After washing in icy water and pulling on her violet tunic, she tried to eat the dry flat bread, washing down tiny bites with leftover broth after skimming off congealed bits of fat. In only minutes, she was ready in her coat and boots, waiting anxiously for her guide.

What if he didn't return for her? Would the men of Ringfort abuse her in the way he suggested? She couldn't believe that her small fortune secreted away was valueless here. Maybe they scoffed at it only to get her to raise her offer.

She needed a dozen things lost in her saddlebags: nutrient bars so she wouldn't be dependent on the food available at remote outposts, a comb to untangle her hair, the unguent for her cracked lips and burning cheeks. Most of all, she regretted the loss of mementos of her beloved family, especially the locket with tiny watercolor drawings of both parents that her mother had given her on her sixteenth birthday. She'd broken the chain many days ago and put it in her saddlebag for safekeeping. She also hated losing the little sewing kit Fane had brought back from a journey to Luxley. Her adopted brother was her leader in childhood pranks and her best friend. She should have confided her plans to him, but she couldn't trust him not to tell their father if he thought her life was in jeopardy. Her quest was risky, but she was doing it for a cause they all supported passionately.

She was waiting as he'd ordered. Even in her luxurious lepine coat, she looked small and vulnerable. What did this defenseless woman expect to accomplish by going to Norvik?

Dare had left his polar stronghold to gather news of the outside world, and he needed time to think about everything he'd learned. His hostage was a burden, but she could open new possibilities for his mission. He didn't know yet how to fit her into his plans.

Logan's daughter could tell him more about Thurlow's struggle with Earth than he could learn in a dozen spy missions, he realized as he bundled her into the swoosha. Earth! He nearly spat when he thought of the planet that had colonized Thurlow more than a millennium ago. Because of the mother-world's insatiable need for energy, Thurlow's economy was in chaos and there was serious unrest among the people.

Once the Earth ships had only been able to approach every sixty-six years, but their new technology now allowed them to navigate almost at will through the asteroids surrounding Thurlow's three moons. The more often the Earthers came, the more they drained the lifeblood of his world.

Dare stealthily led his team through the only exit in the thick wall. Once outside the gate, he mounted the platform in front of the seat, standing to drive his team of yakas away from Ringfort as quickly as possible.

"Are we safe now?" she asked anxiously, but he wasn't inclined to offer her any soothing words.

She must be mad to leave her pampered life in the Citadral to come to such a dangerous place.

Dare burned with curiosity, wanting to know what message she was carrying to him, but for now the violently swirling ice pellets and eerie darkness required his full attention. Even he could get lost if he didn't rely on the small magnetic device fastened to his wrist—his most precious possession. It had been tied around his neck by his mother or father before he was kidnapped by the Zealotes and had stayed with him since infancy. He thought of it as the magic amulet that had made him leader of the Wanderers.

Zealotes! Just thinking of them brought a bitter taste to his mouth. Dare's early years were painful memories, thanks to Warmond, the Zealote who spirited him away as a babe and took him to a compound beyond the Flaming Sea. There he was one of many children Warmond had concealed from the other Zealotes; his plan had been to raise a great army to help him rule the planet. Although Warmond was evil beyond description and was now living out his life in captivity, Dare blamed each and every member of the Order of Zealotes for their practice of kidnapping newborns to swell their ranks. If Logan and Calla, Tia's parents, hadn't discovered Warmond's fortress and destroyed his plan, Dare might have been a prisoner of that evil genius to this day instead of the leader of an army of Lost Ones.

"Are we far enough away to be safe?" Tia called out, her voice melodious—and frightened.

Part of him wanted to slow the team and comfort her, but the daughter of Logan didn't deserve his sympathy. Logan had destroyed Warmond's plot and outlawed kidnapping of babes for the

Order, but as the new Grand Elder, he had devoted his life to making the abhorrent Zealotes into a stronger cult. Though Zealotes opposed the government which had established mandatory servitude in the hyronium mines, their power struggle with the government did nothing to make amends to the Wanderers, the stolen children who had grown up rootless and unwanted, ripped from their families and deprived of their heritage.

After Logan had discovered Warmond's secret fortress and had vanquished him, he sent Zealotes back to evacuate the compound. They took away the newborn infants and many of the slave women who'd cared for them. The older boys led by Dare had chosen to hide from the black-robed Zealotes, fearing them because of tales told by Warmond and renegade Zealotes, and not wanting to be enlisted into the cult.

No one, except a few of his closest and most trusted friends, knew how strong the army of the Wanderers was becoming. Many of them lived at Norvik, the isolated post where they'd at last found a safe, if frigid, haven, but some of his strongest and best men, handpicked over the years, were training at Leonidas, a secret base. All he needed now was a foolproof plan to secure a homeland for the Wanderers. He couldn't help but hope that fate had sent Logan's daughter to him for that purpose. Certainly her life would be worth more to the Grand Elder than a ransom of a dozen equests.

"How long will the trip take?" she shouted over the roar of the wind.

"It depends on the weather," he called back over his shoulder. "If conditions stay this favorable, we can make it in five days."

"Don't jest!" She held her hood shut and scrunched down under the heavy pile of furs he'd taken from the cots where they'd slept, explaining that every man traveled with an adequate supply of robes.

The swoosha was a small wagon on sleds, built high behind the seat she occupied with an overhang on the top and sides to give a degree of protection from the wind. Hides were stretched taut to form the seat and backrest, but the cold made them as rigid as stone. Bundles were stored behind the seat, but Yellow Hair hadn't given her time to see what they were.

He stood on a small planked area in front of her, so close she had to keep her feet tucked under the seat to keep from tripping him as he drove the strange, squat beasts who pulled the swoosha. The fierce, shaggy yakas had frightened her when she first saw them, but relief at not having to trudge on foot quickly overcame her trepidation. Their porcine snouts and short, sturdy legs were nearly concealed by rough coats in shades from red to black, but their long backs and savage teeth reminded her of canines bred for hunting in mountainous areas. She felt safe with this man in control of the team, but she couldn't help remembering the bernit who had appeared out of nowhere to slaughter Doman and her equest.

"Will we come across other beasts?" she called out to her guide.

To her surprise, he backed up and crowded his way onto the seat beside her, drawing the fur robe over his legs without slowing the team of yakas.

"I hope not," he said. "The few bernits who come this far on the Frozen Desert tend to be ferocious—and hungry."

"There isn't room for both of us on this seat." She squirmed, pressing against the side of the swoosha, but she couldn't move away from the pressure of his hip and the spread of his thigh.

"I'm not a yaka. I can't stand out in the wind any longer."

"But you have to drive the team."

"The swoosha is designed to be controlled by sitting or standing. I wanted maximum control until we were well away from Ringfort."

Dare answered her questions tersely, unused to having his actions questioned. The thought of leaving her behind grew more appealing with each kilometer they traveled, but what man could be trusted to escort her back to civilization? If her story was false—if she wasn't Logan's daughter—she was still a woman men would kill to possess.

"Those beasts look too small to pull us very far," she shouted over the turbulent wind.

"Not when eight are harnessed together."

Even through his heavy fur coat, Dare could feel her fidgeting beside him, forcing him to keep his legs uncomfortably close together. He was accustomed to physical discomforts; he wasn't used to a female who didn't defer to his judgment and hold her tongue. The thought of returning her to civilization himself grew more appealing as she tried to extract information from him about their route, the supplies, and the exact location of the Wanderers' stronghold.

He wanted to think about what it meant to his plan to have Logan's daughter as a hostage, but when she did keep quiet for short intervals, he still couldn't concentrate. Dare's eyes ached, even though he'd pulled down his hood, leaving only the narrowest possible slit for vision. The snow pellets that battered his head seemed luminous in the oppressive darkness. The dark days lasted six moon-cycles, and the coming of light seemed an eternity away. In this hostile region, strong men battled the elements and weak ones took their own lives. Was the woman beside him strong enough to survive a polar winter?

Trust came easily to Tia, but she couldn't fathom the thoughts of the man beside her. He seemed reliable and capable; she didn't doubt that he'd deliver her safely to Norvik. But he answered her questions reluctantly and withdrew into himself whenever she tried to learn more about him.

She rode with her eyes closed, finding it painful to look at the furiously blowing ice pellets that never ceased swirling in front of her. When she did glance at her guide, he seemed frozen in a rigid pose on the edge of the seat.

"Will we make a stop soon?" she asked when her stomach started to growl.

"When it's time to sleep."

He spoke in the manner one used with very small children or particularly disadvantaged defectives. She wanted to ask him how it was possible to distinguish day from night, but it was humiliating for the daughter of the Grand Elder to be treated as a nuisance. She lapsed into a stony silence, trying to plan what she would say to Dare Lore.

The leader of the Wanderers was a legendary hero who had led a crusade of children away from Warmond's evil fortress when he was still a child himself. She knew how his band had grown larger and stronger, attracting other lost children and runaways, until they had inspired fear wherever they roamed. Eventually they had been driven to a stronghold beyond the inhospitable Frozen Desert, which had been abandoned years before by Earth engineers hunting for new hyronium mining sites. Dare and his followers were now grown men, the leader himself approaching thirty full-cycles. They were a real army, not homeless children, and they'd proved themselves by surviving.

If their leader would commit his forces to helping her father and the Zealotes, together they could overthrow the government and let the people choose new leadership committed to opposing Earth's demands for hyronium.

The Zealotes had come into being nearly a millennium ago during a time of terrible anarchy. Earlier colonists, sent by Earth to work the mines, had lost faith in the Great Power, the deity whose worship linked them to the mother planet. They had rebelled against working the mines, burnt the books that represented Earth culture, and abandoned civilized customs, turning to crime and lust for diversions. Intent on restoring order to Thurlow, a group of men had banded together. Successful in their efforts, they then had formed the Order of Zealotes, relinquishing most of their political power, and a government was formed. As the current Grand Elder, Tia's father thought it was again time for the Zealotes to intervene in guiding the planet in a new direction. But the Zealotes had lived a peaceable existence far too long, forbidding members to use metal weapons. Unarmed, they couldn't oppose the government alone, and her father might lose his life in trying.

"Tell me about Dare Lore."

She startled him by speaking after a long silence.

"He's a man like any other."

"No, that can't be! He led the Lost Ones when he was only a child himself."

"He's no longer a child." He closed his eyes for a few moments, hoping the stabbing pain across his temple was no more than a simple headache.

"Of course not! But is he a comely man? Do women sigh over him?"

"I wouldn't know," he said dryly, entertaining himself with thoughts of upending her in a drift.

"You've never met him then?"

"I didn't say that." He pulled the fur hood lower over his forehead, but the throbbing grew worse, like a sharp-toothed beast gnawing at his brain.

"If you've met him, then you certainly must know what he looks like," she said.

"By the Great Power, woman, must you chatter like a mindless creature?"

"I'm sorry."

"No, I apologize for snapping. I'm not sure this was a wise idea, taking you to Norvik. Maybe we should go back."

"No, you struck a deal! For twelve equests!"

"You're right, and I am a man of my word," he said in a tone that discouraged further talk.

Dare had never made this trip alone with a female, and the heavy responsibility of keeping her safe made time pass with unbearable slowness. He regretted leaving Norvik, more than a moon-cycle ago, fearing that the disgruntled among his men were busy poisoning others with their doubts. He needed both his forces to succeed, but he wasn't ready to reveal his secret army or his plan for wresting land from the Zealotes.

No matter what he decided, there was nothing to be done until the end of the season of endless nights. More than one moon-cycle of darkness remained, and there was no way he could move his Wanderers out of Norvik before it ended. Even without the women and children in his band, Dare wouldn't risk the lives of his men by traveling in the Frozen Desert during this season.

"We're going to get a storm," he said after a long period of silence.

She couldn't imagine worse wind and cold. Her face burned under the protection of her hood, and her toes ached so badly she doubted she could walk.

There was no sense of time passing on the Frozen Desert: no rising or setting of the sun; no glow from the three moons that hovered over the planet because of dense cloud covering. Several times Yellow Hair had squinted at a round object he had buckled on his wrist, taking it off and moving it around to study it. When she had asked if it was a timekeeper, he answered that it was a navigational aid.

"We won't get lost, will we?" She had never imagined a storm of ice pellets so dense even the ground beneath them was out of the range of vision.

"We should be all right. The trail goes gradually downhill for at least another day's travel, and yakas always go the easiest way, given their head."

She held up her hand, moving her fingers just to be certain she still could. Yellow Hair had been right; a storm was building. She couldn't see her hand at arm's length, and the crudely built swoosha rode the drifts like a small boat tossed about on a violent sea.

"I feel as if I'm getting *mal de mer*," she said with a muffled giggle.

"What?"

"Seasick," she said between the deepest breaths she could muster. "It's an archaic Earth word. I love old languages and old books. My tutors . . ." She stopped, wondering if he knew what a tutor was. She knew nothing about her guide, but he didn't seem to be a man of learning.

"I can read the language of Thurlow as well as any Zealote," he said, the ferocious pain in his head making it a torment to put his thoughts into words.

"Did you go to a school?" she asked.

"If you're going to be sick, give me warning so I can stop," he shouted over the wind, determined not to be drawn into an exchange of personal information. Let her think him uneducated! He had no desire to tell her about his desperate struggle to learn, his continual begging and bartering for books. The Zealotes thought they had a monopoly on wisdom. He was willing to let them believe that—for now.

Dare took comfort in the lives of great leaders before him: Ashover, Dare Blanc II, and Rufus Bar Seine on Thurlow; Alexander the Great, Caesar of Rome, Bonaparte, and Chang Lee on Earth, although he hated what Chang Lee had done in masterminding the colonization and exploitation of Thurlow.

"I won't be sick!" she said, breaking into his thoughts again. "I know the Zealote way of controlling myself."

He groaned in pain and frustration, wondering if any ransom was worth the burden of crossing the desert with this female. Each time he moved his head, pain stabbed his temple like sharpened spikes digging into his skull. He would have to stop soon or risk losing control of the yakas.

The decision was made for him when the yakas swerved suddenly to skirt around an impassable drift. The swoosha capsized on its side, spilling them and their robes into the billowing mounds of frozen moisture.

Tia's first thought was that a bernit had attacked them. She screamed and tried to scramble away, but she was hopelessly tangled in robes and held down by a great weight across her legs. She cried out again, but her hood and the wind muffled the sound so completely, she wasn't sure any sound came from her throat.

"Don't move!"

The yakas shrieked in high-pitched outbursts, the female screamed, and the wind tore Dare's hood away from his face. No accident in the desert was minor, and he plunged forward, frantic to calm the lead beasts and keep them from a panic-induced flight.

"Ho-vay, ho-vay," he shouted, bending dangerously close to razor-sharp teeth that could bite through the bones in his hand as easily as a man could chew bread.

"Ho-vay, ho-vay," he repeated beside one of the lead yaka's ears, pushing aside the matted fur to be heard.

The long hours spent personally training his team proved their worth. After only a few snaps, the lead beasts quieted, transmitting their acceptance of the situation to the yakas behind them.

Tia didn't know what was happening until Yellow Hair staggered back to the swoosha, fighting the wind in a futile attempt to pull his hood over his head.

She scrambled to her feet, nearly blown over by the billowing weight of her coat, and jumped at his back, using her hands like two stiff clubs to knock the fur hood further over his face.

He nearly fought her off. His first reaction was that she was maddened by fear and was trying to kill him. When the hood fell over his eyes, he went down on his knees, ready to do battle until the moment he felt her hand on his arm and realized that she had been trying to protect his face with his hood.

Motioning her to help, he scooped at the drifts already threatening to bury the swoosha. Together they managed to dig it out and right it. Much to his relief, the sled-runners weren't broken, and the harness lines to the first pair of yakas had held.

Tia understood his signal when he motioned to her. She clambered back to the seat, her heart in her throat when he headed toward the team again and was obscured by a wall of battering ice pellets.

"Yellow Hair!"

Without him, she was dead! She was stunned by this harsh truth and plunged after him, following the half-buried team as she frantically tried to find him.

When he saw her, he gestured wildly, ordering her back to the swoosha. She shook her head, struggling to stay on her feet while he tugged the team forward, forcing them to burrow out of the drift and follow him to an area where the wind had temporarily scoured away the shifting mountains of icy downfall.

She imagined a bernit behind every drift and could almost feel lethal claws sinking into her flesh through all the layers of clothing, but when she saw what her guide was doing, she helped.

He staggered back to the swoosha and untied a bulky bundle from the goods stored behind the seat. She hurried to carry one end, shocked by her awkwardness as she tried to flex her arms.

Together they lugged it a short distance, pulling loose bindings that seemed designed to open with one swift yank. They erected a crude shelter, a tent of heavy skins propped up by a framework like the ribs of a four-legged animal and anchored by sharp, heavy stakes. Working in the violent wind, she had to fight for every breath she took, but in her heart, she began to hope for their survival.

When Yellow Hair took her arm and hurried her out of the tent and into the storm, she was dumbfounded. A drift that was knee-high rose to her hips in what seemed like seconds, and he left her standing while he half-dragged, half-led the team of yakas into the thick-skinned shelter.

She started to follow him in, but he pushed her back so unexpectedly she fell, sitting down with ice pellets swirling up to her neck.

He left her there and worked frantically, taking a second great bundle from the back of the swoosha and assembling another tent.

She hardly knew what was happening when she was dragged to her feet and pushed forward. A heavy hand forced her to duck as she was propelled inside the tent.

48

"Why did you put up a shelter for the animals first before you put up one for us?" she wailed angrily.

"If the yakas die, we die," he said, pushing back his stiff, ice-encrusted hood, so blinded by pain that her words of complaint were like whiplashes across his forehead.

"But they can stand the cold!"

"Only while they're moving. They secrete moisture from their pores, even in these temperatures. If they're motionless too long without shelter, heavy ice builds up under their fur, and they suffocate to death. Huddled together in a shelter, they can survive."

Every word out of his mouth came with great effort, and he wanted nothing more than to collapse into oblivion.

She could see almost nothing, but she heard the rebuke in his voice. Unconsciously retreating from him, she crouched beside one wall of the low shelter, surprised by the slipperiness of the skins. She wanted to ask him the reason, but instead she pulled off one glove and touched it, feeling a heavy layer of grease, a natural insulation.

"What do you want me to do?"

"We must eat—drink. Take the rope from my left pocket," he ordered hoarsely. "Tie it to my waist. I have to go back to the swoosha."

"I'll do it. You've done enough already. It's my turn to help."

"You don't know what to get."

"There can't be much left to choose from."

Dare swallowed his pride, knowing he might not be able to get back if the pain in his head grew any worse.

"My pack and a robe." He didn't try to explain. "Tie the rope around your waist and give me the end."

After he had secured the rope around her, she exited the tent. The swoosha was seven paces to the left. She counted them, begging the Great Power not to let her die in this place where her parents would never know what happened. Every step was fresh torment; her toes sent up fiery bursts of pain, but they seemed to be frozen stiff.

There was nothing on the back of the swoosha. She tried to think, tried to remember how far they'd come since overturning in the drift. Not far. Surely not far. It seemed like hours since their accident, but in reality, only a few minutes had passed. She felt rather than saw the jagged furrow where Yellow Hair had led the yakas to a flatter site. Drifts were reclaiming it, smoothing over the edges and filling in the depressions, but she could still follow it. She pushed forward, ignoring an urgent tug on the rope around her waist.

Tia tried to run but only succeeded in limping. By looking at nothing but the ground, she laboriously backtracked until a larger depression showed her where the swoosha had overturned. Falling onto her hands and knees, she dug through the drift, throwing up ice pellets like a fear-crazed animal trying to burrow to safety.

Her hands were so numb she nearly missed the leather-bound pack buried deep at the end of the depression. She dug furiously, weeping with relief as she worked it free of the drift. If she hadn't found it, their life-sustaining supplies would have been lost forever.

50

Dare cursed himself for letting her go and followed the rope to the flap, yanking urgently, commanding her to return to the shelter without any hope of being obeyed. He wanted to run after her—if only to strangle her for wandering off— but the moment he left the shelter, it might be lost to them forever. They could wander for hours and walk within inches of it without seeing it. He held their lifeline, and he couldn't risk trying to secure it to part of the shelter with his fingers too stiff to tie a knot. All he could do was jerk on the rope, his heart pounding with anxiety, and hope she would return safely.

Tia staggered back to the swoosha, grabbing a heavy ice-covered robe and shouldering the pack on her back with straps frozen as hard as metal. Stumbling forward, she dropped to her knees and crawled until a pair of arms pulled her into the murky interior.

"Where were you?" He held her, pack and all, in his arms.

"The pack fell off." Her vocal cords seemed frozen, and she fought for air to calm her heaving chest. "I had to go back to the . . ." She couldn't even remember the name of the crude sled that had brought them this far.

"You found it." He felt the bulky pack on her back.

"I want to be warm," she whimpered.

"I'll warm you," he promised.

Chapter Three

Tia collapsed against him, welcoming oblivion even as it pulled her into a whirlpool of blackness.

"Wake up! Tia, fight it. Don't pass out." He softly tapped her cheek, trying to wake her.

The beast was slapping her, his fingers like metal rods . . . his bare fingers . . . She struggled against the darkness and opened her eyes. "You shouldn't take your gloves off."

"Stay awake," he begged. "We have to get warm before we sleep."

"Never be warm," she mumbled, not quite sure where she was.

"Yes, we will. You'll be surprised how well a polar shelter works."

He was fumbling in the dark, but all she wanted was sleep. While she groped for room to stretch out, he reached above them without standing and pulled at a cord, letting a fine haze of ice pellets flutter into their refuge.

The sudden icy intake roused her more than his coaxing, and she stared wide-eyed as sparks illuminated his face. He was lighting a small stove, only a metal box with vents, but it actually glowed, sending forth the bright promise of heat before she could feel it.

"The fuel is a porous ore saturated with oil," he said. "Our ration for each sleep-stop will only last an hour or so, but it should be enough. Take off your coat and boots."

The glow of the stove was supposed to be bright orange by now, but all Dare could see was a dull patch of hazy light. Few things frightened him after his years of wandering, but his stomach tightened with apprehension at his lack of sight. He tried to convince himself he'd gotten out of the storm in time to avoid permanent blindness, but the agonizing pain in his head wasn't encouraging.

"It's not warming us very fast," she said mildly.

"I can't . . ." Every word sent flaming arrows slicing into his skull. "Can't explain. Shake out your coat away from the stove. Then do mine."

She heard the agony in his voice and saw the desperation on his face. When he clutched his forehead, she hastened to do as he asked, shaking pellets from their garments as best she could in a shelter too low for her to stand.

He arranged the fur robe she'd managed to drag back with the pack, furiously brushing away the ice and covering it with a thin oilcloth tarp from the survival pack.

"Sit here," he said.

This time Tia obeyed immediately.

He was removing his heavy boots, and she did the same, afraid to look at her bare toes, expecting to see signs that they were frostbitten.

Sitting cross-legged, tucking his feet under his legs to utilize his own body heat, he began slowly and methodically rubbing his fingers together to restore circulation, instructing her to do the same.

"Now give me your feet," he hoarsely ordered.

She obeyed and as he massaged her toes, sharp needles pricked her flesh; he was going to crack off her toes one by one. She shrieked, yelped, cried hot tears that seared her face, but he continued rubbing her feet.

"I can't see," he admitted reluctantly after an eternity of rubbing her tortured extremities. "What color are your toes?"

"Red, bright red," she moaned, realizing what she'd said. Her toes were a healthy rosy shade, and she could wiggle them. She wasn't going to lose them!

"And mine?" He stretched out his legs, thrusting them between her thighs.

Without hesitation she gently stroked his feet, beginning with the long slope of his arch and carefully caressing each toe, willing warmth into his icy flesh. His muffled groans told her she was torturing him as he'd tormented her, but he sighed in gratitude when she assured him his digits were as healthy as a newborn's.

"It won't get really cold until night," he rasped, pulling on heavy stockings but setting his boots aside.

She did the same, sparing him the chore of giving her any explanations. "Can we eat now?"

"We have to. Scoop ice pellets into the pan and melt them. We'll only use the ale in the bladder in an emergency.".

They drank their fill of water, then used the residue to thaw meat sticks: wild game stuffed into skins and seasoned with coarse salt. He managed to consume one; she ate three with gusto.

The stove was flickering ominously, and the shelter was less frigid but certainly not warm.

"Can we add fuel?" she asked, knowing his answer would be no but unable to imagine surviving the night without heat.

He shook his head. "Now we have to rely on body heat. Sprinkle ice pellets on the coals to save some fuel for when we break our fast in the morning and close the vent above us."

She struggled with stiff fingers, finally realizing that the smoke hole in the ceiling laced shut much like the waist of her leggings.

Bone-weary and overwhelmingly sleepy, she lay down on one side of the fur robe, expecting to sleep curled under her coat.

"One coat isn't enough," he said, pulling it away. "We have to double up."

"I was fine."

"No, we have to lie close under both coats."

"I can't sleep with you." Her words sounded laughably lame under the circumstances.

"You need my body heat as much as I need yours. Don't act the timid virgin."

"I'm not acting!"

"No, I guess not." His voice was that of a weary, soulsick man. "I'm sleeping under the coats. Join me if you want to wake up again."

"You forget you're my guide! I'm paying you to—"

"I haven't seen any payment yet." He yanked her coat over his, folded the robe on his side into a cocoon, and turned his back toward her, settling down to sleep.

"Oh, no!" In the minutes since she'd extinguished the stove, the temperature had plummeted. She could feel particles of ice forming in her nostrils, and she was going to lose consciousness with or without her coat as a cover.

She crawled over and grudgingly lifted one edge of the pile of coats. He'd left space for the width of her shoulders and hips. She slid under and tried to do what he'd done on his side of the robe, folding it over her feet and head, burrowing into the furs, and making sure not a square inch of her body was uncovered.

He yearned for sleep, a deep, healing slumber to restore his sight and to wash away the horrendous pain in his head, but she wiggled like a ground varmint caught by the tail. He knew she was trying to leave space between them. It wasn't possible, and he hoped she'd soon realize it.

The sleeve of her coat was filling his nostrils with a faint, flowery perfume, keeping him awake as much as her infernal squirming.

"Lie still," he rasped.

"There's no room."

"Lie still." Men quaked in their boots when he used that tone. For a moment he thought she was actually going to follow his order.

Her knee brushed the back of his thigh, and she sat upright, pulling up the coats and leaving his feet exposed.

"Have you no sense at all?" He bolted upright with comets exploding in his brain. "Lie on your side. I'll cover us, and if you move one single muscle, if you even wiggle your toes, I'll tie you up until we reach Norvik."

"You wouldn't!"

If his pain had allowed it, Dare would have smiled in satisfaction when she rolled onto her side in a sleeping position and let him arrange the coats and robe into a snug cocoon.

She was asleep almost before he'd satisfied himself that they were both totally covered.

In the stillness of slumber, Tia kept him awake as surely as if she'd been bouncing up and down on his stomach. Just having her close was enough to rob him of desperately needed sleep.

Pain and cold made him immune to arousal, but it didn't make Dare less aware of the soft, slender form nestled against him. They lay like spoons, her backside pressing against him, her shoulder against his chest. Silky tendrils of hair curled around his throat, reminding him of the time he had found an orphaned newborn felina and cared for it, letting it sleep beside him until the little beast showed its savage nature and sank its teeth into his arm. He'd nearly died of blood poisoning, and he never again took a risk without calculating the effect it would have on his army if they didn't have his leadership.

In his heart they would always be his Lost Ones, having become his responsibility after the Zealote evacuation forces had arrived at Warmond's fortress.

Dare would never forget their escape. The fortress had been hemmed in by marsh, a death trap to all who entered it. The Lost Ones couldn't use the underground escape route which led directly to the Citadral, the lair of the Zealotes. The only other route had been across the Flaming Sea.

Dare had studied it since his early years, fascinated by the great bursts of fire that exploded upward from the seabed, small volcanoes that could burn a boat to cinders in only moments. By the time the Lost Ones had fled from the fortress, he knew the secret of the Flaming Sea. The eruptions almost always occurred at night or when the sun was obscured by clouds. When the sun was high and hot, the odds were much better for a young lad to row a small boat to the far shore in safety.

Dare had made thirty-two round trips over a period of a few days in a small wooden boat that had to be patched with muck from the marsh after every voyage to keep water from pouring through the leaks. Each time he had taken as many boys as possible, returning exhausted and alone. In this way he had become the leader of the Lost Ones. Until recently no one had ever questioned his decisions or his right to make them.

The dissension among his followers troubled him more than the pain in his head. He'd gone on the mission to Leonidas to ready his men for the action that had to come soon. Now a new element had been added to his strategy: Logan's daughter.

Even as he held Tia close, wrapping his arm around her to give added warmth, Dare had more questions than answers.

He needed sleep. Great Power above, he was desperate for sleep! But he couldn't turn off his troubled, turbulent thoughts, and every time his captive stirred in her sleep, he became more aware of her as a woman, a slender but shapely female who fit against him as though they were two halves of one whole.

His discomfort wouldn't be as great if he'd taken her into his bed at Ringfort. He could have comforted—and seduced—her with the easy charm that had never failed with women. But he had felt compassion for her loss of the defective and her mount, as well as curiosity about her willingness to pay him twelve Zealote equests. Those wonderful beasts could carry a man all day without tiring; an army equipped with equests couldn't be stopped. With enough of them, Dare could demand the choicest land to settle his Lost Ones in real homes for the first time in their lives. If she was the daughter of Logan . . .

An evil thought crept into his pain-racked head: what sweet revenge against the Zealotes to ravish the Grand Elder's daughter!

It was an unworthy thought, and Dare despised his momentary weakness. The people of Thurlow had called him Wild Man, the Outcast, and a two-legged beast when they drove his ever-growing band away from settlement after settlement, sometimes taking other unhappy children with them, but no man could truthfully accuse him of being dishonorable. Dare's code was, in its way, as strict as any imposed on the Zealotes by the rules of their Order. He couldn't stoop to forcing himself on an unwilling female.

He would, though, use her in any way he could to secure land for the Wanderers. Not one among them would ever inherit land or a name from their rightful parents. The Zealotes' evil ways had brought the Lost Ones to the brink of desperation.

"You've promised me twelve equests, Mistress Tia," he whispered. "The time may come when your father will beg me to settle for a hundred times that ransom."

Dare awoke, screams piercing the fog in his mind, and instinctively he held Tia close, murmuring into her hair until she was awake enough to make sense of his words.

"You've had a bad dream." The wind howled outside their tiny shelter, and he didn't dare sit up for fear of letting icy blasts creep under their covers. "Hush, hush, little one. It will be all right."

"I'm sorry," she said, then asked, "will that wind never stop?"

"It may blow itself out—at least the worst of the gale."

"I can't bear it."

"The worst storms always come near the end of the six moon-cycles of darkness. The first stories I ever heard were ones about the Power of Darkness throwing fits because his time of rule was running short. They were scary nursery tales."

"Your mother told you—"

"I never knew her. Nor my father."

The bitterness in his voice made her want to slink away, but she needed his warmth, needed to be held in strong arms and told that all would be well.

He rolled on his back, his legs stiff from the cramped position, but he pulled her with him, cradling her head on his chest.

"For warmth," he said, maneuvering her legs between his and adjusting his body to her weight.

Her even breathing told him she was sleeping soundly again, but Dare was too wide-awake to do more than close his eyes and wait for the beginning of another day of travel. He was aroused now, achingly hard, and he slid his hand under her tunic, caressing her back without waking her.

Later, much later, he heard the harsh squalls of the yakas and knew the time for sleep had passed. The beasts wanted to wallow in loose drifts and swallow ice pellets, the only sustenance they needed for a trip of many days since they utilized their stored body fat. When they reached Norvik, he would have to let them gorge on precious supplies of grain, but they would earn it before they reached their destination.

His eyes felt sticky, difficult to open, but it was too dark in the shelter to know whether he was suffering from polar blindness.

"Is it daytime?" She stirred sluggishly, seemingly content to cushion her face against his shoulder. "Oh!" She sat up suddenly. "I never meant to sleep so close to you!"

He felt her move away and become part of the blackness that surrounded him.

"You needed my warmth so don't think any more of it. The yakas are howling to go, but we should eat first. There should be enough fuel in the stove to light it."

"I can do it."

"Can you . . . can you see anything?"

"Not well. Just enough to light the stove. The wind is quieter. What a blessing that is!"

"A blessing, yes." His mouth formed words, but in his mind he was screaming in desperation.

He was blind, and there was no way to know if his sight would ever return.

"Shall I heat more water?"

He realized she'd asked twice.

"Yes."

"I found some bread. Can we make a meal of it? I'll only tear off a fifth of it."

"Do it," he agreed woodenly, trying to consider what his blindness meant to their survival.

She put something into his hand, and it took him a moment to realize she'd given him a portion of the frozen flat bread.

"I guess if we dip it in the heated water, we can chew it," she said dubiously.

"Tia, I have to tell you something. I'm blind—it's polar blindness."

"Can you see my fingers?"

"No, I can't see anything."

"How long will it last?"

"I don't know." He shook his head, relieved that the maddening pain had lessened, but helpless to say anything to quell the fear in her voice.

"We'll wait here until you're better."

"No—you have to know the truth, Tia. That may be never."

"I can't find Norvik!"

"No, but you'll have to be my eyes. First tear off a strip of the tarp. I need something to cover them."

He heard ripping and felt her tie a silky strip over his eyes.

"What is this?" It was slippery—almost sensuous—like the garment that had clung to her breasts when he woke her at Ringfort.

"Lining from my coat. It adds nothing to the warmth."

"Thank you," he said, realizing he'd be indebted to her for much more than a slip of cloth if they managed to reach Norvik.

She followed instructions well, collapsing and packing the shelter, then led him to the yakas, helping him identify the lead pair, still in harness because freeing them might tempt them to bolt. Dare heard her labored breath and knew the work was taxing her strength, but she didn't slow down or fail him. If the stench of the beasts' droppings offended her, if working in the inhuman cold pained her, she didn't complain of it. They worked as a team until he told her to hand him the reins.

"You can't see. I'll have to drive the team."

"No, you won't. You can be my eyes. If you look at the amulet on my wrist and tell me what you see, then I can drive the team and you'll be my navigator."

"You can't drive the beasts!"

"Yes, I can. They know my voice and my hand. We have no choice."

"I can do it."

"It takes a man's strength."

"I'm not helpless!"

"Nor am I. Sit down."

"You can't see!"

"I'll follow the trail."

"There is none!"

She could see that although the wind was still blowing in energetic bursts, visibility had improved. Being able to see in all directions didn't comfort her. Great mounds like shifting dunes in a sandy desert were continually changing shape, making the frozen wasteland seem alive with menace.

He flicked his small whip against the planks at their feet, and the yakas inched forward, slowly freeing the swoosha from the drifts around it.

The yakas were nasty beasts, foul-smelling when confined and given to bolting in the wrong direction, but she wanted to drive them, needed to prove she wasn't a helpless female. Although he never said so, Yellow Hair thought she was only the pampered daughter of the Grand Elder. His mocking deference, his self-satisfied assurance, his patronizing ways all told her what he thought of her. If she weren't so frightened of the endless icy vista, she would have liked to see him plunge headfirst into a drift!

She followed his directions in using the magnetic device, shifted her weight to left or right when he gave the order, and maintained a stony silence.

She was pouting and disliked herself for doing it, but he was treating her like a spoiled child. Watching his sure moves and calm acceptance of his blindness, she was reminded of her father and brother, both so sure of themselves, so strong and intelligent, so ready to correct her faults! Was this how it felt to be a man's woman, forever dependent on his will? Even if the reins would bite into her hands and the yakas would jerk her arms from their sockets, at least she'd know how it felt to take control. She didn't want to be coddled or protected! She wanted . . .

What? What was this intense longing that made her want to lash out at the man beside her? Olan, her betrothed, never spoke to her as Yellow Hair did, never treated her as a child or was disrespectful to her. Neither Olan nor any other man had ever stirred such strong emotions in her before. A lack of interest in the young men she knew had prompted her father to arrange a marriage for her with Olan. Tall, broad, and robustly healthy, Olan would father the kind of children so desperately needed on Thurlow. She'd been impressed by Olan's essential goodness, and she had agreed without hesitation to the match out of love for her father. The Grand Elder of the Zealotes deserved a flock of sturdy grandchildren. Olan was kind and gentle, and he had never made her seethe with anger or bristle with hurt pride the way Yellow Hair did. She had never really considered how she felt about him; agreeing to marry him made her father happy, and that was what was important to her. Betrothals were binding on Thurlow, and marriages lasted a lifetime. She'd never considered that she'd agreed too hastily to the match to please her father. She cared for Olan, but he stirred no strong feelings in her. Would her father have been disappointed if she'd refused Olan?

She was quiet and still, which Dare had wanted the previous day, but now her silence annoyed him. He wanted to hear her voice, to feel connected to another human being. He'd spoken a few times to the blind Zealote at Ringfort, and he'd met other sightless people in his travels. But nothing had prepared him for the sheer isolation of perpetual darkness. He felt cut off from humanity, no longer a part of the real world. How must she feel, knowing her survival depended on a man who couldn't see?

"Read my amulet again, I've changed my mind," he said, thrusting his wrist in her direction. "I'm getting tired and I'll show you how to control the team. Just in case."

Tia took his place and grabbed the reins. There was more to the task than she'd realized. The swoosha could capsize if she let the team swerve too suddenly, but too firm a hand on the reins made the beasts balk.

Her arms ached after a while, and holding the reins meant she had to expose her hands to biting winds so severe her gloves did little to protect them.

"Tell me when you're tired," he said. "You're doing well."

The beasts skirted a high drift with little urging from her; then suddenly one of the lead beasts howled in a shrill, almost human voice. The swoosha was tossed from side to side, shuddering to a stop as Yellow Hair grabbed the reins from her.

"I didn't do anything!"

"Tell me what you see!"

A burst of wind battered her face with ice pellets, but she stood and strained to see ahead.

"I can't see! Wait, the lead animals seem to be fighting. There's a great commotion!"

The team didn't respond to his forceful commands, and all the beasts were squealing now, making sounds of extreme distress.

"Crawl forward on your hands and knees," he ordered, "but don't get too close to the yakas. Don't move unless you can see where you're going."

Tia scrambled to obey, crawling down the line of beasts without questioning his reason for telling her to do it. The howling grew louder, but so did a scratching noise, like blunt toenails on ice.

"Don't go any farther!" he shouted urgently.

She looked ahead and knew why he had stopped her. The lead pair had disappeared, suspended by their harnesses over an ice crevasse wide enough to swallow the team and the swoosha.

"Back up very slowly," he called out.

She did, but not before she saw the drama taking place at the edge of the drop-off. The second pair of yakas were biting and tearing at the leather straps, trying to release the lead team from the harness.

She scrambled desperately toward the rear of the swoosha and threw herself down behind it, grabbing the back support and trying to use her weight as an anchor to keep the sled from slipping forward. The lead beasts let out a horrible shriek, and the swoosha shuddered. For an instant she thought they'd be thrown forward into the crevasse; then Yellow Hair was beside her, adding his strength and weight to hers.

"You did the right thing before I even thought of it," he said, the astonishment in his voice all the praise she needed.

"They were biting through the harness. The leaders fell."

Dare tore off his blindfold and pulled her into his arms. She was a blur, pale-faced and indistinct, but he could make out her reddened cheeks, her frightened violet eyes, and her blue-tinged lips.

"Thank the Great Power! I can see!" He held her close, pressing his lips to her cold forehead. The polar blindness had passed.

When they resumed their journey, Tia was grateful that Yellow Hair's sight was restored, as skirting the ice crevasse had taken them many kilometers off course. She also felt an inner warmth that had nothing to do with the robe pulled up to her nose.

Much later, when the yakas were bedded down and a small, smoky fire was warming their shelter, Tia started to talk about their near disaster.

Pam Rock

"We should be dead. Our survival is a gift from the Great Power," he admitted. "Usually a team will follow their leaders, even if it means plunging to their deaths."

"Why did they stop?"

"Maybe they knew they were pulling the Grand Elder's daughter," he teased.

She didn't like his comment, but Dare couldn't tell her the whole truth without making it sound like a boast. He understood what it meant to be a leader of men or yakas. When he had chosen his lead team, he had put beasts just as strong and cunning right behind them. Legend had it that yakas could sense weakness in their leaders and would ruthlessly eliminate them if they failed in their role.

Were his own men sensing weakness in him? Would they eliminate him as ruthlessly as the yakas had cast off the leaders that led them to the crevasse? Even more importantly, could any man but him lead the Wanderers to the home they desperately wanted?

Dare slept deeply in the cramped space, storing up strength for the days of trial to come.

Every time Tia closed her eyes, she saw the yaka team and heard the gnawing and scratching that had sent the leaders to their deaths. The great, bottomless crevasse might disappear in the next polar upheaval, and it could have been her body that was swallowed forever. Her father would never have known what happened to her; her mother would have mourned for her only child until the day she died. Fane would have blamed himself for not learning of her plan and preventing her foolishness. Olan would grieve her loss, and she suspected he would also feel sorrow because he wouldn't be able to fulfill the Grand Elder's expectations.

She didn't cry; she vowed not to shed another tear until she had vindicated herself and succeeded in her quest.

If she had died, she would have spent the rest of eternity with Yellow Hair. A warm, tight feeling welled up in the lower part of her body, and she huddled closer to him.

Chapter Four

"We're here."

Dare touched her shoulder, relieved when Tia opened her eyes and peered ahead to see where they were. It had become more difficult to wake her each time they stopped. He doubted if she even remembered the last two nights they'd spent huddled together for warmth. He would never forget them.

"Where is the wall?" She strained to see through the haze, but all she saw was a huge drift, not unlike countless others they'd had to skirt on their trip.

"There are none."

"But if this is Dare Lore's fortress . . ."

"Do you think the Wanderers need to worry about intruders in this place?"

The yakas were howling excitedly, but Yellow Hair silenced them with a long, high-pitched whistle. Apparently it was a signal for humans as well as beasts, as the drift proved to be a building. Tia watched as the front cracked, sending loose ice cascading to the ground, and a wide double door parted. The team raced forward without prompting.

They entered a cavernous structure, more barn than human dwelling, and the pungent odor of confined beasts made her wrinkle her nose.

Yellow Hair left her and hurried toward the pair of men who had opened the door. A russet-haired, rough-looking youth came over to unharness the yakas, gaping at Tia as though he'd never seen a female before.

"What a relief to—" he blurted out, interrupted when Yellow Hair shouted at him to join the other men.

Yellow Hair embraced the younger man and led all three of them far enough away from her so that she could not overhear them. Then Yellow Hair ended the conversation quickly and walked back to her.

"Where are the rest of the buildings?" she asked, leaving the swoosha and confirming that a large section of the place was devoted to housing animals, not only yakas but a great herd of penned bovine and domestic animals of every description. She understood now how an army could survive in such a desolate place.

"Most of the settlement is underground, partly in natural caverns and partly in man-made excavations," Yellow Hair explained. "Only animals can survive above ground during the dark cycle. The drifts piled up around this building have formed a natural wall of thick ice that never melts. It's enough natural insulation for the beasts, but people have to stay below the surface to keep warm. That's where the original rooms were built, and the Wanderers have enlarged the complex."

Tia threw back her hood, relieved to be out of the wind that made the frigid outdoor temperatures unbearable.

"This way," he said, leading her to the rear of the building, then down a broad stairwell into a gloomy corridor.

"I need to see Dare Lore right away."

"You will soon, but not now."

"I've come so far, and it's taken so long. Surely he'll make time to see me. You needn't take me yourself. Just show me the way to his headquarters."

"That's not the way things are done here, Tia. This isn't the Citadral."

He made several turns, leading her through a labyrinth of stone-floored corridors. Her uneasiness grew when they didn't meet another soul. She tried to remember the number of turns, anxious to know where she was even though there was no possible escape alone across the Frozen Desert.

What if the man she sought was hostile toward her? Tia looked up at her guide, his golden hair matted by the hood he'd thrown off, his face set in a pensive scowl. Would Yellow Hair feel any obligation to escort her back to civilization if the leader of the Wanderers wouldn't listen to her?

"I'm deeply in your debt," she said.

"No doubt you'll discharge your obligation in due time," he said, using a formal tone that made Tia uneasy in his company for the first time since his temporary blindness.

"I can only pay you if you come with me to the Citadral." She felt miserable with guilt, again using what could be an empty hook to fish for his services. How would she persuade her father to give this man the outrageous payment of twelve equests? For the first time in her life, she was afraid of approaching the Grand Elder of the Zealotes.

Her only hope was to succeed in her appeal to Dare Lore; then her father might find it easier to forgive her and discharge her debt.

"How large is this place? How many people live here?" she asked. They'd passed many closed doors, and the subterranean silence was unnerving.

"No questions," he said, sounding almost savage in his refusal to answer.

"I insist you take me to Dare Lore immediately," she said, trying to mask her apprehension.

He turned down a narrower corridor, making her scurry to keep pace.

"In here." He opened a rough plank door and stood aside to let her enter, at the same time turning up the gas in a light fixture on the wall. "Someone will bring you food and fresh clothing. You'll see Dare Lore soon enough."

Before she could protest, he backed out and closed the door. The room was a sleeping chamber, but to Tia it had the bleak look of a prison cell. She rushed to the door to call after Yellow Hair, but an ominous click turned her blood to ice.

He'd locked her in.

Dare hadn't wanted to leave her. Walking away from her without any explanation was like severing one of his own limbs. He would never forget the way she'd curled against his chest, warming him and being warmed, putting her trust in him and never suspecting the treachery in his heart.

It wasn't too late to let her go. Until he revealed her identity to his followers, he still had the option of returning her to her father without ransom demands.

In an agony of indecision, Dare stopped and pressed his forehead against the corridor's rough stucco wall, grinding his teeth and clenching his fists as he struggled with his conscience. For almost twenty full-cycles, since he'd first led the Lost Ones away from Warmond's evil fortress, his every waking thought had been of their welfare. He had no life of his own, no identity except as the leader who had vowed to win a homeland for the Wanderers.

Fate had brought the Grand Elder's daughter to him. He was almost sure her captivity gave him the bargaining power he needed to wrest Zealote lands from Logan. Negotiation instead of warfare: He was preparing his men for battle, but he knew peaceful ways were more lasting. He'd held off the rabble-rousers in his army, promising them a better life if they did things his way. Was there ever a war that didn't sow bitter seeds of hatred and revenge?

He was a warlord who didn't want his people to suffer the agonies of armed conflict. His hostage might enable him to meet their needs without bloodshed and death. His course of action was clear now, but he'd never experienced such emotional turmoil in making a decision.

He needed to reveal his identity and hear the

reason for Tia's rash journey to find him, but a weariness deeper than bodily fatigue urged him to rest first. He needed to strip off his filthy garments and scrub his body; he needed to eat his fill of hot food and refresh himself with steaming mugs of honeyed mead. Even more, he needed to steel himself to betray Tia's trust.

While Dare lingered in the corridor, doing battle with his conscience, he knew his men would be carrying out his whispered orders, bringing food, hot bathwater, and clean garments to Tia. She'd slept an alarming amount of time since his polar blindness receded; he tried to convince himself she now needed time alone to recover from the cold-induced sleeping sickness.

Dare hurried to his own chamber, knowing his followers would understand his need to rest before seeing them. He was greatly tempted to crawl under his fur-covered bed and let oblivion heal his spirit.

Opening the door of his carpeted bedchamber, he turned up the gaslight and dropped his heavy coat on the floor.

"Welcome home, Dare."

The woman's voice sent shivers up his spine.

"What are you doing here, Angeline?" he asked, although he recognized this as her latest ploy to attract his attention.

His visitor stretched like a felina on his bed, her raven hair falling over her bare shoulders in a silky cascade. She smiled and sat up, causing the transparent material of her emerald tunic to stretch taut over her prominent nipples. Laughing softly, she parted her legs, bunching the garment between her sleek thighs.

"I thought you'd need my special warmth to

make you forget your frigid nights in the desert."

"How did you know I was back?" He looked away, picking up his coat and hanging it on a wall peg.

"You know I have the gift of foresight."

"More likely you've corrupted one of the stable workers."

"I only want to make you happy, Dare. We can be wonderful together if only you'll—"

"Get out, Angeline."

"Someday you'll hurt my feelings, Dare. You know I'm the only female here who's worthy of sharing a leader's bed. You tired long ago of the little peasants who amuse your men."

She slid off the bed, swaying her hips and sweeping back her hair, running the pink tip of her tongue over her lips, painted crimson to exaggerate their natural fullness. The women of Norvik called her a witch because her eyes seemed to change color, one day dominated by green and gold glints, the next, a hazy brown that masked her thoughts.

"I should have you disciplined for playing the wanton," he said impatiently. "Go cover yourself, and don't try your tricks on me again."

"Will you make me scrub cooking kettles?" She hooted in derision. "A brave warrior would take a whip to my backside."

"Out!" He held the door open. "If I see you wearing indecent clothing again, you'll muck the bovine stalls for a moon-cycle."

She sauntered out. "Someday you'll realize that we belong together."

Dare slammed the door, his blood roaring in his temples. He was sorely tempted to break his own rule against corporal punishment. He'd never turned down a young person who asked for asylum with the Wanderers, but it had been an evil day when Warmond's own daughter had begged him to take her in. She constantly stirred up trouble, tempting men to neglect their duties and tormenting them for spite. He suspected Angeline of being in league with the troublemakers who wanted an immediate bloody confrontation with Logan, but he'd never been able to find proof of it.

Warmond had secretly broken his own vow of chastity long before Logan reformed the Order and encouraged his members to mate. Warmond had fathered only Angeline. She had been raised by Perrin, a kind and upright Zealote who had married Angeline's mother after she was freed from slavery in Warmond's fortress.

Angeline was one of many runaways who'd appealed to Dare for sanctuary with the Wanderers, a request he never denied because so many who came were sent by parents frantic to save their sons from servitude in the mines. But she was the only one who'd joined because a stepfather was too good and kind.

When the Wanderers left their polar outpost, Dare planned to take Angeline back to civilization and force her to leave his band. He was repulsed by her lewdness, but he didn't underestimate her ability to stir up trouble.

The room was small but not exactly a dungeon, Tia decided. The walls were whitewashed, and the narrow bed was covered with a thick reddish fur. A small water closet had cold running water, a chunk of yellow soap, and squares of flannel to use for bathing. She soaked a cloth and pressed it to her temples, trying to stay calm and think through her situation.

She was honest enough to admit that only her pride was injured. She'd come on an urgent mission, but Yellow Hair acted as though it were a minor matter that could wait. After she spoke to Dare Lore, she wouldn't need to depend on her guide anymore. He'd agreed to bring her to the leader of the Wanderers, and instead he'd confined her in a locked chamber. Who was he to imprison her? What authority did he have to treat her this way? Well, one thing was certain: he didn't deserve a payment of twelve equests!

She was startled by a knock, even though she'd fostered a small hope that Yellow Hair would return so she could vent her frustrations. Her heart skipped a beat when she opened the door and saw the man who'd occupied her thoughts.

"I only came to see if you're comfortable," he said in the tone of a man making an excuse.

"If you really cared about my welfare, you'd take me to Dare Lore this instant!"

"You'll find I don't respond well to ultimatums. You could do your cause more good by telling me your reason for coming here."

"You know I'll only speak to your leader! Who are you? Have you even told him I'm here? You expect a payment of twelve equests, even though I'm no closer to accomplishing my goal than I was at Ringfort."

No one had ever treated her as he did! He showed her no respect. His speech was blunt, and his manners were appalling. His unkempt mane cried out for a comb, and his jaw was as bristly as his temper.

"I came for answers, not questions. If you have nothing to say—"

"Don't go. For twelve equests, you should at least let me know when Dare Lore will see me— if you have his ear. I haven't seen any sign that you're a welcome visitor here."

"You've made it clear that I'm not welcome in this room." He left abruptly, closing the door with a resounding thump.

Tia paced the little room, but even this minor exertion was exhausting. Sinking down on the cot, she wrapped the robe around her, letting her limbs go limp and her thoughts wander.

She fervently wished he would return. She should have said much more about his overbearing ways!

For all his faults, though, Yellow Hair had warmed her through the polar nights. She remembered only too well his broad shoulders and his firm muscular legs. Locked in his arms, the last thing she'd noticed before falling asleep the last night in the shelter was the way his breath whispered against her eyelids, caressing her lashes and tickling the side of her nose.

She wished her memories of the trip were sharper. She had a vague recollection of sleeping on top of him, her legs squeezed into the space between his, but reality and fantasy were all jumbled together in her mind. Had he really pressed his mouth to her ear and crooned soothing words to calm her fears? Had she only imagined his fingers entwined in her hair, gently untangling strands that had been matted by her hood?

Shivering under the heavy robe, Tia felt her courage ebbing. The man she had come so far to see might laugh at her proposal and think she was a foolish girl. He was probably a rough sort, no better than the men who'd scorned her offer back at Ringfort. Perhaps his legendary army was only a handful of ruffians interested in nothing but their own pleasure. What would happen to her if the stories about him were only myths, pretty tales invented by girls hungry for romance?

No matter what rough treatment he might mete out to her, the worst punishment would be knowing she'd been a fool to seek him out.

"Are you going to sleep forever?"

Tia bolted upright and stared at the woman beside the bed.

"There wasn't any point in knocking. You were locked in."

"Who are you?" Tia asked her visitor, who was robed in black, her face partially hooded, reminding Tia of the older Zealotes who clung to the ancient manner of dress. Raven hair framed a stunning face, not beautiful but exotic, with sharply etched features and full, pouty lips.

"I'm Angeline and I've brought you clean clothes. I had a pail of hot water, but it was too heavy to lug all this way. You're not too highbred to wash in cold, are you?"

Tia couldn't remember bathing in anything but warm, scented water at the Citadral, but her long trip had taught her to make do with whatever was available. She shook her head, not sure how to answer this blunt-speaking woman.

"Why are you here?" Angeline tossed a bundle of clothes which she had draped over her arm onto the bed.

"I have to see Dare Lore."

"See him?" She frowned and raised one dark

brow, staring with an intensity that made Tia feel like squirming. "Why?"

"I really can't tell anyone but him. I'm sorry." She apologized automatically, then wished she could take it back. If everyone at Norvik was as rude as Angeline, this place was more unpleasant than Ringfort.

"Why aren't you with him now, if you're so eager to talk to him?"

"Yellow Hair—my guide—wouldn't take me to him. He locked me here instead."

"You've never seen Dare?"

"No, of course not."

Angeline walked over and fingered the rumpled violet tunic Tia had worn so long. "I've never worn this color. Do you think it would suit me?"

"I don't know. . . . I suppose it would."

"I could take you to Dare right now—or you can wait until he accidentally hears you're here. That could take a moon-cycle."

"I can't wait that long!"

"Well, I'm the only one you're likely to see, stuck away in this corner of the labyrinth, and I'm supposed to lock the door when I leave."

"Please, don't. . . ."

"Are you asking me to risk a whipping from Dare?"

Tia paled under the woman's close scrutiny. "You make him sound like a beast."

"I'm not afraid of him, but if I'm going to risk disobeying him, I have to have an incentive. I think that shade of violet would look wonderful on me, don't you?"

"No doubt it would." Tia hated the greedy look on Angeline's face, but not even a tunic made by her mother meant as much as the chance to see

Dare Lore right away. "It's yours if you'll take me to him."

"I'll take you as far as his chamber. Maybe he won't think to ask who brought you there, and you must promise not to mention my name. It wouldn't be a good idea to betray the person who will be bringing you your meals," Angeline warned.

"All that matters to me is seeing Dare Lore."

"Change your clothes, then. I'll wait for you."

"I'll just give you my tunic." Tia pulled it off, uncomfortable removing even that article of clothing under the watchful eyes of this stranger.

"Strip to your skin and wash yourself. Do you want to present yourself to Dare smelling like a yaka?"

"No, of course not."

Tia had never had anyone stare at her body with such appraising eyes, as though the woman wanted to discover any physical flaw.

"Your breasts are full, but not so comely as mine, I think. You have little-girl nipples—pink buds like that will never excite a real man."

"You have no right. . . ." Tia was as embarrassed as she was angry.

"I'll leave if you like, but I don't think you'll find anyone else willing to lead you to Dare for the price of a soiled tunic."

"Stay," Tia said reluctantly, retreating to the tiny doorless water closet.

Even there she couldn't avoid scrutiny. She could feel Angeline's eyes on her as she stripped off her leggings and hastily washed her travel-weary body.

The change of clothes was nondescript but clean and comfortable: a gathered brown skirt laced at the waist, a simple white tunic, and a shawl woven in stripes of russet and gold. Tia slipped her bare feet into the shapeless leather slippers and started to untangle her hair with a comb that had been tied up in the bundle of clothing. She struggled with the tangles while Angeline rolled up the violet tunic and concealed it under her robe.

"Enough of that," she said. "I can't wait forever for you."

"It's been so many days since I lost my comb. . . ." Tia tossed her new one on the bed, realizing that her appearance meant nothing to the other woman. "You're right. I must see Dare Lore right away."

"Follow behind me and don't make a sound," Angeline warned. "I shouldn't be doing this, and I don't want to be stopped before we get there."

"I understand."

"Here, take the key and put it in your pocket. You might want to lock yourself in when you return."

Tia had a peculiar sensation, almost as if Angeline had said, "if you return." She took the key, tucking it away in a pocket of the skirt.

Angeline closed the door after them.

Only a few dim, widely spaced gas lamps on wall brackets illuminated the corridor, but Tia was sure they were going in the opposite direction from the way she'd entered the underground complex.

"Quiet," her guide ordered, but it was an unnecessary warning. Tia wanted only one thing: to meet Dare Lore. She wouldn't do anything to attract attention to herself.

After several turns they came to a corridor that was down three steps from the others. The ceiling was lower, and the only illumination was a wax stick burning in a wall fixture with a globe.

Tia hesitated, not liking this narrow, dank hall. She let Angeline move several paces ahead while she debated whether to turn back.

"Hurry. Do you want me to get caught?" Angeline urged.

"Why would your leader use a chamber here? This section looks half-finished."

"It is, but a leader needs privacy." She took Tia's wrist and pulled her forward to a door that was bolted on the outside.

"Let me go," Tia said, trying to pull loose but unable to break the taller woman's grasp. "This door has a lock like a prison cell."

"Be still! This is the back entrance, the one Dare uses for private interviews. Do you want to fuel the curiosity of a hundred idlers on your way to see him?"

"Perhaps I'll just wait for him to send for me."

"We struck a deal. You won't get your tunic back from me."

"Keep it, then. I'm going back." Tia tried to yank free while Angeline used one hand to slide back the bolt and open the door.

"I have a visitor for you," she called, propelling Tia into the room with a vicious jerk on her arm.

A black-robed figure rose to face her, knocking over the writing-table chair where he'd been sitting.

"Are you Dare Lore?" Tia asked, knowing the answer before the words were out of her mouth. This man was old, his face seamed with gritty lines and his bushy eyebrows white and shaggy over piercing black, mad eyes.

"Female!" He made the word sound like a curse.

"I've made a mistake," she said apologetically, backing toward the door with her heart pounding.

"Bitch!" he howled, springing toward Tia with the quickness of a serpent and grabbing a handful of her hair before she could scream. "How dare you come here!"

He yanked so hard Tia thought he'd tear her scalp off, pulling her face so close she could feel drops of spittle on her forehead.

She screamed hysterically and tried to lash out at him, but he dropped his hands to her throat and cut off her cries for help.

Kicking and pushing, Tia struggled against him, but his thumbs were cutting off her air. Sparks of light danced behind her lids, and she fought even harder.

"Let her go, Burek!"

"Castrating bitch! She deserves to die!"

The steely fingers released her, and Tia gasped for air, backing away from the madman and into a pair of strong arms. She was pulled into the corridor; then her rescuer slammed the door and thrust home the bolt to imprison her attacker.

"Are you crazy? He could have killed you!"

"Dare?" was all she could whisper as she stared up into the face of a handsome, dark-skinned man with close-cropped black hair and puzzled brown eyes.

"Dare Lore wants to see you. If he hadn't sent me to fetch you, Burek would have killed you."

"But why?" She sank down to her knees, massaging her throat and trembling from her near brush with death.

"Because you're female. The old renegade is insane. Didn't you think there might be a reason for the bolt on the door?"

"Yes, but she wouldn't let me go—she yanked me into the room."

"Who?" The man bent to examine her bruised neck, then helped her stand.

"Angeline said she'd take me to Dare Lore if I gave her my tunic."

"She didn't want your tunic—she wanted your life. Burek is one of the runaway Zealotes who took refuge at Warmond's fortress. Dare let him join the Wanderers in exchange for teaching our men the art of making weapons."

"But why kill me?"

"Burek kept a slave woman at Warmond's fortress, a poor creature he tortured one time too many. When he passed out in a drunken stupor, she castrated him with his own dirk and ran away into the marsh to die. Now it's suicidal for any woman to go near him."

"Why would Angeline lead me there?"

"In her way, she's as crazy as Burek." He let Tia lean on his arm, slowly walking back toward her chamber. "She must have heard that a beautiful woman came here, and in her jealousy she thought Dare had chosen you to be his woman."

"She and Dare are—"

"No, she repels him as she does all decent men. She's the daughter of Warmond, and lately she's shown signs of being as evil as he is."

"Who are you?"

"Jonati, Dare's lieutenant and friend."

"How did you find me?"

"I went to your room to bring you to him. You were gone, and I had a feeling something terrible had happened. I was checking the corridors when your screams led me down to the unfinished section."

"May I see Dare Lore now?"

"He'll want to hear what happened to you immediately, if you're up to it."

"I'll have to be," she whispered hoarsely, not too proud to cling to his arm.

Chapter Five

Tia had given much thought to what she would
say to the leader of the Wanderers, but now
that the time was near, her mind was a blank.
The image of Burek's savage face stayed with
her, and she couldn't stop looking over her
shoulder.

"He can't get out," Jonati assured her. "You're
completely safe with me."

"I can't thank you enough. I owe you my life."

"You're not indebted to me. I'm only sorry you
had such a horrible fright. Most of us here aren't
the least bit scary."

They descended several flights of steep, curving
stairs into a high-domed cavern. Dark green rock
walls marbled with silver formed a natural cathe-
dral with catwalks above and tunnels leading off
in several directions. A lean, shaggy-haired young
man in black breeches, high boots, and a gray

tunic passed them with a nod of his head and a curious glance at Tia.

"I didn't expect anything like this," she said, awed.

"We have what we need to survive," Jonati said bitterly. "Everything except sunlight, moon glow, blue skies, fertile soil, and the freedom to come and go without being harassed and driven away."

She followed him into a tunnel braced by wooden beams, then through an arch into another man-made corridor.

"This place is so large."

"The engineers who built it expected to find hyronium to meet Earth's quota, so the government didn't spare any expense."

"Did they find it here?"

"No, all they found were base metals and natural gas, nothing Earth wanted. When Dare brought us here, it had been abandoned for at least fifty full-cycles. We made it habitable because we had to, but the metals have been a blessing. Only the Zealotes think the planet is better off without them."

"Only as weapons," Tia was quick to point out.

"No matter. We find most villages more than willing to trade food and other necessities for the weapons and implements we make here."

He stopped and opened a door. "Wait here," Jonati told her, closing it before she could see into the room.

"What took you so long?" Dare felt as though he'd been waiting hours.

"There was a problem. Angeline pretended to take the Zealote woman to you, but instead she tricked her into Burek's room," Jonati answered.

"Is Tia all right?" Dare asked, the blood draining from his face when he thought of the possible consequences.

"Frightened but not hurt. I got to her just in time."

"Thank the Great Power! No man ever had a better friend than you, Jonati. What possessed that she-fiend to try to kill Tia? Letting Angeline join us was the worst decision I've ever made!"

"Don't blame yourself. She looked like a homeless waif when she first came to you. You've never turned down anyone who had no other place to go."

"I may have to start," Dare said, furious at Warmond's treacherous daughter. "I should have that witch driven out of Norvik. Let her try to scheme her way across the desert."

"You won't, though."

Dare stared at his lifelong friend, then shrugged. "If I do, the malcontents here might rally to her aid. It's just the excuse they need for open rebellion. I can't allow anything to divide us, not now when we're so close to success."

"While you were gone, Becket was the most vocal about his complaints. The food is wretched; man isn't meant to live without sunlight. He only said things that bother all of us from time to time, but he's been seen whispering with others."

"I wish I had a clearer picture of how many support the faction that opposes us. And more importantly, who the leader is—I suspect Becket. We're so close to success, Jonati! The government is losing its grip. There couldn't be a worse time for a faction within the Wanderers to stir up trouble."

"I can't believe there are large numbers who are

talking against you. I'll find Angeline and make sure she doesn't make any more moves against your captive."

"Lock her in the cell next to Burek's for the time being. I'll deal with her as soon as I can. And find out who defied my orders and told her about Tia's arrival. It's probably one of the three on stable duty when we arrived."

"Are you ready to see Tia?"

"Send her in," Dare said, sounding more ready than he felt. His palms were damp, and being unsure of himself was a frame of mind so foreign to his nature that he dreaded this meeting more than he feared losing his own life. It went against his policy to practice fraud, and he felt like a man waiting to be judged for a felony. He had a wild urge to fall on his knees and beg Tia's forgiveness for not revealing his identity sooner. Since returning, he'd thought of little but their nights in the polar shelter, and he couldn't believe he'd held her so close and not sampled her sweet lips. That denial was tormenting him now. He'd never felt so drawn to a female and had never dreaded anyone's anger and scorn so much. The burden of leadership often demanded sacrifices, but he'd never paid such a high price for the sake of the Wanderers.

Dare sensed her fear when she stepped into his chamber, and it only made his guilt worse when Tia smiled in relief and greeted him as a friend.

"Yellow Hair! I didn't expect you to be here, but I'm so glad you are. A horrible woman promised to take me to Dare Lore, but she took me to a madman instead. He nearly killed me! I'm so sorry I didn't trust you to arrange this meeting."

She looked around, as though expecting to see a third person, then frowned in puzzlement.

"Jonati said Dare would be here."

"He is."

"No, you can't be. . . ."

He stepped closer, and she looked at him with dismay.

"I'm Dare Lore," he admitted, pained by the hurt in her eyes.

"You're a changeling—a twin brother! Or are you an illusion? My mind must be playing tricks on me."

"No, Tia." Her unwillingness to accept the truth only made it more difficult for him.

"Why did you pretend to be Yellow Hair?"

"You gave me that name. I never liked it, but I would gladly make it mine for life if that could change things."

"You deceived me."

"I'm deeply sorry, but Ringfort wasn't the place to tell you."

He had ordered that she be given clothes, and these drab ones were perhaps the castoffs of a girl grown too tall to wear them, but Tia was more beautiful in humble garments than any other woman in costly finery. Her hair streamed over her shoulders, a rich sable mane so silky his fingers ached to touch it. He'd seen her violet eyes sparkle in anger and the little bow above her lips deepen when she pouted. He thought he knew her moods, and he'd expected to face monumental anger, the worst her temper could produce. Nothing had prepared him for the stricken look on her face, for the pain that clouded her eyes.

She slowly raised her chin, biting her lower

lip to stop it from quivering, and looked into his eyes.

The legendary Dare Lore certainly was a comely man, she thought miserably, as her eyes traveled over his brushed golden hair and his clean-shaven face. Her cheeks burned at the memory of the question she'd asked him. She felt stripped of pride, her trust destroyed and her heart ravished by betrayal. Until that moment, she hadn't known how much deceit could hurt.

"Please sit," he urged.

Her instinct was to refuse anything he offered, but her legs were trembling, and she needed time to compose herself. Tia gathered the limp shawl tightly around her shoulders and sat on a chair with a backrest and legs fashioned from massive antlers. It was one of several like it clustered around a dark round table. Except for the fur-covered bed, the room reminded her of the one her father used to confer with his closest counselors.

"I'm sorry Angeline put your life at risk. Living underground takes a toll on all of us, but that doesn't excuse what she tried to do. I guarantee she won't trouble you again. Now I think it's time you tell me your reason for wanting to see me."

"I could have told you at Ringfort. Why bring me here?"

"Telling me there wouldn't have changed my plan, Tia," he said regretfully. "I wanted to spare you the distress of traveling here as my prisoner."

"Spare me! You're telling me I'm your captive after I came here in good faith to—"

How could she beg for his help now? She was

the daughter of the Grand Elder; she didn't know how to behave as a supplicant, especially not a captive one.

"Tell me why you wanted to see me, Tia." His voice was husky and persuasive, coaxing not demanding, but they both knew he held her in his power.

She looked down, seeing only his close-fitting brown breeches tucked into high boots, but she felt his eyes on her, vivid blue and penetrating.

Slowly, and she hoped regally, she rose to her feet and looked into his face, trying to see the warlord, not the man who'd held her in his arms and shared his warmth during those five long polar nights.

"You must know something of the situation on Thurlow. Earth's demand for hyronium increases each time one of their vessels arrives, and now their technology allows them to come almost at will," she said.

Dare nodded, watching her soft pink lips, fearing that what she had to say would separate them even further.

"Only one mine is still producing, but to meet the quota, men are now required to work through the planting season, sometimes with only one moon-cycle of release time to work on their own holdings."

Dare was surprised by her news; none of his sources had told him that the term of servitude had been increased so drastically.

"I take it the Zealotes are still exempt from service," he said harshly.

"The Order is dedicated to—"

"Yes, I know. Learning, philosophy, the arts, things too lofty for the common man."

"You make it sound like an evil thing to pursue wisdom!"

"Not evil, but not much help to the people of Thurlow."

"That's not true! Even now my father is negotiating with the government to right some of the great injustices—"

"This I don't want to hear. I can't accept the child-stealing Zealotes as humanitarians."

"My father changed all that! Babes are no longer summoned or kidnapped into the Order. My own adopted brother, Fane, was the last. Zealotes marry now. It's the sacred duty of every member to beget healthy children."

"Your father is no hero to me. What has he done for the disinherited, the Lost Ones?"

"You ran away with them! You never gave the Zealotes a chance!"

"We escaped from the cult that robbed us of our families, our land, even our names!"

"My father is a good man! He's trying to persuade the government to resist Earth's unreasonable demands."

"How will he do that? Your father lives in the past."

"He's changed—and so have the Zealotes—but he needs help."

"He sent you here to ask me to help him?" Dare sat down on the edge of the bed, stunned by the audacity of the Grand Elder.

"No! He doesn't know I'm here. Please, Dare. . . ."

"I think I liked it better when you called me Yellow Hair and only wanted me to risk my own life for your father's sake. You've heard rumors that I have a large army, and you want me to use it to further his ends." He stood again and paced without looking at her.

"Not his ends—the welfare of Thurlow. You live here too. You can't be indifferent to what's happening: people going hungry, the economy in shambles—"

"You've told me what you want," he interrupted brusquely. "What are you offering in return?"

"I'm sure my father would reward you. . . ."

"Are you also sure he'll pay me the twelve equests you owe me?"

"I hope he will," she said with less assurance.

"Hope! You were willing to let me risk my life, and you only 'hope' your father will pay your debt?"

"The Wanderers could be wiped out too, if all of Thurlow erupts in violence."

"Or my people could be the only survivors."

"That's cold-blooded!"

"Only practical," he said, wishing he could wipe the stricken look from her face and make her smile at him with warmth and longing.

"At least consider what it could mean if your army helps my father replace the government and break Earth's hold on Thurlow."

"Have the Zealotes grown too weak to fight their own battles?"

"Their numbers are too small, and they're poorly armed. The rope is still the Zealotes' choice of weapon."

"You've given me much to think about," he said in a cold, formal voice.

He stood very close, but she was a world away from him. He wanted to put his hands on her, to grasp her slender shoulders and feel her tremble against him, but it wasn't to be.

For an instant his face softened, and she thought he'd take her in his arms. She opened herself to him for a fleeting instant, wanting to feel the whisper of his breath on her eyelids again, but he hardened his expression and turned away.

"Why did you bring me here?" she asked.

"As a hostage."

"Do you want my father to deliver the equests in exchange for my safe return?"

"More than that, Tia. For the present, you'll have the best accommodations we can provide. Someone will come to take you to your chamber."

"But we've . . ." she started to say, but he left without closing the door. She was too stunned by his abrupt departure to follow him into the corridor. A statue carved of stone could leave its pedestal more easily than she could have moved to pursue him.

She didn't know if minutes or hours had passed when Jonati finally came for her.

"I think you'll like your new chamber better," he said.

He led her to a door nearby, but she couldn't react to his kindness or show appreciation for the snug, carpeted little room that was to be her prison.

"You'll have everything you need here," he assured her. "Just ask, and we'll do our best to provide any comforts you would like. Our traders do better each time they go out. There's hardly a man on Thurlow who doesn't want a sword or dirk these days."

"They're illegal," she said woodenly, forgetting the trouble she'd had procuring the one Yellow Hair—Dare—had taken from her.

"These are lawless times," Jonati said, leaving her and quietly shutting the door.

She expected to hear the metallic click of a lock, but none followed Jonati's departure. To be sure, she opened the door a crack. There wasn't a lock; the only security fixture on the door was a small dead bolt on the inside.

This small token of trust only made Tia more despondent. She could leave the room, but there was nowhere to go. Even if she wanted to sacrifice her life in a futile attempt to escape across the desert, she had no idea where she was in the underground labyrinth. She would be seen and caught long before she reached the surface.

"Damn you, Dare!" She pounded on the solid plank door, then flung herself on a bed covered with a thick, soft blanket woven from the fleece of woolies.

Her instinct was to cry, to howl against her fate, but she remembered her vow to remain strong and to fulfill her mission.

She plucked some soft white fibers from the bedcovering and rolled them between her thumb and fingers, crushing them into a hard ball, then blew it from her palm.

This wasn't the end of her quest. Dare could imprison her and demand a ransom from her father, but the struggle between them was only beginning. She wasn't ready to concede victory to him.

Dare wanted to smash something. He needed to go to the training room and grapple with one of his strongest men or do combat with one of the best swordsmen, but he was too angry to trust himself not to draw blood.

One person did deserve his fury. He ran up the curving stairwells to the room where Angeline was confined. When he reached it, he slid the bolt and slammed the door open.

"Do you have any idea what you nearly did?"

Angeline was sitting on the bed, her knees pulled up to her chin, her eyes murky and hooded.

"You didn't need to bring her here. You have me."

Anger and jealousy made her voice ugly, but at least she didn't flaunt her body or jest about whippings she knew he'd never administer.

"I've always respected your intelligence, Angeline, even when your behavior was abominable. No longer! Your stupidity nearly ruined my plans. Do you really think I brought the Grand Elder's daughter across the desert in the dark season just to mate with her? I could have done that much more conveniently at Ringfort."

"Logan's daughter?" Her voice trembled, and she stood, putting out her hands as though to ward off a blow.

"The perfect hostage fell into my hands by chance," he said scornfully, "and you nearly ruined our opportunity to bring the Grand Elder to his knees."

"Forgive me, Dare. Please forgive me!" She fell to her knees and pressed her forehead against the top of his boot. "I deserve whatever punishment you decide on."

"Get up, Angeline," he said, embarrassed by her overly dramatic gesture. "You're being ridiculous."

"Ridiculous?" She barely whispered the word, but her cheeks blazed with color and her eyes glazed over, the mottled brown revealing little of her thoughts.

"You're confined to this room for three days on short rations. Then, if Jonati decides you're penitent enough, you'll be assigned to scullery duty indefinitely."

She dropped her chin, hiding her face from him, but he could see her shoulders trembling with anger.

"You're responsible for Tia's safety. Warn your friends away from her. If anything happens to the Grand Elder's daughter, you'll be driven out of Norvik."

"Alone—in the Frozen Desert?" Her shock wasn't feigned.

"Yes, and one more thing. I don't want to set eyes on you again. Stay away from me unless you want to spend the rest of your days in this chamber."

"Not seeing you is the cruelest punishment of all!" she cried out. "That woman does mean more to you than a chance to best Logan."

"You don't know what you're saying." He turned away and left her in the locked room.

Tia couldn't complain that her captors were unkind. On the second day of her imprisonment she had been given a pale yellow robe so soft that wearing it was like wrapping herself in a cloud. Even better, Jonati had brought her a thick leather-bound volume of stories. The costly book of Earth myths was finer than any in the Zealotes' library, and she had felt weak with confusion when she saw Dare's name inscribed on the inside cover. The Zealotes had kept a love of books and learning alive on the planet, but few people outside the Order had access to such fine works. Sharing it with her had been exceedingly generous.

But Dare was still a beast! Had he thought he could atone for his betrayal with the gift of a book? She had almost cried then, but she had refused to give in to her moment of weakness.

Not even the beautiful tales in the book had distracted her from longing for her home and family. She missed her own room with its appointments: her ornately carved wooden bed and matching chiffonier, her polished steel mirror, and her petit point footstool.

She had tried to keep her mind on trivial things because it hurt too much to think about her family's and her betrothed's worry and fear. Guilt was like a boulder pressing on her heart. She had grown so sick of her own company during these past nine days that she could do nothing but pace the brightly woven rug, wondering if her feet would wear away the vivid greens, browns, and reds in the intricate pattern.

Nothing was worse than being Dare's prisoner! She needed a hero to rescue her, the kind of man she'd imagined Dare to be before she met him, but she couldn't find solace in the hope of being rescued. The thought of scholarly Olan attempting such derring-do almost brought a smile to her lips. He didn't even know where she was, and for that she could only blame herself. Dare would keep her captive until it served his purpose to release her. And each passing day put her father in greater danger.

Her thoughts wearied her and she longed for something greater than freedom, more satisfying than the security of home, more fulfilling than the love of her family. But when that longing focused on visions of Dare, she raged against herself, against fate, and especially against her captor.

The next time Jonati came, she would persuade him to bring her a pen with writing fluid and paper, telling him it was a fancy of hers to compose verses. She had a plan.

Dare stared at the scrap of paper, trying to feel anger instead of the painful longing that ate at him like a ravenous beast devouring him from within.

"You have to admire her resourcefulness," Jonati said. "If that note had gotten into the wrong hands, she might have found her rescuer."

"I suppose there are quite a few here who would smuggle her back to civilization for the reward Logan would give."

"Fortunately none of them were working in the kitchen."

"I wonder how many notes she's smuggled out under dinner plates."

"This was the first," Jonati said uncomfortably. "I gave her the paper and quill just yesterday at her request so she could entertain herself writing poems. I'm sorry for being so gullible."

"No, don't apologize. I would have done the same. Just take them away and let her know we'll be watching her more carefully. Assign a guard to watch her whenever she leaves her chamber." Dare was so weary his head ached, but each passing day brought him closer to the time when the dark season would end and he could send a messenger to Logan. He didn't have time for the aching sense of loss that filled all his waking hours.

"She never leaves her room, Dare. Maybe you should talk to her."

"No, that's not a good idea." Dare turned his back to Jonati, dismissing him.

When Jonati took away her writing tool and paper, he also took Tia's last hope of finding someone to help her escape.

"Walk the corridors," he suggested when she complained of boredom. "You're not confined to your room. This place seems dismal, but there are things to see: the foundry, the venting system. . . ."

"I'm never going to leave Norvik, am I, Jonati?"

"Of course you are." He rubbed his hands together, then wiped them on the sides of his reddish-brown breeches.

"I've never seen you fidget before."

"I'm worried about you, friend Tia. You shouldn't be alone so much."

"You're the only one here I want to see, and there's nothing more for us to say to one another, is there?"

When he left, she paced feverishly. Her long hours of solitude had given her time to think. She had one more idea, and if it succeeded, she'd be done with plans and quests forever.

"She seems to like you," Dare said impatiently. "Talk to her, tell her she's being a silly fool!"

Jonati studied his friend with concern but didn't answer.

"Do something to make her eat!" Dare demanded.

"Do you want me to take two men to hold her down while I force soup down her throat?" Jonati was one of the few people who dared use sarcasm with Dare.

"No, of course not. What should we do? You know her better than I do." His flush gave away his falsehood. He knew Tia better than anyone else; she lived in his mind, and thoughts of her were consuming him.

"She hasn't eaten for four days, and a dead hostage isn't worth much. You might try tempting her with a special treat."

"Try that," Dare ordered.

"I have." Jonati shook his head. "I think you'll have to go to her yourself."

The flat bread Dare carried was still warm from the oven, and the sweet preserve he'd spread on it was the last of a small hoard they'd traded for a bag of metal ingots before the dark season began.

He knocked but didn't expect an answer. Her door wasn't locked, but if it had been, he would have smashed it off the hinges to go to her.

"I brought you fresh bread," he said, closing the door behind him and moving to the bed.

He sat beside her, breaking off a small bit and holding it near her lips.

Tia turned her face away, but not before he saw the violet shadows under her eyes, the pale shading that emphasized their color. Her face seemed leaner, her cheekbones sharper, but she was even lovelier than he remembered.

"Please, Tia."

She pulled herself up, although it seemed to take more strength than she had to spare.

"It's delicious." Dare chewed with a show of relish, although it could have been a dab of sawdust for all the pleasure it gave him.

"A drink?" He held a mug of warm milk laced with honey to her lips.

She shook her head, closing her eyes. "I want only water."

"I'll bring you some."

She swung her legs over the edge of the bed, wrapping the yellow robe around them and wishing she had the energy to conceal her thin, pale feet.

She drank when he put his arm around her and held the cup to her lips, but his touch made her tremble from something more than hunger.

"Leave now," she said.

"No, I'm staying until you've eaten what I've brought."

"I won't!"

"Oh, but you will," he said, brushing her forehead with his fingertips.

"Please reconsider helping my father. You know he only wants what's best for everyone on Thurlow."

"I don't want to hear your pleas."

"You're cruel, insufferable. . . ."

This was the hero whose reputation had lured her to Norvik in hopes of helping her father, the golden warrior who was all she'd ever dreamed of in a man. Yet her self-imposed starvation hadn't touched his heart. Part of her admired him for not letting himself be manipulated, but she longed to see compassion on his face instead of the poorly veiled scorn.

Dare heard her words, but her eyes were telling another story. He'd been right to avoid her, even when stories of her fast had kept him awake at night. Sometimes he felt like her hostage, not her captor, and blood thundered in his ears when he

105

thought of the consequences of possessing the Grand Elder's daughter. She was Logan's daughter, flesh of his flesh, child of his heart. Tia was the one woman on the planet who could have a disastrous effect on his long-cherished plan.

Could she be his? The violet depths of her eyes seemed to beckon him, but the price of surrendering to his desire was one he could ill afford. He couldn't put his heart in the delicate white hands of the Grand Elder's daughter, nor could he promise to support her father's cause. His first obligation was to the Wanderers.

With superhuman effort, he stood and turned away. He picked up the bread, sticky with bright red preserves, and tore off a small piece.

"Eat this now," he ordered.

She accepted the morsel, feeling as though her will had been ground into dust. She hadn't thought he'd let her fast so long, and there was no further reason to defy him in this way. She couldn't help her father by dying.

He fed her, silently insisting she finish the last crumb, then handed her the honeyed milk.

"Drink all of it."

She didn't understand what was happening. Weak and incapable of resistance, she felt as helpless as a newborn. Yet part of her mocked her subservience, urging her to hurl the unwanted cup across the room.

"I'm going now," he said when the milk was gone. "But if you don't eat a goodly portion of every meal, I'll be back."

After he left, she thought of all the things she should have said, scathing remarks to put him in his place. Hunger had addled her brain, making her give in to a man who didn't deserve her respect.

She wanted him to come back so she could tell him how much she hated him!

Her sacrifice hadn't accomplished anything, except to make her so weak she'd wanted to feel his arms around her more than she'd wanted food. She almost hated herself more than him!

Night and day meant nothing to the Wanderers in their subterranean hold, but Dare had long ago set up an inflexible schedule for sleeping. Only the weapon-makers who worked a late shift at the forge and those on night guard duty were exempted from being in their sleeping chambers.

He followed his own rule, pacing like a caged lepine as he remembered each moment with Tia. What wouldn't she do to enlist him in her father's cause? Did she understand what she was asking? His whole life was invested in securing land for the Wanderers. What would happen if he used his now-powerful army to aid a Zealote cause?

He was angry at himself for letting her fast so long. She'd taken food from his hand, but he didn't feel any sense of victory. Every skirmish with Tia drained him, and he began to doubt his own steadfastness.

As soon as she recovered her strength, life was going to change for the Grand Elder's daughter. It was time she understood more about the Wanderers, and one great source of their strength was shared labor. No member, himself included, was too lofty or too privileged to be exempt from the chores of everyday existence.

He couldn't purge thoughts of the beguiling Tia from his own mind, but he could take steps to occupy her with something besides her father's cause.

Chapter Six

Every fifth day Dare met with his Council of Six, the men responsible for arming and training the Wanderers' army. They gathered around the table in his chamber after the day's first meal: Jonati, his second in command; Theobar, the rusty-haired weapon-maker; Henus, small and shortsighted, the supply master and keeper of records; Cyrus, thin and scholarly, the planner of routes who knew the geography of the planet as well as the palm of his hand; Gregor, an olive-skinned giant who oversaw the physical training of the army; and Garridan, the master swordsman.

Although Dare loved them all as brothers, only Jonati, Henus, and Cyrus knew of his second army at Leonidas. The fewer who knew, the less chance there was of a careless word slipping out in the throes of anger or passion.

They argued as equals. Dare weighed each man's opinion before making a decision, but today they were talking in circles, their words hardly registering on his weary mind. Was one of them a leader of the malcontents, speaking against him behind his back? He watched each man's face as he spoke, wondering if the bonds that had held them together since their childhood in Warmond's fortress were weakening.

Jonati he would trust with his life, and Gregor was surely as loyal as he was unimaginative, content to follow any decision Dare made. Henus fought a greedy streak in his nature, but Dare had never known him to put the welfare of the Wanderers second. Cyrus, more than any of them, wanted a piece of land on the map he carried in his head. Theobar was a genius with his hands, insisting that each weapon struck on the Norvik forge was the finest men could make. Garridan was as skilled in using a sword as Theobar was in making it, but Dare frowned when the swordsman started speaking.

"I say we strike out immediately," Garridan argued. "We have the Grand Elder's daughter. We'll never be more ready." He pushed away the coal black hair falling over his forehead, revealing the vivid scar that had replaced his left eyebrow. A swarthy man of medium height and build, he had the quickness of a lightning flash when he held a sword in his hand.

"Are you volunteering to cross the Frozen Desert before the dark season ends?" Dare asked him.

Several men laughed at the folly of such a course.

"I'm only calling for an end to all this talk," Garridan said defensively.

"Only Dare can lumber about on the Frozen Desert like a bernit," Gregor said, enjoying the joke because his bulk had earned him the nickname of Gentle Bernit.

"I want a decision made," Garridan insisted, red-faced and testy.

Dare had made his decision, but he wasn't ready to have it be common knowledge.

"We can do nothing until the end of this mooncycle," he said, standing to dismiss his council, "but reassure your men the time is near."

"Stay, Jonati," he said when the others had filed out. "I've made a decision about the Grand Elder's daughter."

"You've changed your plan to negotiate with Logan?"

"No, it's Tia who concerns me. I'm weary of her antics; she has too much time to plot mischief. I want her put to work."

"With the others?" Jonati pursed his lips, his dark eyes skeptical. "The malcontents will have easy access to her."

"I've thought of that—but we haven't tried to keep her behind locked doors. Let her do something to earn her bread. We'll see if the daughter of a Zealote can handle a few menial chores."

"What if Angeline—"

"Tia is safe from her—for now."

"Just to be sure, I'll have someone keep an eye on her wherever she is. I'll pick trustworthy guards to take turns at all times and tell them to listen carefully if she talks to anyone," Jonati said.

"Yes, do that. Assign her to kitchen duty, so she'll never be working alone. Not even Angeline would dare make an attempt on her life with Mother Macy as a witness."

The thought of those delicate white hands chopping up tubers was disturbing in a new way, but Dare hoped his obsession with Tia would pass when she was hidden away in the kitchen and out of his sight.

The knock made Tia's heart lurch, and she barely managed to call out her permission to enter. A girl had collected her tray some time earlier, and it was too soon for the next meal. She wanted to see Dare almost as much as she dreaded another meeting, but the prospect of facing him made her blood race. She resented that he hadn't taken pity on her when she had been wasting away from hunger.

No matter how hopeless it seemed, she had to continue trying to persuade him to aid her father. She was a hostage, a pawn in some secret plan of Dare's, but she couldn't give up. She tried to hate the man who was thwarting her mission, but she even failed at that because of her growing attraction to him.

Jonati, not Dare, entered her chamber, and she tried to hide her disappointment. He was her only friend in this forsaken place, and she owed him more than her life.

He was carrying a bundle, but she had little interest in gifts.

"I'm glad to see you," she said.

"We thought," he began hesitantly, not explaining who 'we' were, "you must be weary of these four walls. Beginning today, you'll have some duties to perform. It will make the time go much more quickly."

"Anything is better than sitting all day." She was grateful to him for not reminding her that she was free to wander wherever she pleased. Although she wasn't afraid of meeting other Wanderers, she was wary of being exposed to the anger they held against the Zealotes.

"Put on these clothes. I'll wait in the corridor."

In her eagerness for a change—any change—from the dull sameness of her days, she'd forgotten to ask what her duties would be. The garments were unappealing, but she started dressing, stripping to her skin to pull on an ungainly one-piece undergarment with long sleeves and legs to her ankles. A panel over her backside had buttons to open and close the seat, and she giggled at such an awkward arrangement. The rough, homespun fabric, more gray than white, was itchy, and she hoped she wouldn't embarrass herself by scratching when others could see her. Next she pulled on a long, loose-fitting white jumper of even coarser material that left the sleeves and bottoms of the undergarment showing. In place of the lightweight slippers she'd been wearing, she stepped into sandals with thick rope soles.

She went out to Jonati, eager to escape the stifling boredom of her solitary room. Perhaps, with luck, she could find someone who would help her foil Dare's plans for her. She still had the currency secreted away in an inner pocket of her coat.

Jonati took her to the crowded kitchen, where a score of workers dressed in jumpers like hers was scurrying about under the direction of a lean, leathery-faced woman with pale silver braids coiled around her head.

"Mother Macy, this is Tia. Dare wants her to help in the kitchen."

Mother Macy was the oldest person Tia had seen at Norvik, although she was perhaps no older than her own mother.

"Mother Macy cared for us at Warmond's fortress. She loved us well enough to join us when her husband disappeared," Jonati explained.

"That vile Zealote was my slave master, not my husband, as you well know, Runny-nose."

"It keeps us humble to have Mother Macy here," he said, laughing. "She remembers us as children and reminds us of our flaws."

"Be gone from my kitchen before I whack you where it will do some good," she said, not hiding her smile as she waved a long-handled wooden spoon at Jonati. "Get back to work, all of you!" She thumped the spoon on a wooden chopping block for emphasis. "Now, Tia," she said in the same breath, "what can you do to make yourself useful? Bake bread? Make cheese or butter?"

"I haven't had much experience," Tia admitted. "I could set plates on the tables."

"You have to work your way up to the easy jobs. You can begin by washing tubers and cutting off the sprouts. Let me warn you, our supplies of everything but cheese and milk are getting low. No nibbling and no hiding food in your pockets, or you'll sorely regret it. I'm not so kindhearted as Dare, and he never interferes in the running of my kitchen."

"What is your baby nickname for him?" she asked impulsively.

"Dare Lore has always been Dare Lore," Mother Macy said thoughtfully. "I don't believe he ever was a child, not inside where it counts."

Tia was sent to a musty-smelling, low-ceilinged cubicle and told to fill a huge basket with the softest, most shriveled purple tubers. The chore of sorting out enough took longer than she would have guessed, and her back ached from bending over the coarse bags. Filled to the brim, the heavy basket was almost more than she could carry, but she struggled back to the kitchen and began the wash-up, cutting off pale, wormlike sprouts. The water was icy, and her hands ached with cold before she finished her chore.

All the cooking was done on two massive black stoves, the interiors serving as ovens for pan after pan of unleavened bread. When the doors were opened to remove the finished pans, the heat was as intense as a blast from a forge. Only the huge funnel-shaped vents kept the temperature in the kitchen bearable, and Tia's hair was sticking to her face and neck long before her first job was done.

Except for Mother Macy, the kitchen workers were youthful: boys with unshaven cheeks and girls still self-conscious about their budding femininity. They slyly flirted, making the work seem like a lark, except when Mother Macy let fly with her spoon and sent a particularly negligent helper scurrying back to work clutching his—or her—backside.

The head cook was a good-natured tyrant, and no one seemed to bear her any ill will for her infrequent chastisements. Tia tried to do her work inconspicuously, but she did notice a sober-faced young man standing against one wall who never seemed to take his eyes from her. Later another, shorter and broader, took his place, and Tia was sure that every move she made was under scrutiny.

In spite of the hard work, there was camaraderie in the kitchen, and the young people were willing enough to include Tia in their chatter.

"You're young to be working so hard," she said to a boy named Petsy who seemed to get in more trouble than all the others combined. "Dare must be a hard man."

"Not hard, but fair and brave and just. I only wish I were old enough to start training for his army," he said, praising the leader until Mother Macy called him to help lift a boiling cauldron from the stove.

After all the shifts were served in the dining hall, the helpers had their meal at a scrubbed plank table in the kitchen. Tia was so tired, she could hardly lift a cup to her lips.

"If you think we work hard, be glad you're not in the scullery," her new friend Petsy said, gesturing at an open doorway at the far end of the kitchen. "Long after we're sleeping in our beds, they'll still have scrubbing up to finish. Course, most of 'em are there as punishment, so you can't feel sorry."

Tia went to bed, exhausted and certain of one thing: The young people who labored in the kitchen loved Dare beyond all reason. No one there would help her get back to her father, not even if her conspicuous watchdog weren't there.

A dozen times a day Dare resisted the impulse to race to the kitchen and assure himself that Tia was all right. Had he assigned her to a duty too soon after her fast? Was she strong enough to do the unaccustomed labor?

115

"She's doing the work with goodwill," Jonati had reported after her fourth day in the kitchen. "You were right to give her something to do."

Dare wanted to believe his lieutenant, but he wasn't satisfied. Tia was accustomed to a pampered life. The stifling heat of the ovens and the dankness of the storage rooms might be more than she could endure. He thought she'd regained her strength after her fast, but her deeply shadowed eyes haunted him.

After yet another night of torment, tossing and turning in his bed, he had to satisfy his curiosity. Putting on a seldom-worn robe, he let the rough brown hood fall over his face and went to the kitchen to see for himself.

Standing in the doorway, he saw Tia stirring the contents of a huge pot, her face flushed as she struggled to keep the coarse-grained mush from sticking. Her hair was braided in a thick coil that hung down her back, and she looked lost in the oversize jumper that all the kitchen workers wore.

This wasn't what he wanted for her, but even in the ugly garments, her beauty stunned him. Would her face grow leathery like Mother Macy's? Would her tiny waist thicken and her hair grow lank and dull from the dreariness of subterranean life? No matter how hard he tried, he couldn't imagine anything diminishing Tia's beauty.

Tia saw the hooded figure loitering in the doorway. Her first impulse was to confront him. She was sick of being watched! With so much work required to feed all the Wanderers on the dwindling supplies, Mother Macy could give the ever-present spies some useful chores.

The tireless head of the kitchen called out an order, and Tia hastened to obey, forgetting the sentinel at the door. She tried to work her hardest, not from fear of Mother Macy's heavy hand, but because she respected the woman for laboring so hard herself. Mother Macy had a mission of her own: the health and welfare of her Lost Ones.

Tia couldn't complain about her treatment. The youthful workers were congenial, but they didn't know what to make of her. Mostly they ignored her, especially when she asked questions about Dare.

The work was hard and the hours long, but Tia refused to let a single whisper of complaint get back to Dare. If he expected kitchen chores to break her spirit and make her forget her mission, he was going to be disappointed.

Each day seemed longer than the one before it, and worst of all, Tia hadn't found a single person who was dissatisfied with Dare's leadership. She had to make contact with someone who could be bribed to help her escape if all her efforts to enlist Dare in her father's cause failed. The dark season was over at the end of the moon-cycle. Traders would be sent out to barter for badly needed supplies, and she had to manage a way to go with one of them.

The helpers in the kitchen never mingled with the scullery workers. If there were malcontents at Norvik, Tia decided they must be among those assigned to punishment duty washing dishes and scrubbing pans. The more she thought about it, the more important it seemed to make contact with one of them, even if it meant she had to do something to be assigned to the scullery herself.

The prospect dismayed her, but she decided it had to be done.

"It's not my turn to wash these disgusting tubers," Tia loudly complained the next day, surprising everyone around her into gaping.

"I'll trade jobs with you," Petsy offered, sounding gallant as he tried to keep her out of trouble.

"No, thank you," she said for the benefit of her stunned audience. "I don't know why I should have to slave to feed a bunch of overgrown boys playing at being warriors."

The room grew deathly still, and Tia was afraid her co-workers would hurl their chopping knives and blocks at her.

"You shouldn't say that!" A mousy girl who hardly ever said a word to anyone cried out in anger, stepping forward to confront Tia.

"I'll say what I like," Tia said as arrogantly as was possible when her knees were trembling.

"You—you—you Zealote!" the girl shrieked.

Tia seized her chance, much as she hated what she had to do. Stepping forward, she slapped the girl's face, a resounding blow that hurt Tia's hand—and her conscience.

"Enough of that!" Mother Macy grabbed Tia's braid and pushed her facedown on one of the age-stained wooden counters, raining blows on her arms and shoulders where she was less protected by the bulky jumper. "I won't have such behavior in my kitchen!"

The stinging whacks brought tears to Tia's eyes, but the humiliation was far worse. She'd never been beaten, not even spanked when childhood naughtiness might have warranted it. She broke her tormentor's hold and lunged for the long-handled spoon, snatching it away and breaking it on the edge of the counter with superhuman effort.

"Enough of that yourself!" she said spitefully, feeling rotten to the core for provoking such an ugly scene.

"I won't have a spoiled brat in my kitchen," Mother Macy said in a deadly calm voice. "From now on, you'll do scullery duty."

Tia saw her ever-present guard hovering close but at a loss for what to do.

"On whose authority?" she asked haughtily.

"My own. This kitchen is my command, and Dare won't trouble himself over an ill-tempered chit like you."

Tia was banished to the scullery immediately, made to sit on a stool without supper until the others came to begin the evening cleanup.

A chunky young woman named Bellareda was in charge of the scullery, and she singled out Tia for the worst jobs: scraping scraps into a bin to be taken to the yakas; scrubbing the crusty interiors of big kettles; polishing blackened exteriors until they gleamed; digging into the depths of greasy, tepid water to find the eating utensils that had needed soaking.

Tia was too harassed to notice her fellow workers; she would no sooner look up from one greasy pan, than another would be shoved into her sink. Her hands shriveled and her feet ached from standing in one place so long.

When the last pan was scrubbed and every dish had been returned to its place, the scullery crew was allowed to make a meal of cold stew served on chunks of dry bread. Each worker had a cup

119

and a hook to hang it on; when they finished, there were no dishes to wash.

Tia was too exhausted to think, but at last she had a chance to look at her fellow sufferers. They were, without exception, older than the kitchen help, and with one exception, all were men.

Her stomach knotted when the dark-haired female sauntered toward her, and she knew she'd made a terrible mistake.

"What would the Grand Elder think? His daughter scrubbing dirty dishes!"

"Angeline."

"I thought you swore not to mention my name to anyone." Even in her shapeless work jumper, Angeline looked like a sharp-clawed lepine poised to strike.

"That was before you tried to kill me!"

"What nonsense! I only wanted you to be warned. Norvik is anything but safe."

"It is, if you keep away from me!"

"Oh, you're safe enough as long as your shadow-keeper hovers in the doorway."

Angeline pointed at the ever-present guard, and Tia realized that Dare would soon have a report about her abominable behavior. She felt sick with embarrassment, and there was no possibility of talking to any of the men in the scullery while Angeline and the guard were watching. She might have to spend countless horrible days scrubbing pans before she had a chance to sound out a potential rescuer.

Tia was roused the next morning by a girl with a tray of food, a privilege she hadn't enjoyed since becoming a kitchen helper.

"Does this mean I'm not to go to the scullery today?" she asked, torn between dread of returning and fear of losing her last chance to find help in escaping.

"Oh, no. You must hurry. Bellareda is cross enough about the tray. She doesn't allow her workers to break their fasts until the first meal's scrubbing up is done. It isn't sitting well with her that someone higher up insisted."

After eating her breakfast, Tia was soon up to her elbows in slippery water, her hands stinging from the harsh soap.

"You're in trouble," Angeline whispered in her ear, bringing her a big pot with browned remnants of the morning mush sticking to the bottom. "Bellareda said to bring you all the worst kettles. She doesn't think scullery slaves should have breakfast in bed."

Tia attacked the pot with a scrub pad made of links of metal, hardly daring to look around now that she was in the bad graces of the mean-spirited woman who supervised the scullery. Her only hope was to make contact with another worker while they ate, but she was kept at her sink when the others had their meal break.

She straightened, arching her back to relieve the stiffness, and reached for the pot Angeline was bringing her. Suddenly Angeline seemed to trip, lurching forward, spilling icy water from the kettle down the front of Tia's jumper.

"I'm sorry," Angeline said for the benefit of the supervisor. "Oh, here, I tripped on this spoon." She pulled the utensil from the front of her jumper, daring Tia to contradict her version of the accident.

121

"Get the mop, Angeline," Bellareda ordered, ignoring Tia's soaked condition.

Icy water saturated Tia's jumper, making it sodden from her chest to her knees. There was an unnatural hush in the room, and she realized everyone was waiting for the daughter of the Grand Elder to cry or try to pin the blame on Angeline.

So angry her spine stiffened and her hands balled into fists, she was determined not to provide more entertainment for anyone.

Slowly and deliberately, she walked to the racks where kitchen cloths were hung to dry and lifted the jumper over her head. She squeezed out the water as best she could and draped the garment to dry, trying to pretend she wasn't the focus of every eye in the room. Then she returned to her duties, ignoring everyone. She looked up only once, seeing a hooded figure in the doorway.

When Mother Macy ordered Tia to her chamber to change her clothes, she wondered what the next step up the ladder of punishments was. No one had rebuked Angeline, so somehow the fault had been assigned to her.

She changed quickly into the plain skirt and tunic, clasping the striped shawl around her shoulders because she was still shaking with cold. She sat, huddled on the bed, waiting for the next blow to fall.

In the communal dining hall that evening Dare knew he was being surly with his friends, but he couldn't explain his behavior, not even to Jonati. He felt bested by Tia's display of dignity; he smarted even though it was she who took the dunking at Angeline's hands. Had anyone besides him seen the naked defiance in her eyes?

Did she know it was he who spied on her behind the hood? Was she defying him to do his worst when she calmly cast aside her jumper and went back to scrubbing pans in a sodden undergarment? Surely she had to know how the sight of her luscious curves would inflame the senses of any man! No female could be as innocent as she seemed!

His orders had been specific. She was to serve him, and only him, at his table. He waited, hardly daring to breathe, as the servers began carrying out bowls and trays laden with food.

Tia followed the others carrying a single plate heaped high with more food than he would have taken for himself from the common bowls.

"They said I'm to serve you," she said, putting the plate in front of him without meeting his eyes. "I don't know if it's a reward or a penance."

He didn't know how to answer her; having her so close was his penance, not hers.

"Tonight's a feast night," he said. "I've ordered the ale kegs tapped to lighten people's spirits. It's been a long dark season, but we're nearly at the end."

"What does this have to do with me?" she asked woodenly.

"Only that you keep my mug filled," he said curtly.

"As you wish—sir."

"It seems you have yourself a serving wench, Dare," Garridan called out from his chair two places down. "A comely one, at that."

Dare ate in silence, with little appetite for the slabs of bread and cheese or the thick stew she'd heaped on his plate.

"Take this to the children's table," he ordered Tia after he'd eaten only a small portion, "and fill another mug so I can drink while you fetch refills."

He didn't know why he was shouting his orders or why it seemed so important to make a show of dominating this woman.

"You're not yourself tonight," Jonati said, speaking softly so no one else could hear. "Are you sure it's a good idea to have Tia here?"

"She's our captive, nothing more. She's caused trouble in the kitchen and chaos in the scullery, so let her see how she likes taking my orders."

"I hope you know what you're doing." Jonati turned back to his own supper, his back stiff with disapproval and his eyes silently censuring.

"Don't interfere," Dare said, not hiding his surly mood from the friend who knew him best.

The ale was dark and foamy, and Tia had to wait in line as others filled pitchers, one allotted to each long table. Clearly there was a rationing system on strong drink, but the two men in charge of the kegs said nothing when she filled a second mug for Dare.

She took it to him, stepping behind him to serve it over his shoulder. The first mug was already empty, and she wondered if the leader of the Wanderers had a weakness for ale.

"This mug is dirty," he said loudly. "Return it and bring me a clean one."

The mug was clean; she wanted to argue but sensed she'd be playing into his hands that way.

"I'll exchange it—sir."

He wanted to brood alone; he regretted beginning this game and liked himself not at all in the role of drunken tyrant. But once begun, there was no way to stop. An apology would show weakness; begging for forgiveness would betray his heart.

At least the ale was creating a friendly buzz in the room. Interest in Tia waned as full pitchers of ale led to relaxed gaiety and alcohol-inspired jests.

He saw the children hustled off to bed, and the atmosphere in the room became more rowdy before Tia returned to him.

"You've kept me waiting overly long," he said gruffly.

"Others were in line ahead of me. Did you want me to demand a place at the head because Dare Lore has a greater thirst than others?"

"I want you to hold your tongue and serve me," he said, slurring his words even though the ale hadn't touched his senses yet. "Get a fresh pitcher and set it by my hand, so I won't be kept waiting again by your lazy ways."

She went back to the kegs, this time stepping to the head of the line. "Dare Lore wants me to bring him a pitcher immediately," she said.

A round-faced young man with a gap where two front teeth should have been chuckled to the other keg-keeper and filled a pitcher so full the foam cascaded over the edge.

"Now don't spill a drop," he warned. "It's not often we tap the ale kegs."

Why was Dare ordering her around like a slave? The other servers worked at a leisurely pace, laughing and sipping ale themselves. She'd come to Norvik as an ambassador from her father, albeit an unauthorized one, but Dare Lore was doing everything he could to humble her and break her spirit.

She hurried back to his table, so angry the ale sloshed over the sides and dripped onto her skirt.

"You've wasted good ale by carrying it carelessly," Dare said when she came up beside him.

Jonati had vacated his chair, as had the massive, olive-skinned man on Dare's left.

"The man at the keg filled the pitcher too full."

"Don't blame others for your mistakes," he said, saying what his farce required, not what was in his heart. "At least see if you can pour it without soaking the table."

"You saw me in the scullery," she accused him. "You were the coward who covered his face with a hood!"

"Take care how you pour," he said, choosing to ignore the insult that no man would dare say to his face.

"You spied on me! You saw that witch dump filthy water on me, and you did nothing!"

"Angeline is still in the scullery and will be until she leaves here. You've been promoted to my service. Now fill my mug."

"Yes, master," she said in a sweet, fawning tone.

Tia lifted the heavy glazed clay pitcher and, before he could react, emptied the foamy brown liquid on his flaxen head and down the front of his tunic.

Sputtering, with the bitter liquid stinging his eyes, he pushed his drowned locks away from his face.

In one quick move he stood and flung her over his shoulder, knocking the pitcher from her hands, shattering it into hundreds of pieces on the stone floor.

She squirmed and kicked, clawing at his back in panic, but he walked resolutely between tables of surprised spectators toward the door, for the second time carrying his captive out of a crowded room.

Chapter Seven

"Put me down!" Tia cried, but her plea fell on deaf ears.

Trembling with fear, she flailed ineffectively at his back. Her eyes lost focus and her head reeled. She became too dizzy to distinguish the pattern of the flagstones in the corridor, but she knew where he was taking her.

He held her easily with one arm, his grip on her thighs as unbreakable as stout leather bindings. Storming into his chamber without breaking stride, he slammed the door shut and secured the latch, then tumbled her facedown on the tawny fur bedcovering.

"What are you going to do to me?" she gasped, barely able to catch her breath as she scrambled to her knees and raised her hands defensively. "Are you going to . . ." The words stuck in her throat.

128

"Am I going to what?" he asked harshly, his chest heaving as though he'd been carrying an extremely heavy load.

"Whip me?" For the first time in her life she was truly frightened at the prospect of physical punishment.

"What gave you such a thought?" His face was more anguished then angry.

"Angeline said . . . when she pretended to take me to you . . ."

"After all that witch has done, you believe her sick fantasies?"

"She did seem afraid."

"Angeline isn't afraid of me or anyone else. Surely you're not naive enough to swallow her lies?"

"I think the man who kidnapped me is capable of anything!"

He lifted his arms and pulled off his tunic, exposing his chest with golden hairs stickily matted by the ale down to the damp front of his laced breeches.

"Why are you disrobing?" His naked torso made him seem larger and even more threatening.

"Because I'm soaked to the skin with ale," he thundered, flinging the sodden garment to the floor and kicking it aside.

She could hear his breathing, like the ragged gasps of a man who had run many kilometers. He moved to the very edge of the bed, towering over her like a vengeful warrior.

With her legs tucked under her, there was no dignified way to retreat. She held her spine rigid, refusing to cower even though the taste of fear was nasty on her tongue.

Cupping her face in his hands, he sank to his

knees in front of her, sensitive to the quivering of her slender form and the distrust in the violet depths of her eyes.

He'd never been angry in this way, never been so aroused that he wanted to unleash the savage beast in his nature on the object of his passion. He couldn't focus on anything but her proud, sweet, beguiling features swimming before his eyes.

"In the name of the Great Power, do you think I would lift a hand against you in anger?" he asked.

He knew in his heart of hearts that he could not—would not—ever bring harm to her, no matter how much she tried his patience or provoked his rage. His only thought in carrying her away had been to remove her from the scene as quickly as possible so Becket and his malcontents didn't think he had no control over his hostage. Her frenzied resistance had fueled his fury until he felt like a volcano ready to erupt. Still, she was as safe with him as she would be in the secureness of the Citadral where her father ruled. He would cut off his own hand before he raised it in anger against her.

Straining to calm himself, he watched her breasts rise and fall and her lower lip tremble, hating the very real terror he saw in her eyes. But there was more in her expression, something frightening and arousing and more potent than the most dangerous weapon.

"Do you?" he repeated, running his thumb along the soft side of her cheek.

"No," she whispered, pursing her soft lips as she uttered the word, melting Dare's anger when her deep violet eyes met his.

"Is this punishment?" He touched his lips to hers, brushing against them so lightly it was like being tickled.

When he backed away, she rubbed her mouth to make the tingling go away. He leaned forward again and held her fingers, gently nibbling her knuckles.

"Am I hurting you?"

She shook her head.

"Is this painful?" He captured her hand in his and moistened her lips with the tip of his tongue.

"No."

He reached behind her and broke the bit of yarn she'd unraveled from her shawl to tie the end of her braid. Working slowly and carefully, he knelt in front of her and loosened the plaits until her hair lay like a veil around her shoulders, the sable strands kinked from braiding.

He was still breathing hard, and there were tremors in his thighs, as though he'd been kneeling for hours instead of moments.

"Why did you do that?"

There wasn't an answer he could give her, and his control snapped like a cord stretched to the breaking point. He took her in his arms, covering her lips with his mouth, kissing her as he'd longed to do so many times, even when she was up to her elbows in scrub water, her face shiny from the exertion. Once started, he was powerless to stop, claiming her mouth with hungry, demanding kisses, his tongue urgently probing between her slippery-smooth teeth.

Tia heard a strangled cry and only belatedly realized it came from her own throat. His kisses befuddled her mind, and she reacted without thinking, letting his tongue caress hers. She

was more afraid of the way he made her feel
than she ever had been of his anger, but she
was swept along like a leaf in a gale, powerless
to resist.

His hair was softer than she'd thought it would
be, and she combed her fingers through it, not
stopping when the last strands slipped out of her
grasp. His back was warm and taut, and she let
her hands wander to his lean waist, hanging on
as the force of his kisses rocked her whole body.

All her daydreams seemed like silly, girlish
imaginings, pale shadows of desire compared to
Dare's assault on her senses. She slid her hands
upward over his rib cage, softly whimpering in
pleasure as he crushed his mouth against hers.

Her hands were cold, but they generated a heat
as all-consuming as a fireburst on the Flaming
Sea. Her eyes were closed, but his were famished
for the sight of her, fascinated by the arch of
her brows, the blush of her cheeks, the dusky
thickness of her lashes. He kissed her more passionately, trying to absorb her essence, frantically savoring the innocent welcome he found on
her lips.

One busy little hand invaded a vulnerable spot
under his arm, making him gasp and resist the
urge to double over. He'd long ago forgotten his
childish weakness. She stroked the fine hairs nestled there until he pulled away, unable to bear
another instant of tickling.

His torment gave him only a moment's respite from his overwhelming desire for her, but he
forced himself to stand and turn away from her.

"No, this can't be." He sounded like a man who'd
swallowed sand.

"Dare . . ."

She'd never before said his name as an endearment, and the longing in her voice was a new, much sharper torment.

"Why?" she asked, compelling him to look at her again.

Her lips were swollen, challenging him to taste their sweetness again, but he dug his nails into his palms, resisting although the cost of doing so was a pain unlike any other he'd experienced.

"Dare, answer me! Why . . ." She couldn't put her burning question into words; she could hardly believe her own boldness in wanting to know why he'd stopped.

"Tia, my goals aren't your goals; my dreams aren't yours."

"You're saying a man and a woman must be of one mind?"

"No! But I despise everything you represent!"

She felt wounded, as though a knife blade had severed some vital link to her heart, but, heady with passion, she couldn't stop the flow of dangerous words.

"Then join me! Help my father stop the government! Help him stop the exploitation of Thurlow's people!"

"Do you expect me to become your father's puppet—to dance to his orders like one of his craven Zealotes? I have my own destiny!"

"If you'll help put down the evil that's corrupting Thurlow, my father can aid you in fulfilling your destiny."

"Your father and his kind denied me my destiny! My heritage! The Zealotes took everything away from me when they kidnapped me. In my nightmares I see my mother, exhausted from childbirth and terrified of the fiends who came to steal her

133

babe. Only she doesn't have a face, Tia! Even in my dreams, my mother is nameless and faceless! Do you have any idea how that feels?"

"My father had nothing to do with it! The only time he ever accompanied Warmond he did so to investigate why so many babes were disappearing."

"Your father is a Zealote, no matter what changes he's instituted in the Order. It's well known that he only betrayed the old ways because he wanted your mother! He abolished celibacy so he could marry! Otherwise the Zealotes would still be riding at night, stealing innocent babes to add to their ranks!"

"That's not true! When he saw how few healthy children were being born, he knew it was the Zealotes' duty to mate. You don't know my father! He's an honorable man!"

"Where were his priorities when the Wanderers were driven from village to village across the face of the planet? We've fled across seas, over mountains and deserts, even through the Valley of Sunken Craters. Three of our people died there by their own hands, driven mad by thirst."

"If you knew him . . ."

"I have no desire to know the Grand Elder of the Zealotes. My business with him concerns a payment of twelve equests—and the ransoming of a hostage."

"That's all I am! Your hostage!"

"I've never deceived you about that. You became my captive as soon as I saved you from certain death."

"You agreed to bring me to Norvik."

"That didn't change your status."

"My father will pay my debt," she said bitterly,

realizing that he would have to sacrifice far more than that because of her rash, foolish attempt to help him.

"We'll see. If he does, then I'll talk to him."

"Do you want to sell your services? Is that all you are, a mercenary?"

She wanted to wound him because she could hardly stand the pain of his rejection.

"I'm not for sale," he said angrily, "but I'm not a fool either. I would negotiate with the Power of Darkness if it could atone to my people for the wrongs they've suffered."

"Then you are willing to make a deal with my father?"

"You never cease, do you?" he asked, pacing the room. "Did you expect to come here and rally my warriors to your noble cause? Were you going to ride at the head of my army, banner in hand like some legendary Earth saint on a crusade?"

She wanted to say something to stop his hateful words, but how could she penetrate his shell of anger? No one had ever spoken to her the way he did. Her blood was boiling, but she didn't know whether passion or anger was consuming her.

"Perhaps we're more alike than you're willing to admit," she cried out, standing and bracing herself as though she expected a punishing blow.

"How so?" He stopped his pacing, his naked torso damp from the heat of his feelings for her.

"We both received a good dunking today," she said.

Her laughter was forced, a hesitant little giggle generated more by fear than good humor, but it acted as a soothing balm on his frayed spirit. Remembering the way she looked with her wet

135

undergarment clinging to her form, the ungainly drop seat sagging like an old man's breeches, he smiled spontaneously.

"I've seen wet avians that looked less bedraggled than you did," he said, managing to make his voice sound teasing.

"At least I don't smell like the inside of an ale barrel!"

He laughed at himself. "I probably invited my dunking!"

"You did!"

"But you were foolish to provoke Mother Macy. What did you expect to accomplish except to get your pretty little backside reddened by her spoon?"

"I was tired of the kitchen."

"You preferred the scullery?"

"I didn't know Angeline was there."

"You did know scullery duty was a punishment. I think you wanted to sound out the workers there. What did you hope to accomplish?"

She looked away.

"Never mind, I think I know. You thought you'd find a troublemaker willing to take your bribe and help you escape from me."

"You can't get away with holding me hostage!"

"You would trust a malcontent with your life just to spite me?"

"I trusted a nameless ruffian to bring me here!"

"I think you found my warmth pleasing enough on our travels." He faced her, his hands on his hips as though daring her to deny it.

"I would have endured the stink of a yaka to keep warm!"

"The scent of an ale cask must be more pleasing than that."

"I think not!"

He took a single step closer, his arms folded across his chest. He had to put her out of his mind. She was, after all, only a chit of a girl, and he felt eons older, hardened by the life he'd led. He neither needed nor wanted the burden of caring about her. He only had to cast his glance at any unattached woman among the Wanderers, and he would have a willing partner to share his bed. In fact, it was his duty to have a son someday, but he wanted his children to live on the surface, on land that belonged to him. There was no place for any female in his life right now, especially not one who had a hold on his heart or a claim on his loyalty. The daughter of the Grand Elder was as unobtainable as the most distant star.

"Tia . . ." He meant to try again to explain his sense of duty to his people, but his mind went blank.

"Do I have your permission to go to my own chamber?" she asked.

"Yes." He gave her leave but didn't move aside to let her move toward the door.

"Do you have new duties for me tomorrow?"

"No, I think not. You'll be safer in your own chamber."

"Then that's where I should go."

"You should."

"I will, then." Her feet seemed rooted to the floor, and it embarrassed her to realize she was staring at his torso, admiring the tiny lip of his navel above the lacings of his breeches. His chest hair was dry now, as golden as the mane on his head.

"Tia . . ." He didn't know what he meant to

say, but her name rolled off his tongue, sweetly imploring her to come closer to him.

"Dare . . ." Her cheeks grew hot as she remembered his lips on hers, and she unconsciously touched them, surprised by the tenderness of the flesh around her mouth.

She was so small and yet so womanly that not even the rough homespun garments concealed the swell of her lush breasts. He moved closer, crowding her so she had to tumble backward onto the bed or come into his arms for support. He spanned her small waist with his big hands, lifting her against him until her feet dangled and her sandals fell off.

It seemed natural to cling to him, to circle his neck with her arms and wrap her legs around his thighs.

His kiss was long and slow and gentle, and his hands slid under her bottom, pushing her against him. She knew that equests had organs that grew huge and hard when they mated, but her only knowledge of human males came from helping her mother with Zealote babes. She felt the rock-hard swelling at his groin, even though her skirt was bunched against it, but was afraid to cast her eyes downward.

He lowered her to the bed and sat beside her, stroking her cheek for a long while until she put her fingers over his, finding his tenderness torturous to bear.

"When you're kind, it hurts more than when you're harsh," she said, wondering if he would understand.

"It's not my intention to be rough on you."

"Then send me back to my father."

"I can't, Tia."

138

He slumped forward, his elbows resting on his thighs, his eyes averted.

"You can! You're the leader of the Wanderers. Your people respect you. I don't want to be your captive!"

"What do you want to be?"

Your woman! she wanted to cry out, but the same pride that had surfaced when Angeline tried to humiliate her kept her from speaking now.

"What, Tia?" He pressed, his face so close she could see the faint beginnings of golden bristle.

She couldn't answer.

He kissed her just below her lips, then on each corner, toying with her like a man sampling a honeycake, wanting it to last as long as possible.

Blood roared in his ears, and he'd never felt such an urgent need for a woman, yet he felt unmanned, his strength sapped by the emotions tormenting him.

Did she but know it, her power over him was making him as weak as the smallest babe, ready to sell his soul for her sake. Yet he didn't dare show it, not with Logan's daughter.

He found the neckline of her tunic and slowly ripped it down the front, expecting—needing— cries of protest or indignation to make him stop. Instead she looked into his eyes and slipped the ruined garment off her shoulders, letting it crumple around her hips. Naked to the waist, she'd never seemed more like royalty or less like a frightened captive.

The single gaslight on the wall of his chamber gave her skin a golden glow, but he felt shamed for looking at her exposed breasts. He covered them with his hands, as though he could undo the outrage of tearing away her tunic, but still

139

she didn't react with anger. Instead she covered his broad hands with her small, work-reddened fingers and pressed his palms against her hard nipples.

"Why did you tear it?" she whispered, her eyes riveted on his face.

"Forgive me."

"Tell me why."

"I tried to shame you. Instead I've humiliated myself."

"No."

Perhaps she did know the power she had over him. He groaned and moved her fingers away, cupping one breast and kissing the pink bud that sprang to a peak under his touch.

She lay back, giddy with excitement, not knowing what to expect. His tongue scorched a trail to her other breast, his teeth nipping at the tip until she squealed in confusion, torn between stopping him and begging him to consume her.

He parted her knees with his strong leg, wedging his knee between her thighs until she was riding it, her groin tightening and pulsating against the pressure.

He kissed her more insistently, trying to lose his qualms, his doubts, in the heat of her body. Her hands were tangled in his hair, making his scalp tingle, and her lashes brushed against his cheek. Every nerve in his body was warring against his sense of right and wrong, and he shuddered at the conflict raging within him.

She ceased being his captive and made him her prisoner, chaining him with his own lust. Her hands grasped his shoulders, her nails biting into his flesh, but he was insensitive to pain, her own and his.

"Dare, Dare . . ."

Her voice was a hushed whisper, but it penetrated the fog of desire that clouded his mind. He pushed himself away, stunned that his legs were so wobbly that they barely supported him.

She instantly felt a loss so great that the physical ache threatened to engulf her. Looking up, she searched his eyes for answers, probing the icy blue depths even as she raised her arms, inviting him to return.

"Dare—"

"I overstepped my bounds," he said in a dull voice that masked the turbulence he dared not show her.

"I wanted you to—"

"Don't say anything else, Tia. Don't give voice to anything you'll regret later. This doesn't change anything."

"Is this how you treat all your captives?"

"You're my only captive," he said, "and I almost regret the day I led you out of that frigid wasteland."

"Are you sorry I didn't perish with my shadowkeeper and my equest?" she asked, sitting and covering her breasts with her arms.

"No, not sorry . . ."

"Well, I am!"

He quickly turned away and went to a chest, sorting through the contents and pulling out a soft white tunic sewn by an admirer which he'd never worn for fear of encouraging the woman.

"Cover yourself," he said harshly.

"This is too fine to be prisoner's garb." She fingered the delicate silky fabric.

"Wear it, woman! Can't you once obey without giving your own interpretation to a thing?"

"Is that what I do?" She looked at him with pain-filled eyes. "Have you had your use of me for this day?" she asked, her tone as wounding as her words.

"I won't call upon you to serve me again."

"So I will be going back to the scullery."

"No, do as you like with your days. Only I want you to sit by my place at the table each evening so I can gauge the extent of your mischief."

He took her elbow, amazed at the delicacy of it under the sleeve of his oversize tunic, and guided her to the corridor.

There, standing less than ten paces from his door, was her guard, one of the men who took turns watching her every move.

"So my days are my own," she said with bitter irony, running toward her chamber with her shadow-keeper hurrying behind her.

Dare closed his door and flung himself down on the bed without extinguishing his light. The bedcovering felt warm from the heat of her body, but his heart was encased in ice. He'd learned early to deal with pain and humiliation; his life as a child in Warmond's fortress had been a series of daily tortures with only one goal: to build strong soldiers. Dare had always longed for something more in his life: a tenderness he only now recognized as love.

Tia had brought that into his life, but nothing had prepared him for the desolation, the torment, of loving the Grand Elder's daughter.

Chapter Eight

Her small chamber now seemed like a sanctuary rather than a prison, and she bolted the door, trying to pretend she could shut herself away from Dare.

The sleek black coat her father had given her was hanging on a hook, and she slipped into it, hoping its warmth would stop her trembling. The single gas lamp made her shadow larger than life on the cold stucco wall, and without thinking she began a familiar childhood game. Using her arms and hands, she made a ferocious shadow-beast, wiggling her thumb to pantomime a snapping jaw. She tried to growl like a lepine, not caring whether the ever-present guard outside her door thought she was mad.

In truth, the dark shadow on the wall reminded her of a muslin-and-sawdust felina, a child's lump-ish plaything. Tia's talent wasn't up to creating a lepine's frightening leer or its stealth in stalking prey.

She sat on the edge of the bed, her legs straight out like sticks, and wished she were a little girl again. How wonderful it would be to forget about her disturbing captor and his hellish stronghold; how comforting to lose her apprehensions in a world of make-believe. She smiled, remembering the many games she'd played with her brother. Fane had always made her act the role of the Outsider in their mock wars, and he played the Zealote warrior who subdued her with his rope. Once he'd been too zealous in vanquishing her, leaving a rope burn on her cheek. She'd tried hard to conceal it with her hair, but their tutor was too sharp-eyed. Her dear adopted brother ate his supper standing up, and Tia suffered more in sympathy for his sore bottom than for her own aching face.

She didn't really want to return to childhood, but she was homesick for her family and deeply sorry for the distress they must be suffering. The only way to justify running away from them was to sway Dare to the Zealotes' side.

Her cheeks burned when she remembered Dare's accusation: that she wanted to ride at the head of his army like some legendary heroine. It was the truth in what he said that hurt. How often had she imagined leading the Wanderers through the broad gateway to the Citadral and enlisting them in her father's cause?

Was it naive to believe she could help her father? What right did Dare have to make her feel so inadequate and confused? She couldn't lose faith in herself! There had to be a way to help her father. The time would come when

Dare had to see that his own people were threatened by the government's corrupt alliance with Earth.

The chamber was too warm to wear the heavy coat for long. She hung it back on the peg and idly put her hand in front of the grille near the floor where a faint flow of warm air kept the room from being uncomfortably frigid. Somehow the Wanderers made air move from the overheated forge to the living areas, but she didn't know the means. Once Jonati had offered to show her more of the workings of Norvik, and her lack of interest had been a mistake. If she ever got back to the Citadral, she should at least be able to tell her father what was happening in the Wanderers' stronghold.

If she ever got back! She crawled under the bedcovering, but her mind was like a water wheel turned by a flooded stream. Images kept whirling through her head, and she couldn't stop thinking of Dare. Her lips were tender from his kisses. Her breasts tingled, and she slid her hands under the fine fabric of his tunic, putting them over her bare mounds of flesh. Touching made them even more sensitive, and she didn't want to feel the way she did.

He had no right to kiss her! And yet she knew he hadn't forced himself on her. She'd been thrilled by the smooth warmth of his back under her hands and the power in the arms that held her. When he looked down at her, the angry set of his mouth dissolved, and the habitual scowl etched on his brow showed only as a faint line. Dare was a comely man, but that didn't explain why she wanted to bunch her fists between her thighs to stop the incessant throbbing.

The daughter of the Grand Elder couldn't be reduced to ignominious surrender! Shame and failure gnawed at her, but she was more determined than ever not to accept defeat.

The next morning Tia refused to open her door to take the food sent to break her fast, but Dare had expected no less. He wasn't afraid of a new hunger strike. If she didn't appear at the evening meal as ordered, no door on Thurlow was strong enough to keep him away from her.

He spooned his tasteless mush, gloomily surveying the huge cavern where many hundreds could dine together. A score of gas lamps on the catwalk above illuminated the rough plank tables, but the dark walls swallowed the light. This was a dangerous time in the full-cycle; not even his strongest warriors were immune to the black depression that settled on people during the dark season. Dare kept their hands busy and their bellies satisfied, but he couldn't work miracles. He couldn't bring sunshine to the underground settlement.

"You're morose today," Jonati said, lingering over his hot herbal drink. "Maybe you need to consult with Mother Macy."

"Potions and purging won't help what ails me."

"Maybe not." Jonati rubbed his chin and grinned into his fist. "They're whispering about you in the sewing room."

"I don't care about female gossip. Don't they have enough to do getting the army ready to move?"

"They say Dare sleeps alone because he's infatuated with the Grand Elder's daughter."

"I don't have time to listen to nonsense." Dare stood to leave just as the kitchen helper Petsy raced up to him.

"Dare, they need you in the scullery!"

He ran, almost glad for a crisis to take his mind off Tia.

Kitchen helpers and scullery workers were clustered near the door between the two areas, and Mother Macy seemed to be keeping them at bay, waving her spoon like a baton.

"That witch has cornered Bellareda behind a sink," she shouted over the din coming from the scullery.

"Angeline," Dare said under his breath, cautiously stepping up to the entryway, only to jump back when a heavy kettle crashed against the door frame.

"Angeline!" he called out loudly. "Stop that now!"

She stood, her hands on her hips, her raven hair wildly framing her face. "Come out, cow," she called to the terrified kitchen supervisor hiding under one of the big metal sinks. "I have what I want now."

Dare motioned to the frightened woman, and she crawled out on her hands and knees, her face so red the blood under her skin seemed to be boiling.

"She tried to kill me!"

"If I wanted you dead, you'd be dead," Angeline shrieked, rushing toward Bellareda and kicking her backside so hard the woman squealed in pain.

Dare grabbed Angeline from behind, holding her arms to her sides until she relaxed against his chest, pushing her bottom against his groin and purring with satisfaction.

147

"You came to me at last," she whispered, glaring at the mass of faces peering into the scullery from a safe distance.

"Have you lost your senses?"

He pushed her toward the drying racks and grabbed a strip of cloth long enough to secure her hands behind her back.

His face hot with anger, Dare propelled her through the crowd of curious workers, not slowing until he maneuvered her up the two flights of narrow stairs to the corridor where Burek was confined.

Sliding free the bolt on the chamber next to the madman's, he nudged her into the room with his knee.

"Why do you behave this way?" he asked angrily, roughly untying her wrists, then pushing her shoulders to seat her on the one wooden chair in the chamber.

"Now you're acting like a real man," Angeline said, her eyes appraising him under hooded lids. "I knew you'd come to me eventually."

"I haven't 'come' to you, but I've had enough of your vile behavior."

"I have been naughty." She snickered suggestively and wiggled on the chair. "Doesn't your hand itch to—"

"I've had enough," he said, his voice deadly soft. "You disgust me, Angeline. The thought of touching you sickens me. I never want to lay eyes on you again, and to that end, you'll be confined in this room until the first trading expedition can take you back to civilization."

"You can't make me leave you!" Her face contorted with pain, and the blood left her cheeks. "You can't!"

"That's the way it has to be. You're a danger to everyone here."

"Bellareda provoked me! What kind of leader are you, condemning me without a hearing?"

"Then say what you can in your defense," he said woodenly.

"You don't know what goes on in that scullery! That cow was going to push my face into the scrub water!"

"Did she do it?"

"I didn't allow it!"

"What did you do to provoke her?"

"I only made a commotion so someone would send for you. I knew it was time for you to break your fast. Don't you see, Dare, I can't live without you! If you want me sweet and prissy like Logan's daughter, I can be that. I can be the only woman you'll ever want!"

"Please, don't, Angeline. I haven't done any-thing to make you think—"

"It's because of her."

The venom in her voice sent shivers of apprehension down his spine; he'd never had greater fear for Tia's safety.

"The Grand Elder's daughter is a hostage, noth-ing more."

"Then show me that she means nothing to you." She stood and slipped the loose straps of the kitchen jumper over her shoulders, pushing the bulky homespun down to her ankles.

"Stop, Angeline."

She shed the shapeless undergarment like a serpent slithering out of its skin, standing naked before him.

"Does she have nipples like dark, rich berries? Is her secret place as thick and silky. . . ."

Dare backed toward the door, disgusted by her evil, conniving nature.

"Together there's nothing we can't do," Angeline pleaded, her voice shrill with urgency. "With me by your side, you could rule all of Thurlow. I'm all the woman you'll ever need, Dare!"

"When I want a woman," he said in a deadly calm voice, "I'll do the choosing."

The rest of the day seemed to last forever. Dare looked forward to the evening meal with the single-mindedness of a starving man, and it took all his self-control not to go to the dining area an hour before the appointed time.

When he finally assumed his place at the head table with his Council of Six, he sent Jonati for an extra chair to place beside his, hoping against hope that Tia would join him without coercion.

When she did belatedly arrive, she was carrying a babe, one of the few born during the dark season. Although his men were free to wed whenever they liked, there were dozens of suitors for every unclaimed woman. Many, like Dare himself, were holding back, waiting for a time when they could establish a family on land of their own. Births at Norvik were few and far between, but Dare adored each little creature, vowing to see that every one of them would someday have a real home.

Tia was smiling at the little face that bobbed in front of hers, laughing when the babe grabbed at her nose. Dare's throat ached with longing at the thought of someday fathering a precious new life, and he couldn't imagine a sight more beautiful than Tia ripe with child, her belly swollen by his seed.

Tia looked up from playing with the babe and met Dare's eyes, startled by the intensity of his gaze. How would it feel to carry his child, to present him with a strong, brave son or a beautiful, spunky daughter who would wrap him around her little finger?

She blushed and hoped he couldn't see her pink cheeks in the dim light. Since her betrothal, she'd thought a great deal about children, hoping she could fill the Zealotes' nursee with sturdy grandchildren for her father to enjoy and spoil. She'd given little thought to the means of conceiving them, trusting that Olan would be as gentle and considerate as possible in planting his seed. She'd never dreamed a woman could burn with desire, never known a man could make her ache with longing just by casting his eyes in her direction.

The young mother beside her reclaimed the child, leaving Tia alone under the searchlight of Dare's stare. She wanted to hurry to his side, but pride held her back. He was her captor, not her lover. She had to obey his orders, but he couldn't command her heart.

He motioned to her, gesturing at the empty chair beside his, but she pretended not to understand. Squaring her shoulders, she walked slowly toward an empty place at a table in front of his.

"Do you want me to bring her here?" Jonati asked, grinning.

"No, let her keep the place she's chosen." Dare nodded at her, conceding her small victory with a barely perceptible smile.

My darling Tia, he thought with grim satisfaction, you'll be spending more hours by my side than you can even imagine. He didn't begrudge

151

her the illusion of freedom for a few fleeting moments.

"It's not like Garridan to miss his supper," Jonati observed.

Dare reluctantly looked away from Tia, but not before he watched her dip a bit of bread in the stew and tuck it between her soft pink lips. He envied that morsel of food, wishing he could feel the slippery inside of her mouth and the bite of her teeth on his tongue.

"I haven't seen him today, have you?" Jonati asked, breaking Tia's hold on Dare's attention.

"Gregor, have you seen Garridan?" Dare called over to the trainer.

"Strange to say, some of the lads said he was absent from the drills. Mayhap his bowels are acting up. A weakness of his, you know."

Dare finished his meal without tasting the food, his eyes rarely leaving Tia although his mind was uneasy about the master swordsman. He watched with relief when she left the dining hall; with the season of light near, he could ill afford the distraction of the Grand Elder's daughter.

Hours later, Garridan was still missing, and Dare became concerned and started looking for his council member.

He finally knocked on the plank door of Tia's chamber, the last place he'd intended to look. Would he discover Tia missing too?

"Come in. It's not locked."

"It's wiser to bolt your door at night," he said, although, in truth, he was the only real threat to her chastity. His men were well disciplined, accustomed to working off their urges in the rough and tumble of the training room.

"If I were wise, would I be here?" Tia asked, an impish grin tugging at his heartstrings.

"Well put." He grinned back, wishing all their moments together could be lighthearted. "Are you cold?"

"Cold? Oh, my coat. You'll think I'm silly, but touching it reminds me of home. My brother Fane had to kill a black lepine to save his own life. My father had it made into a coat for my eighteenth birthday."

Her love for her family hit him like a blow to his midsection, and he envied her. His whole life had been consumed by a burning desire to have a place to call home, not only for himself but for all the Lost Ones. She was drawing comfort from her loved ones, even though they were far away and unable to help her.

"Why are you here?" she asked, letting the coat sleeve fall from her fingers.

"Angeline is missing," he blurted out.

"She left on her own?" As fervently as she wanted to be gone from Norvik, Tia didn't believe it was possible to survive alone on the Frozen Desert without protective gear and a guide.

"No, Garridan, our arms instructor, is missing too. We're trying to determine if others left with her." Dare didn't succeed in keeping the uneasiness out of his voice. It hurt to know that one of his most trusted lieutenants had left in secret with Angeline, but his anguish was balanced by relief to see Tia still there.

"I'm still here, and I haven't seen Angeline. I'm sorry about your friend Garridan," Tia said, although she couldn't understand why her heart reached out to Dare. "Betrayal hurts."

"Yes. I'm sorry for some things too, Tia. I hope you know that."

She wanted to ease his conscience and smooth away the worried frown on his forehead, but she sensed that tenderness would break down all the barriers between them. Much as she longed to feel his arms around her, she couldn't afford any show of weakness.

"Well, I'm the last person who would run off with Angeline," she said unnecessarily, finding it hard to draw a deep breath while he hovered over her, his gray tunic unlaced to reveal a deep V sprinkled with golden hair.

"There are many demands on my time now," he said, wishing he could speak of the things that were in his heart. "So I'll warn you now. Be prepared to leave in three days."

"Three minutes is enough warning. I'm not burdened by possessions to pack."

"I'll have someone bring the things you'll need for a long trip."

"You're taking me to the Citadral?" she asked hopefully, pretending she wanted nothing more than to be quit of him.

He solemnly shook his head no.

"I'm just a pawn in some wicked game you're playing! Isn't there any way I can persuade you to help my father?"

"Are you offering what I think, Tia?" He clenched his fists, wondering if any torture was as debilitating as denying himself the solace of her flesh.

"I'll do anything to help my father."

She had an image of herself as a sacrificial maiden, stretched naked on a cold stone mound, Dare standing over her.

"You're no good to me as a martyr," he said harshly, retreating while he still had willpower enough to put a closed door between them.

During the next few days, Tia felt in the way no matter where she went. In a community of many hundreds, she was the only one without purposeful work. No one stopped her when she wandered through the underground labyrinth, intent on seeing anything that might interest her father, but people were constantly rushing past with barely a nod. Men were working extra hours in the huge cavern where weapons were made, the intense heat of the forge circulated by giant fans. The Citadral, more than any place on Thurlow, clung to the old ways, but now that Tia had seen the broiling hell of technology that produced the Wanderers' weapons, she cherished even more the traditions of the past.

Finding her way to the schoolroom, she listened to the children's lessons, surprised by the advanced knowledge of geography and history taught to all but the youngest babes. When she offered to help in the classroom or nursee, she was politely refused. She had to believe Dare was trying to keep her isolated from the mainstream of life at Norvik. She felt more like a captive than when she was locked in her chamber.

Nor had she seen Dare. Either he was too busy to take meals with his people, or he was avoiding her. She'd never been so lonely, but, increasingly, it was the leader of the Wanderers who filled her thoughts, not her own dear family.

Finally Jonati brought word of their departure, leaving her a heavily loaded backpack along with clothing for the trip. Tia tried on the sturdy brown leather breeches and jacket and an unbleached tunic woven from the fleece of woolies, surprised at how well they fit. With the greatcoat, gloves, and boots she'd brought with her, she was properly outfitted to cross the Frozen Desert again.

She hardly slept a wink all night. Not only would she be traveling in the direction of home, she would see Dare again.

Her heart skipped a beat when she saw him the following morn. He was standing by a team of yakas, supervising as two youths harnessed the beasts. His hair was pulled back and held by a leather cord, making the planes and angles of his face appear harsh. But when he looked at her, his eyes softened for an instant, the pupils luminous blue like pure, deep pools.

"You ride with me," he said brusquely, turning his back to her.

"I'd rather ride with Jonati," she said, wanting to hurt him because her own pain was so sharp.

"You don't have that option." He bent to test a strap, refusing to meet her eyes.

"You don't want me to forget I'm your captive. Are you going to keep me prisoner the rest of my life?"

"Not if your father and I can come to terms," he said dryly, walking to the rear of the swoosha and testing the fastenings on the load. "Put your pack here."

She threw it at the conveyance, wishing she had the nerve to throw it at his stubborn head.

"When he pays you the equests, you have to free me."

"No, Tia, I don't." He looked at her then, his unrelenting frown giving her cold chills. "Don't entertain false hopes."

The great barn echoed the shouts of men and the squeals of the yakas, but all Tia heard was Dare's ominous warning.

"You can't keep me captive the rest of my days!"

He stared at her, looking as though he wanted to say more, then turned away to finish his preparations.

"Dare!" she called out to get his attention again.

"Get into the swoosha. We'll be leaving soon."

"If my father refuses to pay the equests, are you going to kill me?"

He recoiled as though he'd been slapped, staring at her in disbelief. "How can you ask that?"

"It's my life you're using as a bargaining chip. I have a right to know!"

He looked at her with so much sadness in his eyes that she wanted to take back her question. Instead she turned away and sat in the swoosha.

Dare couldn't answer questions about her future, not when the success of his mission might depend on keeping her hostage. He walked through the huge surface-barn, checking on men and animals and shouting encouragement, but his heart was a chunk of ice, ready to shatter from the pain of not being able to claim her as his woman.

His woman! She was his captive, subject to his orders, but he wanted her to come to him willingly, to accept him not as a captor, but as the man she loved. He wanted nothing more than to spend the rest of his life with her.

He was letting fantasies cloud his senses at a time when everything depended on his judgment. He tried to forget the hurt in her eyes, but this was going to be the longest journey of his life.

When the doors were finally open and they went outside, Tia blinked at the brightness of the sun reflected on a glistening white world. As far as the eye could see, the desert sparkled like diamond dust. It didn't seem possible that she and Dare had crossed this endless plain in the dark, battered by swirling ice pellets. Now the vast expanse seemed crowded as she rode in the midst of seven other swooshas, each carrying two men. The drivers raced each other, shouting and laughing like boys let out of school, making Dare seem even more somber as he silently kept aloof from their contests.

The two of them frequently trailed the pack, but Tia saw the others well enough to recognize familiar faces. Besides Jonati and Dare, she knew Cyrus, the geographer, by name as well as three others: Knud, a large, fair-haired, ruddy man who seemed like a younger, pinker version of Dare; Raviv, an energetic, wiry man with tousled brown hair cut short; and Tistur, darker-skinned than Jonati with sleek black hair and a mustache that drooped on the sides of his mouth. The others she couldn't call by name, but it seemed clear that Dare had brought enough men to handle the equests he hoped to get from her father.

Night came gently, with the three moons of Thurlow shining on the horizon. Tia shared Dare's shelter, but he silenced the good-natured jests of his men with a severe frown.

She prepared an evening repast, lighting a small stove like the one that had helped them survive on the trip to Norvik. Dare thanked her for her efforts, reserved and polite in his few words to her, but she much preferred the gruff manner of Yellow Hair.

The cold was less bitter, and the wind didn't howl around the shelter as it had during their previous journey. They lay apart, each wrapped in a greatcoat. Tia felt the chill, but she was afraid she'd never lie in Dare's arms again.

The days seemed interminable. Dare rarely sat beside her, preferring to stand on the platform to oversee his team. Tia had lost all track of time when Ringfort's weathered walls appeared as an indistinct form among the ever-changing drifts.

"Are we staying there?" she asked Dare, pointing toward the frontier post.

"No, we're safer out on the tundra. We'll skirt around it and hope no one is curious enough to give chase."

Tia couldn't pass within sight of the settlement without thinking of her well-loved shadow-keeper and the equest she'd lost. How could she explain her rash action to her father when she'd totally failed to marshal any help for him? What would the Grand Elder say if he knew his daughter was attracted to her captor?

Dare sat beside her then, crowding her against the supports of the swoosha and covering her gloved hand with one of his.

"I'm sorry we have to come within sight of Ringfort. It must bring bad memories."

You fool, she thought, remembering the golden-haired ruffian who'd led her to safety before claiming her as his captive. If he only knew everything that was in her heart! How could

he trade her for equests or whatever else he
wanted from her father, when she belonged
with him?

The men no longer jested with each other, and
it had been several days since Tia heard them
wager on the performances of their teams. The
weather seemed almost mild, the sun making wet
spots on the peaks of the drifts.

They came to their first village on the elev-
enth day. The swooshas stopped as close together as the combative yakas would allow, and the
men gathered in a knot around Dare, keeping
their voices low and gesturing frequently toward
the unwalled village ahead of them. Dare seemed
to be hearing each man's opinion; then he dispatched Jonati and one of the others to scout the
settlement.

"What's wrong?" Tia asked as Dare paced between the halted teams, his eyes locked on the
diminishing figures of his two men.

"There should be a storage tower on the edge of
the village. It's gone—either torn down or leveled
by fire. I don't want to ride in without knowing
what's happened."

The men left behind ate cold rations for their
supper, but Tia was too anxious to do more than
stare morosely at the distant village. Jonati was
her only friend among the ranks of the Wanderers, and she worried about his safety as she
would her own brother's.

"Why send Jonati?" she asked, expecting Dare
to be angry because she was questioning his judgment.

"He's the only man I trust to act as I would."

"Then why not go yourself?"

He looked at her more searchingly than he had in many days. "Like it or not," he said solemnly, "my place is by your side."

"Until you return me to my father?" She couldn't imagine how it would feel to know Dare was facing danger and adversity and not be able to reassure herself of his well-being.

"Until you've served your purpose," he said, deliberately wounding her because every moment with her was a torment.

He'd stood up to many trials in his years as leader of the Wanderers, but none had tested his strength the way Tia did. He wanted to release her because that was the only way she could ever come to him of her own free will. His obligation to the Lost Ones stood between them like a thick wall of ice.

When Jonati and his companion returned, everyone was waiting outside the shelters, too eager for news to bed down for the night. Tia stood beside Dare, anticipating the report with cold dread seeping through her.

"What news?" Dare called out as soon as his two men were close enough to hear.

Jonati shook his head and wearily trudged up to Dare. "The village is all but abandoned. One old ruffian was too ill to travel, and we learned all we could by bribing him with our rations."

"Was there an attack?" Cyrus asked, the thin, shortsighted geographer making notes in a book he always carried in his pocket.

"No, the people emptied the storage tower and burned it themselves. They fled to avoid more service in the mine. The government has gone berserk, impressing even younger boys to work in the one mine that's still operating and forcing every male fit enough to stay on his feet into prospecting crews."

"What does the government expect to buy with the hyronium?" Knud asked bitterly, his young forehead creased by worry lines.

"Power," Dare said. "Earth weapons to keep the people enslaved."

"Maybe we'd be better off if we just stayed at Norvik," the younger man suggested.

"We'll starve there if the villages don't have grain to trade for our weapons. The time for hiding in the bowels of the planet is past," Dare said.

"It's not just that village," Jonati said. "The old man told us that people are on the move everywhere, refusing to help Earth bleed the planet anymore."

"And an Earth ship is coming soon," Jonati's companion warned with the awe of a young man who'd never seen one of the ominous space vessels.

"The government men aren't worried," Jonati said. "They're lining their pockets and consolidating their power at the expense of the people, especially the poor and powerless."

"Is there any news of my father?" she asked in an anxious voice.

"I'm sorry, Tia." Jonati took her hand. "The talks between the Zealotes and the government have been terminated. The Grand Elder has returned to the Citadral."

"You can't believe everything a sick old man tells you!" she insisted.

"We'll confirm the reports soon enough," Dare said.

"Tia, you must be fatigued. Why not retire to the shelter?" Jonati suggested.

"Please let me hear it all—no matter how bad."

"One of our spies reports that the Grand Elder's son is working covertly at the mine, sabotaging efforts to reopen the tunnels blocked by explosions set by troublemakers."

"But that's dangerous! Fane wouldn't—"

"It's only a rumor," Jonati's companion said.

"It's just the kind of thing he would do," she admitted, drained by the terrible news.

The men conferred in hushed voices, but Tia stumbled toward the shelter, too stunned to hear about refugees and rebellions. She lay down, though sleep was impossible, and stared with unseeing eyes at the pale roof of the polar shelter.

Dare found her curled in a ball, her coat and boots still on. Without considering the consequences, he lay beside her and took her in his arms.

"It may not be as bad as it sounds," he said, trying to console her. "Reports can be false; rumors are always exaggerated."

She didn't believe his words, but having him close again was comfort enough to let her sleep.

Chapter Nine

They left the fields of ice behind them and began traveling by foot. The freehold where Dare had planned to leave the yakas for safekeeping was deserted, but the beasts could go no farther. They were already beginning to suffer from the warmer climate. He left two young men behind to care for the penned animals, taking twelve men with him.

Trying to find Dare's stronghold had taken Tia nearly a moon-cycle, but she'd traveled with ease on the back of a reliable equest for most of the distance. Even though the men tried to slow their march to accommodate her, she was hard-pressed to keep up. Each night she rubbed balm on her aching feet and calves, but sheer stubbornness kept her from protesting.

The polar shelters were too bulky to carry without the swooshas, so they slept under the stars,

164

always with two men on guard against marauding refugees.

Village after village was deserted or populated only by the sick and elderly, and Dare chose to avoid them whenever possible, knowing desperate outlaws would be preying on anyone they found in the unprotected settlements.

"Where have all the people gone?" Tia asked Jonati, who walked by her side more often than not.

"Into the mountains and the wilderness. Some may be taking refuge with family or friends in quieter districts."

"I don't understand why they left. Who will plant the fields?"

"No one will. Most people won't try to return until there's an amnesty. The men in this area refused to serve in the mines. When patrol police forces came for them, they hid. Now the whole district has been declared a rebel state. Every man and boy has been sentenced to servitude for life—when they're found."

"How will they survive?"

"The same way the Wanderers did," he answered grimly.

The trip seemed to take ten times longer than it had when Tia first went to Ringfort, but she became a seasoned trekker; by the seventeenth day she was keeping up with the men as though she'd been born a Wanderer.

Dare always bedded down near Tia, but he rarely spoke to her on the march. Jonati was always kind, but Cyrus, the geographer, became her companion more often as the days passed. She never tired of hearing his anecdotes about the places they passed, and sometimes he even succeeded in taking her mind off Dare.

But she couldn't ignore her chafed thighs and her blistered heels from the endless walking, or the midday heat. Carrying her greatcoat added enough weight to her pack to make her back ache.

"Are you well?" Dare asked her one evening when the men were settling down to sleep.

"I'm fine," she lied, realizing how angry she was at his coolness toward her. He scarcely acknowledged her existence most days!

"I'm sorry to push you so hard, but we're in great danger in this district. Jonati's scouts have been bringing in nothing but dire warnings."

He settled down on his ground cover, turning his back and pretending to sleep. He knew only too well that she waited until the men were sleeping to tend her aches and pains, and he longed to rub her poor bruised feet and massage the cramps from her legs and shoulders. If he could have taken her fatigue and discomfort on himself, he would have done so gladly. He'd spent his youth on the road, and memories of the hardships were still vivid. As a woman, she probably suffered most from lack of privacy, but they were living on half-rations, going to sleep with empty stomachs so they could eat their fill before beginning each day's march. So far the polished metal beads and other small trinkets they'd brought to trade for food were valueless. Anything edible was a precious commodity in the district, and the few people who'd stayed behind had none to spare.

"Tia," he whispered on impulse.

"I'm sleeping."

"You're as wide-awake as I am."

"No, my eyes are closed. I need my rest," she said, then started giggling.

"You're not hysterical, are you?" he teased, loving the sound of her laughter so much that his heart seemed to be melting.

"Does it matter?"

"Yes," he said, sobering her with the regret in his voice.

"How far are we from the Citadral?"

"You've made this journey before."

"Then I had an equest—and a map."

"If we can get transportation on the river, the going will be easier."

"That's not what I asked! I can keep up with you without any pity, thank you very much, Master Dare Lore."

"No doubt you can." He stretched out on his back, a smile touching his lips for the first time in many days.

Three days later they found an abandoned over-size barge used for ferrying bovines to market on the River Rexulus, and the men spent a day repairing the ancient craft. They traveled the river by day, but at night they concealed the vessel as best they could and slept on land, doubling the number who stood guard during each shift.

Tia always sat in the middle of the barge, at least partially shielded by her traveling companions. Dare rode in the front, taking turns at one of the long poles that guided the craft. When the day was warm, he stripped off his tunic, letting the sun's rays redden his shoulders. By the fifth day, his back was bronzed and his hair was sun-bleached to an even lighter shade, yet he seemed totally unaware of the striking picture he presented to her. Tia's fingers ached to feel the swell of his powerful shoulders. She wanted to run her tongue down the length of his spine and taste the wind-dried saltiness of his skin. When Cyrus spoke to her, another woman seemed to answer him. She was distracted—and tormented—by the pleasure she took in watching Dare.

As they continued on the river, her blisters healed and her sore muscles were forgotten. She lived for the moment each day when Dare stripped to the waist and took his turn with the pole, his body fluid with motion, his buttocks and thighs straining as he fought the current. Yet, when he looked back at her, she closed her eyes and pretended to doze, too shy to let him see her naked admiration.

During their trip, he felt her eyes on his back, and sometimes, boyishly, let himself bask in her admiration, flexing his shoulder muscles more than necessary and tightening his buttocks into hard, round swells. He was so intensely aware of her that the others ceased to exist for him and he was caught in his thoughts of her until a water fight broke out and someone doused him with river water.

Tia's laughter soon turned to sputtering when a wall of water descended on her front, but before the skirmish ended, she had her revenge, soaking the mischievous Raviv from head to foot. The rough play ended when Jonati tossed the culprit into the river, making him swim after them until Dare showed mercy and had him hauled aboard, winded and somewhat repentant.

The sun was warm and the shore deserted; one by one the men stripped down to the homespun garments they wore under their breeches to let the air dry their soaked clothing. Tia tried not to look when Dare peeled off his breeches and took his place at the bow, his homespun clinging damply to the cleft between his buttocks.

She was soaked too, and her companions were abnormally quiet, waiting to see if she'd strip to dry her garments. Her wet breeches were clammy, and her tunic stuck like a second skin. She accepted these small discomforts, but felt alienated from the men for the first time on the trip. In spite of their past courtesy, their faces betrayed their thoughts. They avidly wanted to see the Grand Elder's daughter naked and shivering in their midst. They were bonded against her in a subtle but demeaning way, and she wondered what would happen if she did expose her body to their hungry gazes.

Then she looked up at Dare, and he turned in her direction. There was no challenge, no mockery, no lust on his face, only tender understanding.

The moment passed, the men became congenial traveling companions again, and Tia realized what it meant to be in Dare Lore's care.

At long last they left the barge, carefully concealing it in case of future need, and began journeying through more familiar territory. She knew they were within a few days' trek of the Citadral.

The next day Dare sent the men on their mission, setting up camp for Tia and himself in a deeply wooded area that offered maximum security. He knew the hardest part of the journey was just beginning: being alone with her while they waited for Logan's response.

Although they seemed to be alone, the troubled times forced Dare to take extra precautions for their safety. They camped at the base of a mammoth pere tree, sheltering under branches that touched the ground in places. He grabbed short snatches of sleep by day, preferring to remain awake at night. She straddled a heavy branch, boosted there by Dare, to watch for intruders while he slept.

With all their energy directed toward survival, they spoke of little else, but one question was tormenting Tia.

"What will you do if my father refuses to give you the equests?" she asked, taking advantage of a contented moment after they'd managed to fill their bellies with roasted pesce Dare netted in a nearby stream.

"I pray he won't." He turned his face away, not wanting her to read the truth in his eyes. He'd instructed Jonati to give the Grand Elder a message that would ensure his men's safe return: If any of them were harmed, Tia's life was forfeit. He couldn't allow her to live if Logan harmed his followers, but the thought of killing her was like a white-hot blade piercing his skull: unendurable but inescapable.

"That's no answer."

He seemed more like a stranger to her now that his men were gone.

"You know your father. Do you honestly think he'll honor your debt to me?"

"He most likely would if I asked him myself. How will he know I'm still alive? Why should he believe what Jonati tells him when I've been gone so long?"

"He can easily overcome my men and torture them for the truth."

"He'd never do that!" She sprang to her feet and backed away, shocked by his suggestion.

"The Zealotes I knew would flay the skin off a man's back with their accursed ropes for less cause than I'm giving him."

"My father isn't cruel! He's forbidden lashings. The practice of carrying ropes has been banned within the Citadral."

"So you say, but that doesn't ensure my men's safety. If Logan lets them go in peace, it's because he recognizes your dirk."

"You sent him that?" She knew her father would recognize it as an illegal weapon but not necessarily hers. "Why not a lock of hair—or perhaps a little finger?"

"You don't know what you're saying." He sat on the edge of his ground cover, emotions warring on his face as he tried to answer calmly.

"What threat did you use to force payment of the equests?" She bunched the edge of her tunic in her fist.

"I don't make threats, as a rule," he said in an ominously low voice, "but I do think the Grand Elder's daughter could greatly benefit from discipline applied to her bare hindquarters."

"Angeline knows you better than you'll admit!"

"The witch knows me not at all. If I had less self-restraint, you would have smarted for slapping that poor kitchen lass."

"I . . . I am ashamed of that," she admitted, embarrassed by her guilt. "But I was desperate."

"Desperate to stir up trouble?" He slowly stood and walked up to her, backing her against the rough trunk of the tree. "You did that by seeking out the Wanderers. Angeline ran off in a jealous rage, depriving me of the services of my master swordsman, Garridan."

"You can't blame me for that!"

"Maybe . . . maybe not." He tasted bittersweet defeat in every skirmish with his captive, but it wasn't anger that made his heart race and his mouth go dry.

"You haven't answered my question," she hoarsely whispered, wanting to reach out and smooth away the angry set of his mouth.

"If your father refuses to send the equests, my dealings with him are at an end."

"But what about me?"

"What about you, Tia? If I send you back without compensation from the Grand Elder, my people will lose faith in my leadership. Does your happiness depend on scurrying home to Papa?"

"You are cruel!"

He was so close she could see his nostrils flare when he took a deep breath.

"Life is cruel, Tia. I can't make it easier for you, but I don't take pleasure in your pain."

She sniffed, closer to tears than she had been since her vow not to wallow in self-pity.

"Will you watch so I can rest for a few hours?" he asked.

"How do you know I won't steal away while you're asleep?"

"I trust you, Tia. Someday you'll learn to trust me."

"Never," she murmured under her breath, but she let him boost her up to the branch where she could better see or hear any disturbance in the woods around them.

*   *   *

The next day, Tia was shelling krozer nuts she'd found that morning, planning to add them to the pan of green berries she was stewing to make them less bitter, when the ground trembled. She dropped a tiny nutmeat, feeling the earth shake beneath her feet; then Dare was shoving her behind him, drawing his sword to face whatever unknown force was advancing on them.

The trees around them rumbled, and the air was filled with dust and debris, as though the shrubs of the forest were being uprooted.

"By the Great Power!" Dare cried out, racing toward the unseen racket.

Tia recognized the thundering as the hooves of a herd of beasts; then Jonati, grinning and triumphant, reared into sight on the back of a massive black equest.

"We did it!" he cried with the excitement of a boy, completely abandoning his reserve for the first time since Tia had met him. "Ten mares, this stallion, and the rusty one Tistur is riding."

Jonati dismounted, turning the reins over to Dare, and excitedly parted the thick, shaggy wool on the equest's flank. There, imprinted on the beast's heaving backside, was the Zealote brand, a Z in a triangle, and a second, rawer mark, the curlicue that indicated the beast had been legally obtained.

"Every one of them broken to the saddle," Tistur, the only expert horseman among them, said.

Knud, more ruddy-faced than ever, was the next to dismount, joking and patting his tender behind. "What's broken is my arse. I've been bouncing on this beast all night, following a madman!"

He playfully punched Jonati's arm and had his earlobe pinched in return.

Dare saw twelve pairs of sharply pointed ears twitch in expectation and could hardly believe his eyes. He knew the Order's broad-haunched, shaggy equests were the finest on the entire planet, but actually seeing the highly prized beasts was awe-inspiring.

"They can outrun any beast but a lepine," Tistur said, "and we've put them to the test getting here. Except for a bit of awkwardness—they can't change course once they're lunging forward—they're living miracles."

Dare walked up to each equest, congratulating the rider and inspecting the animal from massive head to branded flank. An army equipped with beasts like these would be unstoppable against any force on Thurlow, but he knew the twelve were too valuable to use for anything but breeding until the Wanderers owned a hundred times their number. Yet he could hardly believe his good fortune.

"Take care," Tia warned. "They've been known to charge and trample people."

She recognized a brown mare with a pinkish nose and black socks, the offspring of a stallion her father especially prized. Three of the beasts were midnight black, and the rest were shades ranging from brown to deep rust to a creamy tan.

"They seem compatible," she said, surprised that her father had parted with such choice beasts, ones that would stay together on a trail without fighting each other. He could easily have unloaded inferior beasts fit only to be harnessed to a plow. Even the Zealotes' careful breeding couldn't avoid a few misfits, but her father hadn't included one among the equests he'd sent to Dare. She reached up to stroke between the eyes of the familiar mare.

"Have a care," Tistur warned.

She smiled, feeling as though the great beasts were old friends. "I named this one Corella. I saw her take her first steps, trembling on legs like sticks."

"Do Zealotes name their beasts?" he asked.

"Not usually. My father calls it a female whim, but my mother named every beast on her father's freehold when she was young."

Dare was burning with impatience to hear Jonati's report on the meeting with Logan, but he wanted Tia out of hearing first.

"Tistur grew up on a freehold before his parents died, but the rest of my men have had little or no experience with equests," Dare said to Tia, not mentioning that he was a rank novice himself in handling the beasts. "Will you advise them on feeding and watering the animals?"

"First they have to be cooled down. They've been ridden too hard, too fast. See, this one is foaming from the mouth. Caring for an equest is a serious responsibility."

Dare smiled behind his hand; apparently the Grand Elder's daughter did have a gift for something besides stirring up trouble.

Jonati handed her the black stallion's reins, recognizing how eager Dare was to draw him aside.

She saw the glance that passed between the two men and knew they wanted to speak alone. If they were determined to exclude her from their conference, there was nothing she could do. Dare would tell her all there was to know in his own good time—or wish he'd never laid eyes on her!

Dare watched with relief when Tia willingly led the black stallion to a clearing and began giving instructions to the riders. Fortunately Tistur looked on with amusement, not resenting her lessons. Dare hoped it would be a while before she learned that the men had been well briefed on handling equests; it was his order that they get far from the Citadral before Logan changed his mind about any equests he gave them. In fact, the men had been chosen because they were quick learners with gifts for handling yakas and domestic beasts.

"Logan wants his daughter back," Jonati said, his boyish exuberance gone now that they were alone. "He wants you to come yourself and set a price for her safe return. He was incensed that her life was forfeit if we were detained or killed, but he hid it better than most men would have."

"I never doubted that. What kind of man is he?"

"He's a natural leader, accustomed to being obeyed. He hides his frustration well, but his failure in negotiating with the government was a serious setback."

"Is he an angry man?" Dare knew his own weakness: he was more apt to make mistakes when emotions clouded his judgment.

"Angry at his daughter, I would say." Jonati smiled. "She's a handful for any man, but I don't need to tell you that."

"Did you make it clear that the equests are payment promised by his daughter?"

"Yes, he sent them as a show of good faith, not as ransom. He also loaded our packs with foodstuffs, although I didn't ask for it. He wants to meet with you face-to-face."

"What assurances did you give him?"

"Only that you would ensure her safety. You might be doing Tia a favor, keeping her out of her father's reach until his anger cools."

Dare shook his head. "He dotes on her. A tongue-lashing is all she has to fear. Do you think he suspects what we want?"

"No, but he's intrigued by rumors about your army."

"The question is, can we trust him?"

"I think he's an honorable man."

"So his daughter said," Dare said skeptically. "But he's still the Grand Elder of the Zealotes. How far will the Grand Elder go to keep the Order's privileged status?"

"The rumor about his son working undercover at the mine is true, even though the Zealotes are exempt from servitude."

"Is he an idealist, or is he acting on his father's orders, hoping to gain something for the Zealotes?"

Jonati shook his head. "You ask hard questions. Logan didn't reveal his intentions to his daughter's captors."

"How were you treated?"

Dare had spent his childhood hearing horror stories about Zealote dungeons and the lashings members suffered as penance for transgressions against the Order's rules. These tales had made him determined never to let his childhood friends fall into Zealote hands, but as an adult, he realized that Warmond had used fear and terror to control his followers and the unfortunate boys he was training for his army.

"By day we were treated like honored guests, fed delicacies, and given the freedom of the grounds," Jonati said. "At night we were separated, sent to isolated chambers to sleep with guards outside the doors to prevent our wandering. I can give you a sketchy layout, but our movements inside the buildings were heavily monitored."

"I'm leaving for the Citadral at first light tomorrow," Dare said.

"I'll be ready."

"No, Jonati, it's more important that you and Cyrus take the equests to Leonidas. I'll take Tia, two equests, and two men."

"Logan had nothing to gain by holding us, but you're a bigger prize. He could use you as a bargaining pawn with the government."

"No, I'll be safe enough as long as Tia is hidden away. My only question is whether two men can contain her." He grinned at his friend, feeling like a man emerging from a fog now that it was time to take action himself instead of waiting for others to carry out his plans.

She met him as he parted from Jonati, her eyes belying her outward calm.

"You've spoken with Jonati. Now tell me that I'm to return to my father."

"In due time," he said.

"Due time! You have no cause to detain me unless you plan to go to the Citadral yourself and take me with you."

He saw the hope on her face but steeled himself to disappoint her.

"You're still my hostage, Tia," he said, turning away and refusing to speak more with her until he'd had time to weigh all the implications of his next move.

178

Love's Changing Moon

* * *

Tia was so angry she had to find an outlet for her fury. She returned to the equests, working harder than any of the weary, saddlesore men in brushing coats and providing water and fodder. Her father had sent everything necessary to keep the beasts as strong and healthy as they'd been in the Zealote stables, and she cherished a secret hope that he had some plan to reclaim them.

When evening came, she stank like a stable lad and ached in every muscle, but she felt a part of something again. It pleased her when Dare wrinkled his nose and sent her to bathe before supping on fresh flat bread and dried fruit sent by her father.

She awoke at dawn the next day, roused by the activity around her.

"What's happening?" she asked a grumbling young man rolling up his ground cover.

"I 'spect we're on the move again, but I'd rather walk back to Norvik on my hands than bounce around on one of those beasts again."

"Relax and move in rhythm with your mount. When you learn to ride, you'll love it."

The woods around her were green and fragrant, with tiny nosegays of wild blooms springing up in patches of sun between the giant pere trees. She pitied all those left behind at Norvik, and Dare would have to bind and carry her if he expected her to return to the bowels of the earth.

"Whatever your plans for me, I won't go back to Norvik!" she said, approaching him by the stream where he was scraping bristles from his face with a wicked-looking blade.

179

"You won't?"

His mild response made her suspicious.

"Why won't you let me go home?"

"Your father honored your debt," he said, rubbing his hand over a chin still pink from shaving. "But our business together isn't over."

"You expect more payment for my release?"

He saw her eyes narrow in anger and was tempted to flatten the little pout on her lips by kissing her the way he longed to. "Your father can't buy you away from me."

"What, then?"

"Tia, be patient. The last thing I want is to bring you to harm."

"That tells me nothing!" She watched as he slipped his tunic over his head, nonchalantly gathering up his toilet articles.

"Are you going to join my father's cause? If so, tell me! Don't keep me in suspense."

"Would you be willing to stay with me if I aided your father?" he asked on impulse.

"I . . . I don't know what you mean."

"Of course you do. If I aid the Zealotes, will you cook my meals, sew my clothing—"

"You want me to be your slave?"

"Oh, no, Tia. I want to know if you'll be my woman, share my bed, part your thighs when I hunger for you. . . ."

"You're despicable!"

"You're asking me to commit my men and risk all our lives in a cause that means nothing to me. What sacrifice are you willing to make, Tia?" He saw her distress, but it only made him press harder for an answer.

He was asking her to do the one thing she most wanted in life: to be his companion and love. But she'd given an oath to Olan and a promise to her parents; she was betrothed to the man of her father's choice.

"Dare—"

"Yes or no, Tia. Is it such a hard choice? Do you still believe Angeline's tales about me? Are you afraid of me?"

"No!"

"Then do you think I'm too coarse, too ignorant for the daughter of the Grand Elder?"

"You're not being fair! That's not what I think at all!"

"Then maybe my person doesn't please you! Am I too tall? Too short? Do you prefer black hair, green eyes, a bushy red beard? Tell me, Tia, because the workings of your mind are a mystery to me!"

"I like your looks well enough," she said, so angry now that she wanted to put him in his place. "But you're a bully, a beast, a tyrant who must have things his way all the time!"

"You've been so spoiled by your doting father, so pampered by your easy life, that you think life owes you happiness."

She acted without thinking, a red haze of anger clouding her mind. She heard the resounding slap and felt the sting in her hand before she realized she had indeed struck him.

He rubbed his cheek without moving to defend himself, but the look in his eyes was more punishment than she could bear.

"I . . . I didn't mean to do that."

His silence was worse than a blow.

"I won't blame you if you retaliate," she said in a meek voice that seemed to belong to someone else.

Still he said nothing, watching her with eyes that seemed to read her thoughts.

"If you want me to apologize, I will. I'm sorry, Dare. I acted without thinking!"

"Did you?" he asked, turning away from her and slowly walking back to the others. He had his answer, and it hurt far more than her well-aimed blow.

Chapter Ten

Tia wanted to run after Dare, but she didn't know how to explain why she'd insulted him rather than tell him of her betrothal. He would never believe that it was an obligation she didn't want to face until she had to. Because Olan had agreed to go through the lengthy process of becoming a Zealote, she'd counted on several more full-cycles of freedom.

She knew her father would forgive her for running off. He might regret the loss of the equests, but he wouldn't withhold his love because she'd disappointed him. Yet, first and foremost, Logan was Grand Elder of the Zealotes, and when he had reformed the Order he had established new rules governing betrothals and marriages. He would never condone the breaking of the Order's rules, and that was what she would be doing if she didn't honor her commitment to Olan. Her father would be forced to pay a huge forfeiture or see his daughter imprisoned. Worse, he would lose the respect of the Zealotes if he allowed a member of his family to flaunt the law.

She understood why penance had been part of the ancient Zealote way. She would rather face a beating than know her father suffered on her account. She knew where her duty lay. She had to harden her heart against the man she loved.

Dare had given his men their instructions the night before. This morning Jonati and nine others were to take ten equests to Leonidas. Knud and Raviv would go with him, sharing one equest while he and Tia rode the other. The beasts could easily carry double loads, but Dare didn't know if he could stand the torment of riding with Tia. Yet now as he sat on the equest, he knew that, rather than reverse his orders and seem like a vacillating leader, he had to let the plan stand. He doubted it would be any easier to see her in intimate contact with another man.

Dare watched as Tia approached him and Jonati helped her mount. They rode out together and Jonati wished them both good fortune before taking a different fork in the trail.

They traveled in silence for a few moments; then Tia noticed that Dare's legs were stretched taut so his toes could hook into the stirrups.

"You can't ride this way," she said, breaking her silence and looking over her shoulder at him.

"I seem to be doing so."

"Your feet are too low, and you're bouncing like a babe on a knee."

"Worry about yourself," he said gruffly.

"I am. I'm going to slide off if you don't learn

to hold your seat. It's tricky, riding two on an equest."

The two younger men had passed them on a wide place in the trail, and Dare couldn't help noticing they seemed to be more in rhythm with their beast's movements than he was. Yet he was in no mood to take instructions from the Grand Elder's daughter.

"I won't let you fall," he assured her.

"Bounce all you like, then. It's not me who'll be sleeping on my stomach."

Without warning, she slid off the equest's back, landing gracefully on her feet in spite of the great distance to the ground.

"What are you doing?" She'd made him even angrier by giving him a scare.

"Walking. I won't share a beast with an incompetent rider."

"Not everyone grows up playing with the pick of the Zealote's equests."

"Riding isn't child's play, although you're going about it as if it were."

The others were out of sight, and he didn't want his small party separated.

"Give me your hand. I'll pull you back up. We don't have time for games."

"I'm not playing a game, and I'm not riding unless you do it properly."

He had to slow his mount or pass her by, but the equest resented his command, nearly throwing Dare off when it reared up.

"You've a heavy hand and a cruel touch!" Tia said angrily, reaching up and snatching the reins from his hands. "Poor Corella," she crooned. "Some men aren't fit to ride a mare."

The beast grew calm, and Dare admired her

185

gift in spite of his annoyance.

"Get back up here," he ordered, reaching down to grab her.

She easily eluded his hand, but he was more frightened than angry when she crept under the beast's belly and started adjusting the straps.

"Tia, you'll be trampled!"

"Not if you keep your brutal hand to yourself."

He watched dumbfounded when she pulled his foot free of the stirrup, made an adjustment, and positioned his leg as though she were handling an inanimate object, doing the same on the other side.

His face was burning, all the more so when she pinched his hip, making him rear up so she could slide her hand under his buttocks.

"Now hold yourself above my hand," she ordered. "Use your thigh muscles instead of sitting like a lump of suet."

He wanted to throttle her, but she went to the equest's head and gently led it, alternately crooning to the beast and snapping instructions at him.

His face was scarlet with humiliation, and he wanted nothing more than to turn her over his knee and teach her a lesson.

"See, isn't that easier?" she asked. "The first time is always the most difficult."

"What makes you think it's my first time?"

"Generally you're graceful enough, but I've seen bags of meal ride with better form."

"You are a witch!" he said, too stubborn to admit that much of what she said was true.

At last she gave him her hand, all the help she needed to leap astride the beast and settle herself in front of him. She still played the part of drillmaster, sharply rebuking him when he didn't execute her orders with dispatch, but he grudgingly accepted her admonitions, knowing full well he had much to learn about equests.

She didn't blame Dare for being a surly pupil. He was showing great restraint by not throwing her off into one of the spiny bushes that lined their path, the sharp needles on the branches a menace even to the equest's shaggy hide. Yet she wasn't willing to soften her voice or phrase her instructions more tactfully. She was putting a wall of anger between them because it hurt too much to think of what they could mean to each other.

They caught up with Knud and Raviv and easily passed them at a trot. Dare was exhilarated as he felt the power of the beast flow through his own body and was eager to try a full gallop.

"Whatever you wish," Tia said with a laugh.

She gave the beast its head, and they raced down the sandy track, the greenery on either side a blur as the equest made the ground tremble and Dare's stomach lurch.

He forgot everything she'd taught him, clutching the beast's sides with his legs, dropping the reins in Tia's lap, and instinctively wrapping his arms around her.

"Slow down!" he yelled, more winded than the equest, realizing she'd bested him one more time. She stopped the beast and doubled over in laughter.

"You've made your point," he said grimly, wondering if his legs would support him when he tried to walk.

"I'm sorry," she said. "I only wanted you to know it's no small thing to manage a beast like this. You've learned more in one day than some

187

can absorb in a moon-cycle. Please forgive me."

"If you'll forgive me for the unkind thoughts I've had of you."

"How can I, when I don't know what they were?"

He realized his arms were still locked around her waist. He felt ready to ride a lepine if it meant holding Tia this close, feeling her tiny waist and the soft swell of her hips under his hands. Her saucy bottom was wedged between his thighs, and he began to understand what sweet torture it was to share a mount with the woman he loved.

She asked if he wanted to walk to work the kinks out of his legs. He had to decline, however inviting the suggestion was. He didn't want her to see how she was affecting him, pressing against him and firing his lust with the graceful sway of her hips.

The two equests started traveling together again, and Dare encouraged her to offer suggestions on his men's lack of expertise instead of his, beginning to realize how many techniques he had to practice.

They left the sheltered woodland and followed a broad, circular roadway into a more populous area. Villagers here weren't abandoning their homes, but windows were boarded and sandbags were stacked in front of doors. The people were ready to defend what was theirs against the hordes of refugees sweeping down from the troubled north.

They passed small groups of fleeing people, some family groups but others bands of unsavory-looking men. Dare rode with one hand on his sword hilt, thankful that the equests gave them greater mobility than most travelers had.

Everyone they passed was eager to know the location of the patrol police. Strangers shared rumors and begged for scraps of information.

Tia was frantic to hear news of what was happening at the mine, gleaning bits and pieces of information that only increased her alarm for Fane's safety. Everyone feared that the patrol police would send reinforcements to oversee the miners.

"Your brother will be all right," Dare said to reassure her. "He wouldn't do anything rash or foolish."

"Like me," she said under her breath, scarcely able to believe how her life had changed in such a short time.

That night the three moons of Thurlow were obscured by heavy black clouds, and the wind whipped itself into a frenzy. Dare preferred to take his chances outside, even in turbulent weather, but he didn't like the looks of many of the travelers they passed on the road. He could see undisguised envy when they looked at the equests, but the stares directed at Tia were even more dangerous. He needed a sheltered area with a stout wall at his back to ensure her safety. Already she'd attracted too many curious and lustful looks.

They rode until dark, stopping at a small outpost that served as a place for freeholders to sell their beasts and grain in more peaceful times. Now the courtyard was crowded with a motley assortment of fugitives, opportunists, and ruffians.

A high wall of rough-barked timbers surrounded a cluster of small buildings, all of them dark with windows boarded. People were quick to tell Dare that cowardly government

189

time-servers had barricaded themselves inside
for the night, ignoring their duty to provide
a hostelry for travelers. At first they'd tried
to prevent refugees from using the walls for
shelter, but the more aggressive among them
had battered down the gates, chopping up the
timbers to fuel many small fires burning in the
courtyard.

Raviv volunteered to stand guard while the others bedded down beside a wall, but Dare was too
uneasy to sleep. Giving strict orders for the others to stay there with the equests, he wandered
around the encampment, anxious to learn what
he could from the crowd.

There were a number of refugees traveling in
groups with women and children, and Dare saw
a sprinkling of government men in seedy green
uniforms, probably fugitives from military service, and more than a few rough types. He kept
in the shadows, deciding it was wiser to listen in
silence than to call attention to himself.

The moonless night made it easy to conceal
himself but hard to watch for familiar faces. One
burly man did catch his eye, and Dare took extra
care not to be seen after confirming that he was
one of the ruffians from Ringfort, the man called
Guston.

"I had him in my grasp, if I'd but known there
was a price on his head," the half-drunk outlaw
boasted.

"You never saw Dare Lore," a companion said
with contempt. "And if you did, he'd run your fat
ass ragged. You couldn't put your whip around
that lad."

Dare swiftly moved away, avoiding the bright
patches around the fires. The government had

offered a reward for his capture, but he couldn't be wanted on a criminal charge. He was sure of that. It had been many full-cycles since the Wanderers had practiced petty thievery to stay alive. If the government was willing to pay to get their hands on him, it meant they were interested in his army.

Leaving now would be more conspicuous than staying. Later, when most of those sheltering at the outpost were asleep, he'd have to risk sneaking his small band out through the open gateway. If he waited until morning, Guston was sure to recognize him and try to make good on his boast to collect the reward.

He found Raviv awake and alert, standing over the prone forms of Knud and Tia.

"I'll stand watch now," Dare said, "but we'll be leaving as soon as everyone is asleep."

"Why have you changed your plans?" Raviv asked, never one to blindly obey a command.

"I'll explain later."

This time Dare wanted to keep his own counsel, although he couldn't have given a reason for being closemouthed with his own man.

The wind whined around the walls, and drunken voices added to the din of crying children and the weary voices of fugitives. A small scuffle broke out near the gate, but it was settled with fists, and not more lethal weapons.

Dare checked the equests and tied the packs on their rumps. When he saw a good chance to leave, he didn't want the animals to be the cause for delay.

As alert as he was, Dare wasn't sure what sparked the riot, but the sound of smashed crockery was followed by a string of vulgar oaths. Suddenly a private quarrel escalated into a full-scale brawl with screams of anger and the terrified wailing of women and children.

Dare's first thought was to protect Tia, but a heavy body crashed into him, knocking him to the ground. He quickly extracted himself, but the only sign of Tia was her abandoned ground cloth. He plunged into the melee, fighting for a glimpse of her.

Tia had leaped up at the first rumble of trouble, intending to lead the mare to a safer spot, but she was shoved toward the worst of the conflict by some unseen hand, barely managing to stay on her feet. She stumbled over an unconscious form and tried to get back to the wall, but two ruffians pounding each other with fists blocked her way. To her left a brawler was knocked off his feet, landing in the remnants of a fire, sending sparks flying in every direction. Tia was so confused she didn't know which way to turn, and she cried out for Dare, more frightened for his safety than her own.

Two heavy arms embraced her from behind, droping over her shoulders like a yoke, and she screamed in fright, trying to break free. She grabbed at her assailant, horrified when a hot, sticky wetness covered her hand. She collapsed to her knees, pushed forward by the heavy burden on her back.

Dare found her then, her face smeared with blood under Knud's inert body.

"Tia!" He was so sure she'd been mortally wounded that his heart stopped in despair.

"Dare."

As faint as her voice was, it gave him hope. He lifted Knud as though the heavier man weighed no more than a target dummy stuffed with feathers, soaking his own hands with the blood of his follower. Before he could help Tia, she scrambled to her feet, gasping for breath but able to stand on her own.

"Put him on the equest," Tia urged, clearheaded now that she could see that Dare was still alive.

Men were fighting separately and in groups, stampeded into a bloody free-for-all by crazed attackers on every side.

Dare lunged toward the only beast he could see and managed to lift Knud onto the high, broad back, his inert form hanging head down, the only way to get him through the chaos around them.

"We have to find Corella," Tia said, knowing it was impossible even before she said it.

Sword in hand, Dare used the flat of it to open a path toward the gateway, reluctant to inflict mortal wounds on men he could scarcely see. Tia led the equest, her hand tight on Dare's free hand.

Others had the same idea, pushing and crowding to flee the enclosure, and Dare was hard-pressed to keep the crush of bodies from overwhelming both of them. Not even the equest's massive bulk intimidated the throngs trying to escape from the brouhaha.

"It's Dare Lore!"

Dare couldn't see who identified him, but the grating voice was chillingly familiar. Guston was raising an alarm against him.

"Grab him! There's a price on his head!"

The equest lunged through the opening in the wall like a cork erupting from a bottle of spirits, carrying Dare and Tia through the press of people.

A man stepped forward to block their escape, and Dare raised his sword, ready to slash their way to freedom.

"It's me! Raviv!"

Dare quickly formulated a plan.

"Take the equest," he said. "Lead them a hard chase; then do what you can for Knud. We'll meet you at the stream beyond Ennora."

He grabbed Tia's hand and raced toward the back of the outpost, staying close to the towering wall to take advantage of the dark cover.

Tia was breathless with fear, and the wind made her feel like a bit of refuse being swept into oblivion. She gripped Dare's hand, her only lifeline in a world gone mad, and tried not to hinder his flight. It was impossible to see the ground, and she stumbled more than once before falling over a piece of rotting timber. He pulled her up as though she were weightless, giving her courage to keep going.

"Run ahead and save yourself," she begged when a sharp pain in her side forced her to stop a second time.

"They're chasing the equest, not us," Dare said. "Raviv will get away." He paused a moment, surveying the stretch of open land behind the fortress. "Unless someone manages to give chase on the other equest."

"We can't let a stranger have Corella!"

"I'm sorry. There's no choice."

She knew he was right, but her heart ached to lose another Zealote equest, one she'd helped foal and break to a lead.

"Our best chance is that high peak, if you think you can climb it," Dare said, pointing toward what seemed like solid darkness. "They only have

194

Guston's word that he saw me. I don't think many will be willing to look very hard in the dark, not if it means a climb like that in the blackness for a reward the government may decide not to pay."

"Let's climb," she said, gasping for air and hoping she wouldn't slow him down.

They ran across the open field, not stopping to look behind them until they were concealed in the brush at the base of the hill.

The flat area surrounding the outpost wall seemed deserted, but Dare knew a lone stalker concealed in the shadows was much more dangerous than a braying mob.

"It will be a hard climb," he said, trying to pick the safest route on the night-shrouded slope. "Let me go first. Try to use the same footholds I do."

"Lead on," she said with all the bravado she could muster.

The lower slope was steep but firm, and only a few pebbles cascaded down behind them. But the way grew more difficult as they climbed higher, forcing them to scramble on all fours. Worse, there were fertile pockets of earth that allowed the wicked spiny bushes to flourish. Dare stopped to pull a nasty needle out of his hand.

"What's happening? Do you need help?"

"No, I have a needle stuck in my hand," he said, still whispering although he was growing hopeful that no one was following. "The spiny point will break off and fester unless I pull it out intact. Just give me a minute."

"Does it hurt?"

"Yes," he said, sighing with relief when he felt the burning tip leave his flesh.

"What are you doing now?"

"Just trying to pick the best route. There isn't

195

an easy way to get to the top."

The climb to the summit seemed to take all night, but once they reached the peak, they were rewarded by the sound of trickling water.

"Wait here," Dare cautioned. "I'll see if it's accessible."

In moments he was back, leading her to a small runoff. He drank first to test the water's quality, then let her drink her fill by pressing her cheek close to the cold, metallic-tasting waterfall. Next she bathed, scrubbing her face and arms, preferring a damp tunic to the blood that had dried where Knud had touched her.

"Will Knud be all right?" she asked.

"Raviv had enough of a start to get him away, but I don't know how bad his wound was."

"I hope it wasn't as bad as it seemed," Tia said, realizing for the first time how much all the young men in the Wanderers meant to her.

"He's strong as an equest," Dare reassured her, although he wasn't at all easy about his friend's chances.

Dare could hear the weariness in every word Tia said, but he was eager to get off the steep hill before daylight. There were no tall trees to conceal their movements, and he didn't dare remain so visible. Guston wasn't the only opportunist who would be glad to turn him over to the government.

Descending took even longer than climbing. The ground underfoot was treacherous with loose stones and pockets of sandy soil that gave way underfoot. Several times they started small landslides, and in spots they had to cling precariously to deeply rooted bushes to gain their next foothold.

When the slope became more gradual and they could walk upright, Dare heaved a sigh of relief. The first pale glimmer of dawn was showing on the horizon, but they could reach a wooded area before full light if they hurried.

Tia was so exhausted her knees felt wobbly, but she was grateful that the worst was behind them. She relaxed—too soon—and lost her footing, surprising herself so much she rolled past Dare to a precarious stop.

Her shriek seemed loud enough to betray their presence to anyone at the now-distant fortress. He scrambled down beside her, a warning on his tongue, but he was too worried about her safety to bother rebuking her for being noisy.

Tia's fall could have been much worse, but she had a spiny bush to thank for saving her from serious injury.

"I'm impaled!" she yelped as he bent over her.

Her description wasn't far from wrong. Her hip had slid against the wicked spines, and he could tell a dozen or more were embedded in the fleshy part of her backside.

"Don't move," he said, leaning close.

Her breeches had saved her from a hundred or more of the weaker needles, but enough had pushed through the leather to make one rounded buttock resemble a pincushion.

"Pull them out," she begged, trying to reach behind and do it herself.

"Careful. If you break any off flush with your skin, I'll have to dig them out. Stay absolutely still," he cautioned, "and I'll get you loose from the bush."

He carefully snapped each vicious, woody spine from the branch, making sure enough needle still protruded to make removing them from her flesh as easy as possible.

Gingerly she crawled to her knees, accepting his hand so he could help her stand.

"Lean on me," he said urgently. "There's no time for me to remove the needles now. We've got to get out of sight before daybreak."

Every step was a torment because of the pain in her thighs, but she tried to bite back her whimpers.

"Hold on," he said, murmuring encouragement.

They reached the welcome stretch of flat meadowland, and he offered to carry her. She refused, preferring to move slowly in agony rather than again suffering the indignity of being dangled over his shoulder.

Progress was painfully slow, and Dare could see the golden glimmer of the sun peeking over a cluster of low bushes in the distance. By veering right, they could reach the shadowy recesses of the forest in a short time. Otherwise, they could be seen for miles.

"I'm going to stoop," he said. "Put your arms around my neck, and I'll carry you on my back."

"I'm too heavy."

"Not compared to the yoke the government would like to lay on my shoulders," he said, remembering his one arrest before he'd even attained his full height.

Patrol police had forced him to march for a day and a night chained to others with a yoke locked around his neck and wrists. He'd been sentenced to work three moon-cycles in a gristmill by a judge who hadn't allowed him to say a word in his own defense. His crime had been the theft of overripe fruit lying on the ground.

He ran with her on his back, her legs tucked around him and her arms locked around his neck, trying not to cut off his air. She'd always known he was strong, but she'd never suspected he had such reserves of strength and endurance. He covered the ground in long, sure strides, scarcely breathing hard when they entered the shadowy depths of a pere tree grove. Even frightened and in pain, she found it far more exciting to ride this man than a beast.

There were places under the giant branches where the sun never reached, but Dare was reluctant to stop until he found a source of water. Tia wouldn't feel like moving after he did what had to be done, and he had no way to carry water to quench her thirst. In all his years as a Wanderer, he'd never been so ill-equipped for a long trek, and he regretted the loss of his pack as much as the necessity of abandoning the equests.

At least the woods around them provided the best possible place to take refuge. Because it was the beginning of the growing season, he wouldn't have too much trouble finding sustenance. Even before he found a spot to rest, he was able to gather a handful of tasty edible shoots from the same kind of bush that had cruelly pricked poor Tia.

"At last," he said, seeing a ground creeper that only flourished near streams.

Tia's cheeks were wet, although she didn't remember crying, and she wanted to curl up in a ball and sleep a moon-cycle. When Dare led her to a narrow stream with clear water bubbling over the rocky bottom, he had to help her kneel and drink. Her legs were as stiff as broomsticks, and the needles in her bottom felt like arrows burning their way through her skin.

"You'll hate the next few minutes," he warned, leading her to a natural bower under low-hanging branches.

They had to stoop to enter, but once the branch swayed back in place, they were so well concealed a man could pass an arm's distance away and not know they were there.

"Now trust me," Dare said in a soothing whisper. "Look, my hand is nearly healed where I pulled out the spine." He held his palm close to her face so she could see the tiny red pinprick which showed no sign of the ominous reddening of the skin.

He took off his jacket and rolled it into a pillow, laying it on the ground while she watched suspiciously.

"Now loosen the laces on your breeches."

"You don't mean—"

"Tia, you can't walk around like a half-plucked avian."

"I'll just stand here and you can pull them out," she said, taking hold of one of the branches to brace herself.

"If that's what you want."

He reached around her waist and deftly unlaced her breeches, pulling them away from her waist in back.

She shuddered when his large hand crept down under her clothing, pausing for an instant on the cleft at the end of her spine.

"Don't move," he warned.

He pinched the first needle between his thumb and forefinger. He yanked; she shrieked and wiggled away from him.

"It hurts, I know," he said gently, checking the tip of the needle to make sure the sharp point hadn't broken off in her flesh.

"I'll do the rest myself." She tried to twist around to reach her own backside.

"Let's try the next one lying on your stomach," he said. "The sooner they're all out, the better."

She grumbled her frustration but dropped to the ground and buried her face in the well-worn leather of his jacket.

Eager to make short work of it and not prolong her suffering, he didn't hesitate to grasp the next woody shaft, pulling it from her flesh with one hand and through the seat of her breeches with the other. Again the lethal-looking point was intact. He held his breath, hoping he wouldn't have to probe for a tip with his dirk. He was no surgeon, and the thought of cutting Tia's silky skin made his blood run cold.

She ground her teeth together, determined to be stoic, digging her nails into the ground and kicking so hard her booted toes dug a trench in the soft, leafy loam under the tree. A rich, musty odor filled her nostrils, and she tried to brace herself for the next extraction. But when Dare pulled another loose, it smarted so much she couldn't help rubbing her bottom.

"Not much longer," he murmured, gently moving her hand aside.

"Please hurry!"

"That's all of them," he said at last. "You won't like this either, but it'll soon be over."

Before she realized what he was doing, he tugged her breeches and undergarment down to her thighs.

"I have to be sure I didn't miss any little ones

that weren't sticking through your breeches."

Now that the worst was done, he could smile at her indignant sputterings and allow himself to appreciate her creamy smooth backside, still beautiful in spite of the little red marks.

His little finger brushed against the enticing cleft between her buttocks, and he let it linger, sorely tempted to explore between her legs.

"Stop!" she demanded, trying to roll away from his hand.

"Stay still long enough to let me feel for small prickers. Then I'll cover the punctures with pod fluff. It's the best thing there is to numb your skin. You're lucky it's the time for pere trees to drop their pods."

She was too embarrassed to make further protests. Never had anyone fondled her backside, and it made her feel squirmy and unsure of herself.

The pain was subsiding, and he patted handfuls of fluffy pere tree droppings over her bottom. To her surprise, she felt a sense of sleepy well-being.

By the time he carefully covered her exposed skin with his makeshift dressing, she was limp with sleep. Wishing one part of his own anatomy was in the same limp state, he stretched out beside her on the ground, gratified when she rolled against him and cushioned her head on his shoulder.

He didn't want to sleep. Holding Tia close was a fulfillment of his dreams. He didn't want oblivion to rob him of the sweet satisfaction of having her in his arms.

Chapter Eleven

Tia awoke feeling hot and lethargic, slowly remembering where she was. She heard Dare's soft, rhythmic breathing before she saw him stretched out beside her, lost in the deep sleep of exhaustion. How long had it been since he'd done more than snatch quick naps? Her heart went out to him, and she rolled away as quietly as possible, not wanting to deprive him of much-needed rest.

She crept out from under the bower of branches as silently as possible, holding up her unlaced breeches and remembering her embarrassing accident. The pain was gone, but she still blushed at the thought of his intimate touch, not understanding why she felt so confused and agitated.

She didn't want to leave him, not even for the time it would take to make herself more presentable. He was lodged in her heart, a part of her every thought, and she nearly returned to his side because even a short separation left her feeling bereft. Forcing herself to go, she hurried toward the stream, dropping to her knees to drink deeply of the crystal-clear water.

What she wanted was to bathe, but the stream was shallow and rocky with no vegetation along the edges to give an illusion of privacy. She followed the flow of the water, watching for signs of human habitation, but the woods on either side seemed deserted.

She rounded several bends before her short hike was rewarded. The stream widened and flowed into a small pond that seemed designed for lazy swims.

Glancing in all directions to make sure she was still alone, she stripped off her clothing, giggling when she realized the pod fluff was sticking to her backside like down on a newly hatched avian. She took a moment to scrub her undergarment and tunic, laying them in a sunny spot in the hope that they'd dry quickly. Then she plunged into the pond, diving under as soon as she discovered it was deep enough for swimming. The water was cold, but she splashed energetically, loving the sheer freedom of being able to frolic in the water.

Dare awoke and sat up in the same instant, knowing something was wrong even before his mind could focus.

Tia was gone!

He jumped to his feet, remembering the way he'd cushioned her head in sleep, their bodies pressed together as though they belonged that way.

"Tia!" He looked around, calling softly at first, then more urgently.

With a Wanderer's practiced eye, he surveyed the site where they'd slept, then studied the ground around it. He saw her boot marks in the soft loam, but the ground was otherwise undisturbed. He was reassured that no stranger had come anywhere near the bower in recent days.

He followed her tracks, relieved when he saw they led to the stream.

"Tia," he called out again, thinking he'd warn her of his approach so she wouldn't be startled.

The stream was just as he remembered it, but Tia was nowhere in sight. He called more urgently, scanning the nearby woods to look for her.

His heart pounding, he imagined a score of dangers from kidnapping to ravaging by savage beasts that could account for her absence, but none seemed likely. She'd used his exhaustion as an opportunity to escape.

The vein in his forehead throbbed, and he was as frightened as he was furious. Her chance of reaching the Citadral unharmed in these troubled times was nil, and the thought of a ruffian like Guston getting hold of her was worse torture than anything the government could do to him.

His first thought was that she'd try to reach the road, but he forced himself to use the skills he'd been perfecting all his life. When he studied the ground, he saw the depression on the bank where she'd stooped to drink. From there it was easy to read the signs that showed she was following the stream.

He took a deep breath and ran after her, growing angrier with each step he took. Had she fallen on purpose last night by the outpost wall, hoping he'd abandon her to save his own skin? The thought of being apart from her for any reason made him feel like a man in mourning.

The stream widened, and he tried to overcome his anger so he wouldn't miss any signs on the ground. If she was trying to elude him, she was careless about where she walked. An imprint from the heel of her boot clearly showed where she'd gone, but she could have a lead of several hours, judging by the sun.

He saw her tunic and underdrawers first, both weighted down by stones to dry on the shore of a small pond. Then, suddenly, a head popped up above the placid surface, and Tia was walking toward him, wringing out her hair as water cascaded down her beautiful, lithe body.

He'd seen her lush, pink-tipped breasts, but his imagination had never been equal to the vision he saw emerging from the pond. Slender but achingly feminine, she had skin like the soft petal of a rosbiscus bloom, fair but touched with the rosy glow of vitality. She had a womanly sway to her hips, but even naked she moved with a serene dignity that made his throat ache. He trembled with desire, not trusting himself to move closer.

His sudden appearance didn't frighten her. In her heart, she'd been waiting, knowing somehow that this was a predestined moment. Her instinct was to cover herself with her hands, but she knew they'd moved beyond the demands of modesty.

"Is the water cold?" He wanted to fall on his knees and tell her all the things in his heart, but only this inane question came out of his mouth.

"Yes, but I've never felt so clean and refreshed."

"Your clothes don't look dry."

"They couldn't be. I just washed them."

"You haven't . . . ?"

"I haven't been gone long."

He couldn't stop looking at her, and he knew she was giving him a gift, a memory of her that would stay with him until his dying day.

"Give me your tunic," she said. "I'll wash it for you."

The thought of the Grand Elder's daughter scrubbing his soiled clothing in a stream should have filled him with a sense of triumph, but he shook his head.

"You're not my servant."

"If I were, you would have to order me to do it. I would refuse, and you would have to chastise me."

"I couldn't."

"Then it's a good thing for you I'm not your servant. You've gotten your clothes quite dirty."

He watched, mesmerized, while she moved up to him and lifted the edge of his tunic over his rib cage. Her hand was cold when it brushed his warm torso, and he shivered slightly, raising his arms but not helping her.

She was resourceful, standing on tiptoes, so close he could inhale the clean scent of her skin, and extricating his arms from the sleeves. He watched with bemused enchantment while she knelt beside the water, her spine a graceful arch as she leaned forward to pummel his soiled tunic. When she rose to her feet, then bent over to anchor his garment beside hers, his heart pumped double-fast and he thought some strange narcotic was making him hallucinate.

"Now your drawers," she said in a no-nonsense voice. "Do you need help with your laces?"

"That I don't," he said hoarsely, wondering if

she could possibly be as innocent as she seemed. "Why are you doing this?"

"I don't care to travel with a man who smells worse than a yaka."

He laughed and undid his laces. "Am I as bad as that?"

"No," she murmured, turning her head while he finished undressing. "I don't find anything about you less than pleasing."

He handed over his dusty garments, hating to see her laboring over them but willing to play the game her way. He'd never felt quite so awkward, so exposed, and he chose to conceal himself by diving headlong into the placid depths of the pond.

He swam hard, holding his breath underwater until his lungs ached for air, putting distance between the temptation on the shore and his aching desire. Not a minute had passed during their days of travel when he hadn't longed to hold her in his arms. He could hardly bear to sleep, knowing visions of her would fill his dreams, and he would awake so full of love he wanted to howl in frustration.

He'd resisted trying to seduce her because he loved her too much to risk hurting her. Now she was tempting him beyond the limits of his endurance.

"Dare!"

She'd never known a swimmer to stay submerged so long. Tossing the sodden bundle of clothing on the shore, she dove into the water, hoping to find him by following his wake.

He came up so far ahead, she couldn't believe her eyes. He'd moved through the water so quickly, he seemed to possess superhuman strength.

Was there nothing he couldn't do, no obstacle he couldn't overcome?

"I thought you'd drowned," she said, weak with relief.

"Not likely, since I can stand with my head above water," he teased.

"I didn't think of that."

"What did you think, Tia? If I drown, you'll have your freedom."

"I don't want it at that cost." She didn't ever want to be free of this man.

His head bobbed toward her, and she realized he was indeed walking on the bottom, parting the water that separated them.

She knew what was going to happen, and she'd never been so sure of her own heart.

He swept her into his arms, covering her cold lips with his mouth until his heat flowed through her like molten lava, burning away a lifetime of restraint.

"My darling," he whispered. "Stop me now. Run away from me. It's your last chance at freedom."

"I've never had a chance, not since Yellow Hair first took me in his arms."

"I don't want to hurt you."

"You can only do that by sending me away."

He carried her out of the water toward a grassy spot in the sun and let her toes slide to the ground before going down on his knees in front of her.

She hugged his head against her, blinded by the water streaming from her hair and by the tears of joy clouding her eyes.

"I've never bent my knees to anyone but you," he said.

His lips parted in a smile like none she'd ever seen, and all the angry planes and scornful furrows on his face dissolved, making him look even more comely than his image in her daydreams.

She knelt beside him and gathered his streaming hair in her hands, gently squeezing out the water that darkened the thick, golden tendrils.

"I love hair of gold," she said, parting her lips for his tiny, nibbling kisses so sweet and gentle they made her heart swell.

"I love you," he said so quietly his mind seemed to be speaking directly to hers.

"I'll die if you don't, Dare."

"Tia . . ." Her name caught in his throat, and he drew her to the ground, kissing her as though the joining of their mouths would make them one person, inseparable in love.

She thought that being naked with a man would make her timid, but instead she rejoiced because her body could make Dare happy. He made love to her throat, trailed kisses from her chin to her breast, bedeviled her ears with hot whispers, and gently touched his lips to her closed lids.

He was like a blind man learning the contours of her body with his hands, and she was just as eager to touch him. His hard, lean muscles relaxed under her hands, and she found delightful soft spots that quivered in response. She'd never thought of a man's nipples as erotic, but his tiny peaks hardened like pebbles under the tip of her tongue.

She was a minx, running her toes down his calf and giggling when her thumb found the fuzz around his navel. Innocently she teased him, and he was sure she didn't understand how urgently he needed her.

"Tia." He rolled on his back, hardly noticing the prickly grass under him or the intensity of the sun on his face. "This may be the last moment I can hold back."

"I want you, Dare."

"I'm afraid of hurting you."

"I'm not so naive as you think. I know the first time can be painful."

He groaned in an agony of need, afraid her only knowledge came from speculations exchanged by schoolgirls.

"Touch me, Tia."

She snuggled beside him, pressing her lips to his and running her hand down his torso, stopping when her fingers brushed the springly hair on his groin.

"You know what I mean," he rasped.

She sat and resolutely looked, not quite able to believe such a huge part of his body had been concealed in his breeches.

"Touch me," he urged, not knowing how he could bear it if he saw disgust or fear on her face.

"Do you think my love is so shallow I could despise a part of you?"

She bent over him and kissed him slowly with a woman's passion.

Instinct replaced thought, and Tia was in his arms, smothered by kisses, then on her back, clutching his shoulders, so overcome by new sensations she thought she'd die of happiness.

He knew his own strength and feared using it. Tia was small and tight, but so wet and eager he couldn't hold back. He forgot everything except how much he loved her. He heard breathless gasps, but she didn't cry out. He felt her hands clutching his buttocks in a steely grip, but she arched her back to meet his thrusts. If a perfect moment existed outside of myth, he found it when he exploded with an intensity that rendered him senseless.

She ached, she trembled, but she didn't let go. She was swept away beyond the here and now, and Dare was her whole world. His release was so powerful that it carried her with him. Her heart swelled with love, and she wanted the waves of sensation to go on forever.

She suddenly understood the secretive smile her mother sometimes directed at her father, and she also knew why no woman could ever share the real secret of love. It had nothing to do with words and everything to do with life.

"I love you, I love you, I love you," she said, meaning it more each time she repeated it.

"Oh, Tia, this was my first time."

"It couldn't be! You're old!"

"Is thirty full-cycles old?" He laughed and hugged her against him, love pouring out of him like heat from the sun.

"I didn't mean old. I meant . . ."

"I know what you meant." He cradled her in his arms, pressing his lips against her forehead. "My darling, please forgive me."

"You're talking in puzzles."

He groped for words, but couldn't find a gentle way to tell her.

"Am I really your first?" she asked.

"I wish I could say yes. Tia, you're the first woman I've loved, the first to make me crazy wanting you. This was the first time I didn't spill my seed on the ground."

She understood what he was saying and tried

to let him know how much it meant to her. She wanted him to be part of her always. Lifting his hand, she laid it on her belly, surrendering her body and soul to his care.

His heart was bursting with things he wanted to say to her, but a rush of feelings made speaking an effort. He closed his eyes, dumbfounded by the power of sheer happiness, and held her close to his heart.

Her legs were still trembling, and she didn't want to think of anything but Dare's tender smile, Dare's gentle hands, Dare's kisses and caresses.

When he nodded off to sleep, she gently disentangled herself from his arms and sat beside him, smiling at the boyish grin that stayed on his lips as he slept.

Dare awoke and reached for her, disappointed but not disturbed to find her gone.

"Lazy bones, I have your supper."

She stood over him, naked but not self-conscious, shading her eyes against the sun, low in the sky.

He grabbed her ankle, wanting her to collapse on top of him, but she stood her ground, making an exaggerated gesture with her arm. "Your dinner, master."

She'd spread her tunic on the ground and found giant leaves to serve as plates. In the center of the makeshift dining cloth, a nosegay of pink and purple blooms showed how much effort she'd made to please him.

"You've done well." Sitting beside her, surprised at how resourceful she was, he reached for a groundcap, bland but nourishing, and bit the fat white head off the stem.

They ate their fill of sweet-water plant, the delicate green leaves slightly bitter but crunchy. She'd even found some pucker berries, tough-skinned but juicy and thirst-quenching.

"You surprise me," he said. "I could almost believe you've had experience living off the land."

"Cyrus told me many things—when you weren't talking to me."

He smiled sheepishly with no more appetite for food but a great, overpowering hunger to hold her again.

"Our clothes are dry except for your underdrawers. I forgot to spread them out."

"My fault." He watched her lean forward, her breasts silky smooth and lovely.

"There's still a little sun." She kept her eyes averted, shy because she really wanted to scrutinize every line and curve of his body so she could cherish the memory in her mind and heart.

"Very little," he said. "We have to find Raviv and Knud."

"Do you think Knud's all right?"

He looked into her face and saw a compassionate woman, a companion more than worthy of sharing his thoughts. He didn't want to deceive her or build false hope.

"I think he was gravely wounded. We can only hope he'll survive."

"I do hope so. But we can't leave yet. It's still too light."

She stood and shook the remains of the makeshift meal from her tunic, holding the little bunch of blooms to her nose.

"Smell how sweet they are," she said, offering them to him.

He took her hand instead, pulling her close.

214

His face was in shadow, but his expression was passionate, compelling, and so full of tenderness that her heart ached with joy.

"Yes, it is too light to leave." His voice was a husky whisper that caressed her like a velvet glove.

"I found a pretty place near where the berries grow where we can lie together."

"It's not too soon to make love again?"

She shook her head no.

Wordlessly they gathered up their garments and boots, making bundles of them and walking hand in hand into the dark seclusion of the forest. She led the way to a mossy knoll, the ground spongy but not moist.

Neatly, deliberately, he stacked their meager possessions and turned to take her in his arms. They stood pressed together, their hearts pounding and their hands intertwined, savoring a tenderness more thrilling than the act of love itself.

"Tia."

He caressed her shoulders, sending shock waves down her spine, then slowly rubbed her back, lower and lower until he was fondling her bottom, lifting her until her legs were wrapped around his waist.

His kisses were hot and urgent, and his tongue swelled against hers until she gasped for breath and dug her nails into his back.

He lowered her to the ground, then caught her breast between his lips, gently suckling until her nipple throbbed and her eyes misted with desire. He rolled over, settling her on top of him.

She straddled his hips, his erection hard against her belly. She hid her face against his cheek, then nuzzled his ear, running her tongue over the whorls until he shuddered and distracted her, his fingers making her squirm and tighten her bottom.

She wanted to be absorbed, to be part of him, flesh of his flesh, linked by passion and love. When she cried out and begged him to quench her burning fire, he grew very still, tenderly stroking her breasts and belly, moistening her with his finger until she impaled herself.

She felt a surge of power like nothing she'd ever imagined, riding him with frantic urgency, crying out in a frenzy of passion that rocked them both.

They soared above the ground in one last all-consuming thrust, and he saw fiery starbursts behind his closed lids.

Tia collapsed in his arms, so spent her whole body trembled. Air rushed from her lungs, and she burrowed down on top of him, holding him inside her as joyous spasms deepened her satisfaction. She felt as if she'd lived her whole life in anticipation of this joining with the man she loved.

"I knew you were the better rider," he said when he could speak, using levity to keep from crying with joy.

She lay in his arms, their flesh and spirits still joined as the shadows around them grew black and threatening.

From somewhere far away, the tiny voice of duty whispered in Dare's head, but he held Tia closer, kissing her moist forehead and closed eyelids. Nothing that he'd ever wanted could satisfy him like Tia did; nothing mattered except the pure love that bound them together. He had never felt so complete and whole since he'd been ripped from his faceless mother's arms as a babe.

"Rest, my love."

They fell asleep in each other's arms.

Tia awoke first, refreshed after several hours' respite, idly wondering if they'd grown together like roots spliced together to create a new hybrid. She rose to kiss his slightly parted lips, tasting salt and honey on his mouth.

"Sleep, my love," she purred, but a sense of urgency spoiled her contentment even before she remembered Knud.

"Is that what I was doing?" He kissed her soundly and planted a noisy love tap on her bottom.

"We have to get dressed and go look for Corella," she said, wiggling against him, hoping he was strong enough to make her leave this enchanted place.

"I think it's still too sunny," he joked.

"You're right, of course. I'm going to have a sunburn where I sit," she said, giggling.

"Did I mention that I love you?"

He rubbed her smooth flanks, wondering how he had stayed aloof from her so long. She instinctively knew more about lovemaking than he would ever learn. He was satiated and more deeply content than he'd ever been, but he wanted her again, wondering if he would ever draw a breath without desiring her.

"Mention it again and again and again," she said, nipping at his throat above his collarbone.

"What did you say we have to do?" The haze of passion was slowly clearing from his mind.

"Get dressed and look for Corella."

He sat, imprisoning her between his legs, seeing the heart-shaped outline of her face in the dim moonlight filtering through the trees. "We'll never find your mare. Some ruffian has her secreted away by now. A man can retire on what a Zealote equest will bring, especially with half the people on the planet on the move."

"We have to try."

She was the first to stand, limping stiffly toward the bundles of clothing.

She ached, but she'd never had such a sense of well-being. She wanted Dare again, spilling his hot seed inside her. Her cheeks flushed just thinking of their tempestuous joining, but she loved him beyond reason, beyond thought of consequences.

He stood beside her, dressing quickly, trying to recall all the things that had seemed so urgent to him before he made love to Tia.

"I had to abandon my sword on the peak," he said, still too besotted by her wild passion to regret the loss of the weapon, as a warrior should. "We have to get to Ennora as quickly as possible."

"How long will it take on foot?"

"Traveling only at night and avoiding refugees and patrol police, at least five days."

"It's scarcely a day's ride for an equest."

"Tia, there's no chance. Men will kill to get their hands on a Zealote equest."

"I can't lose another," she insisted, remembering she still had to tell her father about her dead shadow-keeper and the slaughtered beast she'd lost outside of Ringfort.

"We can't go back over the mountain. Someone at the outpost would be sure to see us in the morning."

"You're a Wanderer," she said with supreme

confidence. "You'll find an easier way to get back there."

"No, Tia."

"I'm going to look for Corella."

"You're still a captive." He spoke decisively, but he wasn't at all sure he wasn't her captive.

"Then tie me up and drag me where you will."

"My love, be reasonable. There's no chance of finding the beast."

"My mother had an equest that could track."

"Impossible." He tied his laces and slipped his tunic over his head, rolling his still-damp under-drawers into a bundle and putting on his leather jacket.

"Have you lived so long that you've seen every-thing?" She didn't like herself when she was snip-py, but the thought of one more offense against her father was making her edgy and sharp-tongued.

"Tia." He knew what she was trying to do, but the glow of love in his heart was still overwhelm-ing. "We can find a middle ground."

"I don't know what you mean."

"We'll skirt around the range of mountains and try to double back to the outpost without being seen. If we don't find the mare tomorrow, you have to agree to go on and not mention it again."

His face was only a blur in the darkness, but his voice was warm and sensual. Her spine tin-gled, and she stood on tiptoe to press a kiss at the corner of his mouth.

"Agreed," she said.

He took a deep breath, not at all sure he'd won this skirmish with the Grand Elder's daughter.

Chapter Twelve

They walked holding hands whenever the terrain allowed it, their love making the rough trek seem like an enchanted journey. The three moons illuminated the meadowland with a silvery light, adding an extra element of danger but making it easier for Dare to find a safer route at the foot of the mountains to lead them back to the outpost.

Tia's heart was bursting with love, and she wanted to know Dare's every thought. His past was like a book with revelations on every page, and she wanted to commit each precious fact to memory. One lifetime wouldn't be enough to absorb the mystery of Dare Lore, the leader of the Wanderers and her lover.

She pushed aside all thought of the obstacles that lay before them. A love like theirs couldn't be denied. Her father had been the engineer of her happiness for all the twenty full-cycles of her life until she left on her quest to find Dare. Although she understood her duty, she clung to the belief that he wouldn't condemn her to a life of unending torment without the man she loved.

They would have made good time, but every dark nook beckoned them; they could scarcely cover a kilometer without stopping to exchange sweet, urgent kisses. She purred when he stroked the swell of her backside; he groaned in pleasure when she kneaded the back of his neck. Both regretted all the time they'd wasted trying to conceal their love from others and from each other.

Dare's stomach was knotted as it was before each serious test of his leadership, but it wasn't the possibility of failure that made him anxious. It was the cost of success. He wanted Tia for himself more than he wanted his next breath of air, but she was still a bargaining chip, part of his plan to secure a home for his Lost Ones.

At the first gray glint of dawn, they were within sight of the outpost but poorly concealed in a grove of spindly young enip trees. They'd crossed the low range of mountains through a pass to the north and were backtracking to the road, growing more cautious as the chance of meeting other travelers increased.

"Listen," Tia said, laying her hand on his arm to hold him back.

He was tempted to take his small dirk from his boot, but so far he hadn't seen any tangible danger.

"We have to cross the road before the morning traffic begins. The meadowland on this side is too open."

"Just listen a moment." She reached up and touched his lips, standing still as a statue.

221

"I don't hear anything."

Without warning she whistled shrilly, alarming him so much he clamped his hand over her mouth.

"Have you gone mad?"

He cautiously moved his hand, keeping it on her chin in case he had to silence her again.

"Look!" She managed another signal before he sealed her lips again. This time she resisted so emphatically he was hard-pressed to keep her quiet without hurting her.

"Don't you see?" she whispered urgently. "Over there by that cluster of boulders."

He saw but found it hard to believe his eyes. "The mare."

"I knew she would never let a stranger near enough to mount her."

"If I can get behind the boulders and jump down . . ."

"You'll send her into a panic."

"Then what do you suggest, my beautiful tamer of equests?"

"Stay here and don't move a muscle, no matter what I do."

"Now that you've ridden me, are you also my master?" He was glad she couldn't see his grin.

"Whatever you say," she teased, slipping away from him.

The mare's snort was louder now, and Tia's greatest worry was that some ruffian sleeping under the open sky would wake and hear it.

"Hush, Corella, hush, sweet beast," she crooned even before the creature could hear her.

Dare watched, fearful for her safety but fascinated by her plan of action. She outflanked the equest, then approached on the beast's left, the

222

side where a rider had the best chance of mounting. He didn't know whether the breed naturally favored this side or was trained from birth to tolerate humans there. In fact, there were many things he didn't know about equests—and about the woman who fearlessly approached this one.

Tia was greatly encouraged when she saw the saddle and pack still in place on the beast's back. Her chance of success would have been small without a stirrup if she only had Corella's long, shaggy hair to help her mount.

She crooned a low, melodious chant, the same she'd used when the equest had been a foal standing no higher than her shoulder.

Dare's heart was in his throat, and he pulled out his dirk, determined to protect Tia if the beast turned on her. Nothing had value to him compared to her safety.

Tia coaxed and soothed, at last getting close enough to gather the reins. The equest was skittish; no doubt more than one brutal assailant had tried to capture her.

She did it! The mare reared up but quickly conceded the battle. Dare was so relieved he laughed aloud and raced on foot toward his mounted love.

As soon as he scrambled up behind her, they made haste to leave the area. Corella covered the ground like a whirlwind, and Dare was content to hold Tia in his arms and let her manage the beast. He snuggled close, so aroused by her courage and closeness that he wondered if it were possible to make love on a galloping equest. His saner judgment won out, but he brushed aside her streaming dark hair to nuzzle the back of her neck and let his hand wander under her tunic until one firm, warm breast was cupped in his hand. She squirmed and laughed in protest but did nothing to restrain him.

Shortly after sunrise they left the road and plunged into a deserted wooded area to conceal the equest. Tia slept while he kept watch, then awoke and insisted he sleep while she acted as his shadow-keeper.

"You're the only refreshment I need. Lie down with me."

"I won't have some ruffian collecting the price on your head because we dallied together."

"The beast will warn us."

"Maybe not soon enough. You don't have your sword."

"Your love makes me invincible. I need you, darling."

She felt dizzy with desire, but being so close to the outpost frightened her. Love was making her a coward. She couldn't imagine anything worse than losing him now.

"Then have mercy," she said. "I can't ride night and day!"

He grinned sheepishly and claimed a long, gentle kiss before stretching out on the ground, resigned to sleeping alone, knowing in his heart she was right. He couldn't take risks that might bring harm to them.

When she was sure he was asleep, she sat and lifted his head onto her lap, waking him for an instant but quickly lulling him back to sleep with whispered endearments.

When dusk came, they feasted on foodstuffs in the saddlebag and headed toward Ennora, shunning the road until it was dark enough to risk using it.

"I've never seen a government man who isn't too lazy to patrol at night," Dare said, remembering countless nights when he'd led the Wanderers out of threatening situations under cover of dark.

The countryside was familiar now, and Tia was agitated at the prospect of seeing the Citadral again. Her optimism about the future waned as they passed through Ennora, the last village before Zealote territory began.

Dare hadn't been this close to the Citadral in years, but he knew the area like the palm of his hand. He and Cyrus had pored over maps countless times, until he could name every road, trail, and stream without hesitation.

Raviv would be waiting south of Ennora beside a stream so deep it had to be forded. The Zealotes discouraged trespassers by not building bridges.

They carried their boots above their heads as they rode through the chill waters which soaked their breeches. Although they didn't speak of it, both were praying that two men would be waiting for them beyond the ford.

Raviv was waiting at the appointed place. Dare knew the worst before he or the other man spoke.

"I buried Knud," Raviv said. "He was dead by the time I outdistanced our pursuers."

"I was afraid of that," Dare said, his voice telling Tia how much the loss of his friend hurt. "Do you think you can carry out the plan alone?"

"Of course. There won't be any problems."

Tia thought he sounded smug, but Dare seemed satisfied.

Delaying his departure would only make it more difficult. He took Tia aside, out of Raviv's hearing, and put his hands on her shoulders.

"I have to ask you to stay with Raviv."

"I'm going with you! You can't leave me after what's happened."

"Darling, I don't want to, but I have to go on alone. You'll be safe, and I'll rejoin you as soon as possible."

"You can't go to the Citadral without me!"

"I have to." He looked into her face and felt as though his heart were being wrung dry.

"I can guarantee your safety. You can't just walk in alone."

"You sound like Jonati," he said, trying to make light of her concern.

"I thought we meant something to each other!"

"You mean everything to me, Tia."

"Then take me with you!"

"No, I have to do this myself."

"You still think I'm your hostage! You're going to bargain with my father for my return."

"Not the way you mean!"

"Am I still your captive or not?"

"I'm keeping you under my protection for now."

"You're playing with words! I don't need protection from my own father!"

"Tia, please trust me!"

"I want to go with you. I can help you."

"No."

"I see. And what happens to me if my father refuses your demands?"

"You know I won't let anything bad happen to you."

"Will you send me home, no matter what happens with my father?"

"You won't be harmed—not even if your father has me bound in ropes and torn asunder by equests."

"He won't!"

"Legend has it that your mother's life was threatened that way."

"It was my father who saved her. The Zealotes have changed. My father has put aside the old ways." She was furious at him for making her defend the Order, but all she really cared about was staying with him.

"Tia, I'll be back with you as soon as I can." He had to leave. Denying her was agony, and he was in no mood to prolong their parting.

"Tell your man to bind me hand and foot. I'm not going to be a model prisoner!"

"You're not going to be foolish, either."

"Are you ever going to let me go home?"

"Would it be so terrible to stay with me?"

"Yes!" she cried out in anger, hating the lie as soon as it rolled off her tongue.

He called out to Raviv and gruffly gave his orders. "Keep her hidden until I return. Don't risk going near the village or the road. You know where to wait for me."

He mounted the brown mare and recklessly galloped away, feeling as though she'd stuck a dirk in his heart.

Tia wanted to cry out a warning. He wasn't skillful enough to race an equest on the narrow trail, but he was gone before she could take back her angry words.

How could he be so stubborn? Didn't he know she'd willingly be his for life? She loved him! What more could she do to prove it?

Her future was mapped out. As a dutiful daughter she had only one choice: honor her betrothal to Olan and bear the grandchildren that would fulfill all her parents' hopes. But she knew with stunning clarity that she would stay with Dare forever if he would only ask her! She couldn't be both his captive and his beloved mate.

Dare entered the lush, green, tree-studded valley as the sun rose beyond the gleaming white spires of the Citadral. His throat constricted as he rode through the verdant paradise so unlike the dark confines of Norvik. The beauty around him only stiffened his resolve: his Wanderers would have a home.

The massive wooden gate set into the wall was standing open, and no one challenged him as he rode through it into the Zealotes' fabled stronghold.

A lad of twelve or so, a healthy boy with rosy cheeks and white-blond hair, scurried up to meet him, his legs bare under the blue tunic he wore.

"I'm Dare Lore. I'm here to see the Grand Elder."

"Are you alone, sir?" the boy stammered with excitement. "Didn't you bring your army?"

Dare smiled at him. It seemed impossible that he had been younger than this lad when he became the leader of the Wanderers.

"As you can see, I'm alone," he said not unkindly, dismounting from the equest and gladly handing over the reins. He wondered if the day would ever come when he could ride one of the ungainly beasts without suffering a beating to his backside. Tia said all he needed was practice.

Tia! How could he bargain with the powerful Grand Elder of the Zealotes when she was constantly on his mind? He imagined her now, emerging from the pond with water streaming down her flawless body, her nipples puckered from long immersion in the water.

A red-haired youth, older and thinner than the other, with his legs encased in breeches and boots under his tunic, appeared out of nowhere—or so it seemed to Dare's inattentive eyes.

"You're to come with me, sir."

"Who are you?" Dare asked, liking to know the names of those he met.

"Aristotle, the third son of Perrin, sir, but my friends call me Totts."

"Well, Totts, please lead the way," Dare said, remembering where he'd heard the name of Perrin. How could this cheerful, robust boy be Angeline's half-brother?

The youth walked beside him, apparently consumed with curiosity about the Wanderers' army, and Dare hoped the Grand Elder shared Totts's interest. He was bargaining for the future of the Wanderers on the strength of a force no one had seen.

The Citadral grounds were elaborately landscaped with beds of vivid blooms in every shade imaginable. Heavy stone benches lined the walkways, and several old men sat dozing in the sun wearing the traditional black robes of the Zealotes. Dare passed a group of children, both boys and girls, carrying book bags on their backs. The younger ones, dressed in a rainbow of colors, were talking and laughing, occasionally chasing one another in good-humored skirmishes.

"Is it your job to greet visitors?" Dare asked the youth as they approached a large white stone building with astronomical symbols carved in the high wooden door.

"No, sir. I'm a page for the Grand Elder when I'm not at my lessons. He sent me to meet you."

Dare wasn't surprised; no one could pass through the spacious valley undetected if someone in the Citadral chanced to look through the open gateway.

Totts didn't need urging to talk; he loved games of skill and was bubbling over with enthusiasm about a contest involving a ball and a playing field.

Prosperity and happiness seemed to radiate from the building itself as Dare followed the boy into a light, airy corridor with white stucco walls embellished with heroic mosaics showing Zealotes mounted on their legendary equests.

A chubby-cheeked young boy rushed by on legs still pudgy with baby fat, and Dare felt off balance, as though he'd suffered a blow to his midsection. He'd never been in such congenial surroundings, and he was sure no child here ever had to go to bed hungry. This wasn't the place of horrors he'd been told it was when he was a child, not with so many young people moving about so freely.

Totts ushered him into a high-ceilinged chamber, simply but elegantly furnished with heavy gold curtains gracing long, narrow windows. The boy invited him to sit on one of the slender-legged chairs arranged in a casual cluster, but Dare declined, too agitated to sit calmly and await his interview.

The page left, and Dare paced back and forth on a large crimson-and-gold rug that covered a good portion of the highly polished wooden floor.

"Do you plan to wear a path in the carpet?" a melodious voice inquired from behind him.

Dare froze, surprised by the sudden appearance of the woman but much more startled by the familiar throaty tone of her voice. She had to be Tia's mother.

He met her direct, appraising gaze and saw so much of her daughter in this stately woman that his longing for Tia made it difficult to speak. Her mother had tawny hair coiled in a single upsweep and fine laugh lines around her eyes, but her irises were an exotic violet like those that had looked at him in love. She was taller and more full-bosomed than her daughter, but the same radiant beauty emanated from her.

"I'm Calla, wife of the Grand Elder. Are you the man who kidnapped my daughter?" she asked, leaving no doubt in his mind that she already knew the answer.

"Your daughter came to me of her own free will," he said, genuinely respectful of the woman who had given birth to his precious Tia.

"So you decided to keep her?"

Calla's words came uncomfortably close to the truth, and Dare had difficulty suppressing his true feelings for Tia. This wasn't the time to declare his love for her, and her mother's quiet antagonism didn't invite this confidence.

"I'm here to discuss her fate with the Grand Elder," he said with humility. "I can promise you no harm will come to her."

"My husband has been unavoidably detained. He'll meet with you as soon as possible." She started to walk toward the door, then turned back with anguish in her eyes. "Is she truly well?"

231

Dare felt shamed by her motherly concern, but he forced himself to look directly into her suffering eyes.

"She's fine," he said, wishing he could say what was in his heart: that Tia was a wonderful, passionate, strong, courageous woman, a credit to her mother and the joy of his life.

"We have quarters for you. I'll send a brother to show you to your chamber. You may come and go as you please. The hospitality of the Citadral is yours."

She turned on her heel, the hem of her silky blue robe swishing around her slender ankles. Dare felt bereft when she was gone; being in her presence made him feel closer to Tia.

A day passed, and then another, and Dare felt as restless as a caged beast in a traveling wagon show. He understood how Tia must have felt at Norvik, trying to pass long days with only frustration and loneliness as companions.

He couldn't fault the Zealotes for their hospitality. His chamber was spacious and well appointed with heavy green draperies and fine, hand-carved furnishings. The bed was the softest he'd ever slept upon, but lying in it without Tia in his arms was a torment. They'd never made love on a bed with finely woven sheets—never joined their flesh and spirits on any bed but forest loam. He'd taken his beloved on the hard ground with grass in her hair and the sun on her skin, but he wanted better for her. He wanted luminous silk to rustle against her naked flesh; he wanted her to come to him warm and glowing from a bath in scented water.

The Zealote brothers, some robed and some less traditionally dressed in breeches and tunics, were courteous to him but mostly kept their distance. They didn't prevent the younger ones from clustering around him on the grounds, and he was amused by their eager questions about his army. If the Grand Elder hoped to glean information from these eager little spies, he would be disappointed. But Dare couldn't resist talking and joking with them.

Had he made a terrible mistake in leading the Lost Ones away from the Zealotes? His heart was heavy and his conscience uneasy. He'd made a momentous decision with only ten full-cycles of experience to guide him, yet he still believed the Wanderers had a right to the freedom he'd won for them at the cost of great hardships.

The well-being of the Zealotes made him even more determined to succeed for the sake of the Wanderers, but a third day passed without a summons to see the Grand Elder. His repeated requests were met with polite refusals.

Totts inadvertently told him the reason for the delay: Logan had been away seeking information about his son's covert activities at the mine.

Finally, Dare's summons came early on the fourth day.

He remembered the one time he'd seen Logan, but the image was disturbing. The future Grand Elder had been carried to the death pit by Warmond's renegades, and they had encouraged the boys to beat him with sticks. Dare had stood at the back of the crowd, risking punishment himself rather than hit a bound and helpless man.

He was ushered into the council chamber by Totts, the youth sober and subdued as though he understood the significance of this meeting.

Dare didn't know the proper form for greeting a Grand Elder, but he was determined to confront him as an equal, not bending his knee or inclining his head.

Logan stood beside a gilt chair with ornate carvings, but he wasn't wearing any of the trappings of his office. Instead he was dressed in dark homespun with a black shirt open at his throat, the garb of a man who toiled in the fields or worked with beasts.

"You're Dare Lore?"

"I am." He stood stiff and straight, refusing to be intimidated by Logan's greater height.

This Grand Elder didn't need to surround himself with the external symbols of power. Dare immediately sensed his strength of character and inflexible will. He was a handsome man with shoulder-length sable hair muted with gray, his shoulders broad and powerful and his eyes a piercing blue. Dare knew in his heart that he would have a battle winning Tia away from this man.

"Where is my daughter?"

An odd sensation flickered across Dare's forehead, and he instinctively stiffened, making his mind a blank. Logan was an empath, one of those rare people gifted in reading the emotions of others. Dare steeled himself, determined not to open his mind to intrusion.

"You can trust my answers without using your empathic probe," he said severely.

"I apologize. Who taught you to shield your mind against me?"

"No one. Apparently it's my gift," Dare said, not adding that he'd just that moment discovered an empath could be resisted.

"Then I'll ask you again. Where is my daughter?"

"I swear on my life that I've done everything I can to ensure her safety. She'll never come to any harm through me."

"Your words are reassuring, but I'd like to confirm her well-being for myself."

"She's fine now, but she deeply mourned the loss of her shadow-keeper, Doman, and her equest."

"She was quick to promise you my equests." Logan sounded like an irate parent, making Dare feel more at ease with his air of authority.

"Thank you for the payment. Tia said you sent choice beasts, not ones that would be easier to part with."

"Dare, let's speak plainly."

"As equals." Dare spoke too quickly, then feared the Grand Elder would read weakness or a sense of inferiority in his words.

"Agreed. I know what I want: the return of my daughter and your help in overcoming the government."

"So you can rule Thurlow yourself?"

"No, I don't recognize or seek any office higher than that of Grand Elder of the Zealotes. I have a lifetime commitment to the Order."

"What do you think will happen if the government is overthrown?"

"A brief period of anarchy, then new leadership chosen from among the people. Thurlow can't continue as a mining colony for Earth."

"I agree, but it's not my overriding consideration."

"Then suppose you tell me what you want."

"Three things," Dare said, meeting the level stare of the Grand Elder. "First, the Wanderers have been homeless too long. The Zealotes stole them as babes, robbing them of family, name, and inheritance. I want one hundred thousand hektares of fertile Zealote land to resettle my people."

"That's a staggering request," Logan said, his face inscrutable. "How many men can you muster to merit such a huge payment?"

"I can bring two thousand well-trained, heavily armed men to your gate."

"You have a force that size at Norvik?" The Grand Elder didn't try to conceal his skepticism.

"No, only a small percentage live there to produce the weapons we need."

"I've heard you've been trading in illegal goods."

Dare ignored the disapproval in his voice, knowing that prohibitions against metal weapons were part of the Order's code. "We trade to survive."

"Where is this army? This is the first I've heard of a second base."

"Well hidden. There are places on this planet where men have yet to walk."

"Agreed, but I find it hard to negotiate on the strength of a phantom army."

"It's not just my army that's important. I can raise the support of thousands more. Parents have been sending their sons to me to save them from servitude in the mines. There's hardly a village on the planet—except Ennora, where they bow down to the Zealotes—where I don't have supporters."

"Will you let me test the truth of your statement?"

"I will." Dare let his passion flow through him without attempting to block his mind from Logan's probing.

"I believe you," Logan said, "but one hundred thousand hektares is beyond the means of the Zealotes. I can offer fifty thousand."

"Not acceptable. I might settle for ninety thousand."

"Sixty thousand, but that must include some arid land."

"My people will make the Valley of Sunken Craters bloom if it means having their own homes. They're tired of not belonging to family or land, but eighty thousand barely fulfills our needs."

"What of your own family? Would seventy thousand compensate you for your loss?"

"I would give up my share to see my mother's face, but we cannot help you for less than seventy-five thousand hektares of fertile farm and grazing land."

"Done, subject to the approval of my council. You spoke of three demands."

"Land is worthless unless men are free to work it. Only the Zealotes are exempt from servitude in the mines. I want that protection extended to my men."

"Impossible. It takes a man years to prepare for taking the Zealote oath. I can't pass out Zealote membership like ribbons at a children's tournament."

"We don't want any part of Zealote oaths or rules. You only need to extend your protection to the occupants of the Zealote lands you give us."

"I suppose it could be done, if that was your only claim on the Order." He was frowning, his forehead creased in disapproval, but Dare sensed victory. "All this presupposes that your army can tip the balance. This agreement won't stand up if your army proves to be an undisciplined rabble of no use in overthrowing the government."

"Success is certain."

"You're young, Dare. Nothing in life is certain."

"I'm risking my men's lives, my people's future. Your stake is land, which you have in abundance, and power, which you've used too long for the exclusive benefit of the Zealotes."

Dare saw anger cloud the Grand Elder's eyes, and he remembered that Logan had been the Master of Defense, the strongest and most wily fighter in the Order. Yet, if he were to die in the next instant, Dare wouldn't retract his words.

"If we're to be allies, there's no advantage in probing for each other's weaknesses," Logan said with poorly concealed weariness. "What is your third request?"

"To cement our bargain by closer ties, I ask for your daughter in marriage."

"My daughter isn't a bargaining chip! You've overstepped the bounds of my tolerance, Dare!"

"I'm sorry if I spoke too hastily. I don't want your daughter as a pledge of your word. I have . . ." He groped for words to explain to her angry father. "I have tender feelings for Tia, and I have reason to believe she looks on me with favor."

"Have you talked to her about marriage?"

"No, I thought the honorable way was to speak to you first."

"You're asking the impossible."

"I know I can't care for her as she deserves until the struggle with the government is over, but—"

"No, stop before you say more that you'll regret. My daughter cannot marry you. She's betrothed."

238

"I don't believe it! How could a man allow his betrothed to ride without him on a dangerous quest?"

"I doubt he had any say. Olan is apprenticing to the Zealotes. It's an arduous course of training with no time for attending to a future wife, but the contract has been signed. It's legal and binding. I'm sorry you didn't know."

Dare was numb, desperately wanting to doubt Logan's words. How could Tia lie in his arms and open herself to him without telling him she belonged to another man? The pain was paralyzing, and he hated the look of veiled pity on Logan's face.

He looked around him, seeing the elegance of the walls covered by patterned silk and the thick luxury of the carpet woven in a hundred shades of blue, red, and gold. How could he ever have expected the daughter of the Grand Elder to leave the luxury of the Zealotes to live in a primitive cot built by his own hands? He felt a fool, but no humiliation could sap his spirit the way Tia had by not telling him about her betrothal.

"Shall we talk of strategy now?" Logan asked.

Dare nodded, trying to focus on the vast lands where the Wanderers would at last settle.

"There was a plot to assassinate me in Capitol City," the Grand Elder said. "It failed, but don't underestimate the danger involved here. I know of only one way to stop Earth from arming the government with advanced weapons that we can't possibly resist."

"Destroy their reason for coming."

"I know now why you were able to build a band of scruffy boys into an army," Logan said with surprise. "You agree that the mine has to be destroyed before the next spaceship comes."

"It's the only way. I don't have a firm plan to accomplish it."

"When the time is right, I'll send three ancient miners to you. The youngest has seen nearly a hundred full-cycles, but they're kept alive by one thing: hatred of the mine that warped their lives."

"I don't need men; I need explosives and the knowledge to use them."

"I'll supply what you need, and the three old miners will supply the knowledge."

They sealed their pact with a solemn handshake.

"Can I send some brothers with you to escort my daughter home?" Logan asked.

"Your daughter will be returned when our alliance has proven successful, when every member of the Wanderers is settled on Zealote land under Zealote protection."

"It isn't necessary to keep her captive. You have the sacred oath of the Grand Elder of the Zealotes that your terms will be met."

"I'll forfeit my life if she comes to any harm," Dare said, "but she remains with me."

"As a hostage?" For the first time Logan's voice seemed to falter.

"As your representative," he said woodenly. "I've been vigilant about her well-being, and I'll continue to see that she's treated in a way worthy of the Grand Elder's daughter."

"Very well," Logan said in the voice of a man who'd just swallowed a bone. "Have you prepared a strategy for the deployment of your troops? As I see it, our most urgent concern should be taking the mine."

"Yes, I understand your son has been working undercover in the mine," Dare said, mustering all his strength to talk of military matters while Tia's betrayal ate away at his soul.

Chapter Thirteen

Dare didn't spare himself or the mare as he hurried toward the rendezvous with Raviv. Corella was frisky after a few days of pampering in a Zealote stable, but Dare was determined to master the beast. He remembered every word Tia had ever spoken, so he easily recalled her instructions on how to ride an equest.

At first the man and beast worked at cross-purposes, but Dare put all his energy, strength, and cunning into winning the mare's cooperation.

"Obey me, you shaggy bag of bones, or I'll see you hitched to a plow," he crooned, trying to imitate Tia's soothing tone, although he refused to mutter endearments to a creature that smelled like musty boots.

Apparently the creature cared nothing for the meaning of words but much for the sweet sound of them. Corella began responding well to his lighter touch, and Dare experienced the elation of making his body one with his swift-moving mount.

If only women were this easy to master, he thought glumly, hugging his disappointment against his heart like a mantle of sharp-pointed nails. He'd been intimate with Tia in ways that made his cheeks burn at the recollection, but her mind was a labyrinth of secret passages and hidden niches. How could she open herself to his love, knowing she belonged to another man as surely as if his brand were burned on her backside?

The angrier he became, the more he wanted her. He longed to caress her and feel her gently tremble from his touch. He ached to taste the sweetness of her breasts again and feel her nipples harden under his tongue. The image of her mouth taunted him, and he wanted to punish it with soul-searing kisses. His palms itched to feel the graceful curve of her satiny back and her buttocks.

His erotic fantasy soured when he reminded himself of the awful truth: Tia belonged to another man, some craven creature who was training to take the Zealote oath to ingratiate himself with her father.

Dare thirsted but didn't take time to drink from the bladder of water secured with his pack. He was hungry but had no appetite for the golden brown bread and sweet dried fruits a Zealote brother had pressed on him as he left. All that mattered was reaching Tia, but he couldn't imagine what he would say when they met again.

*   *   *

When Dare left, Tia had been on the verge of weeping, but it was rage that threatened to open her tear ducts in a virtual flood. Didn't he know that leaving her behind was wrong, wrong, wrong? Did he think she'd claim sanctuary in the Citadral after all they'd been to each other? Did he think her love for him would diminish when she saw her father again? Or, even worse, did she mean more to him as a hostage than as a woman?

Now she hated each hour spent without Dare and regretted the distance between them as she and Raviv rode slowly but surely, farther and farther from the Citadral where her father and her lover were together in a confrontation that could decide her future and the fate of the planet. What right did Dare have to send her away from their conference?

On the fourth morning of their journey they passed a small freehold. Raviv went to the clay-block house to ask permission to water the equest, but when they resumed their journey, he was surly, binding and gagging her.

She squirmed and tried to dislodge the rag Raviv had stuffed in her mouth. Her wrists were raw from trying to slip out of the ropes he'd used to tie her hands behind her back, and she felt nauseous from smelling the sour sweat of his body coupled with her fear.

"Stay still, bitch," he warned, riding awkwardly in front of her on the equest's back. "If you try sliding off, you'll be riding on your belly the rest of the way."

She tried to scream, but all she could manage were muffled grunts. Anyway, there were no refugees wandering in this forest to hear her. Even in such troubled times, people knew better than to trespass on Zealote territory.

Her only solace was defiance. She lunged at the cruel Wanderer with her shoulder, almost dislodging him from his seat. A poorer rider than she'd first thought, he couldn't entirely hide his fear of the equest. If she could knock him to the ground, she might be able to escape.

"That does it, you she-devil!" He reined in, punishing the beast's mouth so it snorted and reared. "We'll see if you have any fight left after you trot along behind me for a while."

He dismounted and pulled her to the ground, letting out a length of rope from the coil he carried at his waist. He fumbled with the end, failing to make the knot he wanted on his first three tries. At last he had a noose that satisfied him.

"I want to keep you alive," he said, making the loop of rope large enough to slip around her waist, "or you would have a rope collar."

She caught him off guard for an instant and tried to run toward the woods, but he grabbed her before she left the trail. He knocked her to the ground with an open-handed blow on the side of her face, then viciously kicked at her hip and thigh until he managed to control his rage.

"I'd kill you here," he said in a ragged voice, "but you're not expendable like Knud was. We need you to lure Dare Lore to us."

"You killed Knud! You're a traitor and a murderer!"

"I've followed the noble Dare Lore long enough! What has it gotten me? Land? Wealth? A woman of my own? I'll have a long gray beard before any of his promises are fulfilled. Even Garridan, his master swordsman, has deserted his hopeless cause!"

When Raviv had first bound her, she'd been

anxious, worried that Dare wouldn't be able to catch up with them before their trail became too hard to follow. Now Raviv's words made her fear that Garridan, Dare's close advisor who'd disappeared from Norvik with Angeline, was behind the treachery. If Dare came to rescue her, he'd be walking into a trap.

"I'm tying the other end to my waist," Raviv said, savage anger making his boyish good looks twisted and ugly. "Keep up or I'll drag you."

Tia trembled as she watched him mount, awkwardly throwing his leg over the saddle and coming down with an audible plop. He was wiry and strong, but he treated the equest like an inanimate object, trying to dominate the animal without any concept of what was needed to master it.

She limped, trying to favor the side where Raviv's boot had bruised her, but he had no intention of making the trek easy for her. As soon as he settled into the saddle, she had to scramble for her life, running with an agonizing shamble, knowing that one false step would plunge her to the ground, and she would be dragged over the rough forest terrain.

Her foot caught on a dead branch, and she nearly lost her balance, jerking the rope enough to make Raviv look back at her and laugh.

She hated him, and anger gave her the courage to do what had to be done. Waiting until Raviv was forced to slow down at a sharp bend in the trail, she gauged her chances of surviving and decided a quick death was better than falling into a traitor's vengeful hands. She closed the distance between herself and the equest's massive rump, knowing one kick could end her life. Then she gambled on Raviv's poor riding skills.

She aimed as high as she could, kicking at the sensitive area under the beast's braided tail, putting the full force of her desperation into the attack. If the beast retaliated with its huge rear feet, she was dead.

The equest snorted shrilly and reared, suspended for a moment on powerful hind legs. Then it lunged forward with all the speed it could muster. Raviv was thrown to the ground with a scream dying in his throat.

At first Tia thought he was dead; then he moaned. She tried to slip out of the noose around her waist before he regained consciousness, but Raviv's poor knot-tying worked against her. The more she struggled, trying to slither out of her binding, the more it seemed to tighten around her waist.

Much to her horror, Raviv sat up, clutching his head, with blood running between his fingers.

"Stupid, mangy demon! I'll have that beast's heart for dinner!"

He railed at the equest, and Tia realized he didn't know what had spooked the mare. She edged closer, still attached to him by an unnatural umbilical of rope.

"Oh!" He clutched his leg, screaming when he tried to straighten his ankle. "I broke something," he moaned. "Get over here, woman. Can't you see I need help?"

She approached cautiously, knowing he could still hurt her by yanking on the rope. Her waist had a rope burn from the impact when he fell, and she was almost as helpless as she'd been before the equest ran off. At least he couldn't deliver her to his cohorts if he couldn't walk.

He crawled over to a tree, leaning against the ancient upright trunk. "I'll need it bandaged," he said, gingerly trying to take off his boot. "Here, pull it off!" he ordered harshly, wiping the blood from an abrasion on his forehead with the edge of his tunic.

He didn't deserve her help, but to give it, she had to have her hands free. She made a muffled appeal and turned her back, indicating that she was helpless until he untied her.

"Get over here," he said in a surly voice. "I'll untie you, but make one false move and I'll beat you black and blue." He groped around until he found a shoot as thick as his thumb growing from the trunk. He snapped it off, stripping away the leaves to make a whip.

She got down on her knees close enough for him to untie her hands, then quickly stood up, ripping the gag from her mouth and throwing it as far as she could.

"Pull off the boot, but be careful about it," he rasped, waving his improvised whip so the tip bit into the side of her knee.

"A man who needs help should learn to say please," she said, clenching her fists to keep from rubbing the stinging welt.

He looked as if he'd like to beat her until his arm gave out, but he dropped the branch a few inches from his hand.

His bravado gone, he screamed when she yanked on his boot. It didn't budge. She tried again, but this time he begged her to stop.

"I can't stand it," he whimpered.

"Your ankle is too swollen. The boot will have to be cut off."

"What do you know about injuries?" he asked,

looking up at her with his eyes bulging in panic.

"I know how to treat an equest for whatever ails it. I haven't had much practice on humans, but I'm not sure you qualify as one."

"You bitch!" He grabbed the flexible branch and swung at her again, this time only cracking it against her boot but still causing her to shrink back from the blow.

She watched while he took a small dirk from the boot on his uninjured foot.

"You'll never catch the equest, you know."

"We're close enough to where my friends are waiting for us that it doesn't matter. I loathe that foul beast anyway."

She was as far from him as possible, putting a distance of four times her height between them, going as far as the rope allowed. She tried squirming free, but whenever he noticed her working at the rope, he yanked it savagely, more than once plunging her facedown into the dead leaves and debris on the forest floor.

He was sawing at the leather of his boot, gasping in pain, his lank brown hair sticking to his skull from the exertion.

Once she thought he'd fainted, but when she ventured closer, he threatened her with the dirk, making her back off.

"Aiiiieee," he shrieked, dropping the dirk and clutching his leg as though he could wring the pain out of his ankle.

"You'll faint if you try to do the rest yourself," she said, sitting on the ground and watching him, formulating a plan of her own.

"I won't faint because you're going to do the rest," he said. "Find a few stout sticks to hold the bones in place."

"I can't do much searching tethered to you."

"I'm not such a fool that I'll let you wander around. Now get over here."

She crawled the length of the rope and gingerly peeled back the remnants of his boot to get a better look at his ankle. As she'd suspected, it was swollen to double its normal size, and getting his boot off was still going to be a nasty job.

"Can you cut another inch?" she asked.

"If I could, I would have!"

"Then brace yourself. Lean back against the tree trunk. It might help if you bite on a piece of wood."

"I'll use a bit of my whip," he said, using the dirk to cut off a thumb's length from the green shoot. "There's plenty left if you try anything funny."

He laid the dirk beside him to fit the wooden bit between his teeth. Tia yanked on the heel of his boot with strength born of desperation, not pulling but twisting, acting so quickly he only had time to howl in agony.

She grabbed the dirk before he could reach out to stop her and crawled as far as the rope allowed, knowing he would follow on his hands and knees as soon as he recovered from the shock of the pain.

Standing, she sawed frantically at the thick rope, the heavy braids of flax giving way strand by strand with agonizing slowness.

"Bloody bitch! You'll wish you were dead!"

He slashed out, the branch cutting through the air with a wicked swoosh and biting into the ground. His fury helped him recover quickly, and he lunged at her again, sliding on his backside and using his good foot to scramble toward her.

Trembling, she kept working at the rope, backing away as he advanced. Her hands were slippery from her effort, and the rope seemed to have a million separate strands.

He threw the branch at her, narrowly missing her head, and she nearly made the mistake of looking down at it. He was scrambling with superhuman strength, and she remembered how the men had made him swim after the barge to punish him for his pranks. He was swimming on land, forcing her backward on treacherous ground, and she nearly toppled over when her foot caught in a creeping vine. If she fell or dropped the dirk, she was doomed.

"I should have taught you who's boss when I had the chance," he said, changing his tactic and tugging on the rope to draw her closer. "I'm supposed to wait my turn with the others, as if the great Dare Lore hadn't already . . ."

When he pulled on the rope, he unintentionally helped her. She slashed through the last taut strands, nearly falling backward. She got her footing just as Raviv made one last desperate lunge, coming so close to her ankle that she had to kick his hand to gain an urgently needed instant.

She ran until her chest ached, then ran some more, following the trail because she was too frantic to get her bearings in the heavy woods on either side. Her mouth was pasty with dryness, the corners of her lips were cracked, but she plunged ahead. Once she thought she heard water, but she was still too frightened to stop.

At last, when she was breathing as hard as a winded equest, she slipped behind a pere tree and listened for sounds of pursuit. She knew Raviv's ankle was shattered; he couldn't pursue her on

251

foot, but she imagined all kinds of horrible things. The equest might come back—although the beast had no reason to: Raviv had ridden with a brutal lack of concern for the red mare's welfare. Most frightening of all, his friends might find him and pursue her.

She ran again, stopping once to drink from a stream near the trail, then continued down the path until the sky was inky black, the glow of Thurlow's three moons masked by low-hanging clouds. At last, when she wasn't capable of taking another step, she sat cross-legged on the cold ground beside the trail, afraid to sleep.

She tried to guess how far she was from the Citadral, but fatigue made her thoughts fuzzy. She longed to cry on her mother's shoulder, to see her reassuring smile. Would she ever see her family again? Would she live to beg her father's forgiveness and ask his help in realizing the only dream that meant anything to her: to be with Dare forever?

The woods seemed alive with the small rustling sounds of night creatures, and Tia realized she was weak from hunger.

"Oh, Dare, where are you?"

She wasn't strong; she wasn't fearless. Being the Grand Elder's daughter had never meant so little. She was tired, timid, and lost. She didn't deserve Dare's love, but oh how desperately she wanted it!

She slept sitting up, her arms wrapped around her legs and her cheek resting on her knees, awaking with a start in the darkness. Had she slept for minutes or hours? She had no sense of how much time had passed, only a gnawing desperation that propelled her forward.

Following the trail because there was no alternative, she wondered if she'd passed the freehold where Raviv had watered the equest. He'd seemed to know it was there. He must have led her away from Zealote territory if he conferred with another traitor there. Even if she could find it, she wouldn't dare stop for help. Her black-and-white world had been turned upside down. If a man like Dare couldn't inspire loyalty in all his followers, how could she possibly distinguish between friend and enemy?

Stopping for the hundredth time to listen for sounds of pursuit, she closed her eyes and saw the golden image of Dare stepping naked from the pond, his hair streaming down his face and his arms outstretched to welcome her. Would she ever again feel his warm lips locked on hers? She was so lonely her heart was shriveling. She wanted to mold her body to his like the tallow from two burning wax sticks flowing together. It would be easier to lie down to die in the dark woods than to face life without Dare.

She kept moving, numb with fatigue and still in shock over Raviv's treachery. Somewhere, somehow, she had to find Dare and warn him against the traitors in his own ranks.

Dare approached the clearing with a heavy heart. Part of him wanted a confrontation with Tia, but another part dreaded the angry words that had to be said. She'd given him a precious gift that wasn't hers to give. Even if she'd acted out of love, she'd dishonored him. He held the vows betrothing man and woman as sacred; as leader of the Wanderers, he'd never allowed a pledge of fidelity to be put aside.

Anxious to reach the rendezvous after the long delay in seeing Logan, he'd ridden all night without sleep. The shimmering mist of dawn made the forest seem an enchanted place, and his heart ached, knowing he'd never again lie naked with Tia in a sheltered glen, never twist strands of her silky hair around his fingers, never feel the warmth of her skin against his.

"Raviv," he softly called, wanting to give warning to his follower. "Raviv, it's Dare. Where are you?"

Puzzled by the silence, he rode into the clearing, wondering why there was no sign of Raviv or Tia.

He dismounted, stiff but too anxious to care, and looked around for some clue to their absence. He knew how to read his surroundings, and there were no indications of trouble: no crushed vegetation to show there'd been a skirmish; no scattered belongings to testify to a hasty departure.

He did see the charred remains of a small fire and crushed grass where two people had bedded down separately.

He led the equest to a nearby stream, his reason for choosing this site for Raviv to wait with Tia. Two pairs of boots had left impressions on the soft ground, one so distinctive he would know it anywhere. Tia had walked here, leaving a rounded heelprint before she knelt down to drink.

He called again, hoping they'd moved to higher, dryer ground to sleep, but the only answer was the sporadic chirping of an unseen avian. They were gone, and a terrible suspicion left him stunned.

Tia had resources; she'd enlisted him as her guide to Norvik on the strength of the riches her father controlled, and she still had an enormous sum of currency. Was Raviv weak enough to be bribed? Had he taken her to the Citadral?

Dare backtracked to the clearing, his whole body tense with a terrible anger at this betrayal. He didn't want to believe that Raviv would desert their cause, but he knew the power Tia had over him. It was easier to face a man armed with a lethal sword than to deny the wishes of the Grand Elder's daughter.

Pressing his palms against his forehead, he tried to get a sense of time and distance. Tia would want to go to the Citadral, but there was only one trail leading directly to the Zealote's stronghold from where he stood. Their paths hadn't crossed. Dare felt sure Logan wouldn't have been so agreeable to his demands if his daughter had been back under his roof.

Calling on all his skills of observation, Dare slowly walked the circumference of the clearing, seeing what he hadn't wanted to notice earlier. The equest had left an unmistakable trail in the opposite direction from the Citadral, away from the path Dare had followed to the rendezvous.

He was already behind schedule. Jonati would be anxious to the point of sending reinforcements to look for him if he lost more time getting to his secret base. But these considerations couldn't stop him from finding Tia, no matter where she was. He set off on the mare again with great misgivings, compelled to find the woman he'd sworn to protect.

The sun was low, and Tia was beginning to hope she was safe from pursuit. She wandered a short way off the rutted trail to forage for food, gratified to find a bush still heavily-laden with ripe berries. She ate some, then picked a handful to eat as she walked, so weary now that putting one foot in front of the other was like lifting leaden weights.

At first she thought the distant rumble was thunder, but soon the ground was vibrating. She ran for cover and tried to conceal herself in a cluster of slender young trees a stone's throw from the path. At least the sound came from the trail ahead of her. It was unlikely that Raviv or his friends had taken a shortcut through the woods to cut her off by doubling back, but her heart hammered in fear as she watched the equest approach.

The rider passed, long golden locks flowing down his straight, proud back, and Tia's eyes misted with relief:

"Dare!" She ran to the trail and called after him, amazed at his deft touch in halting the mare and maneuvering it to return to her.

She reached out to him, desperate for the solace of his arms, but he didn't dismount.

"I was beginning to believe you'd evaded me. Is Raviv nearby?"

"No, I escaped when he broke his ankle." She didn't like speaking to him at such a distance, and the stern expression on his face puzzled her almost as much as it hurt.

"You escaped from Raviv? You didn't bribe him to escape from me?"

"How can you ask that?"

He leaped down and took his time securing the equest to the trunk of a tree.

"I have a lot of questions to ask you."

He walked up to her, his arms stiff at his sides, and a scowl etched his forehead.

"Your man took me prisoner for his own purposes!"

She saw disbelief on his face and wanted to cry in frustration, but more was at stake than her bruised feelings.

"He kidnapped me so you would follow. It was a trap, Dare, and you can believe me or not!"

His face paled, and she felt his anger like the blast from a forge.

"First Garridan's defection and now Raviv! I'd rather be slain by an enemy than wounded by a friend. Who will be next? Does anyone believe in what we began together?"

He walked away and raised his fists to the sky, but in moments he'd regained his self-control, returning to her with his face an unreadable mask.

"Get on the equest." He offered his hand to help her scale the shaggy beast's side, but his touch was impersonal, that of a groom helping a rider mount. She quickly learned that her place was behind him.

"I see you've learned a great deal about equests," she said, unable to hide her amazement at his improved skill.

"Also about females, and I have you to thank for both," he said. "Now tell me what happened."

He was dressed as when she'd seen him in his chamber at Norvik, his torso naked under a leather vest. She wanted to wrap her arms around him and lay her head against his back, but his severe tone and harsh demeanor discouraged her from touching him. She grasped the back edge of his vest to keep her balance and told him of the events since their parting.

"You should have taken me to the Citadral,"

she said, unable to resist reminding him that he'd hurt her by leaving her behind.

"It didn't serve my purpose."

"Talk to me, Dare! You can't be angry at me because Raviv betrayed you."

"Is that what you think? Is your own conscience so clear?"

He'd never spoken to her with such cold anger, and she was afraid to speculate on the reason.

"What happened with my father?"

"We reached an agreement. I've become his ally against the government."

"That's wonderful," she said. "I can't thank you enough."

"Don't thank me at all. I presented three demands to your father. He agreed to two."

"What two?" She liked this conversation less with each passing moment.

"He's giving the Wanderers seventy-five thousand hektares of Zealote land and the Order's protection to guarantee exemption from service in the mines."

"I can't believe it! That's wonderful for you."

"Not for you? Aren't you the one who brought me to your father's cause? Aren't you proud that you've completed your quest? The Zealotes will tell your story for generations to come. You've risen to the ranks of legendary heroines."

"Why are you being so cruel?" Hot tears ran down her cheeks at his sarcastic tone, but she had to hear everything. "And your third demand?"

"It was a request, but the Grand Elder didn't have it in his power to grant it."

"Dare, I didn't know—"

"You didn't know my senses were befuddled by love? You didn't know I was willing to do

258

anything, even bend my knee to a Zealote, to have you as my own?"

"Stop! Look at me! Do you doubt that I love you?" She pulled on his arm, but he shook her off.

"I don't doubt that you wanted to lie with me. I've heard that females are greatly motivated by curiosity, and your betrothed has decided to become a Zealote before he takes up his husbandly duties."

"That's not the way it was!" She threw herself off the equest's back, landing on her hands and knees, the indignity of her fall making her cry.

He reacted instinctively, sure that she'd broken her neck this time. He didn't mean to take her in his arms; it wasn't his plan ever to hold her close again, but part of his resolve died the moment he thought she was hurt.

"You fool!" he said, going down on his knees to cradle her against him. "For all you know of equests, haven't you mastered the correct way to dismount?"

"I deserve your scorn," she said, trying to pull away.

"Scorn! I feel as if my heart has been cut out of my chest. I'm a hollow shell, just going through the motions of living."

"Then you know how I feel! I only agreed to marry Olan to please my father. He longs for grandchildren. He loves Fane, but I'm the only one who can give him a grandson of his own bloodline. You're not the only one who was snatched from his mother's arms as a babe!"

He couldn't listen to another word. Hearing her speak of the betrothal battered his spirit beyond endurance. He had to give up his last hope: that

Logan had been deceiving him in order to keep his daughter from marrying a Wanderer.

"It's true, then. You're betrothed."

"Did you think my father would lie?"

"No, but I was hoping he had." He released her, too drained to stand.

"Forgive me," she said in a weak whisper. "I didn't want to think about the future. I only wanted to be with you."

"You're still a child, Tia," he said, his head bowed in misery. "I should have known love wasn't enough to bridge the differences between us."

She wanted to cry out that it was enough for her, but fragile shreds of pride were all she had to cling to. She couldn't beg him to keep her with him. The price for defying the rules of the Order was so high she couldn't let Dare sacrifice his honor and his people for the sake of their love. What was more, petitioning the Grand Elder to set aside her betrothal wouldn't free her to be with Dare; being released from a betrothal meant accepting a life of seclusion and celibacy.

She wasn't too proud to cling to him, letting her tears dampen his face.

"Tia—"

"Don't say anything."

He held her, muted by the hopelessness of their love, until at last they had to go on.

"Do you really think I'm a child?" She couldn't look at him as he helped her mount.

"No, you're as much a woman as the female who gave you life."

"You met my mother! Is she well? Is she terribly worried about me?"

"She's beautiful, gracious, and strong-willed— like her daughter. She called me a kidnapper."

"I wish that's all you were."

They rode in silence until darkness made the rutted trail dangerous for the equest; then Dare shared foodstuffs from his saddlebag with Tia.

"How far are we from the Citadral?" she asked before bedding down alone near the base of a pere tree.

"I'm not taking you there." He waited for a fiery outburst but heard only a muffled gasp.

"My father didn't make my return one of his demands?"

"He tried to."

"He promised you a kingdom on Zealote land, and you refused to return me to my home? But why? Surely you know he'll carry out the agreement if he swore a sacred oath."

"I don't doubt your father's word."

The darkness hid his face, but she heard the stubborn resolve in his voice.

"Then why—"

"Your presence is a guarantee. . . ."

"I'm still a hostage!"

"I've pledged my life that you'll be safe. I promise you, Tia, I'll return you in time for your mating ceremony."

"And you're an honorable man," she said, the bitterness of her loss overwhelming her.

Chapter Fourteen

The days that followed made their earlier travels seem like pleasure strolls. Often they had to lead the equest through boulder-strewn gullies or along mountain ledges so narrow the mare left tufts of shaggy hair on the jagged rock walls.

Tia endured the hardships of the trek without complaint, but at night when Dare slept apart from her, she thought her heart would break.

Dare chose the more treacherous and difficult route whenever he could, his confidence still shaken by Raviv's betrayal and Garridan's desertion from Norvik. There was hardly a village on the planet where he wasn't owed a debt of friendship, usually from fathers who'd sent their sons to him to save them from the mines. But when his close companions turned away from him, how could he trust Outsiders? So when he had to pass through populated land, he skirted the villages.

Tia offered him her currency to buy food at isolated freeholds, but he refused it, preferring to barter the metal beads he'd brought from Norvik. He didn't come into the alliance with Logan as a pauper, and he wouldn't accept charity from his daughter.

Days passed with a grueling sameness, but when they stopped to rest, Dare couldn't turn off his thoughts. He watched Tia curl up to sleep on the hard ground and longed to cushion her head on his chest. She silently suffered hardships that would make ordinary men whine like babes; her courage made his heart swell with pride until he reminded himself that she was destined to lie with another man, to carry his children, and to comfort a Zealote in his old age.

When the pain was more than he could endure, he paced in a broad circle around her resting spot, hoping she wouldn't wake and see his misery.

She knew when he restlessly prowled the night, and she ached to call him to her side. But Dare's pride didn't give her the opportunity to offer him solace.

"I don't like the feel of this place," he said one morning when they were crossing an open expanse, avoiding spiny bushes and tangles of ground creepers.

Grit blew into their faces on the arid, sun-bleached plain. They had to cover the mare's eyes with strips ripped from Dare's tunic because an equest's eyes were prone to infection if bits of matter worked under the lids. It was easier to lead the blindfolded beast than to coax it to carry them across unseen terrain, but Dare's impatience was growing with each passing day. He chafed at

263

their slow progress and kept a wary eye in every direction.

"How far are we from Leonidas?" she asked.

"Only a few days. There's one more settlement between us and the camp, but it's an unsavory place even in the best of times. It was a mining town before the ore gave out in the government mine."

She instinctively moved closer to him. He took her hand for the first time in many days, using their dangerous position as an excuse to draw closer to her.

"We haven't come this far to fail," he assured her, "but you must promise me one thing: If anything happens to me, you're to save yourself at any cost. I gave your father my sworn oath to protect you with my life."

"Men are always swearing oaths, taking vows, giving promises. I'm tired of the way you men manage things!"

He laughed, and she realized how much she'd missed the sound of his laughter.

"Make light of it if you wish, but the planet would be a better place if people listened to their hearts," she insisted.

"What does your heart instruct you to do, Mistress Tia?" he asked, baiting her because it felt so good to break the long silence between them.

"It tells me not to share my thoughts with a cold, hard man like you."

"If I were a hard man, I would make you my slave instead of pledging my life to keep you safe."

"At least you don't deny you're cold!"

He stopped and tossed the equest's lead around the branch of a spiny bush.

Her face was grimy, and her hair was in wild disarray with red glints from the sun streaking the rich sable hue. Her clothes were little more than rags, her tunic threadbare and poorly concealing the swell of her breasts. Yet she was so beautiful, his throat constricted.

"Think that if you like," he said.

"How could I think otherwise?"

"You could cast about in your memories."

"I do—every waking moment! And at night you haunt my dreams like a craven creature!"

"Craven? No one has ever questioned my courage!"

"Oh, you're brave enough when it comes to fighting fights and winning for the Wanderers, but you don't have the courage to seize what you want for yourself!"

"And you think I still want you?" He clenched his fists, trying to hold back the torrent of words in his heart.

"You've made it plain you don't, so why torment me? Why drag me across the planet in your wake?"

"To ensure your father keeps his word."

"You know he will! A Zealote's oath is sacred."

"What about the daughter of a Zealote? Is her word worth anything at all?"

"When I said I loved you, I meant it!"

"I love honeycakes and dark, full-bodied ale, razor-sharp sword blades and the companionship of my friends. Is this the kind of love you're talking about?"

She dashed away from him, circling round the equest. He started to give chase, but she took him by surprise, mounting on the wrong side, causing the mare to rear, then stomp the ground so hard it quaked.

He had to scamper a safe distance away until she brought the beast under control, and by then it was too late to stop her. She snagged the reins away from the spiny bush and urged the equest into a gallop, leaving Dare behind in a cloud of dust.

He should have been angry, but he couldn't suppress a rueful smile. She'd left him stranded without food or water, but he felt more like hugging her than tanning her backside as she deserved. He could depend on her to do the unexpected, to bring surprise into his life and make him forget his weighty problems.

He started after her, not running but covering the ground with a warrior's stride. He didn't begrudge her this show of spirit, knowing that he could soon send a thousand men to scour the area and find her. Meantime, he followed the equest's tracks, believing in his heart that she would come back for him when she'd satisfied her need to rebel.

Her heart was pounding, and it took every ounce of strength she had to make the blindfolded mare respond to her commands. When she had a chance to look back, Dare was only a small speck. She planned to go back for him in due time; she loved him too much to make him suffer from hunger and thirst. But first she'd give him a chance to repent of his hard-heartedness. Didn't he understand that her betrothal was like a yoke on her shoulders?

The sun was high and hot, and she soon took pity on her beloved, wanting to succor him far more than she wanted to punish him. She slowed the equest near the first place that offered shade: the base of a rock formation that rose up from the dry desert like folded hands. There was a shadowy recess, the opening of a rough-hewn cave that promised a cool resting place. She hobbled the equest and fed it a handful of grain from the saddlebag, then walked toward the cave to wait for Dare to catch up.

By the time he found the equest, he was foot-sore and less inclined to dismiss her wild ride as a prank. He saw the inviting shade and the entrance to a cave, not doubting that he'd find Tia in the cool depths. He felt eyes watching him as he drank from the water bladder; then he walked toward the entrance, a vision of deep violet eyes drawing him forward.

He heard muffled screams, but not even his quick reflexes saved him. He felt a terrible pain in the back of his head, and pinpricks of light exploded behind his lids before everything went black.

"I told ya one like this wouldn't be alone," a gravelly voice said, chortling over Dare's prone figure.

"Drag him out and let's see what we have," his companion said, releasing his hold on Tia's mouth but tightening his grip on her upper arm, bruising the flesh as he forced her back into the sun.

At first she thought they'd killed him. A smear of crimson blood matted the back of his hair, and he lay still as death.

"Turn him over, idiot, and let's have a look at him."

The man restraining Tia was the tallest she'd ever seen, a giant with bulging arms and great, beefy lips that sprayed spittle when he talked.

"He's a strong one, Weg. Maybe we can sell him at the mine," his companion said.

The big man pushed away his cohort, a cadaverous man with the remnants of a filthy green government uniform clinging to his sunken chest.

"We'll sell him, all right. Do you know who this is?"

"He's too well fed to be one of us gentlemen who's left the government's employ. That's the truth, or my name ain't Bitchin' Hitchens."

"Tell us his name, girlie."

He grabbed her backside and pinched so hard she shrieked in pain.

"A name," he insisted, bruising her again.

"I don't know! He's not with me!"

"Just a coincidence, you both happening along? Or did you have a lovers' spat?"

Dare groaned, giving Tia hope that he might live.

"Maybe the gent would like to introduce himself. Persuade him, Hitchens."

"No!" Tia struggled against his hold, only making him laugh at her hopeless efforts.

"She likes the lad. Let's see if he fancies her."

Dare pulled himself to his knees, gradually able to focus on the giant who was shaking Tia as if she were a child's straw doll.

"Stop!" Dare tried to lunge at the giant, but the skinny man knocked him back with the club he carried as a weapon.

"Give us your name," he said, taking another swing and connecting with Dare's shoulder.

"Only if you let her go." His head was swimming, and he couldn't focus enough to detect his assailant's weakness.

"No good hammering at that one. He's as tough as old leather, by the looks of him," Weg said. "Let's see if a little screaming from the bitch will loosen his tongue."

Tia clenched her teeth and braced herself for the worst, but Dare spoke before the giant acted.

"Dare Lore is my name."

"I knew it!" the giant crowed. "He was servin' a gristmill sentence when I was still in the service. He was just a scrawny kid then, but I never forget a face."

"The government's doubled the price on his head. We're rich," Hitchens said.

"Tie him up before you spend it," Weg ordered. "Do it right tight. He's supposed to be a tricky one."

"What about the bitch?"

"We'll think of a way to make use of her," he said, leering in a way that made Tia's skin crawl.

They tried to make Dare walk, but his legs collapsed. She watched in horror as they bound him on the equest's back like a sack of grain, his head dangling over the side with his hands and feet tied by a rope passed under the mare's belly. With her hands bound behind her, she trudged after the equest, prodded on by the blunt end of Hitchens's club.

They entered a village more derelict than any Tia had seen. The crude frame dwellings were small and poorly built, but unlike many recently abandoned settlements, this one had the look of long neglect.

She was terrified for Dare's sake, afraid his long silence meant he'd lost consciousness. The giant untied him and half-carried, half-dragged him to the door of a shed, stopping to unlock the door with a key from a ring at his waist.

Dare feigned greater weakness than he felt, although his head throbbed with shooting pains and his shoulder ached ferociously. He hoped they would underestimate him in his battered condition, but Weg dashed his hopes when he took a heavy wooden yoke from a corner of the shed and separated the two sections of it.

Dare had worn a criminal's yoke before and knew the agony of the weight on his shoulders. The giant roughly jerked his arms into position, then closed the device so Dare's hands and neck were imprisoned. He secured the two halves by slipping a padlock through rings on the ends, laughing as though enjoying a good joke.

Dare felt the same fury he'd felt as a youth, hating his helplessness and demeaned by wearing a contraption inspired by yokes used on unruly beasts. But now the stakes were much higher than a beating or a term of servitude. He had to get Tia away from her captors and reach his army.

"Don't worry about your girlie," the skinny one tormented him. "We'll see she isn't lonely." He cackled with satisfaction and yanked on Tia's hair, making her scream, to torture Dare.

"I'll be all right," she cried out, trying to offer him some comfort even though her flesh crawled at the thought of one of these brutes touching her.

"Let's do her here," Hitchens urged. "Make the mighty Dare Lore watch while we have our fun."

"Maybe later," Weg said. "First we'll squeeze a few coins out of her while she's still all fresh and pretty."

The giant brought the equest into the shed and hobbled it near a bin of grain, taking time to carry water to the beast but not to his prisoner.

"We'll take her to Hermine and see what she'll pay," Weg said as he closed and locked the shed door.

Hard as it was to believe, some of the ramshackle buildings were occupied, but Tia didn't see any women or children, only rough, filthy men in remnants of government uniforms. She didn't need to be told that the village was a hideaway for deserters, the worst, most dangerous refugees on the planet.

The building they entered was a canteen of sorts with a few grease-stained tables and unmatched chairs in front of a high counter that served as a place to dispense sour ale that made the room reek.

"Well, Hermine, you're not doing much business," Hitchens taunted. "Maybe you need to serve up some fresh meat."

"Who's this?" A scrawny woman with dyed orange hair, a thin, sharp nose, and dry, sore-infected lips looked Tia over with no visible sign of compassion.

"A whore I bought from some flesh traders over the mountains. Thought it's time you got a new servicer around here," Weg said.

"I can hardly keep my own girls working," she said indifferently. "I suppose you want a fortune for her."

"No more than you'll make on her in a mooncycle." Weg ripped Tia's tunic down the front. "Look at them tits. Makes a man wish he had two mouths."

Tia forgot to hold back tears of humiliation and fear. Dare was locked away, perhaps severely

271

injured, and she was being sold like livestock.

Weg pinched the fleshy part of her upper arm, leaving a bruise that purpled almost immediately.

"I've kept Hitchens off her, thinking you'd pay a fair price for undamaged goods. If you're not interested . . ."

"Will you take paper money?" the woman asked.

"Half paper, half coins, if me and Hitchens have a free go with her tonight."

"I'll not pay over thirty."

"She's worth seventy."

"Forty—and I'll be lucky to get my money back in two full-cycles, the way things are."

"You've never had more business. Take her for fifty, or we'll be on our way."

"All right, fifty," Hermine grudgingly agreed.

Numb with shock, Tia followed the woman through a doorway and up a flight of bare wooden steps discolored by years of grime. They went into a room crowded with mattresses on a floor that was as filthy as the steps. A few emaciated girls were sleeping, and one listlessly worked at her stringy brown hair with a nearly toothless comb. They seemed ageless in their misery, but Tia was shocked to see a child, still fresh-faced and wholesome-looking, playing with a crude wooden doll on a corner mattress.

"That child can't be one of your servicers," she said, turning on the crone who'd bought her. "No one could be that cruel!"

Hermine gave Tia a strange look, then ordered her to strip off her ragged clothing.

It was a fresh humiliation to stand naked in front of a woman who thought she owned her, but Tia was docile, knowing how much she had to lose by making a rash attempt to escape before the time was right.

"What's her name?" Tia asked, still staring at the child.

"Esma. Her name is Esma."

The woman gruffly ordered her to a water closet off the hall, telling her to wash off the grime. Tia had no desire to protest. Even though the basin was small and the water, released from an overhead tank by pulling a chain, was rusty, she scrubbed with a square of flannel until she felt as clean as possible.

Hermine returned with folded garments: a garish yellow blouse with a low, frilly collar and no sleeves and a short red skirt with a flounce that barely covered her knees. She laced the blouse, trying to pull it high enough to cover her breasts, but there was scarcely enough cloth to conceal her nipples. These and a pair of worn silver sandals were all the clothes allotted her, and she felt more exposed in the tawdry costume than when she was naked.

She went back to the common room, shepherded by Hermine, and nearly bumped into the little girl just inside the doorway.

"For you," the child said shyly, holding out a pair of ear bobs made of multicolored beads.

Tia didn't want to refuse the gift for fear of hurting the child's feelings, so she took them and fastened them to her ears.

"Thank you, Esma. They're very pretty."

The other servicers, four in all, were awake and dressed in ruined finery that mocked their lack of charms, but none of them acknowledged Tia's existence.

A burly woman with the shadow of a mustache on her upper lip came into the room, and Tia could feel the tension increase.

"This is Sadie," Hermine said as though the woman's scowl explained her role. "Take the others downstairs, Sadie. I need to put some fire in this one before we put her on the floor."

Tia watched the others file out, their eyes downcast, trying to distance themselves from their overseer. The little girl stayed behind, watching with dark saucer eyes that made Tia frightened for both their sakes.

"Please don't do this; I'm not a servicer," Tia begged. "The man I came with is Dare Lore. You must have heard how he helps people. He's hurt—maybe dying, locked in a shed by Weg and Hitchens. Please let me go to him before it's too late."

"Dare Lore—the one who takes in children?" Hermine twisted her fingers in her hair and watched Tia with a spark of life in her listless eyes.

"Yes, that's him. He's saved many runaways and fugitives from the mines," Tia said.

Hermine looked at Tia with anguish. "We haven't much time before that pair of louts come looking for you," Hermine said urgently. "Esma is my daughter. Until a few days ago I kept her hidden in the mountains with her gram, but the old woman died. None of the men have seen her yet, but I can't keep her hidden here forever. I want you to take her away. Weg fancies little girls. He would kill me to get at her. Rescuing Dare Lore will be dangerous, and Weg wears the keys at his waist. I have to give Weg and Hitchens their pick of the servicers tonight, and it's Hitchens who has his eye on you. Weg always picks skinny little Wilsa."

"If only you could drug him—knock him out, then I could get the keys."

"I can do that. It wouldn't be the first time I've laced a man's ale to save one of my girls from abuse," Hermine answered, turning to leave the room.

So many things could go wrong that Tia felt sick to her stomach as she sat in the canteen with the servicers, waiting to be chosen and paid for. Esma, dressed in a faded blue dress that strained against her thin, flat chest, clung to Tia's hand, putting so much trust in her new friend that Tia knew she'd be guilt-stricken if the plan failed.

Only a few men were lounging at the tables when Weg and Hitchens entered. Weg acknowledged the men's nervous salutes, but only Tia looked into his cruel yellow eyes, trying not to think of how it would feel to be crushed under his giant bulk. His arms were bare under a filthy hide vest, and the thick black hair on his belly curled like the underside of a bernit.

Hermine intercepted him, handing both men a cloudy mug of ale.

"Who's the little girl?" Weg asked, his voice thick with lust.

"You're not the only one who sells me flesh. I've been keeping her innocent for when I needed her. The truth is, I'm short on the coinage I promised you. If you'll take your due in government paper, I'll let you be the first with her."

"I hear you," he said thickly, his eyes never leaving Esma's trembling form.

"She's frightened silly, but she's taken a liking

to the woman you sold me. I told her the new one would go with her the first time to see she does things right."

"I had my eye on the one we sold you!" Hitchens protested, his Adam's apple bobbing in his scrawny neck.

"Shut up!" Weg ordered. "I like that—two little ladies for one big man. I want them all night if you're sticking me with blasted government paper money."

"Fair enough," Hermine said, handing Weg a second mug of ale.

Tia held her breath while the giant drained the vessel in one gulp and demanded a third. Hermine had given him enough of the drug to down two ordinary men, but the dose was chancy with such a huge brute. Hermine had told Tia that she didn't dare kill him, or the others might use it as an excuse to trash her canteen and carry off her girls.

Weg grabbed Esma and carried her up the stairs under his arm, pulling Tia along by the wrist. He was mouthing an obscene ditty, his singing no more melodic than the roar of an angry yaka, and she was terrified that the doctored ale wouldn't do its job.

He stripped off his vest, and everything from his shaven head to his gigantic boots repelled Tia. She could only guess at how terrified Esma was!

There was no door, only a filthy curtain that sagged across the opening, and a single wax stick sitting on the floor did little to relieve the oppressive gloom in the unpainted room. Except for another filthy mattress on the floor, the room was unfurnished, and the odor of a thousand sweaty couplings made Tia's stomach lurch.

Would the man never pass out?

He ripped off his belt, letting the ring of keys clatter to the floor. She made note of where they fell but didn't dare grope for them until he was unconscious. He staggered, showing signs of unsteadiness, and an awful possibility hit her. If he collapsed on the bare floor, it would sound like the ceiling was about to fall on those below. She couldn't risk having anyone come to investigate!

"Lie down on the mattress, Esma," she urged, "so the nice man can rest beside you."

She prayed the drug would work—and quickly! Esma obediently crawled to the far edge, pushing aside her fear with a trusting smile at Tia.

Weg lumbered over, ignoring Tia in his fascination with the child.

She looked around, frantic for something to bang on his head if the drug didn't work soon, but the room was bare.

A noisy couple shuffled down the hallway to a cubicle beyond theirs, and Weg reached out, patting Esma's head with his huge, clumsy hand.

"Pretty little thing," he murmured, his words slurred.

Tia held her breath as he stretched out and seemed to collapse, then roused himself to mutter something incoherent. She hardly dared hope until he lay slack and motionless, a deep snore confirming that he slept. She waited a few moments, then gingerly removed the coveted ring of keys from his belt, terrified when they made a jingling sound.

Esma edged her way around the mattress to Tia and clung to her, bravely holding back tears.

How long would he sleep? The hardest part of all was waiting for Hermine to come for them.

Not until every man was paired with a servicer or
drugged into unconsciousness could they risk a
run to the shed. Several times Weg stirred, making
Tia's heart stop in panic, but each time he resumed
his snoring, oblivious to the two of them huddled
together near the door.

It seemed like hours before Hermine silently
slid into the room, motioning them to follow her.
Outside the canteen, she hugged her daughter,
whispering a good-bye in her ear. Tia's eyes filled
with tears; she'd seen too much in recent days to
condemn even a slaveholder, especially one who
was taking such a great risk to give her child a better life. But every second of delay was agonizing
as she fingered the ring of keys, hoping she could
find the right one quickly.

Dare lay in a stupor, the last of his strength
drained by his long, futile struggle to free himself
from the yoke. He'd known it probably couldn't
be done, but he'd dug at the rough wood with
his nails until they bled, trying to find a flaw,
and banged the yoke against the walls, trying to
spring the lock. He was maddened by the thought
of Tia in the hands of the giant and the unsavory
Hitchens, but all his efforts did were further drain
his strength and increase his pain.

He heard a metallic sound, the clank of a key
against the lock, but whoever was trying to enter
was having difficulty. He strained to hear drunk-
en curses to explain the problem with the lock,
hoping Weg was returning intoxicated and less
able to defend himself. Dare pulled himself to his
feet with superhuman effort, planning to ram the
giant with the yoke, even if it cost him his life.

Holding his breath, he heard the lock click open

and watched from a dark corner as the door slowly opened, letting the faint illumination of the three moons enter the shed.

"Dare!"

"Tia!" He managed to force her name from his parched throat; then she was frantically trying keys to unlock the yoke.

"Take the equest and go," he begged, imagining the giant hot on her heels. "Save yourself—now!"

"Are you all right? I've been so frightened!" She wanted to hug him against her and make him forget his suffering, but her heart was pounding with urgency.

The yoke separated, and she lifted it off with difficulty, her heart crying for his pain.

Release brought new agony as Dare tried to force feeling back into his numb hands and arms, but he was terrified that Tia would be caught.

She released the hobbled equest and boosted Esma onto its back, then went to Dare so he could lean on her.

"I'll slow you down. Obey me, Tia. Get out of here, and I'll catch up when I can."

"I'll die before I'll leave without you." She tossed a pair of water bladders and a bag of foodstuffs over the saddle, Hermine's last gift to her daughter's rescuer, and pushed Dare toward the beast.

He had to mount or they'd die. Steeling himself not to faint from the pain in his shoulders, he pulled himself up.

"I told you to save yourself," he said, his last words before blacking out in the saddle.

Chapter Fifteen

They traveled north, reaching a rugged mountain range that had shimmered in the distance even before their encounter with Weg and Hitchens. The towering peaks seemed to form an impassable wall, but Dare guided them through a narrow pass invisible to all but one who knew it was there.

"Leonidas," he said, leading the equest with Tia and Esma on its back into a broad, green valley dotted with row after row of low wooden buildings, the dwellings of his secret army.

Reaching his base seemed to restore some of Dare's spirit, and he pointed with pride at the herds that helped support his forces.

"In this season it's a paradise here," he said with pride, "but when the ice clouds move into the valley, it's not a fit home for women and children."

Tia knew he was explaining his urgent need for more hospitable land, but she'd long since forgiven him for everything but his lack of trust in her. How could he treat her as a hostage, when all he needed to do was say the word and she would sacrifice everything to be his forever?

For the child's sake, she held back the bitter words she wanted to say and docilely allowed Dare to parade her through the settlement. His followers ran out to greet him, saluting him with deep respect and open pleasure, but Jonati's face was grim when he hurried out to meet him.

"Terrible news," he said. "Come to my quarters."

He gave Tia a meaningful look but seemed too agitated to greet her cordially.

"You can speak in front of Tia," Dare said, lifting Esma down and handing her to a long-limbed young woman, instructing that the child be fed and cosseted.

"The government raided Norvik. They've taken everyone away to the mine—even the women and children."

"All our people are enslaved?" Dare's face was ashen, and Tia was afraid he'd lose consciousness as he had when they made their escape from Weg.

"We were betrayed," Jonati said, voicing what Dare already knew. "Someone had to tell them the location."

"We have to talk," Dare said. He gestured at a dark-haired woman standing by the path. "Katrine, this is Tia. Please show her the best hospitality we have to offer."

Tia found herself being led away from the men, handed off in the same way Esma had been. But

281

she wasn't a child in urgent need of nourishing food; she wanted to hear Dare's plan.

"Dare!" she called after him.

He turned for a moment and waved her on.

This was what it meant to be a hostage! He dismissed her as easily as he did a child, not giving a thought to how eager she was to know all that concerned him. She tried to respond to Katrine's well-meant kindnesses, but she felt reduced to the status of a prisoner.

"I've never seen garments like yours," her hostess said as she served up a bowl of steaming stew.

"Pray that you never do!" Tia said fervently, briefly explaining how she'd come by them. "What I wouldn't give for my own breeches and tunic!"

"When you've supped, I'll requisition fresh clothing for you. You can use the mineral bath. It's the best part of living here."

It was dark when Katrine led Tia to the entrance of an underground cavern where a natural hot spring provided bathing facilities for the camp.

"You should be alone," she said, handing Tia a robe to cover her nakedness when she emerged from her bath. "The allotted times for both men and women are over."

Torches set in wall brackets helped Tia see her way down the damp steps carved into the rock of the cavern, but ahead the way was misty. Vapors rose from the heated pool, and she moved with caution, looking for the place where a natural ledge under the water served as a seat for bathers who wanted to soak away their weariness.

She did ache! Weary of soul and body, she could hardly wait to sink into the heated mineral water. Stripping off the loathsome clothes

Hermine had given her, she made a bundle of them, vowing to burn them.

Dare sat where the pool was deep so the hot water could lap over his bruised shoulder. He let his body go limp, hoping his troubled spirit would respond to the relaxing waters. His plan hadn't changed; it only became more urgent now that so many of his people were in jeopardy. If the men were forced into the mine, it wouldn't take long for the poisonous fumes to sicken the new workers. Many young men had joined him just to escape the fate of miners—losing the ability to father normal children. Added to all of Dare's other burdens, this new worry was a crushing one.

He tried to review his strategy, knowing this was his last chance to do so in peaceful solitude, but Tia's image came to him with heart-wrenching clarity. She'd saved his life, and if he succeeded in the plan he'd formulated with Logan, the credit would be hers. But it wasn't gratitude he felt. He ached to hold her in his arms; he wanted her with a raw, compelling hunger that made the prospect of victory seem meaningless.

Bubbles popped and reappeared on the steamy surface of the pool, and Dare concentrated on watching them, trying to relax his weary muscles. He heard the soft patter of footsteps on wet rock and froze, hoping the newcomer would enter the shallow area and leave him in peace. He was too exhausted to be fit company for anyone.

Tia bathed at the spout provided, then stepped gingerly into the hot mineral water, letting her feet and legs adjust to the temperature before she tried to immerse her whole body. At first she didn't know if she could stand the heat, but the medicinal flow from the underground spring worked wonders on the tense muscles of her calves, driving out the fatigue of a long, hard ride.

Gingerly she moved toward deeper water, flinching when she immersed herself more fully. She was becoming accustomed to the heat, beginning to understand why Katrine called it the best part of living at Leonidas. She kept walking, wanting to soak her entire body for hours.

Dare didn't see her until she entered the pool, and even then he was afraid the murky torchlight was playing tricks on his eyes. He smiled when she first recoiled from the heat and was hard-pressed not to laugh aloud when she fanned her bottom, bouncing up and down trying to accustom her tender parts to the high temperature of the springwater.

She was game, as always, slowly moving toward the deep end where he was all but invisible in the shadows. Now there was no doubt it was Tia. His body responded to the delightful sight of her full breasts floating on the surface, buoyed by the water as she squirmed to get used to the heat. He imagined the slightly bitter taste of mineral water on her small, hard nipples, and it took every ounce of self-control he possessed to keep from dashing over to her. Yet he knew that this scene was one he would store in his memory and cherish for the rest of his life, long after fate separated them forever. His pleasure at the sight of her was bittersweet, and he despaired of ever knowing personal happiness in his life.

Tia's first glimpse of the man in the shadows made her heart race with fear. Her experience with Weg was too fresh to allow her to trust any stranger, and she covertly searched for the best escape route. Then the mist thinned for a moment, and she recognized the other bather.

She didn't know whether to approach Dare or to retreat. She was angry because he'd excluded her from his counsels. She was the only one who could represent her father's interests, but he was treating her as a hostage. The man who'd brought her to Leonidas was a coldhearted stranger, not the gentle man who'd made love to her beside another, cooler, pool.

He saw her hesitate and knew he'd been discovered. She had every reason to run from him, but suddenly he knew this meeting was meant to be. He couldn't leave on his mission tomorrow without assuring her that his love for her was even stronger, more compelling, than before.

He slipped off the ledge and walked to meet her, the hot bubbles swirling against his throat and chin as he churned up the water.

"Dare."

"I haven't thanked you for saving my life," he said, realizing how badly he wanted to shower her with gratitude. "It was a rash act, releasing me from the yoke, even though I didn't want you to risk your life for any reason. If my plans succeed, the credit is all yours."

"I don't want credit. Do you think, given a choice, I would abandon you?"

"When I think of losing you, the pain is unbearable," he whispered, afraid to touch her, frightened he would lose control and dishonor them both.

"I know what that pain is like," she said, looking into his eyes and wishing she could read his thoughts. "I was sold as a slave, but it was light bondage compared to the hold you have on me."

"The last thing I want is to cause you pain."

"We can escape together—ride to some distant place and live as though we were the only living beings on the planet."

"We could," he said with a sorrow so deep it made her want to weep.

"We won't, though, will we?"

With painful insight, she knew he would die before he would willingly fail his followers.

"Will it always be this way?" she asked, tears filling her eyes.

He understood what she meant. Both of them were enslaved by claims on their loyalty: her love and respect for her father; his vow to see his people settled on land of their own.

"You should leave me now," he said.

"I'm not strong enough." She wiped away her tears with wet fingers.

"You have to be, Tia. I'm not."

"We have a stalemate, then." She smiled in spite of her aching heart. "I'm not easy to reject, am I?"

"There were times on the trail when I wished myself to be a eunuch."

"That would be a drastic way to shun me."

"I only meant to respect your betrothal, not to shun you."

"You're treating me like a Zealote princess. I'd rather be a servicer than be denied the comfort of your arms."

"Don't talk that way!" He took a step closer, standing so near that less than the span of his hand separated them.

"Dare, my heart will always belong to you. It matters little what other parts of me you claim."

"Your reasoning makes me dizzy! You'll have me believing wrong is right and our love is meant to be."

"It is." She reached out and touched his cheek, then laid her fingers over his eyes, closing his lids so he couldn't see the naked longing on her face.

Her hands were warm and wet, and her touch was like the caress of a mystical force. He couldn't stop himself from locking his arms around her.

"Love me," she whispered, her faint cry a plea for mercy.

He lifted her easily and carried her to the shelf at a place where the water wouldn't submerge them, then took her on his lap in water that swirled around his hips. The hot liquid made her body slippery but also gave it buoyancy, and he anchored her to him with his arms, as though the gently flowing current could snatch her away.

She opened her mouth, and he leaned forward to kiss her, urgently trying to brand her with his hard, hot lips. She pressed her mouth against his, frantic to ease the deep, pulsating need he created in her. She was giddy with desire, digging her nails into the warm flesh of his back, willing him to make her totally his.

Tia's skin was hot from the steamy pool, and he caressed her shoulders and back, wondering how much joy his heart could endure without shutting down. She made him crazy with love, and he wanted to know her body more completely than he knew his own. He wanted her to rub against him and make his nerve ends tingle with desire. He felt her teeth nibbling his earlobe and groaned in the madness of his need for her.

She wiggled closer, straddling his hips with her thighs, pleasurably shocked by the rigidity of his member as it pressed against her soft inner thigh. She squeezed against him, moaning softly as she felt herself losing all control.

"Not so soon, my darling," he whispered.

Her neck was velvety soft under his lips, and he rained tiny kisses on the slender column of her throat. He wanted her so badly he thought he'd go insane if he delayed, but he couldn't bear to begin a pleasure that would have to end. His anticipation made him shudder, but he wanted to carry her with him to a mindless ecstasy.

The rock under his buttocks was slippery, but his need to hold and touch all of Tia made him careless. He lost his seating, sliding under the water.

He came up sputtering, coughing from the mineral salts he'd swallowed. Tia patted his back, squeezed water from his streaming hair, and stoked the fire that had made him forget where he was. She kissed him with aching tenderness and offered him her breast when he'd regained his strength, holding it in her hand as he bent to take it in his mouth.

He kissed and suckled her nipples, making her throb with need as though a heated wire carried the sensation to her groin.

"My love," she moaned, weaving her fingers in the wet hairs of his chest.

She bent and kissed the miniature nubs on his chest, tracing the dark circles with her tongue, then laying her head where she could hear the hammering of his heart. He stroked her belly, loving the delicate swell, and ran his hands over her hips, then down the length of her spine, giving her a delicious shock when he slid his fingers between her legs.

He kneaded her buttocks with hard, urgent squeezes even as he bent his head to capture her mouth again, kissing her with ferocious longing.

"I love you," he repeated over and over, his voice firing her arousal as much as his questing hands, making her feel like damp clay to be molded by his will.

She reached down and felt him shudder when her fingers slid back his sheath. Spreading her legs wide, she buried him deep within her.

He leaned back against the side of the pool with water-polished rock supporting his shoulders, and she seemed to float over him, her hair cascading down to his face as she swayed in passion's dance. Her breasts hung over him like delectable ripe fruit, and he had to close his eyes and clear his mind of the vision to hold back the explosion welling within him.

"I want this moment to last forever," she gasped, but even as she spoke he carried her to an unimaginable height, setting in motion tremors that shook her to the very core of her being.

She felt his moment of climax and dug her fingers into his arms, bracing herself as an incredible shudder rocked her.

They clung together, and he marveled at the convulsions rippling through her. He experienced her joy in a way he hadn't known was possible, straining against her with all his remaining strength so he could absorb the waves of passion still rocking her in his arms.

At last they collapsed together, the water lapping at their shoulders, splashing their faces and enveloping them in the haze.

"We'll drown," he murmured, knowing no man could end his life in a state of greater contentment.

She rose above him, standing on the ledge with water streaming from the dark triangle between her legs, and he knelt to pay homage with his lips.

She laughed softly, suddenly shy because she wanted him to love her in every way. She felt wonderfully wanton and willing to give him pleasure again and again and again. This bond between a man and a woman was a mystery, and she wanted all of it revealed. It was a delight, and she never wanted to be completely satiated.

He stood and held her against him, wanting to indelibly impress her form on his: her lush breasts, her sleek midsection, her taut little navel, the swell of her love-mound.

"I know a niche deeper in the cavern," he said, stepping out of the water and offering his hand to her.

He grabbed his robe and hers and led the way beyond the illumination of the torches to a natural cove hollowed out of the mountain. Spreading both robes, he made a bed.

"Lie on your tummy," he murmured.

He kissed the back of her neck, parting her damp hair and letting his tongue savor the slight saltiness of her satiny skin. Her shoulders trembled, but only because her happiness was too deep to contain. Straddling her hips, he slowly kissed and caressed her shoulders, then trailed his lips over her back until she moaned with pleasure.

Although their cubicle was dark, she could see him in her mind's eye, his eyes liquid pools of desire, his firm lips softened and swollen by passion, his strong jaw erotically bristled as he pressed it against her feverish flesh.

He stroked and kissed her until she cried out with need, so wildly aroused she had to force herself to endure more love-play.

He made love to her legs, rubbing them and kissing the backs of her knees until she was writhing for release, even more eager for his lovemaking than she had been in the pool.

When he whispered a command to roll over, she reached for him, but he laid her arms at her sides.

"I've only begun to make love to you," he whispered, proving it as he caressed her brow with his warm lips.

He tested her endurance far beyond her wildest imaginings, nibbling and caressing her face and throat, then claiming her nipples with hard, sensual kisses. He learned that her navel was ticklish, and that she couldn't stop giggling when he sucked her toes. But he didn't touch the hot, pulsating place where she yearned to be stroked.

"Now show me how you love me," he challenged her, lying beside her on his stomach.

She didn't know touching could be so supercharged with pleasure. She loved the firmness and smooth texture of his skin; she adored it when he let little groans of arousal escape from his throat. His shoulders loosened as she kneaded the hard knots, and her fingers danced over his back with little pats that left him moaning for release.

She hesitated at the end of his spine, not knowing what she wanted—what she dared—to do next, but he arched his backside and tightened his steely muscles until she teased him into relaxing.

In the murky darkness, every sense but sight was magnified, and she reveled in his scent, the soft sound of his breathing, the rhythmic beating of his heart. She adored the strength in his body and the powerful muscles that flexed under her slow explorations. And when she discovered his soft spots, she loved them to distraction.

She knew when the time was right. She lay down beside him and opened herself to his unhurried penetration. She was tender to the point of soreness, but she was so wet their joining was as effortless as it was exciting.

She trembled at the wonder of this man's love and died a little death when he slowly brought her to new heights. His love reduced her to a quivering mass of sensation, even as it gave her existence new meaning.

"Can't you see I belong with you?" she asked before losing her last small hold on consciousness.

Hours later Tia awoke with sunlight filtering through the greased paper that covered the one small window in the sleeping chamber. Her body immediately reminded her of the great burst of passion she'd shared with Dare, but he'd left her to sleep alone yet another night.

She found the clothes Katrine had secured for her: panties and vest to serve as undergarments, thick stockings and calf-high boots that were large but wearable, brown breeches woven of woolie fleece, and a flaxen-white shirt that laced to her throat and covered her arms to her wrists. It was traveling garb, and she dressed quickly, hearing a commotion outside her room.

When she left her chamber, she saw that the whole camp was in motion, every man and woman moving with purposeful industry. Katrine ran up to her, handing her a pack with straps to secure it on her back and a heel of bread with a mug of milk to break her fast.

"I was on the verge of calling you. We're moving out today. I'm so excited! I can hardly believe the time has come at last!"

"Where's Dare?" Tia couldn't think of anything but seeing him.

"He's everywhere. He doesn't miss a single detail once he's given an order."

"I have to find him."

"Try Jonati's quarters. The fourth building down that path. Be sure you eat, though. I don't know when you'll get another chance."

Tia went back into her room and left her pack and makeshift meal there, then raced down the dirt path to one of the nondescript board structures. The door was open, and she went in, breathless from running and eager to see Dare again.

He was alone, standing over a basin and pouring a cup of brown liquid over his head.

"What are you doing?"

"Darkening my hair, I hope." He didn't stop to look up. "Does it look brown to you?"

"You're ruining your yellow hair!"

"That's the idea," he said dryly. "If the dye doesn't take, I might as well tattoo my name across my forehead."

He sloshed another cup of the peculiar-smelling solution over his head, protecting his eyes with a scrap of flannel.

"I'll help you," she offered, standing behind him and wrapping her arms around his naked chest.

"Please don't, Tia," he said.

She couldn't have felt more rejected if he'd slapped her face.

"Perhaps I dreamed last night," she said, unable to conceal her hurt.

"Last night was last night." He stood upright and toweled his darkened mane. "We're moving out, Tia. There's no more time for personal concerns."

"What was last night? Your recreation period?" She didn't know whether to strangle him or beg him to hold her.

"Braid my hair," he said, picking up a wooden comb and trying to force it through his tangled locks.

"Is that an order, Dare?"

"If I make it one, will you obey?"

"Do I have a choice?"

"No choice at all—my darling." He bent and covered her mouth with his, knowing it was a terrible show of weakness on his part but needing to touch her more than he needed food or drink. His torso felt branded where she'd hugged him, and what he'd said had nothing to do with what he was feeling.

"I'll do whatever you ask," she said, trying to hold back tears of relief, "but nothing that you order me to do!"

"I can command thousands, but I have to beg for your compliance?"

She was a saucy she-devil, a fit mate for a man who had the heart of a lepine and the strength of an equest. She should belong to him. Bitterness welled in his throat like sour bile, and he had to avert his head, denying himself even the sight of her. He sat on a low stool, repeating his order in a leaden voice.

"Make it secure so it won't come loose in battle."

Her blood went cold because she was so frightened for his sake. The whole camp was in an uproar. It could only mean that Dare's army would finally be tested on the battlefield. She shivered in spite of the warmth of the room and tried to think of a way to stay by his side no matter what happened.

She combed his hair with trembling hands, wondering how long it would be—if ever—before they would share such intimacy again. She tried to be gentle with the snarls, separating the tangled strands without causing him discomfort.

"I'm not a child. Yank the comb through and be done with it."

She didn't want to hurry with this task, but Dare's impatience forced her to work faster. She divided the damp brown mane into three thick hanks and plaited them into a single braid that fell down his back.

"Thank you," he said, standing when she was done and reaching for a shirt that was a mate to hers—and to all the others the men outside were wearing.

"I've never seen an army clothed in white shirts."

"I want our presence to be visible. If we can intimidate, we won't have to kill. Imagine looking at a field that extends to the horizon and seeing rows of men, their white shirts reflecting the sun and their swords gleaming like mirrors. My army will fill that field, and the one beyond it, standing straight and tall like ripe grain. The best part of having great power is not having to use it destructively."

Tistur appeared at the door. Although it was early in the day, the equest handler's dark face was already gleaming with the sheen of exertion, and he spoke rapidly.

"I've found the lad you need, Dare," he said, noticing Tia and nodding at her with reserve. "His name is Danik, and he came to us from Luxley."

"Send him in."

Tia stared at the young man who came through the doorway and saluted Dare, interested that he came from Luxley, the home of her mother's people.

He was still in his teens, tall and gangly with a shock of unruly auburn hair and an eruption of adolescent pimples on his face.

"Danik." Dare nodded, looking over the youth with shrewd, searching eyes. "Tistur says you're brave, loyal, and absolutely trustworthy."

The lad's face flushed, but Dare took it as a good sign. He didn't want a boy who was too cocksure and full of himself.

"You're being assigned the most important task of all. I've sworn an oath to preserve the life and ensure the welfare of this woman. Do you know who she is?"

"People have been saying she's the Grand Elder's daughter, sir."

His awestruck expression was flattering, but Tia was too puzzled to react to it.

"Yes, she is. You may call her Tia, since she'll be your constant companion, your total responsibility."

Tia opened her mouth to protest, but Dare silenced her with the sternest look she'd ever seen.

"From now until I release you from this duty, your only reason for living is to keep Tia safe. She'll try to slip away—she has a bag of tricks that would confound a wizard—but under no circumstances are you to let down your guard. I'm promoting you to my personal lieutenant, and you can commandeer whatever help you need, whenever you need it."

"But why me?" The boy looked totally overwhelmed.

"Because if you fail, your punishment will be so severe, you'll wish for death. Tia has a kind heart in spite of her rash behavior, and I don't think she'll let you suffer because of her."

"You're terrible!" she cried.

"I've tried binding you with ropes and words, but you still manage to do just as you see fit. Now this young man's well-being depends on your obedience and, Tia, I'm not bluffing. I have to go where you can't follow. I can only carry out my mission if I know you're safe."

"I understand, sir," Danik said, standing taller and looking more mature under the weight of his responsibility.

"Wait outside. Tia will join you in a minute."

"This is the worst thing you've ever done!" she said when her shadow-keeper was out of hearing. "You can't make that boy responsible for what I do!"

"I'm making you responsible for what happens to a youth from your mother's village. He could even be some kin of yours. Will you let him suffer pain and disgrace just to have your own way?"

"What would you do to him? I know you're never cruel or abusive! You are bluffing!"

"No, Tia." He held her shoulders in hard hands, looking into her face with steely detachment. "I mean what I say, and Danik knows it. For both your sakes, I hope you believe me."

The horrible thing was, she did believe him, and she realized he wasn't going to relent on this awful arrangement, no matter what she said.

"I'll never forgive you," she said.

"Leave me now."

The leader of the Wanderers gave her an order, and she obeyed it with a desolate heart.

Chapter Sixteen

The time for words was past. Dare clasped Jonati in his arms, then watched as he rode off with Tistur and four men who'd proven their proficiency with equests. He prayed there was no traitor in their midst. The success of the plan depended on these men.

The moment for which his army had trained was at hand. The seeming chaos in the camp was an illusion; in a few short hours, the whole population was ready to move. This time no one would be left behind to be captured by enemies.

Mounted with Cyrus, the geographer, by his side, Dare watched his people depart in their assigned units. They marched four deep and four across in a square formation, each man heavily armed and wearing a backpack and a thick leather breastplate with Dare's symbol, a tree with deep roots, burned onto it.

The few women and children and the young men who had come to Dare to avoid servitude in the mines followed the main body of warriors in the same formation. Those who were defenseless walked inside the squares of armed men; the children too small to walk were carried in slings suspended from their mothers' shoulders.

Dare knew where Tia was: in the midst of a formation with Danik by her side, prepared to die defending her if necessary. Dare trembled with longing, and only his love for his people kept him from abducting her from the shadow-keeper and riding off with her. He vividly remembered how it felt to hold her slender form against him on the back of an equest, and he fought against a wave of black depression that threatened to engulf him.

The baggage carts followed the units guarding the women and children, and Dare was justly proud of the small, mobile conveyances he himself had designed. They moved on two large wheels reinforced with strips of metal to make them sturdy, but not too heavy to be pulled by the placid bovines in the Wanderers' herds. His best fighters brought up the rear, two units specially trained to be aware of pursuit and ward it off.

Scouts were already moving ahead and on each side of the army, but Dare didn't expect to see any of these stealthy loners. They were mountain men who'd lived in the wild and could follow a man almost indefinitely without being detected.

This was Dare's secret army, and pride in their fitness helped dispel some of his brooding gloom. The plan had been set in motion. He prayed the Great Power would grant him success.

* * *

Dare stayed with his army during the long, tedious march toward the mine, taking care to avoid Tia. Thankfully, she made it easy for him, never venturing far from the small knot of women who were her companions when they made camp at night.

Only Cyrus knew all the details of the plan, and the two men spent the long hours trying to find flaws and anticipate unexpected obstacles.

Finally the day came when Dare had to go on alone. This was the riskiest part of the plan, and if he failed, his army might pay a high price.

"Good fortune go with you," Cyrus said, embracing Dare in his arms as the two men parted under the cover of darkness.

Dare handed over the reins of the equest, the same mare who had carried Tia into Leonidas, and gave his battle gear and pack to Cyrus. Dressed all in brown with shabby leather breeches and a worn tunic, he was satisfied that his disguise was as complete as he could make it.

He hadn't said good-bye to Tia, but he was taking her with him in his heart.

The area around the last and greatest of the hyronium mines was denuded of all foliage, a man-made desert more desolate than any designed by nature. Dare knew his motives would be suspect if he openly approached the forbidding compound, so he had to make certain he was captured in the woods, where any sensible traveler would stay concealed.

He climbed a tall tree to spy out the mine and soon learned the routine of the government men who guarded it. Two guards were constantly riding the perimeter on shaggy, sluggish equests, keeping an eye on the woods where Dare was hidden. They made short forays into the timbered area, perhaps thinking they could catch an intruder unawares. In fact, their pattern was so unvarying that Dare could choose a campsite where they were sure to find him.

As he'd planned, they stumbled over him at dawn the next morning while he feigned sleep under a low-hanging branch.

"Look what we've got here," one of the guards yelled, his voice booming through the woods as he roughly kicked Dare's backside with the toe of his boot.

Dare pretended to awaken, rubbing his bruised rear and groggily protesting the attack.

"Shut your mouth, if you know what's good for you," the other guard said, hauling Dare to his feet and forcing his arms behind him.

Dare allowed them to bind him, although their carelessness made them more vulnerable than he was.

"The director won't mind adding this one to the crew," the first guard said.

They led Dare toward the mining compound, making sport of him for their own amusement by forcing him to run behind the equests. Dare tolerated their crude abuse, knowing the distance was short and the stakes were high.

"Are you addle-brained?" the director asked, confronting Dare in a small, sparsely furnished office that was part of the government section of the compound.

He was an officious little man, restlessly pacing behind an oversize desk covered with neat piles of documents, but Dare didn't underestimate the cold, cunning cruelty he read in the man's eyes.

"I am not," Dare answered, trying to decide whether this tyrant would respond better to brashness or a more humble attitude.

"Then what the devil were you doing so close to the mine?"

"Looking for my brother," Dare stubbornly insisted, deciding to use this half-truth as his excuse. He did think of Gregor as a brother, and he fervently hoped to find his council member safe inside the compound with the rest of the Wanderers kidnapped from Norvik.

"Where are you from?" the director demanded to know.

"Luxley."

Cyrus had suggested this small village as part of his cover story because it was remote from the mine.

"What's your brother's name?"

"Lang." Dare kept his eyes downcast, afraid the keen-eyed director would see some sign of the defiance he felt.

"And yours?"

"Danik." On impulse he gave the name of Tia's shadow-keeper.

"Take him to Compound One. We'll see if his back is any stronger than his brain. No man with any sense would try to find a mine worker."

Dare had seen many deserted mines, but none had prepared him for this vast facility. Across from the director's office, there were two huge enclosures with walkways running along the top of high wooden fences. He saw a guard with a heavy whip and a long club patrolling on one. He desperately needed to be among his own people, but the two stockades weren't connected in any visible way. He could only hope the Wanderers were confined in Compound One, his destination.

His guards opened a small locked door and freed his hands, then pushed him through the opening and slammed it shut behind him. A line of filthy, gaunt men were shuffling past a huge kettle, holding out small glazed clay bowls for a scoop of thick, gray gruel. Dare had broken his fast before his capture and had no stomach for the miners' rations, but a pale, bald man with squinty eyes thrust a dish into his hands and ordered him to get in line.

"Move along if you want time to eat your ration of mush," he said. "Our shift will be starting any time now."

Dare stepped into the slow-moving line and studied each weary, unshaven face he could see. Not one was familiar. He looked around, hating to think of how difficult his task would be if none of his people were in this compound.

He stood alone, making a show of hunger as he scooped the cold gruel into his mouth with two fingers as the others were doing. The unkempt men around him had the outward look of slaves, stoop-shouldered and filthy, dressed in ragged remnants of clothing, but something in their faces—the light of defiance in their eyes—made him think the spark of hope was alive.

When the wide gate opened and a unit of mounted, heavily armed guards gave orders for the men to assemble, Dare saw that the prisoners had a leader.

The man was taller than Dare by half a head, slender but well formed, with broad shoulders unstooped by heavy labor. He was as filthy as any of them, his face and arms embedded with mine dust, but he looked at Dare with achingly familiar eyes. His irises were an arresting shade of violet; he had Tia's eyes. Dare was certain this man was her kin, that he was Fane.

The leader urged the men through the gate, and Dare knew he was imposing order to protect them from the ready whips of the overseers, trying not to give the guards an excuse to abuse the men.

Falling in at the end of the line, Dare managed to stand beside the leader.

"I'll speak to you later," the man said, leaving no doubt about his role among the enslaved miners.

Their task was simple but backbreaking. The huge mountain cavity served as the entrance to the mine and was totally blocked by debris, some boulders heavier than the weight of hundreds of men and others mere pebbles that could be scooped out by hand.

The leader drew Dare aside on the pretext of giving him a heavy mallet to break apart a piece of rock too heavy to move.

"I'm Ian, leader of the miners."

"I know you're Fane, Logan's son," Dare said.

The man looked surprised but recovered quickly. "Don't use my real name, call me Ian. Just listen carefully, and we'll speak more later. This is part of the slowdown the miners began when they tried to escape. They planted charges in the entrance tunnels. Even though many of the men were recaptured, the mine is inoperable until all this rubble is cleared. I don't want that to happen any time soon. Do as little as possible without earning yourself a beating, and when the guards aren't near you, try to add to the debris. Watch the others to see how it's done, but don't take chances. Time is on our side."

Time wasn't on their side, but Dare didn't have an opportunity to speak further with Fane until the weary crew was herded back to the compound many hours later. He had confirmed one thing: none of these men were Wanderers. The people captured at Norvik had to be in Compound Two if they were still at the mine.

"I watched you—you did well," Fane said, carrying his chunk of bread and cup of watery soup to eat the skimpy meal beside Dare.

"I have a lot to tell you," Dare said, "but first you need to know I'm Dare Lore."

The taller man whistled through his teeth. "Your people are in Compound Two. I'd heard you escaped capture. They're an unruly lot, slow to follow a well-conceived plan."

"Your plan, you mean. It remains to be seen if it's well conceived, Fane."

Dare saw a spark of anger in Fane's eyes and was so strongly reminded of Tia that his throat ached. He had to remind himself that Tia was full of tricks, and Fane was far less trustworthy since he had no reason to trust Dare.

"Don't call me that. Government informers could be listening. I suppose it won't hurt to tell you what's going on," he added reluctantly. "When we sealed the mine, we cut off access to huge reserves of hyronium ore stored in one of the caverns. When the Earthers come, they'll bring equipment to refine it on the site and reduce the bulk for shipment back to their planet. Their ship is due any time now."

"Thurlow was better off before they had the technology to come so often."

"Thurlow is a colony and always has been. What we need is to topple the government that kowtows to their demands. If the ore is inaccessible, the Earthers will withdraw their support from the politicians who exploit us and deal with someone who can deliver in the future."

"You're only assuming that. Maybe the Earth ship carries equipment that can move a mountain of rubble."

"I doubt it. They expect to find the ore ready for them as it always has been."

"Your plan is fine as far as it goes, but I've made a pact with your adoptive father. . . ."

"With Logan?"

"Why sound surprised?"

"I'm only surprised my father chose you as his messenger."

"That's not what I am. We have an alliance against the government, but I need to be with my people," Dare said, wanting to hurry explanations because he felt time slipping through his hands. "How can I get to the other compound?"

Fane frowned as though considering the best way to help him.

"There is a way, but it could backfire. If I help you, will you urge your men to participate in the slowdown?"

"The slowdown bought time, but your father has agreed to another plan. We're going to blow up the mine."

"I don't think destroying the mine is the best way. Do you have any idea how difficult that will be? The mine is inside a mountain. There's a labyrinth of tunnels, so many that no one man has seen them all."

"Just tell me the best way to get to the other compound," Dare urged impatiently.

"If you cause trouble here, I may be able to persuade the guards to put you in the other compound." Fane lowered his voice, checking to be sure the guards on the platform above them were out of hearing. "You'll have to risk your hide twice: once when I best you in a fight, and again when the guards mete out your punishment."

"How do you know I won't be the victor, and you won't be the one punished?"

"I trust myself on the first count, and the guards need my cooperation to keep the men from rebelling again."

"So you're their pawn." Dare clenched his fists, welcoming the chance to teach Tia's skeptical brother a much-needed lesson.

"I'm trying to keep the miners alive! What chance do these men have against the armed police who patrol the mine?"

"Maybe it's time for new leadership," Dare challenged in a loud voice. He watched the taller man strip off his ragged shirt, and he wasn't at all reluctant to bare his own body to the waist and trade blows with Fane if it would get him transferred to his own people.

The miners had gradually backed away from the pair, sensing hostility between them and seemingly eager for a fight that would distract them from their dreary routine. Dare eyed them warily.

"You have many friends here, and I have none," he said.

"No one is to interfere," Fane called out to the

others. "Some pleasures a man has to reserve for himself."

The two men circled each other in the broad space cleared by the spectators, and Dare knew this fight was more than a ploy to have him transferred to the other compound, however urgent that was to his plan. He felt confident he could best Fane in any fair fight, but he was too experienced not to size up his opponent before making any telling move. Fane was taller with a longer reach, but he didn't seem as fast as Dare.

"You're foolish to challenge my authority," Fane shouted loudly to attract the attention of the guards.

The pair on the walkway moved around to stand directly over the men, apparently not loath to enjoy the contest for a while before they intervened.

"You're a sniveling coward, bending your knee to anyone who cracks a whip!" Dare taunted, wanting Fane to strike first.

He reeled backward when Fane's blow landed squarely on his midsection, but he'd been prepared and quickly regained his breath. He countered with a hard punch to his opponent's chin, feeling his own knuckles split but quickly pressing his advantage, raining body blows on Fane's chest.

Fane countered with a glancing blow to his head, and Dare knew the fight would end in a stalemate unless he could offset his opponent's height advantage. He lunged and knocked Fane on his back, pinning him to the ground. The taller man struggled to twist away, but Dare had never been defeated in a scuffle that allowed him to use his whole body as a weapon. It wasn't his intention to grievously injure Tia's brother, but he grasped Fane's neck as though to throttle him, hoping the guards would come between them if they thought he was close to victory.

He'd expected a beating after the fight, but a whip lashed across his back without warning, the searing agony so intense he screamed. On his knees, straddling his opponent, he couldn't move quickly enough to avoid the next blow or the next, each one a fiery torment, crackling against his tortured flesh.

"That's enough," Fane shouted as the whip came down another time, crisscrossing the bloody welts on Dare's shoulders.

"The director will have our heads if we disable a fresh, strong worker before all the rubble is cleared away," one of the guards said, putting his hand on the other's arm to stop the beating. "There's other ways to take care of a trouble-maker. Give us something to look forward to."

Fane pulled himself to his feet, blood trickling from a cut on his lip. He put his foot on the seat of Dare's breeches and pushed him forward, knocking his face into the loose grit on the ground inside the stockade, but also putting himself between Dare's back and the whip.

"Get him out of this compound before all hell breaks loose," he warned the guards. "I've got enough to do keeping my men in line without giving them a taste for blood." He spit on the ground, wiping his injured mouth with the back of his hand.

One guard wiped blood from the whip onto his own breeches while the other yanked on Dare's braid to pull him to his feet.

His one involuntary scream had unmanned him

enough; he clenched his jaw, willing himself to stand straight in front of his tormentors and keep silent.

They marched him to the other compound, prodding the small of his back with their clubs and laughing when he stumbled. He tasted his own salty blood as he bit his lip to contain his fury, knowing he was more than a match for the pair. But he had to submit to their cruelty until his plan was set in motion.

Compound Two seemed deserted, but not because it was the time for the men housed there to sleep. Dare staggered into the stockade, reeling with pain, and realized his men were working their shift at the mine.

This compound had the same foul smell of unwashed bodies and poor sanitation as the other did, but a sense of order prevailed that was absent in the miners' stockade. He recognized it as the instinct women have to make a home wherever they are. Makeshift tents had been constructed against the far wall, and the ground underfoot was free of debris. Two females moved toward him, alert for trouble.

"By all that's holy! It's Dare!"

He recognized a familiar voice and collapsed to his knees, in too much pain to let pride stand in the way of getting help.

Mother Macy tended his back in a way that told him she'd grown accustomed to treating the cruel lacerations left by a whip. Her ointment had a narcotic effect, and he slept in one of the makeshift shelters until the men came back at dawn, weary from a long shift clearing rubble and hauling it away.

"What took you so long?"

Dare looked into the shiny olive face of the man who chided him, then embraced the giant Gregor as a brother.

"There's no time to tell you everything," Dare said, quickly explaining the gist of his agreement with Logan. "Here's what has to be done by nightfall."

When all his followers had been told of the plan, a brisk wind was blowing across the compound, away from the entry way. Although he was stiff with pain, Dare felt a stirring of elation at the favorable conditions. Not one of his people had voiced objections to the diversion he wanted to create, and he felt as though he'd come home.

The sun was low when the weary workers were herded back to the mine, Dare among those who were forced to go. But he had every confidence that the women would do exactly as he'd instructed them. Under cover of darkness they were to lay every flammable substance in the compound against the wall concealed by tents, then, one by one, gather the children and creep stealthily toward the gate, staying under the walkway where the guards couldn't see them.

On the way to the mine, Dare stumbled and fell face forward to the ground, feigning unconsciousness even when a disgruntled guard dismounted and started kicking him.

"You won't get any work out of him tonight," an older guard with more authority said, peering down at his prone form. "Looks like he's had a run-in with a whip already. Drag him back to the compound. Give him a day to recover, and if he tries to miss his shift again, whip him again for malingering."

When the gate closed behind him, Dare made sure every soul was accounted for, then lit the fire.

With the guards distracted by the fire, Dare scaled the stockade wall and lifted off the heavy bar that secured the door. Women herded the children away from the burning compound, shuffling away in the military squares they'd practiced so many times, heading toward the relative safety of the deserted government headquarters.

By dawn Dare's forces were in charge of the mine, and all the government men were captives. The leader of the Wanderers was deprived of only one small triumph: Fane had freed the miners from their compound before Dare had had a chance to open the gate and invite them to leave it.

Tia raged at Danik and freed herself from his makeshift halter, but he wouldn't let her leave the security of the woods. A rider approached, and from her place of concealment Tia could see that it was Gregor. She dashed forward, anxious to hear of the Wanderers' success.

"Dare says it's safe for you to come to the mine," Gregor said.

She could see his dark eyes brimming with excitement, and for the first time his face wasn't an impassive mask.

"You and Danik can go there now," Gregor said, then rode away.

Tia walked ahead of Danik on the short trip, trying to pretend he didn't have her on an invisible leash. Of all the things Dare had done, giving her an unshakable shadow-keeper was the most infuriating. She burned for revenge, imagining how satisfying it would be to put a rope around

Dare's neck and lead him back to the Citadral as her prisoner.

When they arrived, Danik took her to a white-washed room in the government quarters and, miracle of miracles, left her there with only a mild suggestion that she stay inside until things were more settled.

She hesitated, wondering if Danik had given her a taste of freedom only to see what she would do with it. The nondescript little room had a cot and a storage trunk, but nothing of interest, not even a window that allowed her to see the sky. She crept out into the corridor and easily found the exit, stepping out in the midst of an orderly bustle.

Men in government green were huddled together, linked by ropes binding their hands behind them. Dare's men were quietly jubilant as befitted young warriors who'd been tested for the first time and gained a relatively easy victory. She quickly learned that a few had suffered wounds, but none had died in battle, thanks to Dare's clever ploy for surprising the guards.

No one paid any attention to Tia, so she hurried through the open area in front of the mine, wrinkling her nose at the acrid smell still coming from the burnt wall. She was so hungry for the sight of Dare that she became frantic when she couldn't find him. Yet she didn't want to ask his whereabouts; she still had some pride, however battered it was.

Two men were standing beside a broad entrance carved into the side of the mountain: one naked to the waist with his hair pulled away from his face; the other taller and more slender with cropped brown hair and clothes so filthy their original color was lost.

"Fane!" Tears of relief welled up in her eyes as she ran toward her brother and threw herself in his arms, heedless of his foul garments. "I was afraid you were dead!"

He lifted her off her feet and hugged her against him, laughing with pleasure.

"What trouble have you landed in now, little sister?"

"I'm being crushed by a man who smells like rotten game!" she said, backing away in mock horror. "Oh, I was so afraid for you!" She hugged him again, her eyes glistening with relief.

Dare knew the jealousy he felt was irrational. She was greeting her brother as any loving sister would after a long separation, but seeing her in another man's arms reminded him of the reality of her betrothal. He hoped never to see the man who would take Tia away from him. He didn't know if he could control the urge to murder him!

She looked at Dare, oddly shy in her brother's presence. Would Fane berate her for not honoring her betrothal in her heart? She didn't want to put it to the test so soon after their reunion.

"It seems I have both of the Grand Elder's children in my custody," Dare said, suddenly wishing he'd been allowed to pummel Fane as he deserved. Even though his ragtag group of miners was scattering as soon as they were fed, Fane still had all the arrogance of a Zealote. Being a leader without followers was doing nothing to make him more humble.

"If you don't object, Master Dare Lore," he said, using Dare's name with poorly concealed irony,

"I'm going to find a place where I can bathe, so my sister won't cover her nose while she tells me of all the things that have happened to her. Everything," he added with a stern look at her.

Tia never thought she'd see the day when she was glad to get rid of her brother. Relief at his safety warred with her need to feel Dare's arms around her, but he turned and walked away.

She gasped when she saw his back, understanding why he'd chosen to leave his torso bare. Horrible red slashes marked his golden skin, and she felt dizzy just imagining how he must have been beaten.

"My darling . . ." she said, too shocked to follow him.

He meant to avoid her, but he heard the pain in her voice, and it was worse than scraping open his wounds.

"Don't cry for me," he said, walking back to her, taking her in his arms and pressing his lips against her brow.

"You're hurt."

"All I can feel is your sweet body against mine."

"Sir, about my responsibility . . ." Danik said, rushing up and stopping in embarrassment when he realized what he'd interrupted.

"You've done a commendable job, Lieutenant Danik," Dare said. "Consider your assignment at an end."

Chapter Seventeen

Dare took her hand in his, his hard fingers caressing her delicate wrist, making her dizzy with love.

"Let me stay beside you," she begged, not knowing how she could endure another separation.

"It's not to be," he said with such deep grief that she would have done anything to ease his misery.

"My father is a forgiving man."

"He might forgive you for dishonoring your betrothal, but not me. He could use it as an excuse to back out of our agreement. The Wanderers wouldn't be allowed to live on the land he promised them."

"He wouldn't do that!" she said, but it was a weak protest, no more than wishful thinking. Olan was undertaking the long, grueling Zealote apprenticeship so he could marry her. The Grand

Elder would uphold the betrothal as a sacred vow of the Order. If Dare defied it, he would become an enemy of the Zealotes. She knew her father well enough to know he was uncompromising on matters concerning the Order's honor.

"Help me be strong," Dare said, pleading for her understanding.

"You're right." Her eyes filled with tears. "The price of our love could be too high."

He wanted to take her in his arms and smother her with love and gratitude, but all around them his people were doing their utmost to lay the groundwork for the culmination of his plan. He didn't deserve to be their leader if he shirked his own responsibilities.

"Don't approach me anymore," he said, forcing himself to say the cruel words.

"Then bind me with ropes and assign a dozen shadow-keepers to restrain me. I'm not strong enough to stay away from you."

"Hear me out, my darling. I'm weaker than you when it comes to denying our love. When I can, I'll come to you in secret."

"There are so many people here. Someone is sure to notice."

"No doubt my people already know that you're more to me than a hostage. It's your brother I'm worried about."

"Fane won't carry tales to our father!"

"He might—if he thought he was protecting his sister from a Wanderer."

"I'll beg him not to! He'll understand."

"No! Promise me you won't mention my name in his presence. He helped me once, and my back is still on fire because of it."

"Fane had you whipped?"

He quietly explained, knowing that each minute he spent with Tia would make their inevitable separation more difficult. Yet time with her was so precious that he valued an hour of her companionship more than his life.

Her face turned stark white when he told her about his beating, making him afraid she might faint.

"I didn't mean to upset you!" He led her inside the quarters where the government's mining officials had lived.

"I just can't stand knowing how you suffered."

"That kind of pain goes away," he said, gratified by the depth of her concern even though he hated seeing her distress. "Losing you is going to hurt a thousand times more."

He left her at the door of the room assigned to her, longing to reassure her again and again but knowing how high the risk was. He never forgot that Garridan and Raviv had betrayed him, and he was too close to success to take chances—especially with the Grand Elder's son already opposed to his strategy.

Tia slept because it was the only way to blot out her misery for a few hours. When she awoke, it was dusk, and her old friend Petsy, the kitchen boy, was at her door. He'd been dispatched to find her and take her to sup, and she welcomed his lighthearted chatter.

"Dare Lore himself sent me to get you," he said, leading the way to an improvised serving table out in the open where Mother Macy was presiding over a huge pot of hot stew served with dry flat bread. "I'm not a kitchen drudge anymore."

"Good for you," she said absentmindedly, hoping to see Dare.

"He's inside the entrance, urging the men to work faster," Petsy said, reminding Tia of his hero-worship of Dare. "He even has the government men slaving with a will. Wouldn't be surprised if some of them join up with us. Not hard to figure out that the Wanderers are a force to be reckoned with now."

She looked for Fane, also without success, and ate her meal with haste so she could explore the mine site.

After she hastily finished eating, she walked through the compound. Dare's genius for organizing was evident everywhere. The people captured at Norvik had bathed and changed into clean garb, only their gaunt faces distinguishing them from the other Wanderers. The guards' quarters had been converted into a home for children and nursing mothers, and the rest of the women had spread their bedrolls in the building where Tia was staying or on the ground a short distance from the men's. The army slept outside as they had on the march, and the rest of the compound served as a prison for the government men who'd been captured. She understood that many of Fane's miners had fled, no doubt eager to let their families know they were alive.

She wasn't allowed to approach the great gap in the side of the mountain where men were laboring to clear the entrance to the mine. Dare had told her that the explosive charges had to be set inside the mine to ensure the collapse of the tunnels. She had to return to her room without a glimpse of Dare.

He said he'd come, but Tia began to think she'd die of old age first. The building had become so quiet she could hear her own measured breathing. She willed him to appear, calling out to him in her head in case there was any truth in one mind communicating with another. Didn't he know she was dying of loneliness because he wasn't with her?

She combed her hair until the ends crackled and refused to stay put, then splashed cold water on her cheeks from a glazed clay basin in the corner, hoping to put some color in her cheeks. There was little she could do to make herself desirable, but she tied the ends of her shirt under her breasts so her silky, slender midriff was exposed.

"Oh, Dare, don't you know how much I need you!" she whispered aloud, burying her face in her arms as she lay on the bed.

"I do, because it echoes my own need," he said, startling her because he'd entered like a shadow, not even making a sound when he opened and closed the door.

She rushed to him and remembered to lock her arms around his hips so she wouldn't touch the welts on his back.

He'd bathed, his hair hanging damply over his shoulders, and in the pale moonlight coming through the window, she could see a hint of the original gold. She pressed her face against his chest, then realized he'd shed his breeches as silently as he'd entered the room.

Their kisses had an urgency that couldn't be denied. They were frantic for the taste of love, for the delight of flesh against flesh, for the fulfillment they could only find together.

He undid the laces at her waist and knelt to slide her breeches and undergarment to the floor, caressing her legs and hips and inhaling her musky scent. He rose slowly, nibbling and licking until he reached her breasts, made so tender by longing that she could hardly bear his touch.

"Now," she pleaded, stopped from backing toward the cot as he lifted her against him and impaled her. She wrapped her legs around his hips, feeling as weightless as a moonbeam in his grasp. She could feel his buttocks flex with every thrust, and she was incredibly excited, biting her lips to keep from crying out.

He thrust harder, penetrating her deeply. Her ears were ringing, and she had to gasp for breath. She lost her handhold on his slippery hips, but he didn't let her fall.

Their lovemaking was like nothing that they had shared before, and she knew she'd never be able to call this night to mind without the heat of passion stealing over her.

He moaned, exploding inside her with a shudder that her body answered. Waves of rushing heat swept through her, pulsating again and again as he held her against him.

When at last he let her slide away, he cradled her in his arms, consoling them both because the separation of their bodies symbolized their inevitable parting.

"I didn't know it was possible to make love standing up," she murmured, letting her fingers wander playfully between his legs, needing to hear his soft, indulgent laugh so she could believe this wasn't a farewell.

"I love you so much, I only need to touch you to feel fulfilled," he whispered, kissing her forehead and eyelids, trailing his lips over her face until he took possession of her mouth with so much tenderness her eyes watered.

"Come sleep with me awhile," she begged.

"I can't, Tia."

"I won't sleep. I'll watch over you and call you before there's a hint of dawn in the sky."

"My place is outside with my men—where your brother can see me."

"You're making him out to be an enemy, but Fane would never do anything to hurt me. Just lie beside me for a few minutes."

"Tia, your brother has told me he doesn't agree with the plan I formulated with your father. We're going to destroy the mine so there's nothing here for the Earth ship."

"Doesn't Fane want that?" She felt a flicker of doubt but didn't want to believe her adopted brother would oppose both her father and her lover.

"He wants to negotiate with the Earthers: strike a more advantageous deal for Thurlow and tap into their technology to make the mines safe for the workers. He's ambitious, Tia. He wants to topple the old government and replace it with his own—propped up by Earth, just as Thurlow's politicians always have been."

She didn't know how to react to what he said. She'd longed to be taken into his confidence, but she wasn't emotionally prepared to take sides against her brother.

"There must be some compromise. . . ."

"None that won't leave Thurlow weak and dependent. This planet is an Earth colony. Until that changes, we're all slaves."

"Fane doesn't believe in slavery."

"I don't know what he believes," Dare said wearily, burying his face in her hair. "I only know what it's like to be homeless, restless, and powerless. It's time for the people of Thurlow to choose their own leader and build a world independent of Earth."

"When you say it, it sounds so right," she admitted.

"I went to your father for only one reason: to get land for my people. But I've come to believe that joining his resistance to the government is right. My people can't be happy on their land while the rest of the planet is under Earth's heel. I can't bend my knee to them, Tia."

"You don't seem inclined to bend your knee to anyone," she said with a smile.

"Only to you." He sank to his knees and wrapped his arms around her legs.

"Dare, stand up," she said, not knowing whether to laugh or cry.

She felt as she had the first time her father placed her on the back of an equest: in awe of so much power and unsure of what to do with it.

"Dare, I love you," she cried out, letting her heart speak for her as he rose and led her to the bed.

They lay in each other's arms, then made love again, slowly, gently, stretching it out until Tia saw an alarming streak of pale light framed by the small window above her head.

"You have to go," she said, hating the words she used to warn him.

"Even if I can't come to you again, never forget how much I love you."

He slipped away quickly, leaving her bereaved.

*   *   *

Dare slept in brief snatches the next few nights, wishing the image of Tia didn't fill his every waking moment. He looked for her wherever the women congregated together but was relieved when she remained out of sight. He knew that she'd volunteered to help Mother Macy and the army cooks with the arduous job of keeping everyone fed, a task that was daunting even with the huge reserves of food at the mine.

He worked the government men as hard as they had worked their captives, but without the cruelty of beatings and scanty rations. Already a number of them had begged to be allowed to join the Wanderers, but Dare refused until each applicant proved himself. He accepted betrayal as a fact of life now, but he wasn't going to make it easy for turncoats to sabotage the Wanderers. It bothered him that no news of Raviv or Garridan had come to him through his network of scouts, but it also made him more wary.

The entrance tunnel was being cleared fast now that Fane's slow-down tactics had been scuttled. In fact, Dare's own men accomplished miracles, eager to do all they could to hasten the day when they claimed their own land.

Dare had one overriding worry: Jonati should have arrived at the mine by now. He was bringing explosives and experts who would set the charges to destroy the mine. This was Logan's greatest contribution to the plan. Without his promised aid, Dare could damage the mine and block the passages using the few crude explosives stored on the site, but nothing there was powerful enough to do more than nuisance damage of the kind the miners had done.

Dare could almost feel the shadow of the Earth ship hovering over the mine. When it arrived, government reinforcements would flock to the site, and he'd have another battle on his hands—one he might not be able to win against a spaceship's superior weapons.

His scouts brought news of a convoy approaching on the evening of the sixth day, and Dare sent four units of his best men out to meet it, passing a restless night himself as he anticipated the arrival.

He longed to go to Tia, knowing he could find sleep in her arms, but her brother was quietly critical of his leadership, still not convinced his father was playing a role in the plan. Dare refused to give him cause to denounce him to the Grand Elder.

The early sunrise the next day promised scorching heat, but Dare put on his shirt for the first time since his beating, finding that it chafed but caused no real pain. If the new arrivals weren't Jonati and his band, Dare wanted his army to look like a disciplined force, not a band of half-naked vagabonds. Except for those clearing rubble outside the mine, every man was dressed in uniform with his breastplate and sword.

Every eye in camp was riveted on the mounted visitors as they slowly crossed the cleared wasteland between the forest and the mine. Keen-eyed, Dare realized as soon as they were visible that something was drastically wrong. Between the white shirts of his marching units, he could clearly see the dark green worn by government forces.

As they moved closer, it was clear there weren't enough men to be a military threat, but they

326

were escorting some prominent people, two darkly garbed figures and one dressed in a dazzling red robe and hood.

He watched dumbfounded as the mysterious figures galloped ahead of the others, reining up in front of him.

"Garridan. Raviv. And Angeline." He spoke their names slowly.

"Greetings from the government of Thurlow, Dare Lore. You have a larger force than I expected," Garridan said, his scar gleaming whitely.

"Since when do you speak for the government?" Dare said, offering Angeline his hand, helping her dismount only because he disliked looking up into her subtly painted face. His attention was still focused on the visage of the man who had once been like a brother to him.

"Since First Citizen Regis offered me land and riches if I deliver your army. You never suspected me of plotting against you at all. I quietly encouraged the vocal Becket and his unhappy friends; all they truly cared about was the gruel in their bowls. I always had bigger plans."

"And you, Raviv—you were one of our most promising new leaders," Dare said, turning to the other man and gazing at him with unconcealed enmity, remembering his treatment of Tia.

"I prefer to follow a winner," the younger traitor said.

"How did you know I was here?"

"There's not much you do that I don't know about, but this time, logic served better than my spies. Your people were taken here from Norvik. You wouldn't be Dare Lore if you didn't rush to their rescue," Garridan said.

Their escort caught up, and they weren't the usual ragtag bunch wearing government green to avoid mine servitude. Each of the ten was tall and brawny with a young, brutal face. They were a handpicked unit, and Dare felt certain someone in authority had assigned them to be the trio's shadow-keepers.

Tia edged close to her brother in the crowd and felt safer by his side. Angeline's shimmering robe and elaborately upswept hair made her seem even more dangerous than when she'd worn a scullery jumper. Her false smile was as dazzling as the crystal bobs hanging from her ears and much more beguiling. Why had she come to the mine with the two traitors?

Fane put his hand on Tia's shoulder and whispered in her ear. "Do you know her? What's her business with Dare?"

Tia told him who she was in as few words as possible, omitting her own run-in with Angeline in the scullery.

"It's not good that she's here," Tia insisted when Fane spoke in admiration of her brittle beauty.

"I'm authorized to speak for the First Citizen," Garridan said, angering Dare when he refused to speak until they were alone.

"I'll go along with your charade for the moment, but you'd better speak quickly. I don't have time to waste on your games."

He led the way to what had been the director's office, where he'd been studying the master plan of the mine. He quickly rolled it up before Garridan could satisfy his curiosity.

"Now tell me why you're here," Dare ordered.

"I will—since even as we speak, my men are spreading word of the government's offer. If you and your army abandon the mine and swear allegiance to the government, this will be yours."

Garridan pulled out a folded square of paper from an inner pocket of his black tunic and handed it to Dare.

"More land than your Lost Ones ever dreamed of possessing."

"The land bordered by the Loggio Mountains to the north and the River Spinx to the south," he read. "As far east as Luxley and west to the Great Sea." Dare looked at him. "A clever forgery."

"No forgery at all. Every member of the Senate signed it. All it needs to be legal and binding for all time is my signature—a precaution First Citizen Regis inserted for my protection."

"Much of that land is occupied already."

"Some has been abandoned. The government will confiscate the rest. It's up to you whether you allow any of the previous settlers to stay in your territory. You can do as you like—even call yourself king. All the government requires is an alliance. The terms are spelled out in the deed."

"I still think it's a trick."

"Your people don't. Listen—I can hear their excitement. My men must be more convincing than I am."

Dare ran outside to his people, who now looked more like a mob than an army as they milled about, arguing and debating the government's offer.

"Listen to me!" he shouted. "Nothing has been decided."

"Have you ever thought the Earth ship might burn us all to cinders if we destroy the mine?"

329

an angry dissident yelled. "I say take the government land and be done with hauling rocks in this hellhole."

Some voiced support, but most people seemed more confused than convinced.

"We can't take the word of these traitors!" a female voice called out. "They don't know the meaning of truth."

Dare raised his arms for silence, and those who were accustomed to his leadership helped quiet the others.

"This decision is the most important we've ever faced. Every one of us must consider the consequences."

"Are you dodging the issue, Dare?" one of his men challenged.

"My Council will consider the government's offer and share their advice with me," he said.

"I came for an answer from you, Dare," Garridan said, speaking loudly for the benefit of the crowd. "I won't linger here in this hellhole while you mull and ponder and weigh consequences like an old woman choosing a bolt of fabric. This offer is only good until the sun is at its zenith tomorrow."

"It won't take Dare that long to break his word to the Grand Elder!" Every eye followed Fane as he walked up to Dare. "If there ever was a pact. I haven't seen any proof of it. Where are the explosives? Does anyone here understand what's involved in destroying a mountain of ore?"

"Jonati will bring everything we need, unless your own father has delayed him with treachery."

"The word of a Zealote is a sacred bond. But we only have your word that Logan ever gave it."

Fane stood with his legs apart in the stance of a challenger.

"My word is as good as any Zealote's."

"Then make your decision now. Are you going to sell out to the government and condemn this planet to another thousand years under the thumbs of unscrupulous politicians?"

"I'll make my decision after the Council members voice their opinions. That's the way of the Wanderers."

"You're trying to throw out a smoke screen."

"Are you challenging my leadership?" Dare's voice was steely.

Tia had known there was tension between Dare and her brother, but she couldn't believe their hostility. She knew Fane wanted to negotiate with Earth on behalf of a new government, and Dare thought their hold on Thurlow had to be broken. But why did they seem so antagonistic? Surely there was ground for compromise!

"Fane, please don't do this," she pleaded, rushing to his side.

He shrugged her off, so intent on Dare he didn't seem to hear her.

"I think you'll throw your lot in with the corrupt government," he said. "You'll destroy all hope for progress on Thurlow. You'll sell out for a plot of dirt! Do you dare defend your treachery by going against me, one on one?"

Dare didn't want to accept Fane's challenge— how could he harm someone Tia loved? But he had to defend his honor in front of his followers.

"To death?" Dare asked.

"To death!"

Someone handed Dare a sword, but he waved it away. "I don't need the advantage of a weapon no Zealote has ever mastered."

"I'm not bound by the Order's rules against metal weapons, and I have mastered this one!"

Dare saw the glint of metal in Fane's hand, the point of the dirk catching the glare of the sun. He only had to reach out, and someone would lay a weapon like it in his hand.

"Fane, no!" Tia tugged on his arm, unable to believe the tableau in front of her: her brother and the man she loved coldly deciding on the means they would use to try to kill each other.

"Tia," Fane said without taking his eyes off Dare, "his plan to consult with his advisors is only a ruse. He'll accept the government offer and make a mockery of the miners' sacrifices. I've dedicated my life to overturning the corrupt officials bleeding the planet. I'm not going to let an upstart Wanderer tip the balance of power in their favor again."

"You don't know Dare! Please, don't fight!"

"If the Wanderers side against the Zealotes," Fane went on, speaking softly for her ears only, "the Order will fall—everything Father holds sacred will be ground into dust. Your own betrothed will become a refugee. Is that how you want to live your life—sheltering in caves and digging roots to survive like our ancestors did before the Zealotes brought order to the planet?"

"You don't know that will happen!"

"I know men. Dare will sacrifice anything, if he thinks it's for the good of his people."

He stepped away from her and called out loudly, "I'm ready, Dare, unless you're afraid!"

Tia shuddered as an audible hiss reverberated through the crowd, every eye staring uneasily at

the two men. Fane's words had cast doubt on
Dare's courage. It was a grievous insult, and she
despaired of preventing a fight.

"You should be the one who's trembling," Dare
said, reaching out for the dirk one of his followers held ready.

"Then you accept my challenge—to the death—
for the leadership of all the men assembled here?"

"If you think you can win men's hearts through
murder, you're a fool," Dare said so softly only
those nearby could hear him. "But I accept your
challenge." He felt Tia's eyes pleading with him,
but he couldn't let her brother destroy all that
he'd worked for.

The two men circled each other warily. Dare
knew he'd bested Fane in their last fight, but
they'd been unarmed and not committed to spilling blood. Fane's longer reach could be a telling
advantage, but Dare had fought real battles while
Fane was cosseted by the Zealotes as a youth.

"Gregor, stop them, please!" Tia begged the
giant trainer of men as Dare slashed at Fane's
arm and connected, causing a bright red streak
to soak his sleeve.

Dare was sickened by Tia's cries of horror as
her brother's blood flowed freely, but the choice
to fight had been forced on him. He couldn't
refuse the challenge and remain the Wanderers'
leader.

Tia watched in horror as her brother retaliated,
arcing his weapon, slicing at Dare's face and only
narrowly missing it.

"Stop," she cried, but her voice was drowned
out by the sounds of the crowd as they jostled
each other, jockeying for a better view of the
fight.

"Gregor! Take Tia away!" Dare commanded, dodging his opponent's dirk.

He swiftly backed away from the slashing blade, but he was off balance when he stepped onto a patch of loose rocks. His feet lost purchase, and he fell to the ground, his dirk flying from his hand.

Eluding Gregor's grasp, Tia rushed to Dare as Fane stood poised to plunge his weapon into his disarmed opponent.

"You'll have to kill me first!" She threw herself on top of Dare and hung on so desperately that he couldn't loosen her grasp without doing her great harm.

Time stood still as Tia clung to Dare's neck, her body stretched on top of his.

"Move, Tia. I'll let him stand and return his dirk," Fane breathlessly argued.

"No! If Dare dies by your hand, you'll have to bury me beside him!"

Dare saw his opponent back off, his arms slack at his sides, as Gregor lifted Tia away. Dare felt for and found his weapon, and all he had to do was make one oft-practiced lunge to plunge the blade deep into Fane's vital organs.

His rage urged him to make a final end to the challenge, but he heard Tia's heartbroken cries over the roar of blood in his head. He dropped his arm by his side, letting the dirk fall to the ground.

"I could have killed you," he said to Fane.

"And I can kill you now."

Dare turned his back and walked away. The knife thrust he expected never came, and his people scattered to the duties that had been interrupted by the arrival of Garridan and his entourage.

"What will you decide about the land?" Tia asked, running after him. She didn't know whether Dare would hate her or thank her for interfering.

"I'll take the issue to my Council, just as I said," he answered woodenly, walking away from her with his shoulders slumped in despondency. Tia had saved his life, but she'd also given Fane a weapon to use against the Wanderers.

Chapter Eighteen

A feast was prepared: baked meat pies, dried fruit stewed in a sweet sauce and topped with beaten cream, and freshly baked flat bread. After weeks of eating trail fare herself, Tia knew how welcome the fine dishes would be to the Wanderers. She threw herself into helping with the preparations, but she was troubled by the reason for the extra effort, which, according to Mother Macy, had been ordered by Dare.

Was it a celebration honoring the acceptance of the government's offer of land? All around her people spoke of nothing but Dare's fight with Fane and what it meant to the future of the Wanderers. Everyone seemed to agree that Dare had acquitted himself with honor, but Fane had succeeded in planting seeds of doubt. A few were calling for a show of hands, but most seemed too perplexed to know which course was best.

They looked to Dare to make the right decision, and Tia ached for him, knowing how heavy his burden of leadership was. Yet she would gladly share his distress, if only her betrothal didn't stand between them.

She heard rumors that the blood flow from Fane's arm wouldn't stop, and another that his wound had to be cauterized. She didn't wish suffering on her brother, but she blamed him for forcing Dare to fight. When a young lad came to the kitchen to say her brother wanted a word with her, she declined to go, then felt guilty for refusing. He'd done as his conscience dictated, and so had Dare. That was what made their fight so terrible.

She served the food until she was ready to drop under the hot rays of the early evening sun, but Dare didn't come to eat. She went back to her quarters with a faint hope that he might come to her, but the man stretched out on her bed wasn't Dare.

Fane was pale, but he sat up when she entered. His arm was heavily bandaged and supported in a sling, but before she could inquire about his wound, he asked his question.

"Did Dare bring you here against your will?"

"I don't have to answer you."

"No, but I'll draw my own conclusion if you don't. Either he abducted you, or you wanted to come with him."

"Both." His tone angered her, and she met his gaze with stubborn defiance.

"Then he is holding you as a hostage so Father will keep his word?"

"Yes."

337

"But you want to be with him, in spite of your betrothal?"

"I agreed to marry Olan to make Father happy, but I dread the day of our marriage. I don't love him and never will."

"Does Father know?"

"No! What good would it do? Even if I could persuade him to buy off my obligation, betrothals are sacred to the Zealotes. He'd never break his pledge to Olan."

"I'm sorry for you, Tia." He sounded more like the brother she loved. "But I hope you don't have any ideas about becoming Dare's woman. There could be terrible consequences."

"You're the one who did a terrible thing when you challenged him!"

"Do you think I wanted to? Brawling has never been my way, but if he accepts the government's offer, it's the end of the world as we know it. The government is sure to abolish the Zealotes, and conditions in the mine will get worse, not better."

"I don't know what will happen, but I trust Dare to make the right decision."

"I see there's no reasoning with you." He stalked out, giving her a stern look of reproach before he disappeared.

Dare called his Council into the office he'd appropriated, waiting until all but the shift of night workers were asleep.

"You know the choice we have to make," he said wearily, speaking to the four faithful men and wishing Jonati were there to have his say. "Let me hear what you think."

"We can't trust a government that would send

a traitor on a mission like this. I say we honor our deal with Logan," Gregor said decisively.

"You don't know how much territory is at stake," Cyrus, the geographer, said. "The government is offering us a fourth of the land surface on the planet, a virtual kingdom compared to the Grand Elder's grant. I don't have it in me to refuse, even though it came from Garridan."

Dare listened in silence, keeping his troubled thoughts to himself.

"I agree," Henus said. The shortsighted book-keeper didn't meet Dare's eyes, but his voice was resolute.

"And you, Theobar?" Dare asked the fiery-haired weapon maker.

"I have no love for the Zealotes, but the Grand Elder is sure to honor his oath if we blow up the mine and return his daughter to him. I say refuse the government offer."

"Two for and two against. I think you mirror the sentiments of our people. From all I've heard, the Wanderers are equally divided."

"It's your choice, Dare." Gregor's voice was gentle and sympathetic.

"When the sun is at its zenith tomorrow, I'll announce my decision."

After his men filed out, Dare felt more deserted than he ever had in his life. He knew the antidote for his gnawing loneliness, but he couldn't go to Tia, not tonight and maybe never. Fane was no fool. He knew there was love between them, and he had his father's ear. Would the Grand Elder keep his word about the land if he thought Dare had dishonored Tia during her captivity?

There was an alternative—accept the govern-ment offer—but he couldn't make such a momentous decision based on his need to keep Tia with him. He went outside and paced the grounds, torn between honor and expediency, weighing the importance of his word and the urgency of his love for Tia.

The next day Dare ordered that all the prisoners be confined to the stockade before the sun reached its zenith. For the first time since the Wanderers took over the mine, no one was digging in the rubble. Dare had followed a different course in clearing the entryway, not trying to open the whole passage but concentrating on one side. Now a single man could pass into the poisonous depths of the mine, but he hadn't allowed any of his people to expose themselves by exploring it.

No one had to be urged to congregate; every man, woman, and child gathered before the appointed time. Dare had a wooden box brought out to stand on to raise him above the heads of his people. He wanted everyone to hear his decision at the same moment.

Even as he waited for the crowd to quiet, he was still unsure of what words to use to persuade them. To his left stood Garridan, Raviv, and Angeline, surrounded by their shadow-keepers, possibly to ensure their safety if his decision went against them.

Dare raised his arms for silence, then shrouded his eyes with one hand, focusing on the distant treeline as he had so many times that morning.

At first he thought he was seeing a mirage, a vision of what he desperately wanted to be there. He hesitated before speaking, even though restless sounds from the crowd urged him to get on with it.

340

His eyes weren't playing tricks. A rider broke away from the faraway band of men and equests, speeding toward the mine, not sparing himself or the beast.

"Look!" Dare said, pointing at the rider. "We can welcome Jonati!"

Jonati galloped up, dismounted, and threw his reins to the nearest man, then stepped into Dare's embrace.

"We have it all—enough explosives to blow a range of mountains and a trio of miners only too happy to lay the charges."

"I was afraid for your safety," Dare said.

"We were delayed by bad weather," Jonati said, turning his attention toward Garridan, Raviv, and Angeline. "You betrayed the people at Norvik," he said, pointing to Garridan. "You sent troops to revenge yourself on Dare!"

"He's lying, Dare! Don't let him influence your decision. You can't turn your back on so much land!" Angeline cried out, defending Garridan.

"I can and do refuse the government's tainted offer!" Dare shouted so no one could fail to hear him.

Garridan reached into the pocket of his tunic as though to flaunt the deed in front of Dare one last time.

Tia stood nearby, unable to stay a great distance from Dare even though he hadn't acknowledged her with so much as a glance or a nod. She saw the glint of a blade and blindly reacted.

Garridan struck with the speed of a serpent, lunging at Jonati's back with his dirk upraised. Tia flew at him and knocked him off course. The dirk narrowly missed Jonati, but a furious Garridan turned, bringing the blade

341

up a second time. Dare moved with lightning speed, but he wasn't able to save Tia from the downward thrust that penetrated her thigh.

Jonati quickly grabbed the assailant, twisting his arms behind him as Dare dropped to his knees and took Tia in his arms.

"Get Mother Macy!" he yelled, ripping off his own shirt to staunch the flow of blood staining her breeches.

"I'm all right," Tia moaned, then closed her eyes.

Dare ripped apart the leg of her breeches and hovered anxiously over her as Mother Macy examined the wound on Tia's thigh.

"The blade didn't sever a major blood line, thank the Great Power," the older woman said. She refolded Dare's bloodied shirt into a compact square and pressed it against the slash wound.

"Talk to the people," Dare called out to Jonati, "and don't let them press so close."

He was vaguely aware that Gregor had seen to the disarming of Garridan's shadow-keepers. Garridan and his cohorts were at the mercy of Dare's men. Jonati spoke at length to the crowd, explaining the plan to blow up the mine, but his words were mostly lost on Dare.

"She's unconscious," he said, not reassured when the healer from Leonidas joined Mother Macy and agreed that the wound wasn't life-threatening.

"She's fainted from shock," Mother Macy said. "Petsy is running for my box of supplies. All she needs to bring her around is a whiff of aromatic salts."

"Dare, come speak to the people," Jonati called. "They have questions I can't answer."

Tia opened her eyes, trembling as she remembered the attack. Dare's face was near hers, pale under a sheen of moisture, and he lovingly stroked her cheek.

"Jonati needs you," she whispered.

"Don't try to talk. Mother Macy is doing all she can. You'll be fine."

"Dare, leave me."

"No, I—"

"The Wanderers need to hear your words."

He stood as Petsy ran up with a leather box of supplies and a heavy blanket to use as a stretcher. He knew Tia was in good hands, but leaving her on the ground hurt more than a dozen stab wounds. Tears welled, threatening to unman him before all of his people, but he fought them off and mounted the wooden box, raising his arms for silence.

When he finished speaking, the crowd cheered his decision and bent their knees, renewing their vows to follow him.

Even Jonati's bronze cheeks were wet with tears when the people dispersed, intent on the urgent tasks ahead of them.

"We've less time than they know," Jonati said with solemn urgency. "The Grand Elder's sources within the government expect the Earth ship before the end of this moon-cycle. I've talked at length with the men Logan found to set the charges, but you need to confer with them immediately."

Dare looked into Jonati's eyes; his friend knew how desperately he wanted to go to Tia, and he wouldn't ask this sacrifice if it weren't compellingly urgent. Dare nodded his head and told Jonati to bring them to his office.

When the three men entered with Jonati, he introduced them to Dare as brothers answering only to the names of Venge, Renge, and Sat.

"Vengeance, Revenge, and Satisfaction," Jonati explained. "Between them they survived nearly a hundred full-cycles in the mines."

"I am Sat, and my brothers and I have lived beyond our time in hope of destroying this last hellhole on the planet," the gray-bearded ancient said.

"Venge," he went on, pointing to a rail-thin man with stooped shoulders and a long, sparse beard, "knows more about the power of explosive devices than any man on Thurlow. Renge studied this mine from the inside. He knows every fault, every weakness in the rock walls."

The short, bald man inclined his undersize head but said nothing.

"I'm the foreman, so to speak," Sat said, his eyes nearly lost in the sea of wrinkles around them. "I need a hundred of your best men for outside work, them that's not afraid to scale the heights of the mountain."

"And inside?" Dare had lived in dread of making the decision to send his men in the mine. He knew he would have to be one of them—but without Tia he had no desire to father children. Having to choose the other men was tearing him apart.

"Only Venge and Renge go inside. They won't trust the delicate work to anyone else, not even me."

"Time is against us," Dare said tactfully, worried that the ancient men couldn't work quickly enough.

Sat laughed, a low bitter cackle. "At our ages, every hour is a gift. We've planned this for more full-cycles than you've been alive. Only the Grand Elder was willing to listen to the ravings of three old fools. Now we'll see."

"So be it," Dare said, giving Sat the list of men who were to be entrusted with scaling the mountain with him.

"The Great Power be with you," he said to the old men as they shuffled out.

"How many days do you think we have?" he asked Jonati when they were alone.

"Think in terms of hours."

"Then we have to start moving people away from the mine."

"The prisoners will be a burden," Jonati added.

"Some have asked to join us. I'll go speak to all those in the compound," Dare replied.

"What about those who refuse?"

"We'll open the stockade gate after the last of our people leave and let them fend for themselves."

"Does that include Garridan, Raviv, Angeline, and those who came with them?"

"No. We'll turn Angeline over to Logan and suggest she be sent to the fortress that holds her father, since she was sired by one Zealote and raised by another. When I rejected her affections, she turned to Garridan, not a wise choice. Garridan and Raviv will have to stand trial for their crimes when a new government is established. We'll have to keep them and their bullyboys under guard, until after we have completed our mission here."

Dare was dying for the sight of Tia. He longed to see for himself that she was all right, but love was a luxury he couldn't afford. The thought of seeing a silver-skinned spaceship in the sky over the mine filled him with a sense of mind-numbing dread. If the vessel came before they were ready . . .

He didn't know what the consequences would be, and that made them seem a thousand times more horrifying. Pushing aside everything but his determination to succeed, he went out to face the mountain of responsibility that sat so heavily on his shoulders.

Logan had kept his word and found men who claimed expertise with explosives, but the three wizened old men made Dare uneasy. There was a fey quality about them, an otherworldliness, that made him wish there were another way to accomplish his end. His rational side trusted them to install the explosives, but he also sensed madness in their obsession with destroying the mine.

Whatever happened, Dare had to organize the withdrawal of his people. He wanted the women and children to leave with armed escorts before sunset.

Everywhere he went, people were eager for his words of encouragement; he couldn't begin to speak to all those who brought concerns to him, but his tenure as leader of the Wanderers had been a preparation for this day. He set his army in motion and wasn't disappointed in the way his lieutenants rose to the challenge.

Cyrus and Henus caught up with him as he went over the assignment of equests with Tistur, deciding which of the new beasts Logan had sent bearing the explosives would carry baggage and which were fit for riding.

"We want to tender our resignation from the Council of Six," Cyrus said.

"So you won't be forced to remove us," the

keeper of books added. "But we also want you to know we'll support your decision, whatever the consequences."

"I can't have lazy men on my Council," Dare said with the trace of a smile. "So both of you see to your duties. When have I ever dictated what my closest friends should say or think?"

He embraced both men and felt bolstered by their loyalty.

"I don't ask that you embrace me as a friend," Fane said, walking up to Dare with a determined stride, "but I do offer my assistance if there's any job a one-armed man can do."

"I respect your reasons for opposing me," Dare said, studying the other man's face and wishing his eyes weren't so like Tia's. "There is one thing you can do, but you may not thank me for it."

"As long as you're honoring the agreement with my father, I'll follow your orders."

"Then I make you responsible for escorting your sister to Ennora. The Grand Elder will be there to welcome her home and fulfill the rest of our pact."

"You're a hard man, Dare. I think I'd rather try to domesticate a savage lepine."

Tia chafed at her confinement, but Mother Macy had taken all her clothes, leaving her dressed only in her undergarment, shirt, and bandage. Her wound ached with unrelenting intensity, but not seeing Dare tormented her more.

She needed rest, Mother Macy had insisted, but she was too agitated to surrender to sleep. She knew Dare was honoring his agreement with her father, but where was he? Was he so indifferent to her that he couldn't spare a moment to visit her?

Jonati had come and answered some of her questions but had left her no easier in her mind. Petsy had escaped from his duties for short periods of time, cheering her with his glib humor but unable to tell her much about Dare's activities.

As Tia lay fuming, Mother Macy entered the room and said good-bye, explaining that Dare had ordered her to leave with the other women and children at dusk. She told Tia that the army healer would check her wound in the morning to see if she were fit to ride an equest.

Tia smiled and tried to be agreeable, but inside she raged at Dare. What did all this mean to the two of them?

Fane found her hobbling around the length of the cot, wincing in pain, when he came to check on her.

"Is there anything I can do for my little sister?" he asked with a gentle smile that asked for a return to their former status.

"Find my clothes," she said, quickly covering herself with the bed sheet.

"I've had your pack put with mine, but I'll see that you have everything you need before we leave."

"What do you mean?"

"You're no longer a hostage, Tia. Dare has given me the responsibility of escorting you to Ennora."

"Are the two of you such friends now that you decide my fate between you?"

"All the Wanderers are going there. Father will join us and take you home." He watched her face and didn't see any trace of joy at the prospect.

"So you're my new shadow-keeper. Will you tie me with ropes so I won't escape?"

"Is that what Dare did to you?" He looked angry enough to challenge him again.

"Dare did nothing to me that I didn't welcome with all my heart," she said miserably, "except reject me when I would have willingly fled to the most remote place on this planet to be with him."

"I'm sorry, Tia." Fane sat beside her, cradling her head against his shoulder. "I haven't found love myself, but the pain of it makes me think I'm fortunate."

"Maybe I'll sleep awhile," she said.

"Get as much rest as you can. We're leaving tomorrow."

"Ask Dare to come and see me," she pleaded.

"I can't, Tia. Even if I could find him, I can't ask him to leave his work."

She lay wide-eyed, surrendering to the pain that throbbed in her thigh because it hurt much less than her separation from Dare.

Torches flickered on the mountain as a hundred men dug shallow holes and planted explosive sticks, networking the whole peak with fuse cords.

Dare watched as the slow procession moved out of the camp; all but those essential to the plan hastened to put distance between themselves and the mine.

The three grizzled brothers disappeared into the interior, and Dare hoped that there was time enough for them to do their work. Sat claimed there was one potentially disastrous fault that could render the mine inoperable, and Dare saw the logic in Sat's suggestion as he studied the master plan. The mine would collapse in upon itself, and the small charges scattered over the surface would seal the caves and crevasses that might tempt future generations to reopen it.

In the small hours of the night, the last of the torches followed a tortuous path to the base of the mountain and flickered out. All those who were leaving that night had gone, and Dare urged the weary workers to snatch a few hours of sleep.

He'd seen no sign of the three ancients and could only suppose they were still laboring inside the mine.

His eyes ached with fatigue, and his body felt as though he'd walked a treadmill for a mooncycle. He needed sleep as much as any man, but the urge to check on Tia was overwhelming.

He only hoped to see her sleeping form and hear her soft, rhythmic breathing. The building where she was quartered was empty; all the other women had left, but Mother Macy had insisted that Tia be allowed a night of rest before beginning another arduous journey.

This time she heard him come. She was so quiet, yet so alert, that she could have heard a choor-bug scurrying across the floor on legs no thicker than threads.

She closed her eyes, feigning sleep, knowing he could see her face in the pale glow of the three moons illuminating the night sky.

Dare knelt beside the low cot, watching her sweet face in repose, knowing that memories were all he'd have to live on in a bleak future without her. He only meant to look at her and leave, but she was so beautiful, so composed and lovely, that he bent and brushed her lips with his, a gentle touch meant to give her happy dreams, not wake her.

She moved so quickly that not even Dare's legendary reflexes were enough to avoid being caught in the circle of her arms.

"You weren't asleep!" he accused her, not trying to break away from the soft hands caressing the back of his neck.

"Did you think I could sleep, knowing that you're sending me back to my father as my brother's prisoner?"

"You're hardly that!"

"If I can't come with you, I might as well be in a dungeon."

"You only say that because you've never spent a night chained to a wall with fiery-eyed rodents as cell mates."

"So many things have happened to you, and I'll never hear about them," she said miserably.

"You're the best thing in my life," he whispered, taking her hand and kissing each finger.

"There's no choice now, is there?"

"You have to go back with Fane. Please don't make it harder for both of us, darling."

"If you had decided to accept the government's offer . . ."

"I was sorely tempted, but only because it would have given us a chance to be together."

"If Jonati hadn't come—"

"I still gave my word to the Grand Elder," he said sadly.

"Then you didn't have to fight with Fane."

"He gave me little choice, but you saved my life and Jonati's. You're an extraordinary woman, Tia, daughter of the Grand Elder."

He kissed her lips, the sweetest, saddest kiss she'd ever experienced.

"Lie beside me for a moment."

He knew all the reasons not to, but he slipped onto the narrow space beside her, cradling her head and shoulders on his bare chest.

"I'm not hurting your wound, am I?"

"That kind of pain goes away," she said, repeating what he'd said about his beating. She wanted to hoard every word he'd ever spoken so that she could summon them and admire them as she would precious gems.

He slid his hand under her shirt and rested it on her breast, comforting himself with the soft warmth of her skin. Oddly, he wasn't aroused; he loved her so much that no physical coupling would bring them any closer than they were at this moment.

She relaxed against him, letting a hair tickle her nose as she absorbed the warmth of his chest through her cheek. His mind was making love to hers, and it was so quietly erotic that her body responded with a spasm as satisfying as any she'd experienced when he was pulsating inside her.

He felt her body quiver and held her closer, trying to wish away the streaks of dawn that were even now dimming the star-studded grandeur of the night sky.

Chapter Nineteen

Dare conferred with Sat as the sun began its daily journey across the sky. Around them the last preparations for departure were being made.

"I've reserved three equests for you and your brother miners," Dare said.

"Take the beasties with you to the woods," the old man said, his eyes nearly lost in folds of withered skin.

Dare had an eerie feeling; cold shivers crept down his spine, and it was difficult to look the old man in the face.

"They're fast mounts. After you light the fuses—"

"That's not quite how it will go, lad." The aged voice seemed to be coming from a great distance. "All we've lived for these many years is the chance to seal this hellhole for all time. Between us we've lost fathers, brothers, sons, and grandsons when

353

tunnels collapsed, equipment failed, and spirits flagged. Few men get to choose the time of their departure. We've decided to make ours count for something."

"I can't let you sacrifice your lives!" Dare knew now what his strange sense of foreboding meant. "I'll light the fuses myself."

"You wouldn't begin to know all that has to be done."

"I can't permit you—"

"You can't deny us the joy of destroying that evil place. Renge and Venge are in place. They'll know when I'm ready for them to do their part. Now leave, if you have any love for the people who need you."

Dare clasped the old man's hand and hoped someday to end his life with such nobility.

Tia was among the last to leave the mine site—by design, not accident. She delayed, blaming her infirmity, until Fane was reduced to pleading and threatening. She stiffly mounted the familiar brown mare just before her brother took matters into his own hands and forcibly carried her away.

She had a superstitious dread of leaving Dare behind, even though she knew he would avoid her as much as possible on the trek ahead of them.

He was talking to a stooped old man, too far away for her to hear what they were saying. He was too engrossed to notice she was leaving, but she and Fane were at the rear of the last stragglers. Even the prisoners released from the stockade had an hour's start on them, and her brother was too cross to be a fit companion.

She looked back over her shoulder, praying that Dare would mount his equest and follow, and her heart skipped.

"Fane, look!"

She pointed at the sky, dumbfounded by the sight of a silver capsule high above the mine.

"Dare!" she screamed. "The Earth ship!"

The old man looked up too, and suddenly his years seemed to fall away. He pulled out a metal cylinder with holes that he wore under his faded gray tunic and blew into it. The high, shrill notes hurt her ears; then the revitalized ancient was running toward the mountain, scaling the side like an agile youth.

Dare hesitated a moment, feeling he should help the old men in some way, but Tia's cry roused him from his odd mind-state. He mounted an equest and took the lead ropes of the three he'd reserved for the brother miners, then raced toward Tia and Fane.

"Run for the woods!" he shouted, but his command wasn't necessary.

Following her brother's lead for the first time that morning, Tia kept pace with him as they urged the great beasts across the desolate wasteland.

None of them looked back until they were concealed by the lofty trees at the fringe of the forest. Then their curiosity overcame their urgency to escape, and they gazed up at the bright morning sky.

At first all they saw was a shimmering oval that reflected the sun with blinding brilliance, but the Earth vessel was descending, approaching the mountain as though intending to land on the summit.

Instinctively Dare and Tia maneuvered their beasts until they were so close his leg brushed against her uninjured thigh. Fane didn't seem to notice; he seemed lost in a trance as he watched the vessel from another world.

"Will the mine blow up before they send their shuttles down?" she asked, hardly able to believe her eyes.

"It's out of my control," Dare said, reaching for Tia's hand to keep a grasp on reality.

"It's beautiful," she murmured.

"In the same way a lepine has beauty," Dare said, his voice sounding reverent as he watched the ship descend. "We can't begin to imagine the lethal potential."

"It's a trading vessel, not a warship," Fane said without looking at them.

"That's not a distinction that matters to us," Dare said. "The Earthers are here to drain the lifeblood from Thurlow. What do you think they might do to stop the destruction of the mine and the ore?"

"Annihilate us," Fane answered honestly.

"They're so close." Tia squeezed Dare's hand, but not even her lover's face could tear her eyes away from the mesmerizing sight of the otherworld visitor. She'd seen paintings of Earth ships, but there was little to learn from the exterior details of one of them. No artist could possibly capture the awesome reality of the vessel.

"Now," Dare urged. "Now, Revenge. Now, Vengeance. Now, Satisfaction."

Tia didn't understand his words, but she did feel the urgency flowing from his hand to hers.

Dare didn't know what to expect, but he knew the chance for success diminished with each passing moment. Had three ancient hearts given up at the crucial moment, or had the old men deceived him for purposes of their own?

The spaceship was suspended over the mountain, its descent completed.

Dare strained his eyes, but even with his keen sight, he couldn't see Sat on the surface of the peak. He gnawed his knuckle and squeezed Tia's hand against his thigh, trying to decide if there was anything to be gained by escaping through the woods. Would the Earthers pursue them? If the mine didn't blow, they would need slave labor; if it did, they might want information or revenge.

"Nothing will ever be the same after this," Tia said, her voice soft with anxiety.

They were looking for a great fireburst to tint the sky orange. Instead the ground under them trembled, forcing all three of them to struggle with their mounts. A sound like thunder magnified a thousand times boomed across the empty plain and shook the trees around them. The air filled with grit, a sandstorm of demolished particles, as hundreds of charges reduced the surface of the mountain to a smoke cloud of rubble.

Dare understood the ancient brothers' mission; he steeled himself not to mourn their passing, but he would honor their sacrifice as long as he lived.

"The worst damage will be inside," he said, releasing his crushing grip on Tia's hand and gently patting it.

They covered their faces as best they could, trying to screen out the particles that whipped around them in an artificial sandstorm. The Earth vessel couldn't be seen through the black cloud

Pam Rock

curling up around the mountain and filling the sky above it, but Dare was rigid with dread, knowing the future of the planet rested on the actions of the Earthers in their silver-skinned vessel.

Waiting with their noses still covered to avoid the swirling dust, they didn't speak of leaving. They had to stay until the spaceship made its move.

Fane and Dare dismounted and blindfolded their mounts, then quieted the three riderless equests. Tending the beasts helped them endure the waiting, but Tia could only squirm and fidget, her thigh throbbing with pain and her hand lonely for Dare's touch.

The cloud of dust—harmless in the open air— seemed to hover forever. Their eyes were red and itchy from straining to see the silver oval.

"Do they realize what happened?" Tia asked the question she knew was tormenting both men.

"I don't see any sign of a shuttle." Dare rubbed his eyes, even though he knew the gesture wouldn't bring relief.

"My instinct tells me to leave," Fane said, but he seemed no more willing to turn his eyes away than Dare and Tia were.

"There!" Dare shouted, pointing at a gleaming streak soaring high above the blackened sky. "They're leaving!"

"I don't believe it!" Tia forgot her pain, straining forward over the mare's head so the leafy branches above wouldn't obstruct her view.

"They know the mine has been destroyed," Fane said. "There's nothing here for them—no reason to risk a confrontation when they have nothing to gain. We're safe—this time."

"Do you think they'll come back?" Tia asked.

"This ship won't. It will scurry back to Earth so the politicians can consult and form committees and bluster about budgets and resources."

"You sound so cynical," Tia chided.

"It's the way things are done on Thurlow. I don't believe our species is any more efficient on Earth. But they'll be back."

"I've seen enough," Dare said. "The two of you will be safer if you come with me and catch up with the main body of the Wanderers."

He led the way on a path well trampled by those who had gone ahead of them. Tia let tears wash the grit from her eyes, and Fane showed her the kindness of pretending not to notice.

On the long trek Tia often felt feverish, but her wound was healing well. She could only blame her hot, flushed face and lack of energy on the condition of her heart. She knew that her final separation from Dare lay at the end of the journey.

Dare left Tia and Fane at the camp on the outskirts of Ennora, a village that had long been cordial to the Zealotes. The Wanderers occupied a huge plain and were able to spread out in relative security. Tia didn't open her bedroll or make preparations for the night; she knew she wouldn't be staying with the people who had come to be her friends.

At dusk Dare returned for her. He was mounted with the five men of his Council and four units of armed men wearing breastplates as his escort.

"We have to keep our appointment with the Grand Elder," he said with solemn courtesy, inviting Fane and Tia to ride in the midst of his lieutenants.

Ennora had always been a place where Zealotes were welcome guests. Tia remembered walking through the village as a child, proud to be holding the Grand Elder's hand. There were small shops lining the cinder road, and once her father had purchased a wooden doll for her.

This evening the villagers were nowhere to be seen. The windows of their stone cots were dark, but Tia had the feeling they were watching through the black windowpanes.

Flaming torches illuminated the roadway. When Dare's party drew near, Tia saw that each torch was held by a mounted, black-robed Zealote with a coil of rope at his waist. She'd never seen the Order in their traditional garb, and the spectacle made her shiver with apprehension. The friendly men she admired looked like avenging warriors.

Dare led without hesitation, stopping a few paces from the broad-shouldered leader of the Zealotes.

"I salute you, Dare Lore," Logan said. "You've honored our pact in every way but one."

"Your daughter is with us." Dare's voice was steady but strained.

"Then you've done all that you promised. The spaceship is gone, and the government is in chaos. But before we speak more, let me see my daughter's face."

Tia's equest edged its way between Dare and Jonati, although she was limp in the saddle with no control of the beast.

"Father." She bowed her head, feeling as if the hooded Grand Elder were a stranger instead of her beloved parent.

"Welcome home, child."

He dismounted and lifted her from the equest's back, holding her in his strong arms for a silent moment.

"You're well?" he asked.

She read much more than concern for her health into his question, but she didn't have the strength to do more than nod her head.

Another black-robed figure slipped from the back of an equest, and Calla rushed forward, losing her hood as she swept her daughter into her arms.

"I've been beside myself with worry!"

"I missed you, Mother." She surrendered to her mother's hug, hating herself because this home-coming held so little joy for her.

"We have much to discuss, and little time to waste," Logan said to Dare. "I've secured the use of that cot, if you'll come with me now."

"My men can hear whatever you have to say."

"Bring them, then."

"Am I welcome too, Father?"

"Fane! By the Great Power, I thought the planet had swallowed you!"

The men went to the small dwelling, leaving Tia with her mother, the torch-bearing Zealotes, and the armed units of Wanderers.

"I love Dare, Mother," Tia softly sobbed as her mother led her away from the roadway.

"Oh, darling, that's something you can never tell your father! So much depends on their alli-ance. There's chaos everywhere. The Senate has disbanded, and the capitol has been put to the torch. If your father thought—"

"I know, Mother." She looked toward the cot where the fate of the planet was being decided and openly wept. Dare hadn't even favored her with a backward glance.

The men crowded inside the small common room, Dare with his Council of Five and Logan with Perrin, his closest friend and counselor, and Fane. Logan produced a deed, stiffly rolled and tied with a black cord, symbol of Zealote authority. With silent haste he spread it on a table and moved a wax stick closer so Dare could read the terms.

Dare's heart hammered with excitement; he was hardly able to believe the Wanderers' dreams were realized at last. He read with care, then asked that each of his men be allowed the same opportunity.

When all were satisfied, Logan solemnly took up a plume and dipped it into writing fluid, affixing his signature to the deed, then asking Perrin to do the same as a witness.

"Thank you, sir," Dare said, inclining his head in respect because the Grand Elder had kept his word.

"This concludes our agreement, but we still have mutual concerns," Logan said. "The government has toppled. The capitol has been leveled by fire, and Thurlow is in a state of anarchy."

Logan answered questions from Dare's men and Fane, until he finally raised his arms for silence.

"You haven't said a word, Dare."

"I've listened, but I don't know how it concerns the Wanderers."

"You have the only effective army left on the planet. The Zealotes have neither your army's weapons nor their training to fill the void left by the central government. For many years we've tried to use diplomacy to influence the course of events, but this crisis calls for stronger measures."

"Then it's up to the people to choose their leaders," Dare said.

"I agree, but they need candidates. There must be order and safety first."

"Which I'm sure the Zealotes can provide," Dare said dryly, aching to be done with Tia's father. How long could he stand in the man's presence without repeating his third demand: his daughter's hand in marriage?

"We've become too peaceable," Logan said with a rueful smile. "More importantly, the people will never accept a Zealote as their leader. We've been isolated from the mainstream of life too long. Only a man who's admired as one of the people can lead the unruly Thurlowians. You've proven yourself, not by bringing about the downfall of the government, but by the restraint you showed in using your army. I'm offering you what you could have taken by force: a chance to govern."

"What are you proposing?"

"You take your army to the capital and restore order."

"I have an obligation to the Wanderers. They've waited too long for a home."

"Without an orderly government, you'll spend all your time defending your territory."

Dare understood the situation only too well and knew what Logan said was true. He felt like a man who had relieved himself of one heavy burden, only to be handed a much weightier one. What made him qualified, besides leading a powerful army, was that he had no desire to rule. He only wanted an orderly process for choosing honest, qualified leaders. Accepting the position would demand sacrifice: he wouldn't be with his people when they settled their land. But without Tia by his side, his life held no joy, no purpose—only loneliness and an overwhelming sense of loss.

After much discussion, they reached an agreement on the terms: Dare would take his army to the capital, leaving behind those men with families so the women and children would have protection. Logan pledged the help of all the Zealote builders and craftsmen to erect a city in their new territory and the assistance of agrarian members of the Order to plant the fields and work the herds.

"I'd like a word with you alone," Logan said to Dare after hours of hammering out the details of their new plan.

"I don't have secrets from my men," he said, wearily repeating what he'd said before their conference.

"It concerns a personal matter." The Grand Elder nodded at his son and Perrin, and they left the cot.

Dare knew better than to hope, but Tia was his only personal link to the leader of the Zealotes. Was it possible . . . ?

His hope was dashed as soon as the two men were alone.

"I was taken away from my family as a babe," Logan said, "and the Zealotes took their place. I suffered less than most, but I understand what it means to wonder about the parents who gave you life."

"It's in the past," Dare said, having no wish to share his pain with the Grand Elder.

"To show my gratitude for what you've done, and for the sacrifice you're making to fulfill our

364

new pact, I've had your history traced."

"What are you saying?"

"I know who your mother is."

"That's impossible."

"No, you were stolen by Warmond. He's still imprisoned at a remote Zealote retreat."

"Why would he tell you? He doesn't know what kindness is."

"No, but for twenty full-cycles he's begged to have his library brought to him. I traded his books for information."

Dare's mouth was dry, and he wasn't sure he wanted to hear more.

"Your father died young, but your mother is here in Ennora."

"Warmond could be lying!"

"He could, but he knows I'll have every volume confiscated if you're not convinced that he spoke truthfully."

"Tell me where she is," Dare said.

Dare left his followers on the main road and followed a path of beaten dirt past tiny cots on the edge of the village. Even in the moonlight, the small dwellings had the shabby look of poverty, and Dare felt as if his chest were bound with chains. He wanted to run from this place and forget the Grand Elder's words, but his feet moved forward of their own volition.

Every cot but one was dark; a dim light showed through the greased paper covering a window in the last home on the path. He walked up to a low door and softly rapped, torn between curiosity and a panicky urge to flee.

The woman answered his knock, holding a wax stick so the light illuminated her face.

"You're Dare Lore," she said, her features soft and blurred in the flickering light.

"I am."

"Come in, my son."

She put the candle on a small plank table and motioned for him to sit on a bench beside it, then sat across from him.

She'd once been beautiful, and there was still a luminous quality to her thin, careworn face framed by hair so pale it seemed to have no color.

"You're so like your father, I thought his ghost was on my doorstep," she said with a soft sigh. "There's so much I want to tell you."

"Begin by telling me how I was stolen."

"My child, you weren't stolen!"

"What are you saying?"

"Let me tell you in my own way. Your father was a comely lad, and I loved him to distraction. We married young—hardly more than children—because he desperately wanted a son before his servitude in the mines began."

"Was he pleased when I was born?" He tried to imagine the man who had fathered him, but the image was like smoke blown by the wind.

"He never saw you. The government men came and called his name for a term in the mine. I was still three moon-cycles from my time, and we said good-bye praying he'd be able to return in time for your birth."

"But he didn't?" Dare knew the answer; he saw the sorrow in his mother's eyes.

"He died of a fever that ravaged the miners."

"I should have grown up by your side to give you comfort."

He could sense her pain as though she'd lost her young husband only that day.

"Please try to understand."

She twisted her hands together on the tabletop. He wanted to cover them with his to still them, but he felt too much a stranger.

"I'll try."

"I never had a family, except my old gram who raised me and passed on when I was still a girl. This cot was hers. When your father died, I swore you'd never be marched off like a slave to die in a hateful mine. There was only one way to keep you safe."

"The Zealotes." In his heart, he knew the rest of her story.

"I asked the midwife to request that the Master of Apprentices come to see me while I was still confined. I knew if I waited too long, I'd lose courage. I've since heard that babes were taken from the Outsiders by force, but it was never that way in Ennora. The Grand Elder wouldn't have permitted it. Warmond came—oh, Dare, he promised me so much: that you'd have honor and learning and opportunity. That you'd never go hungry—he knew I had nothing but the prospect of apprenticing myself to someone in need of cheap labor."

He could bear it no longer; he reached across the table and held her hands still.

"I've been so afraid; you must hate me." Tears flowed down her cheeks.

"The Master of Apprentices betrayed you. He never took me to the Citadral."

"I tried to get word of you. I even went there myself. It was before the time when women were allowed to enter the Citadral, and I was so frightened! But the gatekeeper was kind. He told me no one there knew anything about you. Later I guessed what had happened when stories about Warmond's hidden fortress were on everyone's lips, but it was many years before I heard about the Wanderers and Dare Lore who was their leader. My son, what did I do to you? Can you ever forgive me?"

He went to her and took her in his arms.

"You set me on the path of my destiny, and there's nothing to forgive," he said, wanting to ease her pain so he could begin his own healing.

"Warmond kept his word in one way," she said when she could speak again. "I gave you the only inheritance I could, and he vowed never to take it from you."

"What inheritance?" The word seemed meaningless in such impoverished surroundings, and he knew Warmond had never given him anything but grief.

"Your father's name: Dare Lore."

Chapter Twenty

Her marriage gown was as white as moonglow and so soft it caressed her legs like a gentle breeze. Tia endured the measuring and stitching of the bevy of women as long as she could, then begged them to leave her.

"My head is pounding," she said honestly enough, pulling the garment over her head and tossing it aside, even though it embarrassed her to stand in front of them in the nearly transparent undergarment they'd made for her to wear with it.

"Bride's nerves," one of her mother's friends said. "It's only natural, but Olan is a sweet, gentle man. You have nothing to fear."

Tia bit her tongue to keep from screaming at this latest well-meant advice. Everyone around her adored the saintly Olan!

Time heals a broken heart, her mother had told

her, but nearly six moon-cycles had passed, and her longing for Dare was like a knife embedded in her heart. Everything reminded her of him: a flash of golden hair, a manly shoulder bent in labor, the slap of boot heels on a stone floor.

Her only comfort came from riding the brown mare that had carried them both so many kilometers and that Dare had wanted her to keep, even though the animal had been one of the equests Logan had given to the Wanderers. When she was riding, she could pretend Dare's arms were around her, his face buried in her hair.

She felt like a prisoner sentenced to a death blow, awaiting her future with nothing but regret and dread. Quickly slipping into her riding breeches and tunic, she ran through the sedate halls and across the grounds to the stable that housed pink-nosed Corella. Brushing aside the stable lad's offer to help, she saddled the mare and rode off at breakneck speed, through the gate and across the meadowland still yellow from the cold season's blighting touch.

Hours later, she returned, ashamed of bringing the lathered equest back to its stall in such a sorry state. As penance, she watered and fed it, then set herself to the task of grooming the matted hair and muddy flanks.

Fane found her there hours later, sitting on the floor and weeping as though her heart would break.

Dare pushed aside a stack of documents and reports, wondering why confinement to a desk and chair made him feel more saddle-weary than riding a temperamental equest from dawn to dusk. Outside the window of his temporary quarters, New Leonidas was taking shape: simple, well-planned buildings of sunbaked clay blocks where every citizen could feel at ease in the new capital.

After six moon-cycles, the city was peaceful; the violence had been quelled, and most people had returned to their homes and land. Garridan and Raviv were in prison for a long list of crimes committed while they conspired with corrupt government officials, and Angeline was exiled to where her father was confined. Dare felt weary satisfaction, overshadowed by a deep loneliness for Tia that showed no signs of lessening.

"Even an officially elected First Citizen is allowed to sleep," Jonati said, coming into the office with a concerned smile.

"The new Senate should have chosen someone who can read documents at a glance and sign them faster than lightning," Dare replied, knowing even as he said it that he wasn't fooling his closest friend. He'd scarcely slept since news of Tia's upcoming wedding had come to him through a messenger sent from the Citadral on another matter.

"Since you're still here, you probably should read this," Jonati said. "It was delivered by a Zealote, and the Grand Elder's seal is on it."

"Read it to me," Dare said indifferently.

Although Logan had kept his word and was supporting the new government in every possible way, Dare couldn't feel cordial to the man who stood between him and the woman he still loved with an aching intensity that robbed all his accomplishments of their luster.

Jonati broke the seal and read it, frowning as though hesitant to share it with Dare.

"Well, what is it?"

"He requests that you journey to the Citadral immediately."

"He requests!" Dare stood and snatched the message. "Let Logan come to me if he has urgent business."

"It may not be possible at this time," Jonati said, tactfully trying to remind him that Tia's wedding took precedence with her father.

"Then let it wait!" He ripped the letter into shreds and bunched the pieces in his fist.

"It might do you good to sleep under the three moons again. The weather is mild, and you're looking as pale as Henus from poring over pages all day."

"Why are you so set on my going?"

"Logan wouldn't ask unless it's important."

"Go in my place, then. I deputize you."

"Let's go together. On the return trip we'll toss our hooks and lines into a swift-flowing stream and pretend we're Lost Ones again."

"There's a thought," Dare said, realizing his friend had worked as hard and as long as he had to see a semblance of order restored. "We'll do it. And after our business is done, we'll stop in Ennora. You've yet to meet the woman who gave me life."

They left with a unit of men under Danik's command; the First Citizen couldn't risk meeting bandits on the road. Two days' hard travel brought them close to the Citadral, but Dare was willing enough to pass another night in the open. He didn't want to spend a moment more than necessary in the Zealote stronghold. As they rode, he thought of Tia constantly, knowing he'd make her his captive again, given the chance. He prayed he wouldn't see her face and be tempted to undo all the benefits of his alliance with the Order.

Not expecting trouble, he had Danik post only two guards. The rest spread their bedrolls, but Dare was too keyed-up for sleep.

The three moons formed a triangle of heavenly light, but even these distant orbs reminded him of Tia. How many times had he seen her under their glow, her violet eyes luminous with love? The thought of another man possessing her cut more deeply than any whip, and he regretted listening to Jonati and shortening the distance between them.

He wandered away from the others, paying little attention to his surroundings except to know they were a good distance from any inhabited place. A soft rustling sound came from a grove of trees, but he dismissed it as the stirrings of a small night creature. The meadowland around him was quiet, and he walked without purpose toward a small outcropping of rocks.

They struck from behind, four men or more overwhelming him so quickly he didn't have time to counter their attack. They bound his hands and feet but didn't seem concerned when he called out for help.

His own situation was bad enough, but he was filled with dread at his men's lack of response. Were they dead, murdered in their sleep? Or were his captors part of a larger band capable of capturing all of them? He remembered the rustle in the grove and found it hard to believe a small army could approach without being detected.

His captors—there were five, not four—didn't

speak. He didn't know if it would be better or worse if they knew his name, so he held his tongue.

Two men carried him, one grasping his shoulders and the other his feet, running across the meadow toward a forest. Why had they attacked him in the open? Why not wait until he was sleeping?

"Who are you?" he demanded, but no one answered.

They were wearing black: leather breeches that looked shiny in the moonlight and short, hooded tunics that effectively concealed their faces. Dare was suspicious even before he saw the equests waiting in the woods. Renegades from the old government's service might possess a few tired mounts, but not even the most successful bandits could get their hands on beasts like these. They were huge and shaggy but without the stench of poorly groomed animals. They surely came from Zealote stables.

"I'm on my way to the Citadral," he said. "Why take me by force when the Grand Elder is expecting me?"

He would have welcomed any kind of argument, but his attackers were silent, not even speaking to one another.

"What have you done to my men?" he raged, his anger keeping his fear at bay.

They tossed him over the back of a beast, running a rope under its belly so he wouldn't fall off. The last time he'd been subjected to this indignity, he'd slipped in and out of consciousness, tormented by pain and Tia's plight. This time he was fully aware of his humiliation.

They started off, each man mounted, and Dare

could only guess that the man who led the equest carrying him was the leader.

"At least tell me my men aren't dead!" he demanded angrily.

Their stony silence was worse than abuse, although he was uncomfortable enough without added torment. The beast was galloping, giving Dare the sensation of falling, although the ropes prevented it. Riding head-down made him dizzy, and he roundly berated the man who was leading him.

"Only cowards strike at night and hide behind hoods," he said. "Is the Grand Elder behind this? I know you're Zealotes."

The ride seemed endless, although Dare read night signs too well to believe they'd traveled for more than a few hours. Once he heard an echo of hooves that seemed far behind them, but hope of rescue was soon dashed when all was silent again.

At last they reined within sight of a stream and dismounted, hauling Dare to the ground and standing him upright. From the position of the moons, he could confirm what he'd suspected: They were on a direct course to the Citadral. No matter how many possibilities he considered, it made no sense that he was being taken there as a prisoner. If the Grand Elder wanted to detain him, why not wait until he arrived in the morning?

Or did these men intend to murder him? He looked at them with fatalistic calm, trying to find a way through their defenses. They weren't careless as the old government's guards so often had been, and Dare didn't see any way to disable all five, even if they removed his ropes.

Pam Rock

The tallest of the band, the one who'd led Dare's equest, took a rope from his belt and slipped a loop over Dare's head, securing it around his waist, not his neck as he'd first feared.

"We're going to untie you except for this halter," the tall one said in a husky whisper. "You can't escape, but if you try, the consequences will be worse than you can imagine."

This vague threat sounded like boyish bluster, but Dare had been in too many tight scrapes to take it lightly. When two men had removed the ropes, he cautiously stretched, being careful not to make any threatening gestures.

"Now take off your tunic," the leader ordered. "Slowly—no sudden movements. The other end of the rope is secured to my belt, so you have no hope of getting free."

Dare felt cold fingers of dread on his spine and calculated how best to maim his attackers if his worst suspicion was correct. He knew of men who preyed on other men, but had never heard of any who hunted in bands—or who rode the Order's beasts. He slowly obeyed, glad it was still dark enough to give him a slight chance at securing the dirk in his boot.

"I know you must be armed," the leader whispered, still the only one to speak, although one of the men made a little gurgling sound that earned him a punch in the arm from another man. "Throw your tunic aside and sit on the ground. We'll pull your boots and breeches off."

Dare was knocked on his back as two men roughly stripped him, then allowed him to scramble to his feet when he was naked.

"Now walk into the stream."

Did they plan to drown him? He didn't doubt

he could outdistance all of them if he had a chance to swim, but the chance of undoing a Zealote knot was nil.

Icy water licked at his toes, reminding him of the cold season that had just passed. By the time he was knee-high in the freezing stream, two of his captors had joined him, shivering in their clothes, yet keeping their silence.

Dare walked faster, tormented as the swift current swept over his buttocks and belly and rose to lap at his nipples. He bent his knees to end the torture more quickly.

"Stop there!"

He couldn't go farther; the rope restrained him as effectively as a yoke, and he couldn't free himself, even though his captors couldn't see his hands underwater.

Of all the possibilities, he never expected the torment they inflicted on him. Two pairs of rough hands attacked him with brushes, lathering him with strong-smelling soap from the top of his head to the bottom of his feet, immersing him at their convenience and sparing no part of his anatomy. They were breathing hard as they put no small amount of effort into their work, and they were far more thorough than merciful. They ducked his head again and again, until it took all the self-control he possessed not to amuse them by howling in protest.

"Enough," their leader called at last in his falsetto voice, his laughter giving the others a signal to relax. "If he isn't pink and shiny by now, the twigs will do it."

Dare staggered out, so cold he couldn't feel his toes, but totally mystified by what was more a rough prank than true torture. Those waiting for him on the shore were armed with soft-needled branches that they waved in threatening circles above their heads.

They rained soft blows on his flesh, stinging but effectively drying and warming his torso and legs, showing special enthusiasm for his backside. He felt more hazed than beaten when they tossed away their branches.

"Is someone going to tell me what this is all about?" he asked, still standing naked while two men restrained his arms and two others attacked his tangled mane with combs.

"Now the stubble on his face!"

They forced him to lie spread-eagled on his back while four held him down and the fifth scraped his chin and cheeks with a sharp blade, showing a degree of skill that didn't draw blood.

"Bring the robe," the leader said at last. "Dare is as presentable as we can make him."

The garment seemed pure white under the waning moons, and Dare shivered at the exquisite softness of the fabric. They provided sandals in place of his boots, and he found it difficult to believe he wasn't having a weird dream.

"Are you preparing to sacrifice me in some bizarre rite?" he asked.

They found his question hilarious but refused to answer.

"If you give us your vow not to attempt an escape, we'll allow you to ride unfettered like a man."

"You have it," Dare said, finding something familiar about his tormentor's husky whisper.

They removed the rope and allowed him to mount, which also gave him a chance to note that they'd given him the smallest—and no doubt

378

the slowest—of the equests. Did he only imagine a familiar pink nose?

The sky was a deep predawn blue when they caught sight of the Citadral, and Dare had to rub his eyes to believe what he was seeing. The graceful white spires were illuminated by a magical white glow, making them look like slender fingers reaching toward the heavens.

His captors seemed awestruck too, stopping to gaze at the fantastic sight.

"The Grand Elder only displays this marvelous technology on special occasions," the leader said, not bothering to disguise his voice, "or for honored guests."

They raced toward the gate, leaving Dare to trail behind as though indifferent to whether he followed or bolted. The man who had extracted his promise knew his character; Dare rode in their wake, no longer enchanted by the luminous display. He knew the occasion for it, and the thought of witnessing Tia's wedding filled him with the blackest despondency. What evil genius had ordered his abduction only to torture him in the most telling way of all?

The gate was open, although the sky was hovering between darkness and dawn. Once he passed through, Dare was surrounded by his escort. They dismounted in front of a gleaming white building, one he remembered from his first conference with Logan. Without hesitation or explanations, they led him through the door embellished with heavenly signs and down a dark corridor.

"in there." The leader gripped his shoulder in what would have been a gesture of friendship in other circumstances.

Dare stepped into the room, prepared for an angry confrontation with the Grand Elder.

Tia was standing by a long window, the gentle light of dawn silhouetting her slender form. Her sable hair was coiled on her head, and a pale blue gown seemed to float around her legs.

"Dare! I was so afraid you wouldn't come!"

"I wasn't given any choice," he said, his mind reeling from the impact of seeing her again. What kind of torture was this, to be closeted with the one woman he wanted and could never have?

"Were you forced to wear that white robe and let your hair flow around your shoulders?"

Her voice was low and strained, and he could almost imagine that she was withholding tears.

"That and more! I was trussed up and hauled across an equest's back, scrubbed within an inch of my life in an icy stream, whipped with branches until I smarted from head to foot, and forcibly separated from my whiskers."

"I'm sorry you were inconvenienced. I only wanted to see you again."

"My darling, there isn't a worse torture than seeing you become another man's wife!"

Her face was sad one moment and radiant the next.

"You still think I'm marrying Olan!"

"A Zealote messenger at the capital told me the wedding was all arranged."

"It was! Oh, this is my brother's idea of a joke! Darling Dare, how you must have suffered! I'll box his ears! I'll have him pummeled! How could he!"

At first he thought she was weeping; then she let him see her face.

"You're laughing! What kind of prank is this?

I'll challenge your brother, and this time he won't walk away with just a scratch!"

"No, no!" She ran to him, threw her arms around his neck, and calmed him with sweet, compelling kisses, but he broke free and looked at her with blazing eyes.

"You're not marrying . . . I can't believe . . ."

"Don't begrudge Fane some mischief at your expense. It's because of him that I'm not marrying Olan."

He was speechless and confused.

"I was so desolate! Fane found me late one night, crying hysterically in the stable. He was so shocked by my misery, he led me straight to Father and made me speak the truth to him."

"The Grand Elder set aside your betrothal?" He was afraid to give in to the great surge of happiness threatening to overwhelm him.

"No. Fane and Mother both pleaded with him but as the Grand Elder he was sworn to uphold the Order's laws. As my father, he wanted me to be happy, but he couldn't release me from my betrothal to Olan."

"Olan." Dare had never loathed a name so much.

"Olan is a saint! A virtual holy man! Dare, Fane went to Olan and discovered my future bridegroom was no happier about the marriage than I was. He was only going through with the wedding to keep his word to the Grand Elder. After speaking with Fane, Olan approached my father to ask for release from the betrothal."

"Then your father did have the power to set aside your betrothal!" He was enraged at Logan's falsehood when he'd asked to marry Tia as the third condition of their agreement.

"No. It was Olan's request for release that set me free. He wants to be a Zealote scholar and devote himself to the Order in the traditional way, as a celibate. The penalty for breaking a betrothal is a life of solitude and celibacy—exactly what Olan wants. He wanted to please my father, but his calling to follow the old way was stronger. My father could hardly deny Olan's selfless petition, especially when it would bring great joy to me."

"And now to us. I don't have words to tell you how much I've missed you!" He wrapped his arms around her, so weak with longing that only her support kept him from collapsing.

"Now you see that Fane didn't kidnap you to be a guest at my wedding. He brought you because I was dying for the sight of you before you saw my father. His promise to bring you here was the only thing that kept me from riding to New Leonidas the moment Olan's petition was granted. Please forgive Fane for his heavy-handed jesting!"

A flaming ball rose on the horizon, filling the room with golden light, and he lifted her chin, gazing on her beloved face like a man seeing beauty for the first time, unable to believe the wonder of it.

"I do forgive him—and thank him," he said, kissing her with a passion generated through countless long, agonizing days and nights.

"My darling," he said when he could speak again, "I've been a hollow shell without you. If you still love me, I'll be a whole man again."

"If!" she pulled away. "How can you use that abominable word? If!"

"If my rough ways don't displease you too much," he teased in a solemn voice, "I'd like to ask you to marry me."

"I was so afraid you wouldn't ask! I worried you might have found someone else."

"There is no one for me but you, my darling. Expect the three moons of Thurlow to dance out of orbit before I love someone else." He swept her into his arms and regretted that the room contained little besides small gold and brocade chairs and an ornate carpet. How many times had he dreamed of making love to her on a real bed?

"I think," she said, as though reading his mind, "we should speak to my father."

Weddings, he discovered in the next few days, involved more planning than a battle and more patience than he possessed. He'd seen only brief glimpses of Tia, but each encounter made his heart pound like a boy's.

When the sun was high on the fifth day, he finally found himself alone in the same small room where Tia had awaited his coming. He was dressed again in the gleaming white robe, so scrubbed, shaven, and combed that his person seemed to glow.

He fidgeted; he paced. He was so excited he was afraid of waking to find it all a dream. His palms were wet; his knees felt watery. An encounter with kidnappers was child's play compared to the suspense of waiting behind that closed door to be summoned to say his wedding vows.

He heard the sound of rowdy voices and threw open the door to the corridor, not expecting yet another surprise.

The five grinning faces were familiar, but he'd never thought to see his Wanderers' Council of

Five garbed in breeches and shirts in shades of soft blue and pale green.

Jonati laughed and embraced him, while the others crowded around, slapping his back and pumping his arms, explaining that a messenger had ridden day and night to be sure they knew the exact day of his wedding.

When the time came to join his bride, Dare entered a stately chamber scented by huge bunches of dovewood blooms, the buds forced to blossom early in the heated rooms of the Citadral. Dare saw the Grand Elder, majestic in a deep blue robe embellished with star symbols, and his wife beside him in a pale yellow gown, trying not to weep. His own mother stood beside them in widow's gray, her gentle face glowing with happiness. Fane winked as Dare passed, his devilish grin his due.

The Grand Elder said the simple words of commitment that joined them for life, and Dare felt Tia's hand, gentle and steady on his own trembling arm.

While a small group witnessed the marriage vows, the rest of the Zealote community had set tables on the lawn and carried great platters and bowls of succulent delicacies for the wedding feast.

Dare ate when Tia's own sweet hand placed food between his lips, but he was too elated to feel a need for sustenance. She shared her joy with everyone present, bestowing hugs and happy words of thanks while he hovered as close as her shadow, so starved for the sound of her voice that he absorbed it like a man dying of thirst.

Tia's heart swelled with pride. Her beloved

Yellow Hair commanded the respect of everyone with his quiet dignity and manly demeanor. There was hardly a person present who didn't want to grasp the arm of the bridegroom and newly elected First Citizen. Yet she quickly wearied of the celebration: the press of people, the lilting music of pipes, even the sincere good wishes sent their way.

"I yearn to be alone with you," she said for his ears only, delighting in the look of passion that darkened the blue of his eyes.

"What are the wedding customs of the Zealotes?"

"We'll be escorted to our bedchamber by all the unmarried young people banging on kettles and pots."

He groaned. "I like that less than Fane's prank."

Tia saw her mother beckoning and left Dare in the midst of his own friends, giving them a chance to heckle the new groom.

"Mother, I'm so happy!" She hugged her tightly.

"I'm only sorry I failed to see how desperate you were for Dare's love before your brother spoke up. But I can do one small thing to redeem myself. Now listen carefully, because I've planned every detail."

"Do you trust me?" Tia whispered to Dare when she managed to draw him aside again.

"What kind of question is that?" He squeezed her waist and longed for the moment when they could be alone.

"Just tell me you'll do exactly what I say without any questions."

He listened carefully, agreeing with a puzzled

grin that made her want to hug and kiss him.

Following Tia's directions, he managed to slip away from friends and well-wishers and return to the main hall of the Citadral. He found the door she'd described and entered a small utility closet, a storage place for mops and pails. A black robe, cut in the style all Zealotes had once worn, was hidden on a bottom shelf, and he slipped it over his white wedding garb, concealing his face in the cowl.

There were still Zealotes who favored the traditional ways, so Dare wasn't conspicuous walking on the neat cinder path to the gate. He wanted to run and whoop with joy, but he forced himself to move with the sedate slowness of an elderly man, even affecting a slight limp as a reminder not to break into his natural stride.

Once outside, he waited in the shadow of a high wall, growing nervous when his bride kept him waiting. Then, without warning, an equest thundered through the open gateway, pausing for only an instant so he could leap on the brown mare's back behind its black-robed rider.

"Are we stealing one of the Grand Elder's equests?" he asked, hugging Tia against him as they raced across the open meadowland at breakneck speed.

"I seem to remember him paying you for your services with this beast and eleven others. You must keep better track of where you leave what belongs to you, my love."

"There was never a time when I didn't know where you were! Are you going to tell me where we're going?"

"To a place where we can enjoy our honeymoon in peace. My mother has arranged everything."

They rode with less haste when they reached the woods, laughing with excitement and happiness at their escape from the noisy teasing of their friends.

Tia kept their destination secret through a long day of riding, not swayed by kisses, tickles, or his wandering hands. Like all the best of her breed, the mare kept a steady pace, and Tia stubbornly refused Dare's pleas to seek out a secluded glade. They reached their stopping place in the dark of night, not as fatigued as they would have been if they hadn't taken turns napping as they rode.

The quiet village of Ennora was asleep when they passed through it, and Dare realized that more than one mother had been a party to this scheme to give them seclusion and bliss.

He pointed out his mother's cot, dark as it was, and wasn't surprised when Tia wanted to stop there. She withdrew a key from an inner pocket of the dark robe she was wearing, but before entering they quickly saw to the needs of the equest, hobbling it behind the small dwelling with few words between them.

Inside he lit the wax stick on the table, then struck sparks on a small pile of kindling on the hearth.

His throat felt tight, almost as though he'd come here after a very long journey to find his loved ones absent.

"My father was named Dare Lore too," he said, entrusting her with his newly acquired pride of family.

"He must have been a wonderful man to sire such a son."

He reached for her in the orange glow of the fireplace.

"Dare Lore is a proud name. I pray I can give you a son worthy of it." She touched his cheek and brought his fingers to her lips.

"As long as I have you, I'm more blessed than any man deserves to be."

"Are you thirsty? Hungry?" she asked, suddenly shy of the man who'd lived in her thoughts and dreams for such a long time.

"We supped well enough on the food your mother put in the saddlebag." He held her closer and squeezed his eyes shut, feeling her heart beating against his chest. "My love, not a day passed when I didn't long to hold you in my arms."

"I thought I would die for lack of your touch."

Dare took her hand and led her into the bedchamber which was little more than a recess behind a faded curtain. Tia lovingly touched the oft-laundered coverlet and smelled the spicy aroma of herbs hung on the ceiling beams to dry. She realized what a special place this was to Dare.

He shed his black robe and lifted hers over her head, enchanted by her lithe form in the shimmering white bridal gown.

Her lashes were long and spiky, tickling him when he bathed her face in feathery kisses. The fire was burning low, and he longed to see his beautiful bride before the light died out. He lifted the gown over her head, thinking at first that she was naked under it. Touching her back with open palms, he discovered the gossamer one-piece undergarment but at first was dumbfounded by its lack of closures.

She took his hand and guided it to a narrow ribbon nestled between her breasts, and he untied the slippery bit of satin, parting the lacing and slowly sliding the garment down her body, over her hips, until it fell to her ankles. Then, quickly shedding his wedding robe and undergarment, he took her hand without a word and led her to the bed.

The headboard was unadorned and darkened with age, but no bed had ever seemed more beautiful to Tia. She rolled back the coverlet, soft with age and wear, its colors too dim to be distinguished in the faint glow from the embers. She sat on the bed and Dare joined her, clasping her in a tight embrace and lying down with her on the crisp white sheet.

After a few moments, he released her, then held her lightly, his chin against her forehead, the length of his body caressing her naked skin. When he bent his head and kissed her shoulder, she shivered against him, melting under the tender caress of his lips.

He whispered words of love so tender and compelling that tears of rapture moistened her eyes, all the while pressing gentle kisses on her throat and arms, holding his urgency in check even though his need for her was great.

As if of one mind, they lay facing each other, their mouths locked together, their legs entwined.

She had so many things to tell him: promises to make, feelings to explore, joy to express. But she was possessed by love, too consumed by passion to do more than murmur over and over again, "I love you, Dare."

He looked into her eyes and felt limitless joy and happiness.

After so much despair, he'd been given a second chance to affirm his love for Tia and he wanted nothing more than to dedicate his life to her happiness. He desired her so intensely that his whole being throbbed with the need to join with her. Her hands and lips seared his skin; her words made fireworks explode in his soul.

"Love me, darling," she pleaded, taking his hand in hers and guiding it to her hot, pulsating core.

He held and kissed her, caressing her with his fingers and his tongue, as she writhed against him.

"I love you more than life itself," he said, pulling her on top of him. "If I have it in my power to make you happy, I will."

"Oh, Dare! Just when I think it's not possible to be any happier, you surprise me with so much joy I can't absorb it all! I love you, truly, completely, forever!"

She kissed his face and mouth until they were both breathless with urgency; then her hand stroked him and her lips caresed him until his blood was boiling. She slid away and picked up his hand, pressing tender kisses on his palm and holding it against her cheek. She touched the deepest core of his being with her unreserved love.

He took her in his arms and made love to her, and their joining was like the moons calling to the tides: a great, unstoppable surge.

When he moved over her, she clutched at him, matching her rhythm to the powerful thrusts of his buttocks. He crushed her lips, filled her mouth with his tongue, lifted her hips for a final thrust that thundered through her with spasm after spasm of ecstasy. Her heart melted with gratitude for a love so fulfilling.

"Promise me, Dare, that you'll never leave me, that you'll always love me."

He rolled on his back, taking her with him,

already beginning to surge within her again.

"I'll take that as a command from the Grand Elder's daughter," he said and sealed his surrender to her with a kiss.

TIMESWEPT ROMANCE
A TIME-TRAVEL CHRISTMAS
By Megan Daniel, Vivian Knight-Jenkins, Eugenia Riley, and Flora Speer

In these four passionate time-travel historical romance stories, modern-day heroines journey everywhere from Dickens's London to a medieval castle as they fulfill their deepest desires on Christmases past.

__51912-7 $4.99 US/$5.99 CAN

A FUTURISTIC ROMANCE
MOON OF DESIRE
By Pam Rock

Future leader of his order, Logan has vanquished enemies, so he expects no trouble when a sinister plot brings a mere woman to him. But as the three moons of the planet Thurlow move into alignment, Logan and Calla head for a collision of heavenly bodies that will bring them ecstasy—or utter devastation.

__51913-5 $4.99 US/$5.99 CAN

Futuristic Romance

Love in another time, another place.

Dreams of Destiny

JACKIE CASTO

Winner of the *Romantic Times* Reviewers' Choice Award

From the moment he lays eyes on her, Raul burns with an unreasoning desire for the beautiful girl he and his crew have rescued from desert exile. Has she really been cast out by a superstitious people who don't understand her special powers, or is she actually a highly trained seductress sent by enemy forces to subvert his men? More than anything, Raul longs to ease his throbbing hunger in her soft white arms, but is his love a fatal weakness or an unbreakable bond forged by destiny itself?

_3550-2 $4.50 US/$5.50 CAN

Futuristic Romance

Love in another time, another place.

New York Times Bestselling Author
Phoebe Conn writing as Cinnamon Burke!

Lady Rogue. Sent to infiltrate Spider Diamond's pirate operation, Drew Jordan finds himself in an impossible situation. Handpicked by Spider as a suitable "pet" for his daughter, Drew has to win Ivory Diamond's love or lose his life. But once he's initiated Ivory into the delights of lovemaking, he knows he can never turn her over to the authorities. For he has found a vulnerable woman's heart within the formidable lady rogue.

_3558-8 $5.99 US/$6.99 CAN

Rapture's Mist. Dedicated to preserving the old ways, Tynan Thorn has led the austere life of a recluse. He has never even laid eyes on a woman until the ravishing Amara sweeps into his bedroom to change his life forever. Daring and uninhabited, Amara sets out to broaden Tynan's viewpoint, but she never expects that the area he will be most interested in exploring is her own sensitive body. As their bodies unite in explosive ecstasy, Tynan and Amara discover a whole new world, where together they can soar among the stars.

_3470-0 $5.99 US/$6.99 CAN

TIMESWEPT ROMANCE
A TIME TO LOVE AGAIN
Flora Speer
Bestselling Author of *Viking Passion*

While updating her computer files, India Baldwin accidentally backdates herself to the time of Charlemagne—and into the arms of a rugged warrior. Although there is no way a modern-day career woman can adjust to life in the barbaric eighth century, a passionate night of Theuderic's masterful caresses leaves India wondering if she'll ever want to return to the twentieth century.

_0-505-51900-3 $4.99 US/$5.99 CAN

FUTURISTIC ROMANCE
HEART OF THE WOLF
Saranne Dawson
Bestselling Author of *The Enchanted Land*

Long has Jocelyn heard of Daken's people and their magical power to assume the shape of wolves. If the legends prove true, the Kassid will be all the help the young princess needs to preserve her empire—unless Daken has designs on her kingdom as well as her love.

_0-505-51901-1 $4.99 US/$5.99 CAN

LEISURE BOOKS
ATTN: Order Department
276 5th Avenue, New York, NY 10001

Please add $1.50 for shipping and handling for the first book and $.35 for each book thereafter. PA., N.Y.S. and N.Y.C. residents, please add appropriate sales tax. No cash, stamps, or C.O.D.s. All orders shipped within 6 weeks via postal service book rate. Canadian orders require $2.00 extra postage and must be paid in U.S. dollars through a U.S. banking facility.

Name _____
Address _____
City _____ State _____ Zip _____
I have enclosed $_____ in payment for the checked book(s).
Payment <u>must</u> accompany all orders.☐ Please send a free catalog.

TIMESWEPT ROMANCE
TIME REMEMBERED
Elizabeth Crane
Bestselling Author of *Reflections in Time*

A voodoo doll and an ancient spell whisk thoroughly modern Jody Farnell from a decaying antebellum mansion to the Old South and a true Southern gentleman who shows her the magic of love.

__0-505-51904-6 $4.99 US/$5.99 CAN

FUTURISTIC ROMANCE
A DISTANT STAR
Anne Avery

Jerrel is enchanted by the courageous messenger who saves his life. But he cannot permit anyone to turn him from the mission that has brought him to the distant world—not even the proud and passionate woman who offers him a love capable of bridging the stars.

__0-505-51905-4 $4.99 US/$5.99 CAN

LEISURE BOOKS
ATTN: Order Department
276 5th Avenue, New York, NY 10001

Please add $1.50 for shipping and handling for the first book and $.35 for each book thereafter. PA., N.Y.S. and N.Y.C. residents, please add appropriate sales tax. No cash, stamps, or C.O.D.s. All orders shipped within 6 weeks via postal service book rate. Canadian orders require $2.00 extra postage and must be paid in U.S. dollars through a U.S. banking facility.

Name _____

Address _____

City _____ State _____ Zip _____

I have enclosed $_____ in payment for the checked book(s).

Payment <u>must</u> accompany all orders. ☐ Please send a free catalog.

TIMESWEPT ROMANCE
TEARS OF FIRE
By Nelle McFather

Swept into the tumultuous life and times of her ancestor Deirdre O'Shea, Fable relives a night of sweet ecstasy with Andre Devereux, never guessing that their delicious passion will have the power to cross the ages. Caught between swirling visions of a distant desire and a troubled reality filled with betrayal, Fable seeks the answers that will set her free—answers that can only be found in the tender embrace of two men who live a century apart.

__51932-1 $4.99 US/$5.99 CAN

FUTURISTIC ROMANCE
ASCENT TO THE STARS
By Christine Michels

For Trace, the assignment should be simple. Any Thadonian warrior can take a helpless female to safety in exchange for valuable information against his diabolical enemies. But as fiery as a supernova, as radiant as a sun, Coventry Pearce is no mere woman. Even as he races across the galaxy to save his doomed world, Trace battles to deny a burning desire that will take him to the heavens and beyond.

__51933-X $4.99 US/$5.99 CAN

LOVE SPELL
ATTN: Order Department
Dorchester Publishing Co., Inc.
276 5th Avenue, New York, NY 10001

Please add $1.50 for shipping and handling for the first book and $.35 for each book thereafter. PA., N.Y.S. and N.Y.C. residents, please add appropriate sales tax. No cash, stamps, or C.O.D.s. All orders shipped within 6 weeks via postal service book rate. Canadian orders require $2.00 extra postage and must be paid in U.S. dollars through a U.S. banking facility.

Name _____

Address _____

City _____ State _____ Zip _____

I have enclosed $_____in payment for the checked book(s).
Payment <u>must</u> accompany all orders.☐ Please send a free catalog.

Futuristic Romance

Journey to the distant future where love rules and passion is the lifeblood of every man and woman.

Heart's Lair by Kathleen Morgan. Although Karic is the finest male specimen Liane has ever seen, her job is not to admire his nude body, but to discover the lair where his rebellious followers hide. Never does Liane imagine that when the Cat Man escapes he will take her as his hostage—or that she will fulfill her wildest desires in his arms.
_3549-9 $4.50 US/$5.50 CAN

The Knowing Crystal by Kathleen Morgan. On a seemingly hopeless search for the Knowing Crystal, sheltered Alia has desperate need of help. Teran, with his warrior skills and raw strength, seems to be the answer to her prayers, but his rugged masculinity threatens Alia. Even though Teran is only a slave, Alia will learn in his powerful arms that love can break all bonds.
_3548-0 $4.50 US/$5.50 CAN

LEISURE BOOKS
ATTN: Order Department
276 5th Avenue, New York, NY 10001

Please add $1.50 for shipping and handling for the first book and $.35 for each book thereafter. PA., N.Y.S. and N.Y.C. residents, please add appropriate sales tax. No cash, stamps, or C.O.D.s. All orders shipped within 6 weeks via postal service book rate. Canadian orders require $2.00 extra postage and must be paid in U.S. dollars through a U.S. banking facility.

Name _____
Address _____
City _____ State _____ Zip _____
I have enclosed $_____in payment for the checked book(s).
Payment <u>must</u> accompany all orders.☐ Please send a free catalog.

Futuristic Romance

Love in another time, another place.

Golden Conquest

Patricia Roenbeck

Strong willed and courageous, Aylyn fears nothing—until a faceless man begins to haunt her dreams. For the golden-eyed beauty knows that the stranger from a distant planet will never fall under her control. Only when the visions become reality, and hard-muscled Kolt rescues her from a devious kidnapper, does Aylyn surrender to his embrace. But before they can share their fiery desire, Kolt and Aylyn must conquer an unknown enemy bent on destroying their worlds and turning their glorious future into a terrifying nightmare.

_3325-9 $4.50 US/$5.50 CAN